THOSE PRICEY THAKUR GIRLS

Praise for *Those Pricey Thakur Girls*

'It's witty and sparkling, playful and merry, it is like Jane Austen's *Pride and Prejudice* and Louisa May Alcott's *Little Women* run in a blender and served fresh, it is life in pre-liberalised India described sharply but with nostalgic affection.'
– *Tehelka*

'This is no genteel comedy of manners but a smorgasbord of the rough and tumble of life as it is lived in Delhi.'
– *India Today*

'For the third time in a row, she's cracked the rom-com code and given readers a story that's as cuckoo as it is cute.'
– *DNA*

'Chauhan's prose is a mix of wit and colloquial exuberance. This trademark style was evident in her first two novels, *The Zoya Factor* and *Battle for Bittora*, after reading which I decided she was the only Indian writer of popular fiction really worth buying.'
– Livemint

'*Those Pricey Thakur Girls* is not chick-lit... It is fiction, popular fiction if anything else. It is also Jane Austen in Delhi, or rather hints and traces of*Pride and Prejudice* in Delhi in the 80's and just by that you should know that it is a romp of a read.'
– IBN Live

THOSE PRICEY THAKUR GIRLS

ANUJA CHAUHAN

HarperCollins *Publishers* India

First published in 2013 by
HarperCollins *Publishers* India

Copyright © Anuja Chauhan 2013

P-ISBN: 978-93-5029-602-8
E-ISBN: 978-93-5029-968-5

12th impression 2017

Anuja Chauhan asserts the moral right to be identified
as the author of this work.

This is a work of fiction and all characters and incidents described in this
book are the product of the authors' imagination. Any resemblance to actual
persons, living or dead, is entirely coincidental.

HarperCollins Publishers
A-75, Sector 57, Noida, Uttar Pradesh 201301, India
1 London Bridge Street, London, SE1 9GF, United Kingdom
2 Bloor Street East, Toronto, Ontario M4W 1A8, Canada
Lvl 13, 201 Elizabeth Street (PO Box A565, NSW, 1235), Sydney
NSW 2000, Australia
195 Broadway, New York, NY 10007, USA

Typeset in 11/15 Garamond Premier Pro
by Jojy Philip, New Delhi 110 015

Printed and bound in India by
Manipal Technologies Limited, Manipal

in the backseat of an Ambassador car,
four happy girls sing 'ten guitars'
once so close, now living afar,
Minni-Ruhi-Nandu-Anuja ♥

On a still evening in early April, when bees buzz torpidly amidst black-eyed sunflowers and the scent of mango blossom is in the air, one finds Justice Laxmi Narayan Thakur (retd), clad only in his vest and pyjamas, squatting in the grass, busily administering the death sentence to the upstart weeds that have dared thrust their cheeky, encroaching heads in his fragrant dogflower beds.

Judge saab is inordinately proud of his house. A pillared creamy-white bungalow sporting dreadlocks of maroon bougainvillea, it is built on a 4,800 gaj plot along leafy Hailey Road, with the ruins of a fourteenth-century stepwell to the left and New Delhi's poshest commercial district Connaught Place to the right. A seven-feet-high boundary wall circles the garden, topped off with vicious bits of broken glass that gleam in the sun like salt upon the rim of a margarita glass. This precaution is less to discourage thieves (the Judge admits that by the time he finished renovating the original structure, there wasn't much left inside to steal, anyway) and more to daunt the many amorous males spilling out of nearby Modern School, Barakhamba Road, eager for a sighting of Judge saab's true treasure – five delectable daughters, each one more beautiful than the other.

Surveying his garden in the evening, inhaling the scent of wet earth and desi gulab, secure in the knowledge that wife and girls are safe within, the Judge is often heard to observe that the word 'paradise' evolves from the Persian *pairi-diza* which, simply put, means 'walled garden'.

Next door stands the house of Justice Laxmi Narayan's younger brother, identical in every respect, but somewhat shabbier. But then, Ashok Narayan Thakur has only one son and no daughters to lavish their attentions on either house or garden.

Three of these paragons are now 'settled' and only twenty-three-year-old Debjani and seventeen-year-old Eshwari remain at home. The three marriages, truth be told, have depleted the Judge's purse even more than the renovation of the house has, but that is something he doesn't like brought up.

'A, B and C may feel guilty,' he cautions, 'and D and E will definitely feel short-changed. But really, Mamtaji, I have no idea how we will give this younger brigade a decent send-off.'

At which Mrs Mamta Thakur pats his bony shoulder and directs his attention to how thickly the kamini is blossoming along the boundary wall.

A lifetime spent with meticulously organized legal files and court libraries has moved the Judge to name his daughters Anjini, Binodini, Chandralekha, Debjani and Eshwari – a decision that has earned him a reputation of eccentricity he doesn't quite deserve. It has also caused his daughters to harbour a mild (but lingering) grouse against him.

'Naming us alphabetically, in order of appearance, like we were housing blocks in Chittaranjan Park! It's *so* dehumanizing. D'you know, BJ, that that's how Mr Bumble named the orphans in *Oliver Twist*?'

At five o'clock every evening, the Judge puts away his gardening tools and retreats to his quarters for a leisurely shower. When he emerges, exuding happy anticipation and Brut 33, a table fan whirs gently in the garden and a green baize table has been set up with a pack of plastic-coated playing cards. The Judge sits down, samples the tea and snacks that have been laid out, and awaits the arrival of his kot-piece cronies. These worthies usually roll in around six. Until then, Judge saab shuffles the cards hopefully and attempts to solicit his busy family to a game of seven-eights, rather in the manner (says his wife) of a street vendor selling dirty postcards. She occasionally plays two hands with him, never more, because – as she always remarks when she rises majestically from the table – some people may be retired but *she* still has work to do.

But today there is to be no kot-piece. A major event has occurred in the Thakur family, one that has upset all natural order and routine. And it is because of this that, as the Judge unbends from his beloved flowerbeds and straightens out the kinks in his back, Mrs Mamta Thakur hurries out of the house, all silken rustle and important bustle, and tells him to get a move on.

'Hurry *up*, LN, you're still mooning over those flowers! This is such a big day for Dabbu – and it's happening exactly the way Shastriji predicted it would, remember?'

Shastriji is the family astrologer, and relations between the Judge and him have been fraught ever since the Judge chose to name his daughters so arbitrarily. The Fates are greater than ABC, Shastriji had rebuked the Judge, who had unrepentantly asked why, if the Fates were so great, Shashtriji didn't become a full-time astrologer and give up selling Sumeet mixer-grinders on the side? Shastriji had responded by predicting the Judge's imminent demise by a painful, not-very-polite disease, and departed in a huff.

'That pompous pigtail,' the Judge snorts now. 'We should never have told her what he said. The wretched thing has become a self-fulfilling prophecy...'

According to Shastriji, whom Mrs Mamta had consulted after Debjani accidently sat down on a steaming hot pressure cooker when she was five and drove a needle through her own nostril in sewing class when she was ten, Debjani's stars were in a sleep state known as supta vastha. This was what was causing her to walk into walls, forget to dilute her bucket full of hot water with cold before pouring it over her body, and sink her nose luxuriously into roses seething with teething bumblebees. Her stars would remain in supta vastha until she turned twenty-three, and *then* – he had snapped his fingers, his eyes glowing behind his rather spiffy, cherry-red spectacles – she would awaken to fortune, fertility and fame.

The Judge tried to discourage this theory from taking hold, concerned that it would give Debjani an excuse to be a slacker in school and pile up too much expectation of her later, but it caught the imagination of her older sisters. Debjani was teased every time she gazed dreamily out of the window (which was often) and many parallels were drawn with the tale of the sleeping beauty who was awakened by true love's first kiss.

And now, just a few weeks after her twenty-third birthday, Shastriji seems to have proved himself to be amazingly accurate. Because Debjani has achieved the near impossible. She has cleared three rounds of countrywide auditions, conducted over a period of two whole years, to emerge triumphant as an English newsreader on DeshDarpan – India's one and only television channel. Tonight is her first broadcast on DD's national programme, which beams out live from Delhi for all of India to hear and see. While the rest of the world is managing to greet this event with equanimity, Hailey Road is all a flutter.

'Do hurry up, LN, they said she has to report for make-up three hours before the newscast!'

'Mamtaji, I'm the fastest dresser in this *house*,' asserts the Judge, throwing down his muddy khurpee and struggling out of his vest right there in the garden. 'Heaven forbid anything go wrong with Dabbu-ka-debut! But are the princesses ready?'

They are almost ready. In the little dressing room attached to the airy bedroom that Debjani likes to keep scrupulously neat and Eshwari is always messing up, Debjani stands in front of the full-length mirror, while Eshu kneels at her feet, making final adjustments to the pleats of her sister's stiff silk sari.

They make a charming picture. Eshwari is slim-waisted but otherwise full-figured, with buttery skin and straight black hair that falls into her sparkling black eyes in a spiky fringe. She takes after her mother, as do her sisters Binni and Chandu. At home, she is mostly to be found sprawled across various sofas, with the general air of a hibernating creature conserving its energy for the really important things in life. But when she walks the crowded corridors of Modern School, Barakhamba Road, there is a swing to her short blue skirt, a bounce in her thick ponytail, and a sassy smile perpetually curves her generous mouth.

Debjani, on the other hand, looks best at home, hair released from its tight plait and falling in loose curls around her oval face, her lanky limbs relaxed in denim cut-offs and baggy T-shirt, the slight, defensive hunch she adopts when out of the house eased away. She is widely held to be a paler photocopy of the family beauty, her eldest sister Anjini. Both girls get their looks from their father – all oval and honey, with hair that has the lustrous colour and curves of shelled walnuts. But the auntyjis along Hailey Road have long pronounced Anjini's features to be the finer, her limbs fuller, her manner more vivacious. And they don't like their rulings challenged.

'Is it okay now, Dabbu?' Eshu asks patiently.

But Debjani is too busy glowering at the Mole.

This much despised feature is a black spot, the size and heft of a tiny mosquito bite, bang in the middle of her chin. It is so perfectly symmetrically placed that people often think it's fake and that she's drawn it deliberately, in the manner of a simpering Hindi movie heroine. Debjani is mortified by the 'beauty spot'; she finds it appallingly vapid. Besides, she lives in daily terror of it going rogue on her, turning into a witch's wart and sprouting hairs.

Eshwari bounces to her feet and points out for the hundredth time that things could've been worse. 'It could've been right below your nostril, hanging like a bit of dried snot,' she says as Debjani peers into the mirror, frowning at the thing. 'Better that people think you're into sixties' style make-up, frankly.'

'Oh, it's fine for *you* to talk,' Debjani says darkly. 'You don't have a small doggie tick curled up right in the middle of your chin. At HTA, people were always sniggering at it.'

'Well, today all those HTA types will see you on TV and regret ever asking you to quit,' Eshwari tells her. 'Losers.'

'They didn't ask me to quit,' Debjani clarifies immediately. '*I* decided advertising wasn't the profession for me. And it wasn't.'

Still, she has to admit the Hindustan Thompson Advertising executives had looked super relieved when she told them she'd decided to leave. Her fat Bengali boss had wiped his brow and said 'oh fuck' again and again with increasing insincerity. And that ethnic, oxidized silver-studded aunty with the wriggly, sperm-like bindi hadn't asked her to reconsider even once. Instead, she told Debjani that with her 'dreaminess', her 'self-absorption' and her 'lack of initiative' it was probably a good thing she had decided against a career in advertising. Dabbu had ended up feeling quite demoralized.

If you lived out your entire life as a sort of a cut-price Anji didi – she had wanted to tell the sperm-bindi aunty – you would have lacked initiative too.

All in all, if the telegram from DeshDarpan hadn't arrived three weeks after she stopped working, telling Debjani she had cleared the last round of tests conducted almost six months ago, she would have hit quite a low.

'Can't you leave your hair open?' Eshwari asks as Debjani starts to plait it tightly. 'It's your prettiest thing.'

Debjani shakes her head. 'It'll come into my eyes and blind me,' she says sensibly. 'I won't be able to read. This is fine.'

'Okay,' Eshu says a little doubtfully. 'I hope I've been helpful, Dubz. I wish Anji didi was here. She's so good at tarting people up.'

'Oh, please.' Debjani rolls her eyes. 'She hums "Hey There Georgy Girl" every single time she gets me ready. It's like a law or something. Especially the bit about "why do all the boys just pass you by? Is it because you just don't try or is it the clothes you wear?" I'd rather be dressed by you any day,' she finishes.

Eshu stands back and hands her a maroon rubber band. 'Okay, you look lovely. Let's go, let's go, let's go! I'm so excited!'

'Perestroika,' Debjani mutters, taking short mincing steps in her sari, her narrow face intense. 'Dhimmitude. Hu Yaobang. Thiruvananthapuram.'

In the driveway, the Judge's bulbous black Ambassador is spewing smoke. Husky young Gulab Thakur, the girls' good-natured cousin, is working at it with a cranking handle, his bouffant hair bouncing up prettily with every whirl, while the Judge hunches behind the wheel, haranguing him.

'Arrey, give it a good hard whirl, Gulgul! What's the use of all that bodybuilding if you can't even fix a little starting trouble? Fool! Learn how to heat up a cold engine – it's good practice for married life!'

The engine sputters to life and Gulgul springs away, flushed and beaming. Mrs Mamta and the girls get into the car, Debjani very careful of her sari pleats. The doors slam shut and the Ambassador rolls out importantly through the old green gate onto Hailey Road, where a toli of mangy, khujli-infested street dogs sleeping on a sand pile immediately give it a rousing send-off. The entire family of the dhobi who has ironed Debjani's sari for this momentous occasion jumps to their feet and waves. Frail old Mr Gambhir who runs the kirana across the road raises both palms in blessing and the driver of a packed DTC bus, his hair standing on end at the Judge's sudden and supreme arrival onto the middle of the road, slams down his brakes and curses roundly.

'We've got plenty of time,' Mrs Mamta says happily. 'Debjani, you've got your gate pass, na?'

Debjani has her passes safe, the gate pass and the studio pass, both of which declare her to be a bona fide staff artiste at DeshDarpan Studios. She is feeling anything but artistic, though. As the Ambassador circles Connaught Place, turns into Parliament Street and approaches Broadcasting House, panic wraps its hairy hand around her belly and squeezes. Hard.

'I'll be fine, Ma,' she says as the Judge pulls up the car at the gate. 'Where will you guys watch me from?'

'Home.' Mrs Mamta smiles. 'Everyone is coming. And afterwards, we'll come and pick you up and go for chaat, okay?'

Debjani smiles, a slightly lopsided, street-urchin grin that sits oddly upon her angelic face. 'We're here,' she says breathlessly. 'I'm going in. Wish me luck!'

'Aap traffic block kar rahe hain,' growls the truculent guard at the gate. The Thakurs ignore him.

'Best of luck, Dabbu!' Eshu hugs her sister.

'All the best, beta,' Mrs Mamta Thakur says, sniffing. 'Your first words – you said them jumping up and down, trying to get your father to put down your sisters and pick you up and swing you instead – were *my tunn my tunn*. And today your turn has finally come!'

'My first words were *Eshu eat*.' Eshwari grins. 'Anji didi's were *I sabse pritty*. And Binni didi's were –'

'Never mind all that,' her mother remonstrates. 'Today is *Dabbu's* day.'

'Dabbu-ka-debut!' the Judge beams, praying fervently that this newsreading stint works out better than the job in advertising did.

'Traffic is being block,' the guard tries again.

'So, um, bye, you guys,' Dabbu says, turning down the chrome handle and grabbing hold of her sari pleats.

But her family isn't done yet.

'I remember,' says the Judge as he kills the engine and rests comfortably against the steering wheel, 'when we all went to see *The Magik of the Vunderful Vladimir*. In Lucknow, you know. I wrangled VIP passes through that IAS whose son I defended for drunk and disorderly conduct. Vladimir – huge intimidating chap with bloodshot, kajal-rimmed eyes – asked for a volunteer and I raised my hand. He called me up, made me wear a dam' foolish looking satin bathrobe and then shut me in a box. Dabbu started to cry – she was only three years old. When he started to stick swords into the box, she started shouting. I could hear her through the box, although its walls were six inches thick. And when he produced a shiny saw to cut the box into two pieces –'

'She leapt off her seat and charged up to the stage, pulled out a sword from the box and attempted to impale the Vunderful Vladimir,' Mrs Mamta Thakur finishes, her eyes moist with sentimental tears. 'Right through the crotch. The sword was too heavy, though – she dropped it on her own foot. The doctors had to put six stitches.'

'Gutsy,' the Judge says gruffly.

'Bloodthirsty little beast.' Eshwari grins.

'No, no.' Mrs Mamta shakes her head. 'So *gentle*. You used to hit her all the time but she never once raised a hand on you, Eshu.'

'Traffic,' the guard implores. 'Move kijiye. Please.'

'Yes, yes,' the Judge huffs as Dabbu finally alights. 'We are moving. Oho... ahhh... hrmmph! Left the cranking handle at home. You! Guard babu! Can you give our car a push?'

Okay, that was the most embarrassing moment of my life, Dabbu thinks, mortified, as she walks down the pillared corridor towards the green room with small cautious steps, holding on for dear life to the pleats of her sari. How could BJ do that to me? And what was the need to give Ma the wheel and get out and push the car *himself*, thus revealing his pyjama naada and bathroom chappals for all the sniggering guards to see? I bet everybody out there is laughing at me. And then he made it even worse by shouting 'Best of luck, Dabbu'.

Dabbu! But I won't be intimidated, I won't. I'll be coom and caal. I mean, cool and calm. I can *do* this. I've wanted to be a newsreader since I was three. And now I am. I maxed the auditions. I cleared the GK test, the voice test and the camera test. This is not advertising, where I have to be witty every single second. Here I just need to look neat and not hunch, and read from a prepared script. I've got this.

She walks into the green room, her hands clammy but her head held high, and suddenly finds herself navel deep in children dressed in red-and-black striped towels, with knitting needles sticking out of their hair. All of them, regardless of gender, have three little dots painted upon their chins like a 'therefore' sign.

'Er, hello.' Debjani peers through the sea of red and black. 'I'm here for my make-up.'

The sea parts to reveal a bald man with a belligerent air and a hearing aid, sweating profusely in spite of the air-conditioning. He jerks his head at her questioningly. 'Adivasi dance?'

'Um, no,' Debjani says. 'Newsreader. For the English news.'

His expression turns to one of disbelief. 'So early? *Nine* o'clock news?'

'They told me to be here three hours early.'

The make-up man smirks, not unkindly. 'Come back after one hour.' And he goes back to painting large red circles on the cheeks of the children milling around his knees.

Dabbu, her own cheeks red, goes out and stands in the corridor. I must look like such an over-enthu idiot, she thinks, showing up so early, all trussed up in a sari. *Of course* the professionals drift in late. And they probably don't even wear a sari – they just drape the pallu over their jeans or whatever. Why didn't I think of that?

People walk past without giving her a second glance – a short, bearded man with a clipboard, some scruffy technicians, an important looking bearer loaded down with a tray full of steaming teacups that Debjani doesn't dare help herself to, even though she's dying for a cup of tea.

I'll never fit in, she tells herself miserably. What was I thinking? That I could waltz in here and read the primetime news live on DD? I'm going to be a disaster. Just like I was in HTA. My voice is drying up. Maybe I should sneak off and do some voice modulation exercises in the loo? But where is it?

She turns around – and is hit by a strong scent of imported aftershave. A face she knows as well as her own is bobbing before her eyes. Smoothly handsome, ruddily fair and ending in a neatly clipped beard. A voice like growling honey trickles into her ears. Growling honey with exquisite diction.

'Well, hello there. Are you the newbie?'

Debjani nods, overwhelmed. It's Amitabh Bose, she thinks, stunned. *The* Amitabh Bose. The *It is with great sorrow that I tell you that our Prime Minister has been assassinated* Amitabh Bose. The *Today Rakesh Sharma became the first Indian in space* Amitabh Bose. And sure, BJ claims he wears a beard to hide a weak chin and Eshu says she can't shake off the feeling that he farts, sneakily and soundlessly, even as he reads so fluently and flawlessly – but still, he is famous. And he is talking to her.

'Yes,' she replies. 'I'm Debjani.'

'Babejani.' He smiles. 'How nice. We'll be reading together

tonight. They told me to look out for you. Do you want me to show you the ropes?'

She stares up at him, still a little stunned. The 'Babejani' comment is strictly cheesy but this is Amitabh Bose – dare she take offence?

He assumes she is taking him up on his generous offer, turns around and starts walking, and just like that, the spell is broken. He has a large wobbly bottom, the kind (according to Eshwari, the butt aficionado among the sisters) that jiggles about and actually *talks* to people, so that even when the bum-owner's got his back to you, you don't feel socially neglected.

'Are you familiar with the set-up here?' he asks.

Debjani shakes her head. 'I just got the telegram,' she explains breathlessly. 'Saying I was selected.'

'Ah.' Amitabh Bose winks conspiratorially. 'The famous DD telegram! Have you seen the newsroom at least?'

Debjani nods. Frankly, the newsroom had disappointed her. It was a dusty, dingy space, smelling of stale beedi, housed in some squalid barracks behind Akashvani Bhavan. There were towers of dusty cassettes piled all higgledy-piggledy on the floor, and she had found it hard to believe that the news India heard every night, read out with such grace and elan, was put together *there*.

'This is Studio Number 2 to your right,' Amitabh Bose is saying, 'where all the big shoots happen. There's an Assamese dance going on there today. And that's Number 3, from where we do the news broadcasts. Take a look.'

Debjani peers into Studio Number 3. It's not very big, the set is blue, with a rotating globe, a gleaming tabletop and two high chairs. One of those is for me, she thinks, oscillating madly between panic and pride.

'And that's the autocue,' Amitabh points. 'You've had some practice?'

'Yes,' she says. 'I'm not very good with it, though.'

He laughs. 'You'll be fine. Ah, here's young-Uday with our scripts. Go through them, check for grammatical errors, there are usually plenty.' He mock-frowns at young-Uday, who looks dutifully sheepish. 'And see if you have any questions.'

She takes her sheets from pimply young-Uday, who look even more nervous than her, and scans them quickly. Her lines are marked 'Newsreader 2'. I'm Newsreader 2, she thinks happily. This is easy, actually, lemme see, President's visit to an engineering college in Tirunamalli... Foreign Minister's speech at the SAARC summit... Okay, all good... nothing here I can't pronounce.

Back in the green room, the make-up men attack her hair and face, powdering, dusting, spraying. Their hands smell of Charmis cold cream and onion. She demurs a little at how thick they are laying it on, but they assure her that she'll need it under the strong studio lights. There is an awkward moment when one of them picks gently at her mole. 'It's real,' she says apologetically and he smiles in a friendly way. And then young-Uday – who appears to be the floor manager – leads them back to Studio Number 3 and they sit, and he tells her where to look, and the DD News theme music starts to play and Amitabh flashes her an encouraging smile and young-Uday counts down to one and the cameras whir to life and Amitabh says easily in his famous baritone: '*Good evening and welcome to the Friday Night News at Nine. I'm Amitabh Bose...*'

Dabbu takes a deep breath, smiles and says, not at all like someone whose heart has clawed its way up to her esophagus and is about to leap out of her mouth, '*And I'm Debjani Thakur.*'

'Dabbbuuu! I'm so *proud* of you!'

The Thakurs are at Bengali Market, eating chaat. Well, they're holding it and talking excitedly around it but not much is going into anybody's mouth. The chaat-wallah, a thin bronze personage with a grey handlebar moustache, looks at them indulgently and doles out the golguppas extra slowly.

'How was I?' Debjani asks for the fourteenth time since they picked her up.

'I told youuuuuuuuu! Perrrrrfect!'

'I had tears in my eyes,' Mrs Mamta Thakur confesses. 'You were every bit as good as that Bose, and he's been reading for twenty years!'

'Shhush, Ma, somebody'll hear you.'

'The princesses are eating very slowly,' the Judge says to the golguppa man. 'I apologize on their behalf.'

But that mustachioed worthy shakes his head. 'No problem,' he says, nodding towards Debjani with an avuncular smile. 'I saw baby on TV. Read very well. Eat slowly slowly. Golguppe free hain.'

The girls squeal in excitement. The rest of Bengali Market turns and stares.

'Thank you ji.' Mrs Mamta smiles at him graciously. Then, in a lower voice, 'Keep it down, girls. Always be ladylike. All this shrieking isn't good for Debjani's image.'

'I have an *image*.' Dabbu gulps, her eyes widening, and promptly chokes on a golguppa.

'Ey, bring one Campa!' the golguppa man shouts.

Eshwari immediately starts coughing too.

'Bring *two* Campas.'

'Do you think,' breathes Debjani after a tingly swig, 'that the Prime Minister saw my broadcast?'

'Hmm?' The Judge looks up from his aloo tikki. 'Of course, of course. What else is there to see on TV?'

'Be*have*, LN,' Mrs Mamta starts to say but right then a group of boys emerges noisily from Nathu Sweets. A general air of repletion and loosened naada strings hangs about them, they are picking at their gums with toothpicks and eyeing the kulfi stand in anticipation. Then they spot Debjani sipping her Campa Cola and do a double take. Furious whispering ensues.

'Same sari.'

'Mole on chin.'

'You aks.'

'No, *you* aks!'

Finally a large hairy one approaches the Thakurs bashfully. Dabbu pretends to look unconcerned (because what if he just wants to ask the time or something?).

'Excuse me, you are...?'

Dabbu fiddles with her bottle of Campa Cola.

'Yes,' says the Judge a little testily. 'She *is*.'

A huge grin spreads across the boy's hairy face.

'Arrey wah! You are my first famous person! That I have met personally, I mean. Matlab ki, I saw a two-foot bona with three legs in a mela once, but that's not really the same thing, is it?'

'No,' Debjani agrees, 'it isn't. Ma, can we go home now?'

They load up in the Ambassador which, perhaps aware that there is now a celebrity on board, starts up with minimum fuss.

'I'm so happy,' Mrs Mamta Thakur says complacently, biting into her kulfi. 'See the rishtas that will pour in for you now! All the best boys from the best communities – Rajputs, Khatris, Brahmins!'

'Rishtas would have poured in *anyway*,' says the Judge grandly.

He has none of the proper subservience that befits a man with three daughters married and two more to go. At every rishta negotiation, his attitude has always been one of condescension – like he is doing the boys' side a huge favour by bestowing upon them the undeserved jewel that is a Thakur daughter.

Mrs Mamta sniffs. 'LN, we can't act like that whole kaand with Chandu didn't happen,' she murmurs. 'That would be foolish.'

The Judge doesn't reply. The fact that Chandralekha, their third born, threw aside the nice Rajput second lieutenant with the sword-of-honour-from NDA her parents had found for her, and eloped with a shady American-Estonian a night before her wedding, still rankles.

Hacked my nose off in front of the whole biradari, he broods. That too without the anaesthesia that saving on the expenses would have provided! The tent-wallah refused to return the advance, so did that thug of a caterer even though he didn't have to fry even *one* paneer pakoda.

'If she had mentioned only once that she wanted to marry that lalloo Lippik, I would have relented,' he sighs. 'But she never let on, never even hinted. Am I so scary?'

Everybody ignores this plaintive query.

'How do rishtas matter anyway?' Eshwari asks. 'We all know Dabbu is going to marry Moti-the-mongrel and they're going to live happily ever after!'

'That's not funny, Eshu.' Mrs Mamta Thakur frowns. 'She's twenty-three – we have to start looking.'

'Ma, my world's just opening up and you want to shut it down again!' Dabbu looks upset.

'Arrey aise kaise?' her mother says soothingly. 'We'll find you someone nice, beta, like we did for your sisters.'

Debjani and Eshwari greet this statement with a strangled silence.

'Unless,' Mrs Mamta gives Debjani a sly look, 'you have somebody in mind already?'

'I *don't*,' Debjani groans.

'Dabbu turns down everybody,' Eshwari complains. 'For the weirdest reasons – she doesn't like boys who have too much money or boys who have too much muscle. She doesn't like boys who want you to laugh at their jokes. She doesn't like boys who flick their hair back, like *this*.' She tosses her head. 'She doesn't like boys who wear acid-washed jeans, or boys who breakdance. She doesn't like NRIs – too obnoxious; or IFS officers – too pompous. She doesn't like boys who say twunty instead of twenty. She doesn't like any boys *at all*.'

'Clearly, Moti's our man,' the Judge says, not entirely unhappily. Dabbu is his favourite and he is in no hurry to see her wed.

'Shut up, Eshu, I can speak for myself!' Debjani says crossly. 'Ma, I don't like oversmart, flirty guys who think they're god's gift to women. And I don't like freaks. Is that too fussy of me?'

'Have you *ever* had a crush?' Eshwari demands.

'Have you ever *not* had a crush?' Dabbu shoots right back. 'Right now you're crushing on the guy who doles out the tokens at our Mother Dairy, aren't you?'

'Hai, not that pahadi!' Mrs Mamta exclaims, horrified.

'Chinkies are *cute*, Ma,' Eshwari says dreamily. 'All the cutest basketball players are Manipuri, you know.'

'Why couldn't I have had five fine sons?' the Judge wonders randomly in the front seat. 'Instead of five demented daughters?'

'Ma!' Eshu appeals. 'See what BJ's saying!'

'My girls aren't mad,' Mrs Mamta bristles. 'You don't kn –'

'They're making us fight,' the Judge warns her. 'Watch out, Mamtaji!'

'I *hate* show-offs and flirts,' Dabbu says, rather intensely.

'Duly noted.' The Judge nods at her in the rearview mirror.

'I think it's better to have lots of crushes than none at all,' Eshwari asserts. 'It shows that you don't take yourself too seriously.'

'But I don't!' Dabbu insists.

'Well, *I* think it's a self-esteem problem,' Eshwari declares. 'You think people may not like you, so you quickly say they aren't good enough first. That way you're safe.'

'And you think, just because you've taken psychology in class eleven, you know *everything*,' Debjani flashes, her cheeks very red as she realizes that her parents' silence probably means they agree with her sister. 'If I had low self-esteem, how could I have done what I did tonight?'

'That's... different,' Eshwari says slowly. 'I don't know how, but it is.'

'Well, at least meet some boys now, Dabbu,' her mother coaxes. 'You don't have to marry them.'

'She'll never allow herself to like anyone,' Eshwari predicts. 'She'll wait too long and finally end up with nothing, like people at weddings who don't join the buffet queue till really late to show how non-desperate they are, and then get only raw onion rings and rice to eat.'

'Well, I'd rather be like them than like the bhukkads who elbow everybody else out and stuff their faces,' Dabbu retorts, 'and then get the loosies.'

Eshwari, who has a delicate stomach, gasps at this crack.

Debjani grins.

'*I* think you should start looking for a job,' the Judge intervenes.

'People will recognize you instantly – it will help you no end in interviews.'

Dabbu blinks. 'This *is* a job. They pay 500 rupees a bulletin. If I settle into a weekly spot, I'll be picking up 2,000 rupees a month. HTA was only 1400.'

'But advertising was a *career*,' the Judge replies. 'This is a job. Not even a job, a hobby. You need to do more with your life than just sit in front of a camera and read, Dabbu. You have an MA in English, after all.'

'Bauji, please...'

'What about law?' he persists. 'Why can't you do law?'

Yeah, right, Dabbu thinks disgustedly. So I can spend my whole life being compared to *you* and falling short. Which reminds her...

'Ma, did Anji didi call?' Dabbu asks.

Mrs Mamta gives a guilty start. Anjini had called. And said that Dabbu had read well but looked like a first-time schoolteacher – scared and stiff. I thought her supta vastha would end spectacularly tonight, Anji had fretted, but she still looked sort of half asleep. I wanted to reach into the TV and open her hair. Stupid girl. Anyway, I know how to fix this – I'll come over and dress her for the next broadcast myself.

Being a mother of five girls involves a certain amount of mendacity.

'Of course she phoned!' Mrs Mamta says brightly. 'She said you were *too* good. And to say congratulations and a big hug from Antu bhaiyya and her.'

'And Binni didi?'

'She couldn't get through, I suppose,' Mrs Mamta replies casually. 'The line was busy all evening. I'm sure she'll call tomorrow.'

The truth of the matter is that the Judge and Binni aren't on talking terms. Binni is sulking at him. And the Judge, it must be admitted, is sulking right back. They haven't spoken in three months.

As BJ has banned everybody in the house from talking to or about Chandralekha, Debjani knows better than to ask if her third sister called after the broadcast. Instead, she sits back, satisfied.

At home, after Eshwari and she have carried their mattresses to the terrace, laid them out and sprinkled them thoroughly with fridge-cooled water, Debjani lies back on the chilled sheet and stares at the amaltas canopy above her, replaying her big day in her mind, still hardly able to take it all in.

There are four trees in the garden whose branches nod to the terrace: a jacaranda, an amaltas, a harshringar and a champa. The girls sleep under whichever tree happens to be in flower. It is a recent ritual, started last year after the Big Three left and Debjani (finally) got to call the shots at home. She loves the seclusion and the stars on the terrace. These April mornings she often awakens to find tiny, cup-shaped, sunshine-yellow flowers curled up inside her bedclothes or upon her pillow. Sometimes she will go halfway through the day with amaltas petals caught in her long wavy hair.

Thank god it went off so well, she thinks now, cuddling her pillow. I read smoothly, I didn't panic. I didn't screw up. Hopefully they'll give me a regular slot soon. Maybe – her heartbeat quickens as she has a sudden, glad premonition of good things to come – maybe success, fame and perhaps even romance are just around the corner. Maybe Ma's right. Maybe my 'tunn' in the sun has finally come!

2

DD's dumb doll doesn't please at all
Roving Eye

Over the past few months, there has been a lot of buzz around DeshDarpan's so-called 'Operation Credibility'. We have been informed that, under the rule of our shiny new 'Mr Clean' Prime Minister, DD will become more empowered, more autonomous and a lot less incompetent. A brand-new Director General has even been imported from North Bengal and installed at Mandi House. He has been given the mandate to produce entertaining, informational content and (no sniggering please!) genuinely balanced news reportage, of the kind produced by respected public broadcasters the world over.

So it was with a fair amount of expectation that I sat down to watch the news on the old black-and-white office TV on Friday.

Well.

I'll give you the good news first. There's a nice new piece of theme music – produced by Louis Banks no less. It's a huge improvement on the earlier track, which another reviewer had compared to a galloping donkey with a broken back. The graphics have got better. Jazzy little umbrellas and smiling suns pop up on the India map during the weather reports. There is a new revolving globe logo that's rather spiffy. And there is a toothsome piece of fresh maal reading the news alongside the irritatingly plummy-voiced Amitabh Bore. Slightly frozen and clearly overwhelmed at the importance of the job she has been entrusted with, but overall quite sweet really. I almost expected her to thank her mummy and daddy and the I&B minister for giving her this golden opportunity. She read with a perfect Brit accent (rather reminiscent of C3PO from *Star Wars*) and didn't blink even once as far as I could tell, but that's forgivable. What's unforgivable is the news she read out. It was the same old I&B ministry approved, establishment appeasing pap. The Prime Minister has stated that he prefers his boiled eggs runny, the President has decided to name his bull dog Sunny... and so on.

This, at a time when all the nation wants to know is who took how much money as kickbacks in the Defence Guns deal.

This is no re-invention, DD. This is no 'credible offering'. This is yet another gross insult to the intelligence of the viewer. Do you really think our need for genuine news reportage can be assuaged by a makeover as amateurishly fake as the mole on young Dolly Thakur's chin?

'Dhillon meri jaan? Where's the column? All done?'

Dylan Singh Shekhawat, sprawled in his office chair, hammering away at the typewriter with his back to the sublime view of Ballard Estate bathed in sunshine below, doesn't bother to look up.

'Patience, bastard,' he says, his voice a deep, pleasant drawl. 'Hira's bitchy tone is a little hard for me to manage. But I really don't get this – you own the bloody paper. Why can't you get him to write his own damn column?'

Varun Ohri, fat, fair and five feet tall, rests one fleshy buttock against the edge of a conveniently placed desk, and addresses his investigative editor with sweaty candour.

'I'm a third generation rich kid, baby. My manliness has been leached by a lifetime of luxurious living. I can't yell at editors-in-chief – especially ones who went to school with the Prime Minister of India, like our man Hiranandani. I can only plead with his minions. So give me the damn article, pronto.'

'Okay.' Dylan frowns down at the sheet. 'But hang on a sec, I'm forty words short. Let me think.'

'C'mon, c'mon, just wrap it up,' Varun urges. 'I'll get you VIP passes to all the horny movies at the International Film Festival, pukka.'

Dylan looks up and grins briefly. Lean dimples flash on either side of his firm mouth, softening the impact of his slightly hawk-like nose. 'Deal. Here, want to see what I've done?'

Ohri waddles over and scans the typewritten sheet. 'What the fuck! DD bashing? Hira will freak when he sees this. You know he's up to his nose advising the PM on this Operation Credibility.'

'Don't be idiotic, VO,' Dylan replies in a bored voice. 'Hira isn't an old woman. He likes people to have their own point of view. Just because he's tight with the PM doesn't mean he's his ass-wipe.'

'Doesn't it?' Varun snorts. 'You're being extremely naïve.'

'In that case he should've hung around and written his column himself,' Dylan replies. 'Instead of telling me do it. Well, I've *done* it. He said I could write whatever I liked as long as it was show-bizzy – and this is.'

'He meant write something *safe*. About the rise of the star sons Sunny Deol and that new Kapoor kid, or the parallel cinema scene, or about blooming *Buniyaad* or something.'

'Who's Buniyaad?' Dylan asks, genuinely clueless.

Varun Ohri looks at him in frustration. Bloody Shekhawat. Just because he's got some cosy St Stephen's bonding going on with his boss, in this town teeming with journos from St Xavier's Bombay, he thinks he can get away with anything. 'Bastard, winning Bade-papaji's award for Excellence in Journalism has gone to your head,' he grunts. 'I'm telling you, Hira will flip over this.'

'He won't,' Dylan insists. 'He's from *College*, you know. He'll think it's a damn good joke – even if it's on him – and next time, he'll think twice before getting me to write his columns for him.'

This is entirely possible. Dylan Shekhawat is quite the establishment's darling. Even Bade-papaji Purshottam Ohri, Varun's grandfather and founder of the *India Post*, famously known as the Fat Old Man of Indian Publishing, has a soft spot for him. He says Shekhawat reminds him of himself in his prime. As Bade-papaji now resembles a squat, gnarled and chubby hairball, this seems unlikely. But as his 'prime' was *so* very long ago, in a Lahori village *so* very far away, there is no photographic evidence to disprove his claim.

'Look, take it or leave it,' Dylan shrugs. 'Or wait for Hira to rewrite it. I've got a train to catch. It's not like I'll even get a byline for this shit.'

Ohri nods quickly. 'I'll take it. If you're cool about the bawling out he'll hundred per cent give you, why should I care? Anyway, I agree with what you've written. But at least add forty words more, fucker.'

Dylan nods, drumming his fingers on the arms of his chair,

frowning at the typewritten sheet, his dark hair dishevelled. Then
he leans forward and hammers out a short burst of words.

One last piece of advice to Miss Dolly-Dotted-Chin.
Flutter those lashes. You'll look a little less plastic. At the
moment, the combination of your scraped-back hair and
that unwinking, basilisk gaze is frankly scary. Or maybe
that's just because my grandmother told me never to trust a
person who doesn't blink.

'Done!' Dylan gets up and stretches lazily, towering over Varun.
His white cotton shirt partially comes untucked from his pants,
revealing a sliver of lean brown belly below. He tucks it back in
and reaches for a bulging rucksack lying behind the desk.

'Pull it out and stash the carbon, will you? I'm in a hurry.'

'Hot Friday night date, huh, Dhillon baby?' Varun asks
leeringly.

Dylan glances up, suddenly serious. 'No,' he says.

'Oh?' Varun looks interested.

'Have you ever eaten all kinds of oily shit late in the night,
VO? And then rolled over in the morning and seen the congealed
remains on the plate – the chewed up bones or that orange rim of
grease around the mutton curry – and *shuddered*?'

'Oh, yeah. I *own* that feeling.' Varun nods emphatically. 'But
with me it's usually Bikaner ka bhurji straight from the packet, or
sometimes Milkmaid right out of the can.'

'Well, that's exactly how I feel nowadays whenever I roll over to
find my "hot" Friday night date in my bed on Saturday morning.'

Varun looks at him uncomprehendingly. 'Girls aren't food,
fucker. What kind of pervert are you?

Dylan flinches. Then he straightens up. 'Never mind,' he says shortly. 'I'd better hustle or I'll miss the train. I'm going to Delhi.'

'In this weather? You'll broil your balls off.'

Dylan shrugs. 'Hira wants me to work on some stuff out of Delhi. Besides, I'll get to eat some decent home-cooked food. I've had it with this ragda patties shit.'

Varun eyes him speculatively. 'More anti-Sikh-riot sob stories? I wish you'd let that go. It's been more than two years now. Move on.'

'I *have*,' Dylan assures him, scratching the dark stubble on his jaw. 'But the findings of the Special Investigation Commission will be made public any time now. I'm going to the Trans-Yamuna areas in Delhi to cover people's expectations from it. And once the findings are out, I'll record their reactions.'

With that he slaps palms with Ohri, shoulders his bag and heads out, striding quickly through the *India Post* offices – past the receptionist's station, past Bade-papaji's legendary 1920s typewriter gleaming brassily in the showcase, past the great glass doors emblazoned with the words *Truth. Balance. Courage.*

Walking down the dingy, paan-stained corridor, he encounters Mitali Dutta, a tall athletic girl with lashings of kajal, dressed in a block-printed kurta and jeans. She is tugging at the grill of the elevator and trying to light a cigarette at the same time.

'Dyl!' Her sexy mouth, rendered sexier by the silver nose ring that hovers above it, parts in a warm smile. 'Long time. Not running any more?'

'I run in the morning now,' Dylan says, hitting the ground floor button. 'The evenings have become too hot. You look exhausted, Mits.'

'God, yes,' she says, pulling off her scrunchie and shaking out her hair. 'The tapes need to go out by the end of the week, so naturally, it's nuts in there.'

'How's *Viewstrack* doing? Circulation rising?'

'Like the sun,' she replies. 'It's climbing every month. You should get the hell out of print. Seriously. TV is where the action is.'

Dylan nods, not very interestedly. *Viewstrack* is a video news magazine, a recent phenomenon that has taken the country by storm and is giving DeshDarpan its first taste of serious competition. Video cassettes with visual news stories recorded on them can be rented just like movies from video-lending libraries for ten rupees a day – they cover issues ranging from separatism, corruption and environmental damage to astrological forecasts and the extra-marital affairs of Hindi film stars.

'What's your lead story next month? Can one ask?'

Mitali smiles. 'One can ask but one can't tell,' she says archly. 'All I can say is that it's close to your heart.'

'Ah.' He smiles as they emerge on the ground floor. 'You're covering the SIC's findings on the anti-Sikh riots. Top-billing my favourite MP, Hardik Motla.'

She laughs. 'No comments, but if you take me to the Bombay Gym, who knows what I might, er, *reveal* two drinks down?'

Dylan gives her a quick smile. 'That sounds tempting. But I have a date with the Lobster.'

❖

When petite Juliet Lobo met dashing Second Lieutenant Saahas Singh Shekhawat on his Mangalore posting in 1958 and married him almost immediately, both families were appalled. But Juliet and Saahas didn't care – they were happy in their little billeted home and soon they produced Dylan, the 14th Rajputana Rifle's favourite child, practically a mascot.

'You've done the impossible, Shekhawat,' Saahas's Commanding Officer would often marvel, dandling the large-eyed, hawk-nosed, muscular infant. 'You've created a Christian Rajput. What the hell is a Christian Rajput? Either you're meek and mild, or blood-thirsty and wild. You can't be both! Poor confused child – give him a Coca Cola, someone!'

Undeterred, Saahas and Juliet proceeded to create two more Christian Rajputs – Jason Singh Shekhawat and, after a long gap, Ethan Singh Shekhawat. All three boys grew to be tall and handsome like their father, musical and devout like their mother, and extremely creative in their ways of doing mischief – a trait that was their very own and inherited from no one on either side of the family.

With three such energetic creatures hammering away at their defences, the families thawed eventually and the boys ended up spending most of their holidays at their Grandma Lobo's home in Mangalore. They ran about under the banana tree canopies in nothing but baggy shorts, strings of rosary beads bouncing on their sun-browned chests, playing football in the waves, their aquiline Rajput noses ('just like the spouts of those big aluminium kettles, ba!') peeling in the hot summer sun. For more lively entertainment, they tied a thin string to the bell inside the convent and jerked it from their home across the street at midnight, leading the nuns to believe that the chapel was haunted. They phoned the Vaz Bakery and ordered cakes iced *Happy Birthday Suzannah* or *Get Well Soon, Marietta* and derived much merriment from watching them languish unclaimed in the shop window for days on end.

Because Juliet Bai had told them her own love story a million times, making it sound more and more lyrical with each retelling, the boys grew up to be almost naïvely romantic. She also impressed upon them – especially on Dylan, the eldest – that girls were pure, delicate creatures who needed to be cherished, respected and protected. With the result that when Dylan, after seventeen years of living in an all-boys home and studying in an all-boys school, burst upon the co-educational world of St Stephen's College, he was starry-eyed, hopeful and looking for his one true love. This attitude, coupled with his undeniable hotness, skilled guitar playing and prowess at football, naturally caused all the girls to throw themselves at him. He fell violently in love and confessed his feelings in his straightforward style. She led him a merry dance and after three tumultuous months, dumped him for being 'too boring' and took up with a senior who treated her badly. After that he learnt the art of keeping girls guessing. That worked much better. Ten years on, he is a master player, an accomplished flirt, wary of commitment, and the only kind of 'protecting' he is into comes from the chemist and costs ten rupees for a pack of three.

Naturally his mother is worried. She has just quit her job at St Columba's School, where she reigned for twenty years, loved and feared in equal measure by legions of sweaty, spotty and sporty boys (who dubbed her the Lobster and acquired, in spite of themselves, an appreciation for art in her painting and sculpture class). And now that she is finally free to design a tasteful wedding card, plan an artistic church wedding and welcome a beautiful, accomplished daughter-in-law into her all-boys home, her wretched malgado isn't willing to oblige. She frets constantly, to her brushes and bartans, to Mamta Thakur, to fellow passengers on IPC buses.

'When he was little he used to say, Mamma, I'll find a nice girl quickly, okay? And then I'll love her and love her and love her till we have fifteen children! But now, just see, ba, almost thirty years old and thenga to show for it! I tell you, I'll be dead and buried in that Nicholson Cemetery before I see a grandchild!'

A new source of worry, far worse than his multiple girlfriends, is his recent obsession with the anti-Sikh riots that followed the assassination of the late Prime Minister by her Sikh bodyguards. He had been at the Delhi office of the *IP* when a freshly shorn and grievously wounded young Sikh lad stumbled in, babbling about revenge killings, burnings, rape and MP Hardik Motla. Dylan and a colleague from another paper drove down to the trans-Yamuna colony immediately. What he saw there is something he doesn't talk to his mother about. But it has changed him somehow, she realizes. Won him some big journalism awards perhaps, but taken him away from his family like no girl could.

I wish he would just settle down, she thinks. If he were a married man with responsibilities, he wouldn't go about muttering '*Truth. Balance. Courage.*' and seeking justice for dead Sikh women and testifying before Special Investigation Commissions against the Delhi Police.

Still, at least he is coming home for a month. She worries about his health: he's too thin and always forgets to put cream after his bath. Girls don't like scaly boys. He doesn't oil his hair either – suppose he goes bald? And he never cuts his toenails properly; they may get ingrown, and then how will he play soccer and frisbee and go running on the beach? Let alone walk down the aisle with a pretty, kind-hearted, fertile girl.

Juliet Lobo wanders around the house rearranging things, keeping up a little hum of worry. Suppose Jason has missed Dylan at the station? And why isn't Ethan home yet? Doesn't he want to meet his big brother? And Saahas? Where is he? She pops her head into their bedroom and finds the Brigadier polishing his shoes, his moustache imprisoned in a moustache-bund that ties around at the back of his head, pulling up his nostrils and making him look unusually fierce.

'Where are you going, Bobby?' she asks. 'You know you can't drive till your glasses get fixed.'

'To Hailey Road, Bobby,' he replies indistinctly. 'Balkishen Bau is picking me up...' His voice trails away guiltily. 'For kot-piece.'

A reproachful silence follows.

The Brigadier looks as shamefaced as one can with a strip of cloth tied tightly around one's upper lip.

'They will never be home before seven,' he offers finally. 'That train is always late.'

Juliet Bai tosses her head.

'Go, then,' she sniffs. 'And eat *there* only. More mutton chops for the boys that way. Will Balkishen Bau drop you back, or are you planning to stay the night at LN's?'

The Brigadier, greatly relieved, ignores this piece of sarcasm and leans in to kiss her gratefully. 'Don't give those pups my mutton chops, Bobby. And tell Dylan to come pick me up. He should be home by then.'

The Brigadier has timed things nicely, because the boys arrive a full hour and a half after he leaves. They stagger in, flushed and excited, Dylan lugging his rucksack, Jason weighed down by a massive brown cardboard box, his face almost purple with the effort.

Ethan bounces up from the couch, electrified. 'You didn't! How *could* you? How much did it cost! Actually, don't tell – the Lobster will flip.'

'I won't.' Dylan grins. 'But if I eat only breadcrumbs for the next three years I should be able to pay it off. Mamma! There you are!'

'Hai, why should you eat only breadcrumbs, sonna?' Juliet Bai demands, as her malgado scoops her up and swings her around the room like an ecstatic hero in a romantic movie. 'Put me down, stupid boy, what have you bought?'

The two younger boys are almost knee-deep in cardboard and bubble wrap. They sit back finally, sighing, looking reverentially at a large, squat, rectangular, grey blob that looks (to Juliet Bai) like an ugly electric oven.

'What is it?' she asks her sons.

In awed tones, Ethan and Jason tell her. What it is. Why it's so cool. And how it's going to change the face of technology forever.

'Apple makkhan toast?' sniffs Juliet Bai finally, not particularly impressed. 'What's so great about apple makkhan toast? I've made *mutton chops* for dinner.'

<hr>

Over at Hailey Road, the kot-piece game is in full swing. Until a short while ago, the fourth player in the kot-piece sessions was the Judge's younger brother, A.N. Thakur. But the two have had a falling out, and now Debjani is the fourth – and usually the best – player at the table. This is probably because she is completely uninterested both in the conversation and in the snacks doing the rounds.

Eshwari, who makes herself scarce the moment the card table makes its appearance, wonders how she can stand it. 'I mean, Balkishen Bau is just so weird, Dabbu. If I had to sit there and watch him spend half an hour stroking the warts on his nose with the card before he plays it, going *hmmm hmmm hmmm* all the while, I would flip. Doesn't it freak you out?'

'Well, yes,' Debjani replies candidly. 'But he can't help the warts, you know. It's something to do with his liver.'

'And that cough.' Eshwari isn't done yet. 'The way the balgam rattles about inside his chest, like a small animal in pain, it's –'

'He isn't *well*, Eshu,' Debjani says. 'And Ma said that BJ is already so depressed about his fight with Ashok chacha, if his kot-piece quartet breaks up too, he might totally crack. Besides, I like kot-piece. And the Brig is sweet.'

'Oh, I dig the Brig,' Eshwari agrees. 'But still. Poor you. Maybe BJ and the Ant will kiss and make up soon, huh?'

Debjani, privy to more information on the quarrel between the brothers than her younger sister, knows this is unlikely.

'Don't call Ashok chacha the Ant, Eshu,' she says. 'You know BJ doesn't like it.'

'But his initials are ANT,' Eshu points out. 'And he calls me ET, the Extra Terrestrial. So why can't –'

'Well, I don't think they'll be making up anytime soon,' Debjani cuts her short. 'Meanwhile, I'll just have to learn to love the sessions.'

They aren't *so* bad. The snacks are nice. Besides, her partner is usually Balkishen Bau, and she's quite fond of him.

'So how's the celebrity?' Balkishen Bau nods at her now over his fan of cards, like a bulbous, fantastic geisha, his watery little eyes twinkling. 'My chest grew six sizes just watching you read yesterday, beta! Such good English! Bhai, mazaa aa gaya! The line of your chaahne-wallahs outside must have grown too, eh?'

This is a sly allusion to the toli of street dogs that lives outside the gate. 16 Hailey Road has always been imbued with a certain temple-like quality, devout pilgrims have thronged its gates ever since Anjini turned a luscious fifteen, but in Dabbu's reign, this brigade has grown four-legged, panting, mangy-eared and disreputable. They sit outside the green gate and howl. Some of them have mange, and some of them, the Judge is sure, are rabid.

'The GK of those wretched pie dogs will definitely go up now that their champion is reading the news,' the Judge says wryly. 'I don't know why you encourage them, Dabbu.'

'They're excellent security,' she replies diplomatically. It is an answer she has given many times before.

'That's true,' the Judge concedes with a grunt. 'Besides, they hate my tenants with passion. I like that. Keeps them from getting too comfortable up above.'

'They haven't been throwing down that many peanut shells lately,' Balkishen Bau notes. 'What happened?'

'Winter got over, that's all,' the Judge says in disgust. 'We'll be pelted with lychee skins soon. I wish I could just get the chap to *git*.'

'Won't he git?' the Brigadier asks sympathetically.

The Judge shakes his head. 'No, he won't. Which is why I keep hoping that one of these days, Dabbu's Moti will take a chunk out of him. I've been fattening the brute up in that hope.'

Dabbu suspects it's more than that. She thinks her father has a soft spot for Moti. She's heard him humming Hemant Kumar songs to him out on the road a couple of times, and once she saw him chucking Moti under his chin and calling him 'good boy'.

The Judge looks around. 'What's that infernal racket?' he demands irritably. 'Sounds like a pig being slaughtered.'

Debjani jumps to her feet. 'It sounds like Moti. I'll go see. He's such a gentle dog. I hope no one is harassing him...'

Dylan has driven down to Hailey Road to pick up his father at a quarter to eight sharp. He has pulled up at the gate and given two sharp toots of the horn. He is hot and sweaty and itching to get back home and show the boys all the cool stuff the Apple Macintosh can do. He has no intention of venturing inside Number 16, recalling vaguely that this friend of Dadda's has some fourteen daughters, most of whom are of marriageable age. Highly avoidable.

When there's no response from the house, he gets out of the electric-blue Maruti 800 and strides up and down, trying to work up a breeze. 'Come *on*, Dadda,' he mutters. 'Hurry up.'

He is just about to turn on his heel for the third time to go lean on the car horn again, when a low, wet growling sound makes his blood run cold. He turns warily.

A tiny, scruffy cat is crouching in front of his car. Ragged, orangy-black fur, torn ear, dirty rice-like teeth bared in a weedy, unconvincing hiss.

'What the –' Dylan starts to say. And then he stops abruptly. Because this unlovely creature is Hema Malini in a white apsara sari compared to what it is hissing at.

Standing in front of the green gate of Number 16 is a beast that defies all definition. As Dylan watches in horrid fascination, its jaws work, making that wet, muddy, gurgling sound again.

Is it a donkey? he wonders. Looks big enough to be one. But what about that massive snout, that weird lopsided gait, those glittering yellow eyes? And why does it look *naked*? It seems to have no fur at all, which somehow serves to emphasize its horribleness, not to mention the humongousness of its private parts. Dylan eyes these with healthy respect, backing away as the creature pulls back black, slavering lips and bares its fangs, reminding him of the ripe jackfruit he ate as a child in Mangalore – massive white seeds protruding from drippy, yellow, overripe pulp.

The cat backs away too, and comes up with a bump against the wheel of the 800. It gives a panicked yelp, then turns to make its wretched little stand, raising one scraggy, pathetic paw, now looking like Hema Malini trying to ward off a leering, slobbering rapist-murderer.

Baby, you're toast, Dylan thinks. The hound from hell is gonna get you... unless there's something I can do... but what?

He looks around for a stone to throw or a stick to shake but spots nothing. Abruptly, the donkey-dog kicks the action into higher gear by starting to bark. Deafening, bloodcurdling, bone-marrow chilling barks. Drool drips from its massive jackfruit seed teeth. It starts to make small forward and backward lunging moves, working up a nice little rhythm, until finally it hurls itself upon the cat, its black naked tail waving behind it like a flying snake.

Dylan bends smartly and scoops up the cat. The donkey-dog leaps at him, its yellow eyes rolling wildly. He aims a kick at its hairless chest, praying his sneakers will protect his toes, but then abruptly, a look of the most ludicrous surprise crosses the creature's face. Dylan, who has grown up in an all-boys school, knows that look. It is the look of somebody whose balls have just been squeezed. Hard. As he watches, the donkey-dog, now thoroughly cowed, is yanked backward through the green gate, which is then shut smartly in its face. As it sets up an incensed howl, Dylan realizes a girl has taken its place.

'Were you kicking Moti?'

'That thing's called Moti?' he asks in disbelief. 'As in *pearl*?'

'Don't change the subject,' she snaps, tossing her wavy brown hair out of her eyes. 'Were you kicking him?'

'Well, yes,' Dylan admits. 'But only because...' He holds out his arms to display the evidence that will extenuate him, and stops abruptly. The wretched cat has wriggled out of his grasp and decamped, ungratefully leaving his shirt wet.

'Because?'

She says it challengingly, standing with legs planted wide apart and shoulders thrown back, obviously thinking he's some kind of doggie-kicking sociopath. He starts to give an indignant reply, but just then the last rays of the setting sun hit her face and he discovers that her thickly lashed eyes are the exact colour and shape as Pears soap – a scent he associates with his beloved Grandma Lobo. His throat dries up.

'Because?'

But Dylan is just staring. Dabbu, leaning against the gate, breathing a little fast because of her dash across the lawn, stares back. Behind them the sun slips into the feathery embrace of the amaltas trees lining Hailey Road.

'I'm Dylan,' he manages to say. 'I'm here to pick up my father. Brigadier Shekhawat?'

For a moment she looks at him like she's going to accuse him of lying. Then she nods.

'Wait here,' she tells him grudgingly. Then she turns on her heel and reopens the gate. 'Unbelievable! What a *sociopath*.'

'I heard that –' Dylan takes a step forward but she has already shut the gate in his face. He puts a hand to the latch, wanting her to know he isn't really a rabid dog-kicker, but the sound of teeth gnashing from within stays his hand. Neither dog nor dog-protectress, he reflects wryly, will warm to him when he is so thoroughly doused in cat pee.

❖

On Sunday morning, Mrs Mamta Thakur switches on the television at seven-thirty sharp. She sits before it, her hands busily shelling peas over a brass thaali on the table before her. A digital time clock fills the television screen for ten whole minutes and is then replaced by the revolving DeshDarpan logo which undulates on the screen for an agonizing five minutes to some incredibly depressing, keening theme music. It is *very* sad music. Children in houses across the country have been known to burst into tears on hearing the DD theme music play.

'It's horrible,' Eshwari shudders as she ties her thick shiny hair into a high ponytail. 'Like the ghost of a dead baby wailing for its phantom momma. And that logo – it's like a massive unwinking eye – I think it's a conspiracy to mass-hypnotize the whole country into mindless submission.'

Mrs Mamta looks up at her. 'Going jogging, beta?'

'She's wearing a tracksuit,' the Judge says crankily, 'so she can't exactly be going swimming.'

'Stop it, BJ,' Eshwari replies. 'Bye, Ma.'

But the Judge has just remembered something. 'Why,' he asks her, 'did everybody at that match call you Bihari?'

He has recently been to see Eshwari play at a Delhi State Basketball Zonal, and was taken aback by how aggressively she played. The other girls shied away from her, looking rather frightened. Her skin glowed, her eyes were blazing, her shiny black ponytail seemed to float on the wind like a victory pennant. And every time she scored a three-pointer from the centre of the court, raised both arms triumphantly and flashed a sweaty, exultant grin, a crowd of smitten boys cheered raucously from the sidelines: 'Bihari-Bihari-Bihari, hai hai hai!'

'Oh, that's just them being silly, BJ,' she replies. 'You know I

wear all those bright batik T-shirts? The ones I get from Janpath?
I wore one with the Buddha on it for practice and they started
calling me Bihari, because Buddha was a Bihari, get it?'

'He was Nepali, actually,' the Judge replies, still not 'getting'
why his fifth daughter has a nickname that seems more suited to a
Bombay underworld underling than a gently reared young lady.

'Stop at Gambhir Stores and get me six eggs,' is all Mrs Mamta
says. 'Here's three rupees.'

'Oh god, I hate jogging carrying stuff in my hands!' Eshu groans.
Seeing her mother's expression, she sighs. 'Okay, *fine*, Ma.'

She strides out of the house, skips over the sleeping laindis in the
sand pile and starts her jog. It is a cool morning. Hailey Road lies
damp and empty. Amaltas buds crunch below her sneakered feet, and
above her the trees paint the scene a sunny yellow. At Gambhir Stores,
old Mr Gambhir greets her with a wrinkly, conspiratorial smile.

'So!' he crows as Eshwari halts, not in the least out of breath.
'Your sister read so well on TV! She was *too* good.'

Young Mr Gambhir, his anxious looking forty-year-old son,
cuts in with an uneasy smile, 'Er, what are you wanting?'

'Six eggs, please,' Eshwari says. 'Ma said fresh.' Then she smiles
down at the stooped old man. 'Thank you,' she says.

Old Mr Gambhir beams. Always immaculately dressed in
spotless white kurta pyjama, he has presided behind the cash
counter at Gambhir Stores for as long as Eshwari can remember.
He sits right below the picture of the First Guru, the tip of his
white turban almost touching its frame of twinkling, multi-
coloured series lights, inhaling huge amounts of agarbatti smoke
and working up quite a high.

'Poached egg for breakfast, hain?' he asks jovially. 'Judge saab's
favourite!'

'Er, yes,' Eshwari replies, rolling her eyes at her friend Satish Sridhar, who happens to be at the store too, rootling hopefully in the shelf of English movie video cassettes grandiosely titled 'BEST-OF-HOLLYWOOD LENDING LIBRARY'.

Young Mr Gambhir comes back with an egg tray and places it on the counter. His father waves him away.

'How nice to know that after your didi has read the news to the whole of the country, she will go home and eat...' his hand hovers over the egg tray for a moment, then descends on the largest specimen and picks it up with a flourish, '*this*! This Gambhir Stores egg! How proud that makes me feel!'

Satish gives a little snort of laughter which he hastily turns into a cough. Old Mr Gambhir eyes him with stern, beady benevolence.

'Got a cuff, beta Steesh? Here, let me give you two Vicks ki golis instead of one-rupee change.'

Eshwari gives Satish a quelling look and smiles at the old man. 'Namaste.'

She continues her jog along her usual circuit, past the ruins of the Agrasen ki Baoli, all the way down to the T-point where Hailey Road hits the low red buildings and green grounds of Modern School, Barakhamba Road. She has to weave her way around several sand mounds heaped outside construction sites. The sand glitters silver in the sunshine. Eshwari can see tiny pink and brown conch shells in it. When she was younger, Debjani and she would pick out these shells and make necklaces with them. There have always been mounds of sand and stacks of bricks along Hailey Road, because so many of the old-style bungalows are in the process of being broken down and converted into apartments blocks under the family group housing scheme.

'So Dubs's got a real fan club going now, huh?' Satish calls out from behind her, and suddenly there he is, grinning down at Eshwari.

'Yes,' she replies shortly.

'So now you sisters will become even more snooty,' he says as he starts to walk beside her. 'That's all we need.'

'We're not snooty!'

'No?' He grins. 'All of you pricey Thakur sisters look down upon us dicey mohalla guys. Admit it!'

'You're mad,' she says evasively.

Satish and Eshwari have been walking down to Modern School together all their lives. He has always had a certain good-humoured puppy-like quality, but in the last couple of years he's shot up and become all deep and stubbly, so now, Eshwari thinks, looking at him from below her lashes, it's a German Shepherd puppy-like quality. His grins have grown vaguely wolfish, there is a warm glint in his eye, and last year, he asked her to go out with him. 'Be my chick' were his exact words. She had shuddered and turned him down as nicely as she could, explaining that, after the whole fiasco with her sister Chandu, she wasn't allowed to have a boyfriend until she turned twenty-one.

He took it badly at first, but now, more than a year on, their relationship is back on its old 'just-friends' footing. For which Mrs Mamta Thakur, for one, is extremely thankful. She thinks the Sridhar boy is on drugs. He wears black T-shirts with snakes and roses on them, bangs on a drum set and gets his hair cut once a year. He is supposed to be highly intelligent and is studying to be an engineer, but to her he seems distinctly half-witted. Besides, the Sridhars are appallingly clannish. None but a pure Tamil-Brahmin girl will ever be good enough for their darling son. A romance between Satish and Eshwari can only end badly.

'So how're you gonna top Dabbu's act, huh, Bihari? With basketball? India doesn't even have a proper basketball team. You'll have to run away to Bombay and join the movies.'

'Excuse me, that's a really sexist thing to say!' Eshwari exclaims, pulling a face. 'It implies that my options are purely bimboesque.'

'Not true,' he parries promptly. 'You could become a director. A cinematographer. A producer. Don't put your narrow little thoughts into my big broad mind.'

'Jog in front of me and I'll put my narrow little foot into your big broad behind,' Eshwari invites him sweetly. 'Stupid.'

Satish chuckles and ducks nimbly out of the way of her swinging foot.

'You just wanna lech at my butt,' he says coyly. 'Not that I get that. I mean, why this obsession with guys' backsides? Shouldn't you be interested in their, um, frontsides?'

Eshwari turns on him. 'I'm holding *eggs*,' she tells him, starting to open the brown paper packet threateningly.

The ghost of Holis past makes Satish backtrack hastily.

'Or you could top the school,' he says. 'To be better than Dabbu, I mean. Now *that's* doable.'

Eshwari, whose studies aren't her strong point, glares at him. 'I am not competing with my sister,' she says coldly. 'Hence, I do not need to consider any of these stupid options. Directing movies, topping school, etc etc.'

'Stupid people always say *hence* and *etcetera etcetera* when they wanna come across smart,' says the incorrigible Satish and vanishes into the driveway of Number 8 before Eshwari can think of anything to say. She glares, shrugs and picks up her pace – he was slowing her down anyway.

But when she gets into the house, nobody seems hungry. Her

parents are sitting at the kitchen table looking solemn, while Dabbu, still in her nightie, her hair scattered wildly about her, sits between them sobbing tragically.

'What?' Eshwari asks uneasily. 'Did one of the laindi pie dogs get run over again?'

Debjani holds out the paper, her hands trembling, her eyes huge and tear-filled. 'It's the *India Post*.' She hiccups tragically. 'Calling me *Dolly*. Saying I'm en-en-*enthusiastic*. And naïvely overwhelmed. Everybody must be laughing at me. DD'll never call me back to read again! I've never been so hu-hu-humiliated in my life!'

And with that she puts her head down on the table and sobs like her heart will break.

⋅→⊷⊙⊷←⋅

'What ruddy histrionics,' the Judge mutters as he stirs his evening tea. 'I live in a house full of Meena Kumaris. It's just one person's rant in one miserable publication. Will somebody tell that girl she's overreacting?'

Mrs Mamta Thakur puts the teapot down with a sigh.

'You know how shy she is, LN. She's just started to step out of the shadow of her big sisters and bloom a little.'

Mrs Mamta is much given to nature metaphors. She often refers to her girls as birds, who confusingly (but poetically) *bloom*. Anjini was an early bloomer, Binni was a late bloomer. Chandu, she hopes, though she has no news of her, is finally in full bloom. Even in her fervent tête-à-têtes with the Almighty, when she beseeches Him to let her girls reach their full potential, she asks Him to let them 'bloom'. The Judge, though an avid gardener, doesn't like the word. It feels too wishy-washy to him, too fragile and suggestive of flowers. He'd rather his girls grew into something more substantial and well-buttressed – like a row of sturdy sheesham trees, say.

'That Anjini is to blame for everything,' he says now, promptly going off on a tangent. 'Yesterday also, all she could do was criticize. Obviously her magic mirror has started whispering to her about Dabbu's growing fame. Any day now she'll show up dressed as an old crone and try and slip her a poisoned apple.'

'Why are you always so mean about Anji?' Mrs Mamta demands.

'Because she always has to be the centre of attention,' the Judge replies. 'She pushes everybody else out. She always has.'

'She doesn't push everybody out, you always pull her in!' Mrs Mamta flashes. '*I* was talking about Debjani.'

'Well, if Debjani can't handle criticism, she shouldn't be in the public eye,' says the Judge, shovelling devilled Maggi noodles into his face. 'Simple.'

'No, it's not simple,' his wife flares up. 'It's the *India Post*, LN! Everybody reads it.'

'Worshipping at the altar of the god-of-what-people-will-think,' the Judge mutters, chewing agitatedly. 'It's high time she found a worthier deity.'

'Will you please stop talking tough to cover up for the fact that you're upset?'

If I still had a court to go to, the Judge thinks as he swallows, she would never talk back so snappily.

'Nobody will read that story,' he says testily. 'The front page news is all about fresh evidence incriminating the Prime Minister in the Bofors gun case. People will only remember that. And even if they do read the article, please remind your daughter that DD auditions are no joke – even Amitabh Bachchan auditioned at AIR and got rejected! So Debjani must have done *something* right. She mustn't be so upset because *one* person, who was in a bad mood because his wife denied him sex like all wives are wont to do nowadays,' (Mrs Mamta gasps at this random barb) 'decides to pan her. And if you read it carefully, he *isn't* panning her. He's panning DD!'

His wife doesn't reply. Her diamond nose pin is quivering. It is a portent of tears to come.

'Dabbu is sensitive,' she says. 'She *feels* things. And I had really thought,' her voice breaks just a little, 'that her supta vastha was finally over!'

'That rubbish again!' the Judge flares up, really angry now. 'I am disappointed, Mamtaji, that a sensible woman like you –'

'Oh, be quiet,' she cuts him off pettishly. 'Of course I know it's all rubbish hocus-pocus. But I *had* hoped good times were finally here for her, LN.'

There is silence as the Judge scoops up the last of his Maggi.

'So is madam coming to play or what? Or must we spend all Sunday mourning this national tragedy?'

Debjani, stalking into the garden at this moment, hears this last remark. She tightens her lips and pulls up a chair and sits down, her expression distant. Looking at her swollen eyes, her reddened nose and generally woebegone demeanour, the Judge's heart contracts with fiercely protective sympathy. He wants to find Roving Eye and bash her/him to pulp.

'Ha, *there* you are!' he grunts. 'Good, good, the others will be here any moment. Move the fan a little, Mamtaji, d'you want all our cards to fly away?'

'Move it yourself,' Mrs Mamta retorts. 'I'm going inside. I'll send out more Maggi when your friends get here.'

Debjani and the Judge eye each other warily. Debjani has heard enough, throughout the day, to know that her father thinks she is overreacting. And perhaps she is. But she isn't ready to laugh over it yet – the words *wide-eyed* and *breathless* and *thank her mummy and daddy and the I&B minister for giving her this golden opportunity* are playing in her head like a looped cassette. She helps herself to Maggi and says nothing.

The Judge opens his mouth to speak.

'One word about the Vunderful Vladimir and I will run out of this garden screaming,' Debjani says in a low, clear voice.

He gapes at her. These wretched women can all read his mind!

Mrs Mamta Thakur calls out from the verandah, 'They phoned from Rajpur Road. Balkishen Bau is unwell, he won't be coming today. Should I call Saahas Shekhawat and tell him not to come?'

The Judge frowns, disappointed. 'Unwell again! There goes our foursome!'

'And now we must spend the rest of Sunday mourning *this* national tragedy,' Debjani mutters, rolling her eyes. The Judge, pleased that she seems to be rallying, shoots her a dirty look so that she knows things are back to normal.

'Should I call? Mrs Mamta asks again patiently.

'Haan haan, call him – no, wait, it's Sunday. He said he would come straight after evening Mass. We'll just have to tell him when he gets here.'

They look towards to the gate where, on cue, an electric-blue Maruti 800 has just rolled up. The Brigadier emerges, slams the door behind him and makes for the green baize table with the vim of a cheetah that has just brushed its teeth and spotted zebra. But the Judge bounds to his feet and rushes to the gate, gesticulating at the reversing vehicle to stop.

'Stop him, Shekhawat, stop him! Arrey, don't run down those mongrels... my daughter ties rakhis to them! That's better, nobody dead or maimed. Haan, you! Young man! Arrey, what hello-sir hello-sir? Come out of the car. You know how to play kot-piece, don't you?'

⋅━◉━⋅

And we know that all things work together for good, for those who love God, thinks Dylan dreamily, fresh from church, *for those he has called according to his purpose.* How providential, that while he has been racking his brains on how to get a second look at the ball-squeezing girl with the disturbingly tawny eyes, her father himself should urge him in, place him upon a pink cane chair and offer him devilled Maggi and steaming hot tea?

She hasn't acknowledged him, though. She is busy dealing out the cards, her body moving in a smooth rhythm, the cards dropping onto the table without a whisper. She is wearing one of those baggy, boat-necked, striped T-shirts that all the girls are wearing nowadays, the ones that, halfway through the day, slip off one shoulder in approved *Flashdance* style to reveal a smooth shoulder and a pretty strap. Hers doesn't slip, he notices, even when she leans forward and places the diminished pack in the centre of the table. All that's on display are collarbones that curve back into her shoulders in a way that makes him think, inexplicably, of wings. A tiny silver dog hangs from a thin chain around her neck. She's really not my type, he decides. Chalo, I'm glad *that's* cleared up.

'Young man, you have to play! Hurry up!'

'I'm sorry,' Dylan apologizes, looking at his cards hurriedly. 'My grasp of this game is a little rusty.' He plays his turn. Not very well, apparently.

'That's the trump!' the Judge groans. 'Why are you trumping me? I'm your partner!'

'Fool,' the Brigadier crows gleefully as the girl over-trumps the card Dylan has just played. 'We made the first hand, Dabbu! Well done!'

She gives him a small lopsided smile and looks down at her cards. Something about that smile strikes a chord in Dylan's memory.

'Sorry, have we met before, er, Dabbu?'

Her head comes up instantly, twin pools of Pears kindling with anger.

'It's *Debjani*,' she says coldly. 'And we met yesterday, when you were kicking Moti.'

Ah, eye contact at last. But she has already looked away.

'I wasn't kicking that dog, Debjani,' he says pleasantly. 'I mean, I *was*, but only to stop it from pulverizing a cat, a tiny, orangy-black cat with a torn ear, so –'

'There are no cats on this street,' she cuts him short.

'No?' Dylan, master of flirtation, smiles playfully. 'Are you *sure*?'

Debjani flushes and looks away. Is this dog-kicker calling *her* a cat? What a jerk. And why did she break out in goosebumps when he said her name in that deep, disturbingly intimate voice? And how mortifying it is that her father dashed madly across the lawn to commandeer him. What if he thinks BJ is up to some extremely unsubtle matchmaking? On top of that, she realizes, her blood curdling at the potential clunkers this could cause her father to drop, his name begins with D.

She shakes back her mass of wavy hair and looks up at D-for-Dylan indifferently.

'Yes,' she says steadily. 'I'm sure.'

Looking into her eyes, Dylan has the strangest sensation, like his belly has just executed a lazy backflip.

'It's your turn again, Dyl, play,' the Brigadier grunts irately, rocking in his chair, caressing his moustache.

'Uh, sure. Here you go.'

'Why didn't you trump *that*?' the Judge groans. 'Idiot!'

'Whoops, sorry, sir.'

'We lost,' mourns the Judge five minutes later. 'Really, Shekhawat, this fellow is obviously your family idiot.'

'BJ!' Debjani remonstrates, turning a little pink.

The Judge looks slightly shamefaced, then recovers. 'My daughter Debjani is very protective of losers!' he declares. 'When India won the World Cup she was the only person in the country who sat down and fretted about how bad the poor West Indians must be feeling.'

'That's a little unpatriotic,' Dylan murmurs.

'They were just so *sure* they were going to win,' Debjani mutters. 'It must have been really tough for them to accept that they lost. And anyway, we're too cricket-obsessed in this country – what about hockey? It's our national game, you know.'

The Judge waggles his head in an amused see-what-I-mean manner. 'And do you know why she is called Dabbu?' he asks as he starts to deal the cards.

'Why, sir?' asks Dylan with boyish, deferential interest.

Debjani is torn between wanting to slap him and wanting to strangle her father.

'Because,' the Judge chuckles, still dealing, 'when she was a child, although everybody loved the Kapoor clan – Raj Kapoor, Shammi Kapoor, then Shashi Kapoor and Rishi Kapoor – somehow that funny-faced Randhir Kapoor's career didn't click. All his movies flopped. So Debjani decided to like him. She felt he needed fans. She saw *Jawaani Deewani* six times – in the *theatre*. And when *Stardust* reported that his nickname was Dabbu, naturally her sisters started calling her that.'

Way to go, BJ, Debjani thinks resignedly as she picks up her cards. Reveal me as an uncool person who actually watches Hindi films. Next you'll be telling him about the supta vastha.

'So George Harrison must be your favourite Beatle, then?' Dylan asks and can tell, from the way she immediately stiffens, that he has guessed correctly.

'"While My Guitar Gently Weeps" is a *classic*,' she tells him coldly. 'Miles ahead of most crowd-pleasing Lennon-McCartney compositions.'

She's actually serious, Dylan thinks, amused. What a weird chick! But she is retreating behind her cards again – he must say something to stop her.

'Dabbu isn't *that* bad a nickname, actually,' he volunteers. 'I mean, imagine if they'd started calling you Randhir.'

She ignores him, settling back in her chair and arranging her cards. This Bombay import, she thinks furiously, is just the sort of guy I most distrust.

Dylan retreats, not looking at all put out. The circulating fan turns towards Debjani, cooling her hot cheeks. Things *could* have been worse, she admits to herself. At least BJ has been sensitive enough not to bring up the article in the *India Post*. Probably worried that if he does, I may start blubbering in public and embarrass him in front of his friends.

'This is the third time Balkishen Bau has bailed on us, isn't it, LN?' the Brigadier says presently.

The Judge nods. 'Yes, Balkishen the Bloody Bailer. Truly there is something in first letters! My name is Laxmi and I'm a lawyer. Your name is Saahas and you are a soldier. My wife's name is Mamta and she's a mother. Interesting.'

'No, BJ,' Debjani jumps in, realizing this conversation is headed straight for a *D for Dylan, D for Debjani* discovery. 'Firstly, Balkishen Bau is unwell. And secondly, you're just twisting the words around to make it work. If uncle's name was Ajay, you would have said he's in the Army. If yours was Jinesh you'd have said you're a judge. It's just silly.'

'Your name is Debjani and you just called diamonds,' Dylan points out.

Debjani notices with horror that the Brigadier's son has lean dimples in his cheeks. D for dimples, she thinks, appalled. Oh god, don't let BJ notice.

She flashes him a discouraging look.

'Anjini married Anant and they live in Allahabad,' continues the Judge inexorably. 'Binodini married a businessman. And Chandu, that is to say, um... and so on.'

'LN has his own unique theory, as you can see,' the Brigadier chuckles. 'He thinks personality traits are alliterative. And matrimonial choices should be too.'

Laxmi is a loonie, Debjani thinks savagely. Mamta is a martyr. Then she realizes she is just proving her father's point and gives herself a shake.

Her fingers are slim, Dylan notices in the meantime, and there is a silver ladybird ring on one finger. And every time the circulating fan turns its steel head towards her, her hair floats away to reveal delicate lines of shoulder, neck and cheek. He is observing this phenomenon with interest when she looks up from her cards and catches him staring. His stomach, which seems to have acquired the soul of a Russian ballerina, rises to its toes and does a series of graceful, slow-motion somersaults through the air. He looks away, flushing. This is ridiculous.

'And what's *your* name again, young man?' the Judge asks. Debjani stiffens. Dylan opens his mouth to answer but she is too quick.

'Can we *play*?' she says, her voice slightly bored. 'We're really slow today. Only three rounds so far. Usually we manage six rounds in two hours.'

'Hain? What is all this?' the Judge says instantly. 'The family idiot is wrecking our average! Focus, young man, focus!'

'*You're* talking the most, LN,' the Brigadier says laconically. 'Here, look, Dabbu and I have won this hand too.'

Dylan groans inwardly as he looks down at his cards and focuses, focuses.

And so the game continues, more smoothly now that the new recruit has got the hang of it. Twilight steals across the garden, the singing of the birds grows softer until it is replaced by the humming of crickets. Finally, Mrs Mamta Thakur walks onto the verandah.

'LN,' she calls. 'Seven o'clock.'

Dylan looks up, suddenly, absurdly disappointed. He realizes he has just spent thirty minutes totally on tenterhooks, waiting for a girl he doesn't fancy to look at him. And she hasn't. How humiliating.

Abruptly, he decides he won't go home without getting through to Miss Ball-squeezer. Just so he can get her off his mind for good. He waits for the game to end and then leans in and addresses her directly.

'Um, Debjani? I need to make a call please. Could you show me where the phone is?'

'It's inside,' she says, her tone discouraging.

An awkward silence follows.

'Might as well carry that card table then, if you're going inside,' the Judge urges. 'Strong young fellow like you! It'll save the girls having to take it in later.'

So Dylan folds up the table and takes it inside. Debjani holds the door open for him, her mind clearly elsewhere. He notices, as he walks behind her, that her legs in her ragged denim cut-offs are slender, smooth and temptingly honey-brown. There is a thin silver bracelet clasped around one ankle. There's probably some small animal dangling off that too.

'Where should I put it?' he enquires, hefting the table.

'Here, thanks. And the phone's right over there.'

She starts to walk away.

'There *was* a cat, you know,' he says. 'I didn't make it up.'

'If you say so.'

'It had half an ear missing and it was a dirty orangy brown colour.'

'A tortoiseshell, you mean.'

'Do I? Okay, a tortoiseshell, then. One learns something new every day.'

She continues to look sceptical.

'Anyway, you're a fine one to lecture against cruelty to animals,' he says, piqued. 'When you know very well that you grabbed Moti's vitals and gave 'em a good long squeeze.'

She stiffens, looking decidedly shifty, then starts to speak.

'Don't deny it,' he says before she can reply. 'The expression on his face was a dead giveaway.'

She sits down on top of the card table and finally gives him her full attention.

'See, he's a street dog,' she explains earnestly. 'He isn't trained. I wasn't being cruel. It's the only way I can control him when he gets that rabid.'

'He could have bitten you,' Dylan replies. 'You were barefoot. And wearing those, er, shorts.'

He looks at them as he speaks, noticing that much hard work and creativity has gone into the cut-offs. They are deliberately ripped and embroidered all over with stars and ladybirds – what *is* it with this girl and ladybirds, anyway?

A little silence. Debjani slides her hands into her pockets, puffing out the ladybirds. 'These are called Daisy Dukes,' she tells him loftily. 'They're a craze in the US right now.'

'Really?' He grins. 'Hey, that proves your dad's theory – D for Daisy Dukes. *Double* D, actually.'

Her nostrils flare. 'Is that a cheap crack about my cup size?' she snaps.

'Wha...?' Dylan hastily averts his eyes from her. 'No no, no way! Of course not!'

'Good,' she says calmly. 'Because I don't take any shit from guys. I'm a Modernite, you know.'

And deep down I'm just a Columban, Dylan thinks, feeling slightly harassed. A good, convent-educated boy who always makes the mistake of crediting girls with more sweetness than they possess.

'The only reason I mentioned the, er, Daisy Dukes,' he says carefully, 'is because you could've got bitten on your legs.'

She shrugs. 'I covered my hand with a napkin. A cheesecloth napkin. They're very thick.'

There were thick cheesecloth napkins on the card table today. Dylan wiped his mouth with one. He tries not to think about it.

He says, 'At least you admit he's not the shrinking angel you're making him out to be. *What* is he, anyway? Why doesn't he have any hair?'

She crosses her arms across her chest. 'He has khujli,' she says in a low voice. 'Mange. His fur fell out and I've got him all these injections, and it's growing back, but very slowly, and till then nobody will go near him.'

Except you, Dylan thinks, staring at her. Dabbu. Lover of losers.

'Anyway, you'd better make your phone call. And I should go help with dinner.' She jumps lightly to her feet and tilts her head. 'Goodnight.'

And that's when it clicks. Her hair's all open and she has no make-up on and her shorts are a far cry from the stiff kanjeevaram she wore on TV and she's in colour now, not black-and-white, but there can be no doubt after that lilting 'Goodnight'.

'You're that newsreader!' Dylan exclaims. 'Debjani something!'

Instantly, her face clouds over. Then her eyes get all squinty, she straightens herself, suddenly looking much taller, and raises her chin.

'Yes.'

Dylan's head is in a whirl. 'But you look... so different. Your hair... the shorts...' He frowns. 'Is that mole *real*?'

Almost without realizing it, he has moved forward, putting out a hand to the mole he hasn't noticed so far because he's been so taken by her eyes. She slaps his hand away.

'Yes, it's *real*,' she flashes. 'What did you think? That I painted it on before the news bulletin because I want to look like Aruna Irani?'

'Who's Aruna Irani?' Dylan asks, bewildered.

Debjani makes an infuriated noise inside her throat. Dylan Singh Shekhawat, clutching his stinging hand, knows he has never heard a more adorable sound in his life.

'Just make your phone call, okay?' she says. 'And then let yourself out. Goodnight.'

3

The Judge wakes up on Tuesday morning to the melodious sound of koels koohoo-koohing. He smiles, rolls onto his side, opens his eyes to drink in the sight of his front lawn, and gets a rude shock. The garden fauna, which until yesterday consisted only of the aforementioned koels, along with several chirruping sparrows and fluttering butterflies, has just had its numbers swollen by an unwelcome new addition.

'What the devil...?' the Judge demands, springing out of bed like a suddenly switched on fountain. 'Why is that ruddy Gulgul cavorting about naked in my garden like a sturdy gazelle?'

Mrs Mamta hurries over to look. 'He's wearing a ganji and cycling shorts, LN,' she says, sounding disappointed. 'You bhi na, always exaggerating. But Eshwari's right – Gulgul keeps pumping iron only with his arms, so his chest is big and puffy but his legs are like toothpicks and he has no backside to speak of.'

'He's got enough for me to kick,' the Judge grunts, casting about with one hand for his slippers. 'Ah, here they are! What's he doing now?' He goes up to the window. 'He's leaping over the flowerbeds! And picking up my stone pigeons and doing bicep curls with them!'

Snatches of song waft across the lawn. Gulgul's voice is gaspy but game. He is clearly in a very good mood. The Judge, who isn't as 'regular' as he used to be, thinks sourly that the young thug has probably had a really good bowel movement.

'*Ey miss, dey dey kiss. Aa gaya, Love 86!*' warbles Gulgul, his bouffant hair bouncing with every upward flick of his pigeon-dumbbells.

'Damn his insolence!' the Judge snorts. 'Don't pour my tea yet, Mamtaji, it'll get cold. I'll drink it after I've killed him.'

A few minutes later, Gulab Thakur feels bony fingers pressing into his neck. He gives a little yelp.

'Kaminey,' his uncle's voice says tenderly in his ear. 'You think my garden is a bloody home gym? Tell me why I shouldn't break your ruddy neck?'

'Gu-gu-good morning, Tauji!' Gulgul gasps. 'I just looked across from my room and thought ki, I mean, these pigeons are exactly the right weight, and papa refuses to pay for more equipment, s-s-sorry, Tauji.'

'Put those pigeons back exactly where you found them,' his uncle tells him curtly. 'And come in and eat something now that you're here. Uff, bring your bag, duffer. And is that a *guide*? You're studying law from a Jhabvala Guide? No wonder you keep failing!'

Gulgul, somewhat buoyed by the aroma of ande-ka-bhurji, scoops up the despised guide and creeps into the kitchen. The Judge vanishes behind his newspapers.

'Namaste, Taiji,' Gulab smiles at his aunt.

'Arrey, Gulgul. Come, eat something.'

He tucks happily into everything she puts before him, refusing only the cold coffee because, according to his idol Arnold Schwarzenegger, 'milk is for babies'.

'You're not *that* big yet, Gulab,' Mrs Mamta says fondly. 'How soft and huge your eyes were when you were a baby – just like gulab jamuns. And your skin was so fair!'

The Judge thinks privately that this was probably because his childless sister-in-law had picked out the fairest, best-looking baby she could find in all of Delhi's orphanages. And, naturally, one with a penis. Too bad one can't do height and IQ tests on infants. Gulgul has turned out to be rather short on both counts.

'How are your studies going?' the Judge barks.

Gulgul gulps. He has been trying to follow in his uncle's steps and study law, but he is finding it an uphill task. He has already failed the second-year exams twice.

'Quite well, Tauji,' he says weakly. 'Hehe.'

The Judge makes a small disgusted sound in his throat and leaves the table. Gulgul turns large, timid eyes towards his aunt.

'I wasn't running about in the garden just like that, Taiji,' he volunteers. 'I was practising positive visualization. I imagined the flowerbeds are my exams and I am clearing them smoothly, one by one. Then I lifted the pigeons like I was lifting the pressure I am under. That is how bodybuilding helps you in everyday life, you know.'

She hands him a banana. 'So what are you studying for now, beta?' she asks him kindly.

Gulgul's eyes cloud over. His bouffant goes a little phuss.

'Huf,' he confesses in a low voice and takes a great bite out of the banana.

'Oh, *Huf.*' Mrs Mamta nods vaguely.

'Hindu Undivided Family,' Gulab explains. 'Like us. We are all coparceners in Dadaji's estate.'

'Oh, no.' Mrs Mamta is more confident now. 'Your Dadaji

already divided his estate between your father and your Tauji, Gulgul. All that is *done*.'

'Well, you and the girls are all coparceners in Tauji's estate, then,' Gulab says. 'You're a Huf.'

'Sounds like a simple enough subject,' Mrs Mamta says as she clears the table.

Gulab shakes his head earnestly. 'No, Taiji, it is very complicated! Look at this question, for example.' He leafs through his *Jhabvala Family Law Guide*, clears his throat and begins to read.

'A, a male Hindu, dies intestate in 1979 and is survived by a widow W. He has three sons S1, S2 and S3. S1 is a cripple with an adopted son S1S. S2 is a lunatic. S3 converted to the Muslim faith, married a Muslim girl S3W, begat a son S3S and then died during the lifetime of A. S1S fell into bad company and murdered the brother of A over a property dispute. Discuss who will inherit the 5 crore property of A and what the shares will be.'

'How tragic for widow W,' Mrs Mamta says, much affected. 'Three sons – one mad, one crippled, one dead and, even worse, *Muslim*!'

Gulab Thakur clucks reprovingly. 'The question is not one of tragedy, Taiji, but of legality.'

'That's why daughters are so much better than sons,' his aunt muses. 'They're less sickly, too sensible to commit murder and they know there are no gods like Hindu gods, baba!'

'Don't you want to know who will inherit how much?' Gulab asks.

But before Mrs Mamta can reply, Gulab's mother stumps into the room, her bulldog-like face bobbing bizarrely above her cotton-candy-pink sari. She sees her son and cuffs him behind the ears.

'Ow!'

'Eating egg on Tuesday! And who will eat the atte-ka-halwa I made?'

'Mummy, I keep telling you, I have to eat a protein-rich diet,' Gulab replies as he grabs his *Jhabvala Guide* and makes a rapid retreat towards the door.

'He came over because of his studies,' Mrs Mamta says soothingly. 'Some problem he wanted his uncle's help with.'

Bhudevi Thakur sits down.

'I hate her,' she announces.

'Who?' Mrs Mamta asks warily, picking up her embroidery hoop and needle. As long as she can remember, Bhudevi has always hated *somebody*. It's what keeps her going. She organizes her life around the object of her disaffection the way other people organize their living-room furniture around their TV set. And like a TV, she upgrades to a new model every few years. In her childhood it was her elder sister, who had apparently been much fairer than her. She died before Bhudevi got married and her irreverent nieces insist it was their Bhudevi chachi herself who bumped her off. After her wedding, Chachiji focused her hatred on her mother-in-law. After *her* death Mrs Mamta found herself promoted to the spot of Chachiji's Enemy Number 1, and after spending a few unnerving years in this unwanted spotlight, thankfully found herself displaced by a luscious little item called the Hot Dulari, who is employed as cook at Number 13 and (according to Chachiji) flirts with Ashok Narayan constantly.

'Oho, Dulari, who else,' Chachiji replies. 'She is trying to do jaadu-tona on me.'

'No no,' Mrs Mamta protests weakly. 'Aise kaise? Voo-doo, jaadu-tona, it's just superstitious rubbish. It doesn't work. Everybody knows that.'

Chachiji shakes her head. 'She went off to her village for three days saying somebody had died and she had to attend the funeral. And you know what she did there?'

Mrs Mamta doesn't want to know. 'What?' she asks in her most discouraging voice.

Chachiji leans in, her eyes glinting. 'She sat in the front row when they were burning the dead body. She cried loudly and beat her breast – all dikhawa, of course! And then, when nobody was watching, she put her hand into the embers and scooped up a handful of the dead woman's ashes.'

'Why?' Mrs Mamta asks, intrigued in spite of herself.

'She put them into an empty Postman-oil-ka-tin and brought them to Delhi, mixed them with the dalia I take every morning, and made me eat them.'

'*Why?*' Mrs Mamta asks, truly mystified now.

'Arrey, to turn me into a cannibal! Because the spirits of dead people can enter cannibals, na. Everybody knows that. She's trying to drive me mad.'

Mrs Mamta puts down the pretty cross-stitch pansies she is embroidering and looks at her sister-in-law in fascination.

'*How* do you know she's doing this, Bhudevi?'

Chachiji's voice drops to an impressive whisper. 'Because our mother-in-law told me. Today only.'

There is a small problem with this statement. Mrs Mamta articulates it.

'But our mother-in-law is dead.'

Chachiji shoots a distinctly irate look at her sister-in-law. 'Didn't you hear a word I said? I've been turned into a cannibal against my will and now my dead mother-in-law gets into my body and talks to me.'

'But,' Mrs Mamta perseveres, trying to stay calm and reasonable, 'why would the Hot Dulari do that? What would she get out of turning you into an, uh, medium?'

'She's trying to drive me crazy,' Chachiji replies simply. 'That's her plan. She wants me packed off to an asylum so she can live in sin, khullam-khulla, sabke samne, in Number 13 with AN.'

Mrs Mamta cannot for the life of her imagine why *anybody* would want to live with her smiley, slimy brother-in-law. But AN has never lacked admirers. Chachiji, for all her pugnacity, is pathetically smitten with him. And so, clearly, is the Hot Dulari.

'It's the sleazy Thakur charm,' the Judge assures Mrs Mamta whenever she brings up this puzzling point. 'I missed out on it but AN has it in spadefuls – he's the spitting image of our father.'

Mrs Mamta sniffs. She does not particularly approve of her late father-in-law. Pushkar Narayan Thakur had been a handsome, profligate hellraiser, descended from a long line of horny Hailey Road Thakurs. The family had at one time owned almost half the houses on Hailey Road, built on barren land bequeathed to them by the later Mughals for what was vaguely termed 'services to the empire'. Nobody talks about what exactly these 'services' were, but Mrs Mamta suspects they involved gambling, extortion, contract killings and some high-level pimping. Old Pushkar Narayan was certainly guilty of all these vices – he had inherited five houses on Hailey Road and shrunk them down to two over fifty years of debauchery and sloth. He left one to each of his boys and proceeded to die noisily and painfully of liver cirrhosis, three months after his long-suffering wife tumbled to her death while gathering clothes from the terrace of Number 13 during a sudden hailstorm.

'But where will she live in sin with AN?' Mrs Mamta asks Chachiji now. 'Number 13 has just been sold!'

This is true enough. Ashok Narayan has run through his inheritance at a rate that would have warmed the cockles of his dissolute father's heart and the house has had to be sold in order to pay off the debts. All Ashok will retain is one ground-floor flat in the block of residential flats that is to come up in its stead.

'That all I don't know,' Chachiji says crossly. 'I just know what the Pushkarni told me when she ghussoed in my body. I was just looking at that photu of hers, you know the one where she is smiling, holding AN in her arms, when *phuttt*! She dived inside my body through my open mouth. My neck jerked back and my nose-trills became big, and bas, there she was inside me, with her vegetarian appetite and her gassy stomach and all. *You and your husband are doomed*, she said in my head. *I will never let this house be sold. And your whole family is going to fall apart – wait and see!*'

This last certainly sounds prophetic. Things in the family have deteriorated recently. Not content with selling his own house, Ashok Narayan Thakur wanted the Judge to sell *his* house too, as together the property would command a much higher price per square foot. But the Judge categorically refused, insisting there had always been Thakurs on Hailey Road and there always would be, and where did AN think he was going to marry his girls off from? The newly built Maurya Sheraton hotel on S.P. Marg?

Unfortunately, not all his girls see eye-to-eye with him on this. Binni, his strident second daughter, who is in dire need of funds to shore up her husband's family business, heard the whispers of a house sale and arrived hotfoot from her home in Bhopal to urge her father to sell the house and hand over her one-sixth share instantly.

'You *must* help me, Bauji,' she told him stubbornly. 'You put me in a Hindi medium school and left me in the village with Chachaji for six years – that spoilt my chances *forever.* My own sisters think I'm a behenji. I have to be compensated.'

She had conveniently glossed over the fact that this had been done only because her asthma was so chronic that the doctors insisted she live, not in polluted Kanpur, which was where the Judge was posted in those days, but in the countryside.

'Binni, it would be idiotic to sell this house now,' her father said mildly. 'Its value will escalate for years yet.'

'But Vickyji's business needs funds or it'll go thupp! You have to give me my one-sixth hissa *now.*'

The Judge, who abhors the word *hissa* – the many sibilants in it always make him think of a coiled snake, black hood raised and fangs ready to strike – tried to keep his patience.

'Then maybe he should get a job. He had a decent enough job when you married him, why this obsession with business?'

'Vickyji says only incomepoops do monthly income jobs,' Binni declared. 'Vickyji says you need balls to do business.'

'As your twins made their appearance barely ten months into your marriage, I am well aware that Vickyji's testicles are ISI-mark-approved,' her father replied testily. 'But he shouldn't be frittering away their inheritance like this.'

'But Ashok chacha is selling,' Binni pursued. 'Why can't *you* do like he's doing?'

'AN *has* to sell,' the Judge, goaded beyond endurance after a week of this whining, finally snapped. 'I don't. I'm not going to sell the last Thakur house on Hailey Road. Understood?'

Tears immediately slid into her bold black eyes and the Judge took a hasty jab at lightening the mood. 'And if you *didn't* understand, I can explain it again in Hindi. Haha.'

At which Binni gave a convulsive sob and stormed out of the house. She has since filed a case against her father, asking for the partition and sale of the house and the handing over of her one-sixth share. The Judge is livid. It's been three months since they've spoken.

'I'm sorry Binni turned out so bad, Mamta bhabhi,' Chachiji mutters now. 'I would speak to her, but she is too high class these days, acts like she never lived with me for all those years. AN acts like that too – though he isn't too snooty to sleep with the cook.' Her face brightens. 'But the Pushkarni's told me how to fix the Hot Dulari!'

'How?'

Chachiji beams, her puggish face ecstatic. 'I just have to take one of her pubic hairs, stuff it into a halved nimbu, add a drop of AN's blood, then tied a rakhi over it and burn it in the sink. He will lose all lust for her *immediately*.' She cackles happily.

'But where will you get hold of the, er, key ingredient?' Mrs Mamta asks, reeling slightly.

'I'll figure something out,' Chachiji replies. 'Or rather, the Pushkarni will figure something out!'

'Right,' Mrs Mamta sighs.

'*She's* the real reason why LN bhaisaab didn't lift a finger to help when our house was being sold!' Chachiji continues tragically. 'He *hates* Number 13 – because she died there, na! He'll be happy to see it torn down!'

'That's not true, Bhudevi,' Mrs Mamta says sternly. 'LN is not so sentimental. Or superstitious. He is an educated man.'

Chachiji stares at her for a while, her face tense, and Mrs Mamta starts to worry that she has taken her last statement as a sly jab at Ashok Narayan Thakur, who isn't nearly as well educated as his older brother. But Chachiji's mind is on a different track.

'I think-so LN bhaisaab ne bhi koi rakh li hai.'

'What?' Mrs Mamta responds, half amused, half horrified.

Chachiji switches languages to make things more explicit: 'He is keeping some woman also.'

'Why would you say that?'

Chachiji shoots darting looks this way and that and lowers her voice. 'He steals out at night to make phone calls. I've seen him. Cupping the receiver and talking at Gambhir Stores late at night.'

'You must have seen somebody else,' Mrs Mamta says dismissively. 'Your eyesight is faulty.'

Chachiji regards her with resentful pity. Poor Mamta, she clearly doesn't want to accept that it is her husband who is faulty.

'Why don't you ask Anjini's husband to give us a loan?' she asks, changing tack. 'So we can live in some decent place till the flats are built? He is so well off, surely he wouldn't like to see his wife's only brother thrown out into the street?'

'Ab what to hide from you, Bhudevi,' Mrs Mamta says, placing a cup of tea before her sister-in-law. 'There is tension in their marriage. No good news yet, na. How to ask him for a loan?'

Chachiji is stumped for a moment, and then tries again.

'What about Binni? Her husband does business, no?'

'Not very well, though,' Mrs Mamta reveals. 'His pharmacy business had to be sold. And you know,' she pre-empts the next question smoothly, 'we don't speak to Chandu at all. LN has forbidden it.'

Chachiji sips her tea, watching her sister-in-law out of malevolent little eyes.

'But we must have *some* place to live!'

'Our first floor has been rented out,' Mrs Mamta says with finality. 'Otherwise you could have lived here...'

A little silence falls. Mrs Mamta thinks distractedly of poor Debjani, and of how Bhudevi, typically self-involved, has mentioned neither the momentous newsreading on Friday night nor the monstrous article that followed.

'At least give me the *Awara* set!' Chachiji bursts out suddenly.

'What?' Mrs Mamta takes a moment to adjust to this new change in subject. 'Bhudevi, please, you know the Awara set belongs to the eldest daughter-in...'

To her horror, Chachiji begins to cry. Huge sobs shake her bulldog frame. 'Ashok Narayan Thakur never loved me,' she moans, rocking back and forth. 'He blew up all his money on randis, and now on that wretched Hot Dulari – god rot her! May she *die*, may she be eaten by *worms*, may termites gnaw at her *anus*!'

'Bhudevi, calm down,' Mrs Mamta says, distressed. 'Don't say such things please, just drink your tea.'

But Chachiji shakes her head, pushes back the chair and blunders out of the room. Mrs Mamta, mostly unmoved, pours the contents of the cup into the sink and goes into the kitchen to cook the simple lunch that she and the Judge will eat at one o'clock. Her Nepali cook Lachhu has debunked to his village recently, and she and the girls have to do all the cooking and chores themselves – but after listening to Chachiji's suspicions of the Hot Dulari, maybe this is a blessing in disguise. Not that the *Judge* would have been tempted by Lachhu. But Eshwari, now, that's another matter. Eshwari is definitely going through an if-he's-chinkie-he's-cute phase.

Later, when she is sitting at her Usha sewing machine, stitching the embroidered pansies onto a peasant top for Eshwari, the plump black phone starts to ring, causing its pedestal of three fat volumes of the Delhi Yellow Pages to vibrate alarmingly. She picks it up.

'Allahabad se trunk call hai,' the operator's voice says. 'PP for Mrs Mamta. Are you Mrs Mamta?'

'Yes, yes,' she replies, a little concerned. Anji usually phones after ten-thirty at night, when the half-rates apply. 'Please, baat karaiye.'

'Ma?' Anji's breathless child-like voice sounds rather subdued. 'My period started.'

Mrs Mamta sighs. 'Don't worry, Anji. It's early days yet.'

But it isn't. Anji has been married for six years now. And the fact that Binni squeezed out her twins Monu-Bonu in such unseemly haste doesn't help.

'And for the first three years you didn't even try,' her mother reminds her. 'Because Samar was so young.'

Anji's husband Anant was a widower when they wed. Grave, handsome, grieving, trying to look after his six-year-old son. It had all seemed madly romantic at the time. Now Mrs Mamta wonders if it hadn't been just mad.

'You know the doctor said there's no problem as such,' she tells her daughter gently. 'You've got to stop being so tense.'

'Oh, I'm not tense-tense,' Anji assures her, her voice brighter. 'I just thought I should tell you at the beginning of the conversation, you know? Otherwise you'd keep wondering. How are you?'

'Okay,' Mrs Mamta sighs. 'Bhudevi was here, saying she's possessed by the ghost of your dead grandmother and demanding the Awara set.'

Anjini giggles. The Awara set is a double string of diamonds set in white gold with earrings to match, an exact replica of the one Nargis wore in the classic film *Awara*. It is the sparkling star of a long series of episodes involving the ladies of Numbers 13 and 16 Hailey Road.

'Seriously? Like in *Exorcist*? And did you give it to her?'

'Of course not. She has to find a bride for Gulab first. When she does, I'll hand it over. Till then, as the eldest Thakur daughter-in-law of this generation, the set is rightfully mine.'

'Nobody will marry Gulgul,' Anjini says comfortably. 'Not till he finishes his law, and that will never happen. Ma, I actually called about Dabbu. How is she?'

'All right.' Mrs Mamta sits down on the chair by the phone and lowers her voice. 'Did you see the –'

'Article? Yes. Is she very shattered? You tell her that Anji didi phoned to say the article was all rubbish, but she should try keeping her hair open during the telecast. She can buy those pink sponge-rollers from Depaul's and –'

'I'll tell her.'

'And not to wear such thick silk saris. And to practise wearing mascara every day so that she isn't scared to blink. And has she got her threading done? Because I thought her upper lip looked shadowy. Also her bra was strapped too tight, she needs to – actually, put her on the line, Ma, I'll tell her myself.'

'She's gone out,' Mrs Mamta says. 'I'll tell her.'

'Poor Dabburam. Anyway, I almost forgot, I can dress her myself next week because I'm coming to Delhi for a while. I mean, me and Samar are – Anant has to go to the US on work, and we're free!'

Mrs Mamta receives this piece of news with mixed emotions. She loves twelve-year-old Samar, and though his appetite causes the household expenses to swell alarmingly whenever he visits, Anji always subsidizes them. But Lachhu has run away. Besides, she is not sure of the wisdom of having Anji around when Dabbu is so fragile. Dabbu will grumble that Anji didi is trying to turn her into a carbon copy of herself, and Anjini will sigh at all the opportunities Debjani has, living in the permissive eighties. 'Bauji and you were so much stricter with us, Ma,' Anji often says plaintively. 'Eshu and Dabbu get away with murder.'

'That's great news,' she says warmly. 'We'll talk then – you hang up now, these calls cost a lot.'

The old sewing machine starts to act up in the afternoon, the bobbins jittering and the needle spitting out the thread repeatedly. Mrs Mamta cleans, oils and re-threads it patiently, only to have the thread snap again just as she is about to finish. By the time the girls return home, she has managed to give herself quite a headache. Which doesn't improve when Dabbu stalks in, her face stormy, and goes up to her room without saying a word. Eshwari wolfs down a plate of dal-chawal, pulls a philosophical face when she discovers her blouse isn't ready, and then falls asleep on the drawing room couch, still in her school uniform.

At four o'clock, Gulab comes home on his scooter. He parks it in the driveway and hurries into Number 16, breathing hard.

'Taiji, suna? Balkishen Bau is no more,' he announces importantly. 'Chal basey. Just now. Batao!'

Mrs Mamta Thakur, always so placid, gives an involuntary gasp. 'What!'

Gulgul nods with mournful relish. 'He was sixty – but if you take no exercise and abuse your liver, you can't hope to be a long liver. That's why I do bodybuilding.'

Eshwari sits up groggily and looks at Gulab like she can't believe he's for real.

'Is this any way to break such news, Gulgul bhaisaab?' she demands. 'Seriously, don't you have *any* sense?'

Gulab gives a little laugh, rocks on his heels, and pats his bouffant hair nervously.

'Sorry, sorry, I did not mean to be a rude,' he says. 'Taiji, please convey the news to Tauji. I have to go tell everybody else.'

———

Juliet Bai is massaging oil into Dylan's hair as he lounges in the khas-scented blast of the desert cooler, his head in her lap, having evicted his youngest brother from this prized spot. The displaced Ethan is now resignedly tuning his guitar in a corner of the room.

Juliet Bai clucks over the extreme dryness of his scalp, the length of his hair and the new lines around his eyes that only she can see. She regards his thick long lashes complacently and wonders darkly how many girls those full lips have kissed. Just as she is about to ask him this in a clever, roundabout way, Dylan opens his eyes and looks up at her.

'Mamma?'

'What, sonna? Enough?'

Dylan shakes his head. 'No, no, don't stop. I was just wondering, what exactly have you told people here that I do?'

She blinks. 'What?'

He raises himself a little. 'My job. What have you told people – like that judge friend of Dadda's, for example? My son is a – what?'

'Investigative editor,' she replies, looking confused. 'With the *India Post*, Bombay. Correct, no?'

'Correct,' Dylan says, lying back again. 'Just near the temples now... yeah, there... perfect.' He closes his eyes.

So I'm safe, he thinks. Safe from what, he cannot say, but somehow it is extraordinarily important that the entirely forgettable Debjani Thakur does *not* find out that he is the architect of last week's rather (come to think of it) brutally worded article on the new DD.

Juliet Bai looks down at him curiously. 'I haven't told them your salary or anything, if that's what you're worried about. I'm not stupid.'

'I know.' Dylan smiles at her affectionately. 'So tell me all your news, Mamma!'

Juliet Bai sighs. 'Me! Soon I will be –'

'Dead and buried in Nicholson Cemetery,' Ethan chimes in helpfully. 'Before you see any grandchildren.'

She shoots him a nasty look, but before she can say anything, Dylan interjects hastily.

'So how's the love of Jason's life?'

Juliet Bai wrinkles up her nose. The pressure with which she is massaging Dylan's temples grows. 'Wretched girl! Pudding face! Such round-round shoulders she has, like a simpering dumpling. And so shameless! Cheh! He brought her home, introduced her, your dadda and I said hello – what else to do? Then he took her to his bedroom, as cool as you please, and they were locked in there for hours. Just imagine, with your dadda and me at home! Such shamelessness! I didn't say anything – you know how much that Jason can shout – but the next day, when he went off to college, I quietly took my screwdriver and unscrewed the bolt from the door in his room. Next day, he came home with madam and headed straight for his room. I let them go, they shut the door and then, such a yell, such *cursing*, like you've never heard! Jason came jumping out, his face black with anger, mujhe Jesu, what a tantrum! You have no right, he shouted. I told him, I've got a right – *and* a left – and I'll give you both if you don't stop treating my home like some cheap hotel.'

'Mamma,' Dylan says mildly, 'you always dramatize things.

They were probably just listening to music. Jason's too much of a funk to make a move.'

Juliet Bai snorts, yanking so hard at his hair that he groans in protest. 'Which is a good thing! Don't talk like it is very great to have the guts to *make a move*. Half Jason's problem is that he's trying to be as *gutsy* as you.'

'Yeah, that's right, blame me for everything, you always do,' Dylan says resignedly. 'What about Ethan here? Why hasn't he given you any grandchildren yet?''

'*He* only lives for Inter-school Western Music Competitions,' Juliet Bai says dismissively. 'No conversation, no communication. I feed him and wash his clothes and pray for him. Bas.'

She glances at her youngest son as she says this, but he's busy fine-tuning his guitar, holding it close to his ear.

'And you and Dadda?' Dylan asks next. 'Is everything good between Bobby and Bobby?'

She gives him a little push. 'Dadda and I are fine, we walk together in the park every morning. He even comes with me for morning Mass sometimes. Why you asking so many questions, sonna?'

Dylan shrugs, closes his eyes. 'Just. I miss you guys in Bombay sometimes. That's all.'

My eldest, Juliet Bai thinks, brimming over with sudden affection for the large male lounging in her lap. My malgado. Such a nice boy. So responsible. When he was small, he used to go on his cycle and do all my vegetable shopping for me. Always got back the exact change. And he never wasted any food, ate everything on his plate, and if the others wasted, he forced himself to eat their leftovers too. I only had to look at him and say, It's *wasting*, sonna, and he would eat it. Such a good boy – not like these rascals, Jason and Ethan. But sometimes he takes his sense of responsibility too far.

'Stay out of trouble, sonna,' she tells him. 'Why must you only take the government to task? Rest of the journalists have no duty or what?'

Dylan doesn't reply. Below her fingers, she can feel his temples tense.

'So many positive things are happening in India,' she continues. 'Write about that. We've got such a handsome new PM – he's going to dismantle the Licence Raj, do science and technology initiatives, take us into the twenty-first century!'

'Mamma, the twenty-first century is a *time*, not a place,' Dylan points out, his eyes still closed. 'We don't need a PM to take us there. We're gonna get there anyway.'

'You know what he means,' she says crossly. 'You've come here to poke around in Tirathpuri and do more stories on the Sikh massacre, haven't you? Tell the truth.'

'No,' Dylan says steadily. 'The Special Investigation Commission has been doing all that. I'm just here to get people's reactions to the findings of the SIC.'

'My friend Gurvinder Singh was pretty happy about the Sikh massacre,' the incorrigible Ethan volunteers. 'His mother made him cut off all his hair. All the chicks think he's hot now.'

'Ethan, don't talk about stuff you know nothing about,' Dylan says curtly.

Ethan smirks and strums his guitar. Dylan glowers.

'There's chicken biryani with raita for dinner,' Juliet Bai says quickly.

'Awesome.' Dylan relaxes, sinking back into her lap. 'I hope the chicken has at least ten legs, coz I'm gonna eat seven.'

'Chickens should get married to centipedes,' Ethan pipes up. 'Then there would be legs enough for all of us.'

'Dylan should get married,' says Juliet Bai. 'Then he won't be homesick.'

'No,' Dylan says wryly. 'Then I'll just be *sick*.'

'No nice girls in the *India Post* office or what?'

'No, Mamma,' Dylan tells her solemnly. 'No nice girls in the *India Post* office. Only bad-bad girls. In tight-tight clothes with loose-loose morals who will corrupt me and give me –'

'*AID*.' Juliet Bai nods knowingly.

'I was going to say a bad reputation, actually,' Dylan says, startled.

Juliet Bai takes no notice of him. 'They told us all about AID in school, so we could counsel the boys. It's a terrible sickness. The Devil's own disease, they say. See how sick and miserable that Rock Hudson is looking – all because of AID only.'

'He... just... wanted... to... get... *laid*,' Ethan hums softly to himself, fingering his strings. 'But he ended up with *AID*. Oh, it's just so *sayd*... and now he's cold and...'

'Dead,' says the Brigadier, walking into the room, looking pale. 'Gulab Thakur just told me. Poor Balkishen is no more.'

'No more!' Juliet Bai gasps, her hands clutching her breast. 'How? Was he that ill, Bobby?'

The Brigadier pulls at his moustache. 'He missed three card sessions in the last year. Obviously he was gravely unwell.'

So now there is a permanent vacancy in the Judge's kot-piece group, Dylan muses. Debjani Thakur is missing a partner.

There is silence. Ethan has put down his guitar.

The Brigadier squares his shoulders. 'I have to go over to Balkishen's,' he says abruptly. 'Dylan, you drive me.'

He turns and leaves the room.

Dylan rises to his elbows and looks around, a half-comical 'why me?' expression on his face. Ethan cackles.

'This is all Mamma's doing,' he says virtuously, starting to strum his guitar again. 'She has being praying to the Lord for ages to break up Dadda's kot-piece gang. She wants him all to herself to coochie-coo with. And look what miracles her prayers have wrought! First, Laxmi uncle and his younger brother practically came to blows. And now Balkishen Bau has fallen dead! *What*, Mamma,' he sing-songs, shaking one bony finger at her reprovingly, 'this is *not* good what you are doing!'

'Horrible boy,' his mother replies uneasily. 'Go do your homework.'

The Brigadier reappears, wearing a white kurta-pyjama. 'Come, Dylan,' he says. 'Will you come, Bobby?'

She shakes her head. 'But I'll send food, Bobby. They won't be in any state to cook just now. There's the chicken biryani – I'll pack it. Dylan, get off my lap and go get the car keys.'

'Well, at least you're going where the chicken biryani's going, Dyl,' Ethan says as Dylan gets to his feet with a small groan. 'Maybe you'll score a couple of mouthfuls. *I* get to eat bread-butter and Lobster.'

'Pour a bucket of water into the cooler,' his mother says, putting her head into the room. 'And then go and study – all my friends say that since I left school you've turned into a duffer.'

❖

'Isn't it rather morbid of them to be playing cards when their friend's ashes have barely cooled?' Dylan asks his mother the next day, as she propels him towards the car where his father is already sitting and waiting. 'Or at the very least, slightly indecent?'

'It's been two days,' she tells him. 'Trust me, for them that's a *lot*. Thank you for filling in like this, sonna.'

'It's the least I can do,' Dylan returns piously. 'Poor Dadda.'

This earns him a smacking kiss on the cheek, and now here he is, sitting in the deceased's chair, wondering what to call trumps.

'Spades,' he announces finally.

Beside him the Judge gives a smug little grunt. The Brigadier chuckles. Dylan looks across the table to see how his partner has taken his call. But Debjani is hiding behind her fan of cards. All he can see of her are slim fingers and the silver ladybird ring.

Fantastic, thinks Dylan. At this rate, by the end of the month, I might just find out what her sun sign is.

'Um... that's a really unusual ring you're wearing,' he ventures.

'Thank you,' the Judge grunts. 'It's my wedding ring. Entirely ordinary, really.'

Frustrated, Dylan wonders if Debjani has even registered that there has been a change in players. She seems entirely oblivious to his existence.

But he needn't worry. Dabbu *has* noticed that D for Dylan is back. She could tell you what he is wearing with her eyes shut – a casually snug grey T-shirt that hints at a lean, muscled body and jeans with some rather tantalizingly faded bits. She knows he has a strong jaw and an easy pleasing manner and laughing dark eyes that seem to be seeking hers. She hasn't forgotten how flirty he is. And how she got goosebumps when he said her name. Her mother told her that Juliet Bai is always bemoaning the fact that her eldest son has the morals of a tomcat. And he dared call *her* a cat! He's just out to make a summer conquest, she thinks dramatically, something to vary the Bombay flavour. Well, I refuse to make a fool of myself over him. I refuse to make a fool of myself over *any* guy.

And so she drags her mind determinedly back to her woes – the sniggers she's been hearing in the AIR corridors, the pitying looks she's been attracting from her neighbours on Hailey Road ever since that wretched article appeared. How mortifying it is to know her father is right, that the good opinion of others matters a great deal to her. Will DD even call her to read again this Friday? How easy it would be for them to replace her, just as easily as her father has replaced Balkishen Bau with the Brigadier's son.

And then abruptly, and to her surprise, she realizes just how much she is missing the big brown *hmmm hmmming* presence of Balkishen Bau across the table. Balkishen Bau would never have said 'spades' like Dylan has just done. He was the only one among the four players who insisted on calling the four houses by their Hindi names: hukum, paan, eent and chidi. He did it mostly to irritate the other old men, Debjani always felt, because he thought they were too anglicized. Sometimes he even pretended he didn't understand the English terms. And always, after he called trumps, he would wink roguishly at Dabbu, to indicate that the two of them were going to blow the others away. And he loved the way she read the news. He said she was Thee Best. And look at her, so fickle, already forgotten him, sitting here hyper-aware of the Brigadier's cute son, even *glad* that he's taken Balkishen Bau's place. A guilty lump starts to form in her throat.

With the result that when Dylan finally manages to catch her eye, he finds them suspiciously red-rimmed. A little later, he notices that her shoulders are shaking. And when his hand happens to touch the card she has just discarded it is damp, he is sure of it. Debjani Thakur is weeping behind her cards.

He slips a hand into his jeans, extracts a large blue checked handkerchief and, on the pretext of reaching for the devilled Maggi noodles, drops it gently into her lap.

Debbie stares down at the folded cotton square in disbelief. Is this harami tomcat behaviour, she wonders, confused, or just plain niceness? Whichever it is, she can't afford to be picky. She picks up the blue handkerchief and blows into it vigorously.

Hearing the sound of snot being evicted so energetically, Dylan smiles, feeling absurdly happy.

At eight o'clock, he carries the table into the drawing room and sets it down. Debjani lingers, watching him, obviously feeling some sort of explanation is due.

'He would have said hukum,' she offers finally. 'Not spades.'

'Sorry?' Dylan asks.

'And he would have scraped a card across his warts. And winked at me. He was kind and sweet and I'm sorry I said that his balgam rattled and that he was *ugly*!'

Dylan, recalling the homely-looking old gent he had seen lying in state at the electric crematorium yesterday, finally makes the connection. 'You mean Balkishen Bau.'

At the sound of his name, her eyes start to well up again.

'I'm sorry,' Dylan says hastily. 'Er, I can say hukum too, would you like that?'

She smiles at that, a wonky, watery smile. 'Don't be silly,' she says. 'I'm not a baby.'

Dylan feels his belly do its now familiar head-over-heels ballerina flip. It is definitely time to go home.

'I'm glad you liked my ring,' she says suddenly.

He is taken aback for a moment, and then grins.

'You heard me, then.'

'Oh, yes,' she replies serenely.

'So, is it purely ornamental?' he asks. 'Or does it have any significance?'

She tilts her head. 'What do you mean?'

'I mean, is it a doggy ring?' he asks playfully. 'Uniting you and Moti in a bond of puppy love?'

He is trying to find out if I'm engaged or seeing someone, Debjani realizes. She ought to say something witty and sparkling back to him. But what can she say?

'Moti's married to Voti,' she replies, deciding to take the question at face value. 'Voti is Punjabi for wife. And they've just had a new litter – Chhoti, Dhoti and Roti.'

'Chhoti is the small one, obviously.' The long dimples flash as he props himself against the table and crosses his arms across his chest. (Why is he making himself comfortable? Wasn't he leaving?) 'Dhoti has a big white bum, am I right?'

Debjani smiles. 'Exactly!'

'But Roti defeats me. Unless, wait, is he a glutton?'

'He's light brown,' Debjani explains. 'Sort of wheat coloured. So.'

'Of course. Actually, that was a stupid guess. Because Moti would've given you a *pearl* ring.'

'You sound like my father.' Debjani makes a face. 'He says I'm going to marry a dog. D for dog, you know.'

And then she instantly wants to gag herself, because D for Dylan! Oh god, what will he think? Her cheeks turn an incandescent pink.

She is so transparent, Dylan thinks, amused. Her thoughts

might as well appear in neon across her forehead for everyone to read. He starts to make some casual reply but just then, a fair, top-heavy young man shambles into the drawing room, looking supremely disgruntled.

'Bhai, yeh Meenakshi Seshadri cheating karti hai,' he declares.

'This is my Gulgul bhaisaab,' Debjani says to Dylan, who has just done a double take at the sight of Gulgul's gargantuan biceps.

'Hello, bicep,' Dylan says fascinated, then hastily corrects himself. 'I mean, hello, bhaisaab.'

'Good joke, good joke.' Gulgul smiles graciously as he casts an assessing look over Dylan's body, puffs out his own, far larger chest, hauls his cycling shorts a little higher up his skinny bum, sits down on the sofa and elaborates on his theme. 'Haan, toh this Meenakshi, she looks like she is wearing an *Amar Chitra Katha* outfit – you know, only a white cloth floating on her upper body – but agar close-by se dekho toh she is wearing a full-sleeved, neck-to-waist skin-coloured blouse! And I'm rewinding and rewinding and looking and looking and wondering ki, bhai where is her *toondi*? Batao!'

Debjani chokes.

'What's a toondi?' Dylan asks, totally at a loss.

'A navel,' Debjani manages to say. 'Gulgul bhaisaab, I'll just see Dylan out, and come and chat with you, okay?'

'Hain? But... I needed a favour from you, Dabbu.' Gulgul clears his throat and the tips of his ears turn a delicate shade of pink. 'I came to ask specially.' In a louder voice, he addresses Dylan: 'Can you excuse us, please?'

'Of course, I was leaving anyway.' Dylan nods formally at Debjani and walks out of the room.

Debjani is suddenly disappointed. 'What *is* it, Gulgul bhaisaab?' she snaps.

'Nothing, nothing.' He kicks off his sandals and, drawn by some irresistible urge, shoves his large foot into the ballet slipper that Dabbu has just discarded to sit cross-legged on the sofa. 'Hehe! Look at my foot in your shoe, Dabbu!'

As Gulgul's leg is skinny and hairy and the ballet slipper deep purple and pointy, this is not a pretty sight, but Gulgul appears to find it fascinating. He arches his foot up and down, lost in a reverie, humming a happy little tune.

'*What* did you want to talk to me about, Gulgul bhaisaab?'

'Oh, yes!' He looks up. 'Er, Dabbu, see... you know I'm serious about my bodybuilding, na?'

'Yes.' She nods impatiently, peering out at the garden.

'Ya, well, I was reading Arnold's book on bodybuilding – and in all the pictures in that, the men have no hair.'

'Okay,' Dabbu says uncomprehendingly.

'They are all chikna and oiled, so all the rips and cuts show... And I am toh, you have maybe not noticed, quite, uh...'

'Hairy,' Dabbu supplies, tapping her foot, wondering if she can still catch Dylan at the gate. 'I've noticed.'

'Yes! And I can't wear a skin-coloured blouse like Meenakshi Seshadri. So, I was thinking...' He pauses, and then continues in a rush, 'Can you wax me? Not everything, just the chest. If I go to the parlour they'll laugh at me – I'll pay whatever it costs, of course.'

Debjani stares at him, speechless. One moment you're flirting with a tall dark handsome man who wants to know if you're engaged, and the next you're being solicited to make intimate contact with your short cousin's thick black chest hairs. Such is life. Gross. Grim. Avoidable.

'But chest hair is so manly,' she says weakly.

'Please, Dabbu. It's to help me attain my *dream*. I want to open my own gym one day! I'm going to call it Gulab's Gym. Cool, na?'

He fixes his large gulab jamun eyes upon her beseechingly. The very hairs of his eyebrows seem to quiver in a tremulous 'please'. Everything about him is supplicating. And path blocking. She gets the distinct impression that he isn't about to let her go anywhere until she says yes.

'Okay,' she says in a strangled voice. 'Come over early tomorrow morning. We'll do it in the kitchen because I have to heat the wax.'

Gulgul beams.

'You're so *good*, Dabbu. So kind! Not like Eshwari... not like Binni... not like Anjin –'

'You're welcome,' she cuts him short. 'Now can I have my shoe back?'

Putting it on, she rushes outside.

It is dark in the garden. Debjani comes out to find that Dylan is being interrogated by the two old men, who have him backed up against the green front gate.

'So you think journalists should be answerable to nobody, eh? Not to the government, not to the judiciary?'

'No, sir,' Dylan is replying steadily. 'I think the press *should* be answerable – but only to its readers.'

'To its corporate masters, you mean!' the Judge snorts. 'You people can't see the big picture. Every third division BA with a pencil in his sweaty hand thinks he is a journalist nowadays! You have no concept of the law – that's why your reportage of courtroom trials is so botched up. You should all be made to get a law degree before reporting on legal matters.'

'And all lawyers should get an MBBS before defending doctors, I suppose,' Dylan replies pleasantly. 'And judges should attend IIT for five years before presiding over a civil engineering case.'

The Judge gives a short bark of laughter. 'Perhaps.'

'BJ,' Debjani calls out. 'The cricket highlights are coming on TV.'

The old men's eyes light up. Without a word, they hurry into the house. Debjani finds herself alone with Dylan.

'Don't mind my dad,' she says with a slight roll of the eyes.

'Mine is just as bad.' He grins.

A little silence. Dylan looks over the gate at Voti nursing her puppies upon the sandpile.

'They look drunk,' he says softly. 'Look at their eyes, totally glazed over. And their tummies are as tight as drums.'

Dabbu stands next to him watching the puppies too, completely tongue-tied. There is something a little too intimate about the situation, she feels. The puppies make tiny slurping sounds, then one by one, let the nipple slip from between their teeth and fall asleep, their tiny mouths slack.

'Hardworking little buggers,' Dylan says, his voice a husky whisper. He turns to her, his dark eyes warm, and her pulse jumps crazily. God, what is this?

'So, are you reading the news again this Friday?'

DD hasn't yet informed Debjani when her next broadcast is to be. Or *if* it is to be, she thinks miserably.

She lifts her chin. 'Of course. Why wouldn't I?'

'No reason,' he replies quickly. 'Just, you seemed so upset over your Balkishen Bau.'

Debjani frowns down at the sleeping puppies. She is feeling like a bit of a fake. She twists her wavy hair into a thick rope over one shoulder and looks up at him impulsively, making him think yet again, for some inexplicable reason, of wings.

'Look, I don't want you to get the impression that I'm a very good person.'

'Huh?'

'Because I was crying over an old uncleji,' she explains. 'You might think I am very nice. But I'm not. Not really. It's just that it suddenly hit me that he was dead... really, actually, *dead*... and the sun was setting, and frankly I've been moping about a nasty review of my newsreading in the *India Post*. So it was probably thirty per cent Balkishen Bau, seventy per cent nasty review. Actually, eighty per cent nasty review,' she amends scrupulously.

Dylan doesn't know what to say – this is more honesty than he has encountered in a while.

She squares her shoulders and looks up at him. 'Perhaps you saw it?'

He tenses. It's a question he has been dreading.

'The newscast? Yes.'

She fixes her luminous eyes on him.

'Did *you* think it was dreadful?'

'Uh, listen, Debjani, I –'

'It *was* dreadful,' she bursts out. 'I knew it!'

'It's not your fault,' he says hastily. 'The stuff they give you to read is such crap, I'd look like a zombie too if I had to read it out.'

'I looked like a *zombie*!' she says tragically.

'Not a zombie, just a bit, er, wooden.'

'Like Pinocchio!'

He somehow manages not to laugh. Instead, he reaches out and squeezes her shoulder lightly. 'Stop being such a tragedy queen! Where's your ball-squeezing spirit?'

It is meant to be a friendly, encouraging gesture. Only, it doesn't play out quite like that.

Because his hand is large and warm and strong. Which sounds calming, but the effect it has on Debjani is completely panic-inducing. Act *casual*, she tells herself chaotically. Say something. People in Bombay probably touch each other all the time to emphasize a point. Hell, people in Delhi touch each other all the time to emphasize a point! It doesn't mean anything.

'It's the autocue,' she says with credible composure. 'In the auditions, we read from sheets. That thing freaks me out.'

Meanwhile Dylan is having the weirdest urge to touch her bare shoulder again. Because her skin is smooth and firm and cool and because... Because I'm feeling *guilty*, he realizes. Of course, that's it. I'm feeling guilty because I've screwed up this poor girl's life with that hastily written, unnecessarily personal piece, and now I'll feel like crap until I fix things.

He slides his hands into the pockets of his jeans and says, his voice a little unsteady, 'So, I have this idea. I know a way in which we can lick this little problem.'

'How?' Debjani asks, her voice agonized. 'I've tried to practise, but the more I practise, the worse I get.'

The long dimples flash. 'Tomorrow. I'll pick you up at ten. We'll kick the autocue's ass. You won't regret it. I promise.'

4

'Gulgul bhaisaab, you'll have to be brave.' Dabbu is hot and sticky and quite fed up. 'Take your hands off your chest please!'

But Gulgul, standing with his hands covering his torso in a classic posture of outraged modesty, shakes his head vigorously. The removal of the very first strip of wax has brought tears to his eyes and options to his mind.

'I'll shave it,' he says. 'It won't be so smooth, and I'll have to do it every day, but that's okay.'

'Don't be silly,' Debjani, a girl with a mission now, tells him firmly. 'I spent ages heating this wax, I'm not going to waste it. Now stand still and take a deep breath – see how nice it looks where I pulled the hair off?'

But it doesn't. It's all goose-pimpled and red. Gulgul gulps miserably, he is feeling a little faint in the hot kitchen.

'You know, Dabbu, I don't think-so that you are doing this correctly,' he says, looking down at the used strip, thick with a furry layer of uprooted hair. 'I think only qualified beauticians know how to do this. Isn't that *skin* along with hair? Maybe that's why it is hurting so much!'

Debjani gasps at this ungrateful attitude. 'It's hurting because you're so *hairy*,' she tells him unkindly. 'Now shut up and bare your chest or I'll call Ma to hold your hands back.'

But Gulgul continues to cover his nipples coyly.

'I'll put ice on your chest afterwards,' Dabbu says wheedlingly, wondering how she gets herself into situations like this. 'And then we'll massage in some cold cream and you'll see how chikna you look! Even through this little strip I can make out how well-defined your chest is!'

Gulab Thakur perks up a little at this.

'Definition is very important,' he says. 'Definition is everything. The skin must be so thin that the *veins* show. Bulk is for apes, Arnold says. Bulk is noth – *owwwccchh!*'

This outraged howl brings Eshwari running to the kitchen.

'What are you *doing*, Dabbu? Oh, gross! Avoidable! Avoidable! Why did I have to see that? What an ugly sight! Those used strips could sell in Jagdish Stores as carpeting!'

'Good you're here,' Dabbu says calmly. 'Help me finish. Two more strips should do it.'

Ten minutes later, a cowed and hairless Gulab Thakur slinks out of the kitchen, clutching ice to his denuded chest, and the sisters sit down to a cup of tea in their bedroom.

'That was scarring,' Eshu says darkly. 'What a sight to wake up to! I'll probably have the worst day of my life now.'

'Oh, it'll be a good day, you'll see,' Dabbu sings sunnily as she sinks back into bed.

'You're very chirpy,' Eshwari remarks, yawning as she yanks at the school belt hanging out of the bottom of her closed cupboard door. The cupboard flies opens and all its contents tumble out in a massive heap upon the floor. 'Damn.'

'I bet that's how Japanese people's guts spill out when they perform a ritual harakiri,' Debjani says. 'Why don't you ever clean that cupboard, Eshu?'

'I will,' Eshwari says, rummaging through the heap for her school uniform. 'What are you doing today?'

'Oh,' Debjani says, her cheeks turning a slow, sure red as she picks out a lime-green peasant top from her meticulously neat cupboard and holds it against her body. 'I'm going to the Brig's house today – his son's offered to help me hone my autocue technique.'

Eshwari's eyes narrow. 'Which son is this? Aren't all his sons still studying? Except the harami one – but he lives in Bombay, no?'

'He's here on holiday,' Debjani says, adding a pink sling bag to the lime-green top and studying the effect in the mirror. 'He came over with the Brig, we got talking and he said he'd give me some tips.'

'The harami one!' Eshwari squeals, sinking into her clothes heap. 'What d'you mean you got *talking*? I thought he was no talking, only cocking!'

'What rubbish!' Dabbu splutters.

'When did he come home? How'd I miss him? Is he devilish?'

'He's okay,' Debjani answers, her cheeks burning. 'No horns or forked tail.'

'And the rear view?'

Debjani's eyes get a faraway look.

'Nice,' she admits. And then covers her ears as Eshwari emits a glass-shattering shriek.

'You said nice! Oh my god, you like him! You like someone! Dabbu likes someone! Dabbu likes someone!'

'Just a bit,' Debjani cautions.

'Just a bit? Or just a butt?'

'Well,' Debjani shrugs. 'I don't *know* him yet. I mean, I don't know if he's honest and kind and brave – my three *essentials*, you know. But I guess he's cute.'

Eshwari grins, satisfied. 'So all this sajjing and bajjing is in the harami's honour,' she crows. 'Umm... for your deflowering today, may I recommend the white cotton Sheetal bra and the Nancy panties with the pink dots?'

'Shut up. It's not like that. You think what I'm wearing is nice?'

Eshwari looks at her, standing before the mirror in the lime-green peasant blouse, with pink sling bag, dishevelled sticky brown hair and wax-spattered grey pyjamas.

'*You're* nice.' She grins. 'Yes, I like it. But lose those pyjamas and wear your shorts. And one silver payal. And remember to stay on your toes when you're sitting in the car, so your thighs don't press fully upon the seat – otherwise they'll phailo and look huge.'

◆━◆━◆

At eleven sharp, Dylan, freshly shaved and wearing a body-skimming T-shirt that his mother assures him makes him look exactly like Michelangelo's David but with clothes on, drives up to the gate of 16 Hailey Road and sounds the horn smartly.

Debjani's parents, whose eyebrows have already risen upon hearing her plan for the day, now look even more concerned.

'Cocky chap,' the Judge grumbles even as Debjani's heart starts to beat a little faster. 'When is he going back to Bombay? How long is he here for?'

Debjani murmurs 'Ma, I'm going' as casually as she can and walks out to the verandah. And runs smack into Dylan, who'd meant for the horn to be an announcement, not a summons.

'Whoops, sorry,' he says, putting out a hand to steady her. 'Hope I'm not late?'

'Oh, no,' Debjani shakes her head, feeling idiotically breathless. Because he is *looking* at her. Like looking at her is something worth doing thoroughly. 'Come.'

But Dylan just stands there, still holding her hand, still staring down at her.

'What?' she says, feeling her face start to flush.

'Nothing. Just... you look really nice today.'

Debjani, worried that her father might bounce out any moment and ask Dylan what his 'intentions' are, replies stiffly, 'Thanks. Shall we go?'

Dylan looks undecided.

'Should I say hello to your parents first, d'you think?' he asks doubtfully. 'This feels a little high-handed.'

'Oh, let's not make a big production out of it!' she says hurriedly. 'It's not like this is a date or anything.'

The warm light in his eyes dies. Abruptly, he lets her hand go. 'Okay, let's go.'

He drives them silently around the Connaught Place outer circle, keeping his eyes on the road. He is suddenly rather annoyed. The trouble with girls, especially the prettier ones, is that the moment you give them even one compliment, they start thinking you're madly in love with them. Why does she feel the need to clarify that this is not a date? I don't want to date her, damn it! I'm just trying to undo the damage my review may have done to her obviously low self-esteem.

'Why do you even want to read the DD news?' he asks abruptly as they pull up at a red light. 'It's just a bunch of ministers cutting ribbons and patting each other on the back.'

She tilts her head. 'Sorry, but do you know of any other TV channel in this country?'

She's so *smart*, isn't she, he thinks, irritated. Why doesn't she wear anything other those skimpy denim cut-offs? How am I supposed to think with those legs on display?

'There's a lot of stuff coming up nowadays,' he says as he turns a corner. 'People are finding ways to get around DD's stranglehold. Video news magazines, if you're hung up on the visual media. Or there's print.'

'But no one else has DD's reach,' she points out. 'If you feature on DD, especially on DD English, you're seen across the country. Do you know, after my first broadcast, we went for chaat to Bengali Market and the chaat-wallah didn't let BJ pay because he recognized me!'

'So this is about fame?' he says, sneering slightly. 'Are you hoping to get a break in the movies? Or just casting the marriage web really wide?'

Debjani stares at him in disbelief. Just because he's helping her a little, he thinks he can ask intensely personal questions?

'Don't you know,' he continues, 'that DD is just a government tool? That after her bodyguards shot down the PM in '84, DD broadcast footage of her party workers chanting *Blood for Blood!* and *A Life for a Life!* on national television? And that led to the massacre of 3,000 Sikhs in Delhi alone?'

What a pompous know-it-all, Debjani thinks. And I don't even think that's true. At least, I don't remember it being *that* big a deal.

'Think what you like,' she shrugs. 'And I wasn't the only one who wanted to read on DD. The entire university rushed off to audition as soon as they turned twenty-one. When I got through, two whole years later, I was thrilled.' She adds snidely, 'Why do you sound so resentful, anyway? Did you apply and not get chosen?'

Dylan chokes.

'I'm an investigative editor at the *India Post*,' he tells her loftily. 'I think more people would know me than *you*.'

Dabbu, still smarting from the nasty review his newspaper's given her, starts to tell him exactly what she thinks of the *India Post*. But then the window of the car next to them rolls down and a woman with a tiny baby in her arms calls out excitedly.

'Hai-ho, you're the new newsreader, na? I recognized you from the mole on your chin. So pretty! Is it real?'

Dabbu smiles and nods. Dylan glares. The light changes, and the Maruti 800 shoots ahead.

'You were saying?' she murmurs.

'Never mind,' he snaps.

Why, if he dislikes my job so much, is he helping me? Debjani wonders, irritated. Eshu would say it's because he's in lust with me, but I see no sign of lustiness so far. Am I his good deed for the day? Like mine was Gulgul bhaisaab? Does he pity poor pathetic me? How humiliating!

She is still thinking these panicked thoughts when he pulls up outside a pretty bungalow, half obscured by leafy banana trees, a few minutes later. He stalks into the house, making a point of not opening the car door for her.

Dabbu wanders in behind him, looking uncertain.

'What's that lovely smell?' she ventures as she enters through the heavy teak front door.

'Huh? Oh, it's Lobaan,' he says offhandedly. 'Frankincense. Mamma lights it every morning...'

But Debjani has already been grabbed by a tiny, sweet-faced lady, with dimples exactly like Dylan's. 'It keeps out the evil bugs *and* the evil spirits,' she explains. 'You must be Mamta's fourth girl. *Such* a sweet face, ba! Just like the Madonna's.'

'Hi, aunty.' Dabbu turns slightly pink. 'Ma says hello.'

'Mamma, we'll be in my room,' Dylan says shortly.

His mother looks up and says something in a sharper tone in Konkani. Dylan says something curt in reply.

'What was that?' Debjani asks as he walks her into his room, a neat, sunny, blue and brown space.

'Don't bolt the door,' he says, rolling his eyes. 'And no sitting on the bed. So I told her this was strictly work.'

But Debjani has run up ahead to his desk. 'You have a *Mac*?'

Dylan, much gratified that she is so impressed, manages a nonchalant shrug. 'Yeah. And today it's going to double as a teleprompter.'

Quickly, he explains it to her. He's got the text ready, articles he's written in the past, and she is to read it aloud sitting six feet away, just like in the DD studio.

'I'll keep scrolling it down for you,' he says, turning to the computer, 'at reading speed. Is the font big enough?'

There is a tug at his arm. He turns around and is startled to find twin pools of Pears alarmingly close to his face. This close, they're almost scary.

'Thank you,' Debjani says sincerely. 'And sorry for that stupid remark at my place. It was dumb.'

'Yeah,' he agrees, somewhat distantly. 'It was pretty dumb.'

'I don't know how to talk,' she offers apologetically.

'But you're a Modernite,' he reminds her.

'I'm sorry about *that* crack too,' she says. 'And for holding up a this-is-not-a-date flag. I realize it was presumptuous. I mean, obviously you have a girlfriend.'

Dylan, trained journalist that he is, knows that statements are questions. But he doesn't want to answer this one.

'What a big word,' he says lightly. '*Presumptuous.* I bet you go around saying presumptuous things just so you can use *presumptuous* when you apologize and impress the other person with your usage of *presumptuous.*'

'Oh, please,' Debjani dismisses this with unconscious snobbery. 'I know much bigger words than that.'

And so they begin work. Dylan has typed out the transcripts of his latest interviews with the residents of Tirathpuri on his Mac, and he opens one of these at random. Debjani twists her hair into a rope, pulls it onto one shoulder, looks intently at the screen and starts to read.

'*The last two years have brought some healing to the family of Rajbir Singh and Satinder Kaur. After living in the grounds of the Indraprastha Stadium for the first three months post the riots, they shifted out to a tent behind their local gurudwara. Now they are back in Tirathpuri and are slowly rebuilding their ten feet by sixteen feet home. Rajbir Singh weaves string beds and his wife works from home knitting sweaters for a local NGO. When asked about her hopes from the SIC, Satinder Kaur's eyes well up with tears. "My Simarpreet was only fifteen. Her favourite colour was bright yellow. She was wearing a new yellow and pink dupatta the day those daanavs came..."*'

Debjani stops. 'Daanav is a Hindi word,' she says.

'So?' Dylan asks without looking up.

She says, not without pride, 'So, since I'm allowed to make copy changes at DD, I would change it to demons – or maybe devils.'

'Okay,' he shrugs.

Her voice grows stronger and more assured.

'*And now she is gone and no SIC report can bring her back. But yes, I do want to see Hardik Motla hanged by the neck until he is dead. If I get that closure, I will finally be able to move on and be a cheerful mother to my two young sons...*'

And so it continues. The next article is about Indo-Russian trading ties and Debjani reads through it glibly, her confidence growing with every sentence. Dylan is a good driller, calming and unobtrusive, scrolling the text smoothly, blinking every now and then to remind her to blink, but otherwise managing to act like he isn't there.

'That was very good!' he says finally. 'You've got into the rhythm of it. You seem completely un-self-conscious now. I think we deserve to break for lunch.'

'Tell me something about yourself,' she asks him impulsively at the dining table, over the fish curry and rice that Mrs Shekhawat has laid out. 'Something *real*, so I can decide if you're honest and brave and kind.'

Dylan lowers his glass. 'Why is that mandatory?' he objects mildly.

Debjani flushes. She can't believe she has laid bare her list of qualities-my-dream-man-must-have so blatantly.

'Oh, because my father says those are traits all Rajputs must possess,' she says.

'Really?' His brow furrows. 'I know lots of Rajputs who are slimy and cowardly and cruel.'

'*Son*na.' Mrs Shekhawat has just entered the room, bearing a plate of freshly fried papad. 'Don't be rude.'

'That's okay.' Debjani picks up a papad and crunches into it.

'I was just asking him about his childhood, aunty. What kind of stuff did these boys get up to?'

Dylan racks his brains to recollect a brave childhood deed and draws a blank. 'Let me see...'

'Arrey, what will *he* tell!' Mrs Shekhawat sits down at the table and pulls the plate of rice towards herself. '*I* will tell you, puta, these boys, what *rascals* they were!'

Dylan eyes his mother in exasperation. How excited the Lobster is. She is reading all kinds of major significance into the fact that he has invited this Dabbu for lunch. It's sad, really.

'Mamma...' he says, waving a serving spoon at her warningly.

'Now you've spilt curry on the tablecloth! Cheh, you boys are so clumsy. That's why I have to have such plain tablecloths, Debjani – you must be wondering – though I've always admired the pretty embroidered ones your mother lays out.'

'She embroidered them herself,' Dabbu replies, pleased. 'Right after she got married, when she was pregnant with Anji didi. Cross stitch and satin stitch on casement. It took her ages.'

'Debjani embroidered her own shorts,' Dylan puts in blandly.

'Really!' Juliet Bai glances down at Dabbu's Daisy Dukes, her expression rather doubtful. 'How pretty! Maybe one day,' she clears her throat meaningfully and takes a bold leap, 'one day you will embroider a cloth for *this* table, hmm?'

There is a strangled choking sound from Dylan. Dabbu smirks.

'See, puta, we had this old uncle Donny – Donald Noronha, my mother's first cousin from her mother's side. All the Noronhas were randy, but this Donny, he was the randiest. He was a bachelor and forty-plus, but all the women were mad about him. Heart-breaker, hymen-breaker we used to call him –'

'Mamma!' Dylan exclaims, scandalized. 'Go make a bhindi painting or something!'

'See how he talks.' Juliet Bai sniffs. 'Philistine. He was *dreadful* in art at school.'

'I was dreadful because my mother was my teacher,' Dylan groans. 'Who wouldn't be?'

'Art is as important as politics, isn't it, Debjani?'

'Er, yes,' Dabbu responds.

'That machine of yours,' Juliet Bai continues, nodding towards Dylan's room, 'is meant to be used for *art*. Not for typing out articles.'

'You're right enough there,' Dylan concedes wryly.

'See!' Juliet Bai beams triumphantly. 'So one day Donny Noronha started sniffing around Dylan's and Jason's piano teacher, Miss Patsy. Such an innocent girl! So pure! So quiet! That devil Donny broke her heart and spat her out like a chewed up wad of sugarcane. Dylan and Jason were furious. And two days after that, he confiscated their football – he said it had crushed his cock.'

'He ran a poultry farm,' Dylan clarifies straight-faced as Debjani splutters into her food.

'So what these rascals did no, they pooled their Christmas money and got 200 beautiful gilt-edged wedding cards printed reading *Donald Noronha weds Daisy Duck*, complete with date, time, venue and his phone number as RSVP, and mailed them to everybody on the church's mailing list.'

Debjani gasps. 'That's... *evil*. Did people actually believe it?'

'Oh, no.' Dylan grins reminiscently. 'But they pretended to. He wasn't very popular, you know. They kept congratulating him wherever he went. And phoning him up. And sending him presents of little rubber duckies. He was apoplectic. Miss Patsy thought it was damn hilarious, though. It's the first time we saw her laugh in months.'

Mrs Shekhawat leans forward triumphantly.

'Now isn't that a sweet story?'

But Debjani simply smiles enigmatically in reply and asks Dylan if they can go back and practise some more. Dylan, much to his irritation, finds himself on tenterhooks for the rest of the day, wondering if he's passed her 'test'. What does this girl want, anyway? A Param Vir Chakra? A certificate of good character stamped by the Vatican? Maybe he should tell her that he won the Excellence in Investigative Journalism Award instituted by the Press Club of India last year. But how to work that casually into the conversation?

'So? Am I honest and kind and brave?' he asks finally, as he halts the electric-blue Maruti 800 outside 16 Hailey Road. Moti's entire family are wagging their scraggly tails, waiting for Debjani to emerge.

Debjani turns to look at him, the slanting rays of the setting sun lighting up her face.

'You're evil,' she says. 'And cunning. And rude to your mother. *And* probably lusting after Miss Patsy yourself.'

'That's true enough,' he admits. 'She was...' he sighs, '*phenomenal.*'

Debjani discovers within herself a newfound hatred for all piano teachers.

'But I did help you with your newsreading. *That* was kind.'

'Nah.' Debjani shakes her head, flashing her street-urchin grin. 'You just wanted to show off your brand-new Apple Mac.'

Dylan opens his mouth to protest. She raises her eyebrows challengingly.

'You were right,' he remarks. 'You really don't know how to flirt.'

Her eyes widen. 'I said I don't know how to talk. I never said I don't know how to *flirt*.'

'So you *do* know how to flirt.' He grins.

'Wha...? Ya... no!' She shakes her head. 'You're confusing me.'

'Do you know,' he continues, squinting down at her, 'that when the sun hits your eyes they're the exact same colour as Pears soap?'

She wrinkles up her nose. '*Orange*?' she hazards. 'That's just creepy. Also, you're calling my eyes orange and *I'm* the one who doesn't know how to flirt?'

His lips twist into a smile but his eyes stay intense, looking down at her, glittering strangely. Debjani's heart starts to slam slowly against her chest. Harami alert, her brain panics. Harami alert.

'Listen!' she says. (Extra loudly, she realizes.)

'Listenao,' he replies invitingly.

'Thank you so much,' she says sincerely. 'You were such a help. And I had a lovely day.'

'Oh, let's not make a big production out of it,' he says mockingly as he reaches up to touch her cheek gently. 'It's not like it was a date or anything.'

◈

Debjani, all flushed and buzzing, enters the house to find Samar Vir Singh, her lanky twelve-year-old step-nephew, sprawled across the sofa, his forehead furrowed in thought, eating wafers and playing Chinese Checkers against himself. Her high evaporates, instantly replaced by a faint headache.

'Well, hello, summervine,' she says as enthusiastically as she can. 'Did you come,' (clinging to a faint hope) 'alone?'

Samar shoots her an ironic look. 'Of course not,' he says, his long mobile face creasing into a conspiratorial grin. 'Anji-ma's in the kitchen.'

'Fabulous,' Debjani mutters as she sinks down on the sofa next to him and kisses him soundly on both cheeks.

'Where's Eshu?' Samar asks.

Dabbu pulls a face. 'Is she still your favourite mausi, you horrid creature?'

'She's not my mausi at all,' he replies seriously. 'We aren't related by blood.'

Dabbu tweaks his ear. 'She's still in school. Basketball practice. Can I play one side?'

He nods. 'You can be red. Red is winning.'

'That's very generous of you,' Debjani replies. 'So, how've you been? What's the action in Class 7B?'

Young Samar studies her intently. 'Aren't you going to meet Anji-ma?'

'I'll go in a bit,' Debjani says airily, thinking, not for the first time, that Samar Vir Singh is an oddly perceptive child. 'Hmm, you're right, red is winning. Take that!'

Samar frowns and bends over the board. Debjani collapses back into the sofa and wonders how long she can hold off the inevitable.

Not very long. Before Debjani's flock of little red soldiers can lay claim to the green triangle across the board, Anjini emerges from the kitchen, exuding Poison and her helplessly appealing kiss me-crush me aura. She is wearing a filmi-looking floral top over her ripe bosom, and – Debjani realizes with resignation –

Debjani's new custom-tailored bootcut jeans. She advances, arms outstretched, a smile of great sweetness upon her face, warmth spilling from her eyes.

'Dabburam! My baby!' she exclaims. 'TV starrrrr! How are you, baba? Why don't you ever talk to me on the phone?'

'Hi, Anji didi,' Debjani says with a tight smile. 'Nice jeans.'

Anjini gives the tinkling laugh that always sets Debjani's teeth on edge. 'They were right on top of the dhobi pile,' she explains. 'They're nice, Dabbu, fitted waist and all. Bit loose though, I have to keep pulling them up.'

Debjani chokes. Anjini clicks her fingers. Her nails are immaculate, painted a delicate shade of seashell pink.

'Maybe a belt – oh, Chabbu's school belt, let's see if I can still get that round my waist... Where is she, anyway?'

'Not back from school yet.' Samar springs up from the sofa. 'I'll go wait for her at the gate.'

'That boy is crazy about Chubs.' Anjini rolls her eyes.

Mrs Mamta Thakur enters as he leaves the room, still in her flowered dressing gown, looking harassed. She has every reason to be. Anjini has just spent the entire morning telling her about her latest how-to-get-pregnant strategy.

'First I thought I would fast,' Anji had explained. 'But then I thought my motive might be tainted, that I might just be doing it to lose weight and *pretending* it was to please God, you know?'

Her mother nodded. Anji has done this before. A sixteen Saturdays fast, a month of Mondays fast. She's even done a maunvrat – a no-talking fast – for two whole weeks, something the whole family remembers quite fondly.

'So now I have *sworn* to become good.' She perched herself on top of the kitchen counter, her eyes glowing with the fervour of those who swear mighty oaths. 'Really, really *good*. I realized I'm not getting pregnant because I'm not a good person. It's a punishment. So now I am going to eschew all vanity, all competitiveness and all jealousy totally, and spread kindness and sunshine and happiness wherever I go.'

Mrs Mamta looked at her apprehensively. Ever since she can remember, Anjini has slotted her own sex into two categories: the vast majority category that she dismisses as a) not as pretty as me, and the extremely tiny minority category that she allows to be b) as pretty as me. Similarly, the vast majority of men falls into a) smitten by me, while a tiny smidgeon serves out their notice period in b) not yet smitten by me. It is a simple universe and Mrs Mamta is not sure it can handle the revolution Anji is planning.

'That's, uh, good,' Mrs Mamta Thakur had said cautiously. 'But you're only human, you know, Anji. Don't be so hard on yourself. Both your father and I feel you're making too much of this pregnancy thing – the doctors have said, na, there's nothing wrong with you. And Anant has fathered a child before. If you just relax, it will happen.'

'It *won't*.' Anji shook her head gloomily. 'It's all so clear now. I spent too many years making everybody's boyfriends fall in love with me, and now just see, Binni's sturdy uterus has squeezed out twin babies and totally neutralized my straight nose, my delicate collarbones, my C cup breasts, my tiny waist, my thin top-of-the-knees, my peachy skin and everything.'

Seeing how upset Debjani is now looking, Mrs Mamta concludes that Anjini's attempt at 'goodness' isn't progressing too well.

Into this thickened atmosphere enters Chachiji, her bulldog-face glowing. Her every step is accompanied by a melodious *chham-chhamming* sound, causing her sister-in-law and nieces to look down at her rather horny feet clad in blue and white Bata chappals.

'Payals!' Dabbu exclaims. 'How lovely, Chachiji! And so heavy! Must be expensive?'

'AN got them for me,' Chachiji says with a nonchalance that fools nobody. 'Three thousand rupees.'

'They're gorgeous,' Mrs Mamta remarks.

'You should get a pedicure,' Anjini advises.

'He said they are a nishaani of his pyar and I should never take them off,' Chachiji elaborates triumphantly. 'He put them on my feet himself.'

'You really *should* get a pedicure.'

'Be quiet, Anji.' Mrs Mamta frowns.

But Chachiji is talking to Dabbu. 'The totka worked,' she says excitedly. 'I did it and next day only he got me these payals – and he was so *curt* to the Hot Dulari, I can't tell you!'

'Terrific!' Dabbu gives her a hug.

'I'm going shopping now.' Chachiji gets to her feet melodiously. 'Bye now.' And she *chham-chhams* out of the room.

'Can't wait to show her new bauble to all of Hailey Road,' Anji says sapiently. But Mrs Mamta is glaring at Dabbu.

'She told *you* about that totka?'

Dabbu nods.

'The nimbu and the blood... and the pubic hair?'

Anji gasps. '*What?* This is delicious!'

'Yes, she did,' Dabbu says defensively. 'And I told her to go for it. I like Chachiji. Everyone is so mean to her – especially Ashok chacha – and I'm glad she did it because now everybody's happy.'

Her mother shakes her head. 'She's a bad influence, Dabbu. She'll fill your head with rubbish.'

'I'm not *stupid*, Ma,' Dabbu replies hotly.

'Yes, but it was irresponsible of her to tell you such things,' Mrs Mamta says, quite distressed. 'You're an unmarried girl – chhi.'

'Well, *I'm* married,' says Anji, her eyes dancing. 'Tell me the totka again, Dubz, what was it? Blood and pubes and *nimbu*? Ugh!'

But Mrs Mamta changes the subject. 'Where's that Eshwari? It's almost dark.'

'They've extended the practice timings by half an hour,' Debjani replies. 'She'll be back soon.'

Anjini wriggles deeper into the couch and looks speculative. 'Are you sure she isn't seeing someone?'

'Pretty sure.' The thought *has* crossed Dabbu's mind, several times, but just out of habit perhaps, she doesn't want to agree with Anji.

'I never played basketball,' Anjini muses. 'Bauji didn't approve of it back then.'

And *that*, Debjani thinks, is history rewritten Anjini Thakur style. You didn't play basketball because you weren't good enough to make it to the team. Why blame poor BJ?

'How's Amitabh Bose?' Anji asks next. 'I *love* his voice! Whenever he speaks, I feel little responsive quivers in my... um... stomach. Did he flirt with you?'

'No,' Dabbu replies stiffly.

Anji just stares at her, wide-eyed and uncomprehending.

'He seemed really nice, though,' Dabbu adds.

Anji gives a little scream of laughter. 'He would have flirted with *me*,' she says. 'I would've made him. God, you're such a *nun* – Dubz the Demure. When is your supta vastha going to end? You're almost a year overdue!'

Debjani glowers.

'These jeans are really comfy!'Anjini says next, tucking her knees up under her chin. 'But like I said, loose.'

'They're made of a new kind of material,' Debjani explains. 'It stretches.'

Anjini pulls a face. 'Still! Not bad for me, right? I'm the mother of a twelve-year-old!'

'He's not your *biological* child,' Debjani points out.

'Don't say that,' Anjini hisses immediately, her head whipping around, looking for Samar. 'He's really sensitive.'

'He's outside, didi, relax. So, should I unpack for you? Pull out something for you to wear?'

Anjini's face clouds over. Her lower lip trembles. She says, her voice rising to a higher pitch with every word, 'You'd *think*, when you come to your mother's house after so long, that your sister could share her *jeans* with you.'

Debjani hastily tries to stem the flow. 'Anji didi, it's okay, just wear them –'

But Anjini has got to her feet.

'Ma!'

'What, beta?'

'Can you give me a track pant or something? Dabbu doesn't want me to wear her jeans!'

Mrs Mamta turns harassed eyes upon Debjani.

'Dabbu?'

'Ma, I never said –'

'I thought she wouldn't mind because all she ever wears are those stupid shorts she cuts up! No, Ma, don't shout at her. She's all messed up because of the *India Post* article. I understand. She has to take it out on *someone*.'

And leaving Debjani open-mouthed, Anjini flounces over to the music system and starts to look through Dabbu's and Eshu's carefully arranged collection of cassettes and records. 'Don't you have any Abba LPs?' she sniffs. 'Or The Seekers? Or Cliff Richards? What is this Bryan Adams? And Dire Straits? And *Wham*? Is that even a band? This man looks pukka gay.'

Eshwari, who has just entered the room, leaps to the defence of her beloved George Michael. 'He is *not* gay,' she declares hotly.

'I can tell,' says Anji expertly. She points a perfectly manicured finger at the two smooth-faced men with plucked black eyebrows on the *Wham – Fantastic* cover. 'This one's the chick, this one's the man. So how are you, Chabbu? And how come that bunch of amaltas? Who gave them to you?'

'My nephew,' Eshwari says. 'He was waiting for me at the gate.'

Debjani watches sourly as Anji clucks over Eshwari, frowning at her stained T-shirt, approving of her fringe, asking about her love life. While chattering away, she also manages to unbuckle Eshwari's school belt and clip it around her waist. 'It fits,' she says smugly. 'Dekha? I didn't have to loosen it at all.'

Eshwari, catching the stormy expression on Dabbu's face, hurries over to her as soon as she can. 'How'd it go with the harami?' she whispers. 'You still think his butt is cute?'

'Oh, what does it matter,' Debjani whispers back petulantly. 'Now that Anji didi has come, the world will revolve around *her* again, and we'll have to listen to bloody Abba for the next seven days and get non-stop unsolicited advice, and be told that all our choices – whether it's music, clothes, men or movies – *suck*.'

Eshwari giggles. 'Do you think the harami will hit on Anji didi? Everybody does.'

Debjani feels a surge of irritation. It's all a joke for you, isn't it, Eshu, she thinks. While for me it's – it's what? she asks herself, appalled. Serious?

'Where's Samar?' Anjini demands suddenly.

'Playing with the puppies,' the Judge says, entering the room. 'He's talking of adopting one.'

Anjini rolls her pretty eyes. 'Uff! Why are there so many laindi dogs outside the gate? And such ugly ones too! It makes our gate look really lower middle class. Bauji, shall I call the MCD office – that Sharma uncle was so fond of me, remember – and tell them to send some workers to take them away?'

'Don't you *dare*,' Debjani hisses, jumping up.

Anjini turns around, raising her delicately arched eyebrows. 'Oh, are they *your* laindis? Arrey, sorry, Dabburam, how about we get that big naked one fixed at least? The procedure's quite painless, I believe.'

'No messing with that dog's balls!' the Judge roars suddenly, making everybody jump. 'What is a male without his manhood, huh? He'll turn into a wimp and be killed in a dog fight before the week is out! Besides, it'll be too expensive.'

'Oh no, Bauji,' Anjini says. 'It's not very expensive at all!'

'You're quite the expert, I see,' the Judge snorts. 'You women just like to emasculate all your men, and that's the truth. You want us to curl up and purr and talk to you about crochet patterns and Princess Diana's pregnancy and what not! Well, nobody's going to touch Moti's gotis on my watch. Is that clear?'

Anji's nostrils flare. 'What are you trying to insinuate exactly?' she says, the colour in her cheeks suddenly hectic. 'That because I can't have childre –'

'Arrey, no no.' Mrs Mamta goes over to her quickly. 'Of course not, Anji, don't be so sensitive!'

'Just leave that poor dog alone,' the Judge growls.

An awkward silence falls.

Finally Anji says, with artificial brightness, 'Uff, really, I miss you girls so much and when I come you just sulk at me about everything! Your mongrels will stay unfixed, Dabbu. And Chabbu, that Georgie Porgie is not gay. Happy?'

◆◦◆◦◆

That evening, there is an indefinite power cut and a lively family circle forms on the terrace. The girls carry rolled-up gaddas up the stairs, a glass bottle filled with fridge-cold water to dampen them with, packets of potato wafers and a blender full of cold coffee. Even the Judge promises to come up upstairs presently and appreciate the blooming amaltas.

'There's a gym in our colony now,' Anjini announces, flopping down on the gaddas once Eshwari has sprinkled them well. 'I've joined. The owner begged me to – everybody follows my lead, na. And now Rocky Singh the instructor ignores everybody else and just gives tips to *me*. It's so embarrassing. Do you know what he said to me yesterday?'

Dabbu is fairly sure nobody said 'what' but Anjini provides the answer anyway.

'Ki Mrs Singh, is that new newsreader on TV your elder sister? She looks so much like you!' She screams with laughter.

'It's probably the juvenile behaviour,' Eshwari quickly murmurs into Debjani's indignant ear. 'Makes her look younger than you.'

Dabbu gives a snort of laughter.

'What, what?' Anji looks hurt. 'What did you say? You girls have so many secrets. It's not fair.'

'Nothing,' Eshwari says, turning up the radio. 'I'm trying to tune in to Yuvvani for *A-Date-With-You*. But the static's terrible.'

'Expecting a request?' Anjini says knowingly. '*Basketball babe in the Number 10 shirt, without you my life is dirt!*'

'More like *Kot-piece queen, I love you so, our boring dads will never know*!' Eshwari murmurs. Debjani gives her a dirty look.

Anjini pricks up her ears instantly. 'What's this? What's this?' she says, delighted. 'Somebody's crushing on Dabbu?'

'No!' Debjani shakes her head vehemently.

'So lucky,' Anjini sighs. 'You'll probably have a love marriage. Not like me, bundled off to the first bakra on the block.'

Mrs Mamta frowns. 'That's not right, Anjini. You chose Anant yourself – such a handsome boy.'

'But I wanted to have a career first!' Anjini protests. Her voice becomes wistful. 'I wanted to be an airhostess with Indian Airlines. You know, travel the world, meet new people.'

'Binni didi says you just wanted to meet the Prime Minister,' Debjani remarks. 'I mean the now-ka-Prime Minister. That your favourite fantasy was sashaying into the cabin, bending over and breathlessly asking, *What can I get you, captain?*'

Anji doesn't get angry. Instead, she smiles secretively.

'I'd have hooked him if I'd met him,' she says, as though stating a simple fact. 'I'm prettier than the wife – definitely.'

There is silence.

Whatever happened, wonders Mrs Mamta wearily, to being good?

'I think Antu's having an affair,' Anjini says next with relish.

Mrs Mamta sighs. Eshwari smothers a yawn. Why does she pretend she wants to talk about *me*, Debjani thinks, nettled, when all she really wants to do is talk about *herself*?

'Antu bhaiyya's not the affair types,' Eshwari offers comfortingly. 'He's probably just overworked or something.'

'Fat lot *you* know, Chubs.' Anjini immediately takes offence. 'The girls in his office all dote on him. Actually,' her voice grows speculative, 'I wouldn't mind if he *had* an affair, it might spice up our marriage...'

'Why are you here, Anjini?' her mother asks suddenly. 'Tell me. What has happened?'

Anjini shrugs and looks up at the amaltas, her brown eyes clouding over.

This whole thing is Harrison Ford's fault, she broods. She had been so eager to see his latest Indiana Jones film that she went to see it with Anant's boss. Okay, maybe that wasn't very smart because the man was a total despo and she knew it would make Anant cross, but she was angry with Anant because... well, she has forgotten what it was she had been angry with him about. Anyway, she took the house keys without realizing it and he was locked out of the house when he came home from work, and while they stood arguing about it on the doorstep, a delivery man arrived with fifty exotic orchid stems, flown in specially from Thailand, bearing the card of their pimply Eureka Forbes salesman with whom Anji had flirted one day because she had been so depressed after meeting all the glowing, pregnant-for-the-second-time mothers during the parents-teachers meeting at Samar's school. She tried to explain this to Anant, thinking, with her usual optimism, that perhaps a showdown would be *good* – it would lead to angry words and lots of tears and drama and a deliciously tempestuous reconciliation.

But instead, he folded his arms, became all silent and tight-lipped and left for the US without saying a word to her.

'Oh, nothing, Ma,' Anji sighs. 'Everything's fine. I was just missing you guys, that's all. Tell me, should I get my hair permed?'

The green gate kunda clangs musically just then and Mrs Mamta looks down at the driveway. It is the Judge, coming back from a walk. His body language looks just a little furtive to her, and for a moment she wonders if Chachiji is right; maybe he really does sneak off to make phone calls and arrange rendezvous with another woman. Stop it, you're thinking like Anji, she tells herself sternly.

The Judge appears on the terrace presently, slightly out of breath. He looks at the little party on the mattresses and smiles. 'Mamtaji, your nest is full tonight!'

Anjini springs to her feet. 'Bauji, you never let us sleep outdoors when we were young!'

'You never asked,' he replies simply. 'All you ever wanted was a desert cooler for your room and when I organized that, there were endless arguments about whose turn it was to fill water in it.' He makes talking gestures with his fingers. '*Kichid kichid kichid.*'

Anjini's face falls.

'LN, see the flowers!' his wife steps in quickly. 'Aren't you glad we planted so many trees around the house?'

The Judge nods. He looks across at Number 13, beyond the boundary wall. 'That building is going to be six floors high. The trees will help block it a little, I suppose. Even then, I don't think you will be able to sleep up here any more.'

'How bad are Chachaji's debts anyway?' Anjini asks. 'And what on earth did he do to – ouch!'

This, because her mother has just pinched the soft flesh of her upper arm.

'I feel bad I couldn't do more for Ashok Narayan,' the Judge says heavily.

Debjani rolls over onto her stomach and hugs her pillow. And encounters Eshwari's huge black eyes looking right into hers.

'Tell,' she whispers.

Debjani smiles, feeling a ridiculous surge of heart-tightening excitement.

'There's nothing to tell,' she whispers back.

'What did you *do*?'

Debjani doesn't reply. Instead, with a sudden, dramatic movement, she rolls onto her back and stares up at the stars. 'What colour eyes would you guys say I have?'

Eshwari looks puzzled. 'Brown,' she says. 'Everybody has brown eyes. Or black eyes. That is, everybody Indian.'

'Oh, I don't know about *that*,' Anjini puts in. 'A lot of people say my eyes are the colour of brandy. Some say sherry. And some say aam-papad.'

'Those are all the same colour!' Eshwari looks unimpressed. 'It's just a fancy way of saying brown! We're not goras with blue and green and grey and brown eyes to pick from! No, Dabbu?'

To her surprise, Dabbu looks unconvinced. 'Oh, I don't know,' she murmurs. 'There are subtle nuances to each shade...'

Eshwari looks at her in disbelief and her black eyebrows snap together. She says, lowering her voice to a whisper, 'So what colour eyes did the harami say *you* had?'

'He didn't,' Dabbu whispers back, going bright red and feeling thankful for the darkness. 'We just practised reading... he has a Mac.'

Eshwari looks like she wants to shake her.

'Why are you so *careful*, Dabbu? Can't you just admit you like him?'

'His hands are nice,' Debjani replies. 'Lean but strong – and he types really fast.'

'Hey bhagwan! So now you like his hands too – how long will it take you to like the whole package?'

'I don't know,' Dabbu says again.

Eshwari glares at her, exasperated.

'Besides,' Debjani points out prudently, 'why should I put myself out there? I have to know if *he* likes me too.'

Eshwari groans, picks up a bottle of water and hits herself repeatedly on the head with it.

Chachiji is at Number 16 for tea and sympathy. Sitting hunched over the kitchen table, ladling spoonful upon spoonful of sugar into her cup, she tells her sister-in-law and nieces the tragic tale of her day so far.

A.N. Thakur is out of town and Gulab's law exams are on. He spent the whole night holed up in his room, studying, and early in the morning, Chachiji went to Birla Mandir to pray for him.

'Let him pass this time, Lord!' she begged. 'Once he is a qualified lawyer, he will free me from the humiliation of being married to a man who is sleeping with my cook!'

'You don't know that he's sleeping with the Hot Dulari, Bhudevi,' says Mrs Mamta. 'Think of your new payals! It's all just your veham.'

'You're *much* prettier than the Hot Dulari,' Anji assures her earnestly. 'She's so flat-chested and dark.'

Chachiji sniffs dolefully. 'It's not about looks, ladkiyon. She has done jaadu-tona on him – he can't help himself, poor man.'

The ladies of Number 16 receive this remarkable statement with diplomatic silence. Chachiji continues her tale of woe.

She bought flowers and a coconut for ten rupees. She spent

over an hour in prayer. Then she fed the cows outside the temple. And when she finally came home in a cycle-rickshaw, she found Gulab still fast asleep in the downstairs room, *Hindu Undivided Family Law* spread across his chest, his mouth wide open, eyes shut. He had missed the Bar examination.

'It's all that wretched Hot Dulari's fault!' Chachiji declares.

'What?' Dabbu is mystified. 'How? He's the one who overslept! How can it be *her* fault?'

Chachiji glares at her. 'She should have woken him up!' she snaps. 'I found her boiling eggs in the kitchen, humming *Humne tumko dekha, tumne humko dekha* under her breath. I'm going to sack her.'

But Dabbu's mind is travelling along a different track.

'And what about Gulgul bhaisaab? He's lost a year, surely?'

'I'd sack him too, if I could,' Chachiji grumbles. 'Adopted that fool from the gutter and look how he repays me! May he get *worms*! May he rot in *hell*. May termites gnaw at his –'

'Anus,' Anji finishes comfortingly for her. 'We know. Don't worry, Chachiji. Have another cup of tea.'

'Arrey, what tea,' Chachiji says tearfully. 'You haven't heard the whole story yet. When I shook the good-for-nothing awake, do you know what he said to me? Not I-am-sorry-mummy, not I-am-an-idiot-mummy, but *good*, I'm glad I missed it. I don't want to do law anyway, I want to open a *jim*!'

'*No!*' Mrs Mamta says weakly.

'Don't tell me!' Dabbu manages.

'But I *am* telling you!' Chachiji says morosely. 'The father has gambled away the roof over my head and now the son wants to hobnob with large naked men in chaddi-baniyan!'

'You know,' Anji says slowly. 'That's not such a bad idea,

Chachiji. Gyms are becoming very popular nowadays. And Gulgul really knows his weightlifting.'

'He wants to call it Gulab's Gym,' Debjani tells her aunt hesitantly.

Chachiji stares at both of them, bug-eyed. 'You two *know* about this? You've been encouraging him? Of course you've been encouraging him. Horny girls wanting to see muscular men coming and going the whole day! Well, you won't. My Gulgul is not going to open a jim, he is going to be a lawyer!'

Mrs Mamta Thakur frowns. 'Now, Bhudevi, that's enough. Of course the girls didn't know!'

'*I* knew,' Debjani says, firing up. 'Why can't Gulgul try running a gym? It won't cost much. He can keep studying law on the side. He already has a really good music system and all the mirrors he needs. You just have to buy him some weights, Chachiji. And maybe a desert cooler.'

'I'll buy him sixty kilos of sandalwood to be cremated in,' swears Gulab's unnatural parent. 'Wretched, wretched boy. And shame on you for encouraging him.'

Mrs Mamta tries to calm her down. She explains that all she really needs to do is buy Gulab an alarm clock. 'And forget about sacking Dulari,' she says soothingly. 'AN's just bought you those lovely payals – which means he *loves* you – in return, you must show that you trust him. Sacking this woman is below your dignity. Besides, you need all the help you can get today – you have to move out, remember?'

Today is indeed the black date the builder has set for the demolition of Number 13 (no wonder AN has made himself scarce, thinks his sister-in-law darkly). The crew arrives with their bulldozer at the dot of ten, very loud and bossy, and starts arguing with Chachiji about why the house hasn't been emptied yet. Mrs Mamta hurries over, calms Chachiji down, and officially invites her to come and stay in their annexe for the time being.

Chachiji, instead of being grateful, as Mrs Mamta privately thinks she ought to be, moans about how her evil sister-in-law is making her stay in 'servants' quarters' and drops broad hints about wanting to stay in the main house.

'I'll share with Debjani,' Chachiji suggests craftily. 'She likes me.'

'That won't be possible,' Mrs Mamta says firmly. 'Debjani already shares with Eshwari. You had better stay in the annexe only. The three of you can spread out nicely there.'

Mrs Mamta isn't entirely happy with this arrangement, because Ashok is unsavoury, Chachiji unstable, and even Gulgul, though he himself is sweet, has some very overfriendly, over-muscled buddies. But what to do? Family is family.

It irritates her when the Judge says the same thing, though.

'Family is family,' he states pompously. 'We must stand together.'

'Oh, it's all very well for you to talk,' Mrs Mamta says pettishly. 'You'll never talk to Ashok about his disgraceful behaviour, you'll just shut yourself up in the study. It's me who has to do all the socializing with your stupid sister-in-law and your randibaaz brother.'

Later in the day the girls help Chachiji move in and set up her kitchen. Satish Sridhar, who has surfaced briefly between his many engineering entrance exam classes, pitches in to help. Eshwari and he stagger back and forth between the houses, carrying boxes and bundles of all shapes and sizes.

'This is kinda cosy, huh, Bihari?' He gives her his endearing wolf-puppy grin. 'Me-and-a-you-and-a –' he peers into a box, 'a garam masala grinder, a toaster, a pressure cooker and something that's quite possibly a sexual pleasure enhancement device. Basically, everything one needs to set up a modern home today!'

'Shut up, Steesh.' Eshwari rolls her eyes. 'And hold your side higher – the carton's tilting.'

'I can carry the whole thing myself, you know,' he assures her. 'I'm strong enough. I'm just letting you help coz getting so close to you feels *nice*.'

Eshwari lets go of her side of the carton abruptly.

Satish curses, recovers, weaves around for a bit, then grins at her manfully. She twinkles back.

'All good?' she enquires.

'Of course not,' he pants. 'I'm studying engineering, not weightlifting. Get your side again, c'mon.'

Eshwari smiles and grabs her end of the carton.

'Phew!' says Satish. 'Where's that ape Gulgul when you need him?'

'Don't even ask,' Eshwari replies. 'He's fully in the doghouse – must have sulked off somewhere.'

They walk along for a while.

'I love that perfume,' Satish says presently. 'Sometimes I can swear I smell it when I'm swotting over 3-D engineering drawings in the middle of the night. What's it called?'

His eyes are friendly as he towers over her, but Eshwari can feel her cheeks go hot. The meaningful grin is just a flicker away, and lately she has started responding to it. There is a certain intensity lurking behind it that quickens her pulse, and causes her to doodle E-for-Engineer at the back of her history notebook.

'Anais Anais,' she replies matter-of-factly. 'Don't get too fond of it though, it's too expensive to use on a regular basis. I'll be switching to something cheaper soon.'

'Oh?' he replies.

And they let it go at that.

—◆◆◆—

When Dylan and his father drive over the next evening, both in a state of pleasant anticipation, albeit for different reasons, they are confounded to find that a floral cushioned cane sofa has pushed the green baize card table off centrestage. Around the sofa are grouped six besotted men of varying ages and types, and upon it is seated a vision of beauty dressed in a sleeveless pink chikankari dress, with the table fan (no longer set on circulation mode) pointing squarely at her, taking delicious liberties with her cascading curls of hair.

Looking at her, Dylan gets the weird sensation that he has wandered into the pastry section at Wenger's bakery. Everything is just so ripe and moist and creamy and temptingly displayed.

The six men certainly seem to be standing with their noses pressed against glass. One of them, a scholarly-looking man with slipping spectacles, is speaking.

'*So* nice to see you again, Anjini! Yesterday only, when my father-in-law was having a heart attack, I was remembering you and speculating that the word *angina* – which is a chest pain you get when your heart muscles do not get enough blood – is probably derived from the Sanskrit root *anjini*. Haha!'

'How naughty of you,' Anjini murmurs, eyes sparkling beneath demurely downcast lashes. 'But I know you dashing IPS types – always putting the ladies under cardiac arrest.'

Much appreciative laughter. Nobody, Dylan notices in amusement, bothers to ask if the man's father-in-law is alive or dead.

'How many days are you here for?' asks another admirer.

Anji turns her body towards him with the air of a hostess proffering plump little cupcakes on a tray. *Please have some. Oh please, do have at least one.*

'A week at least,' Anjini replies. 'My son was bored of Anji-ma's cuddles – he wanted his nani-nana.'

A wistful silence greets this utterance – the little circle is clearly imagining being cuddled by Anji-ma.

'Jijaji nahin aaye?' gulps a thin, stringy man with a bobbing Adam's apple.

'No,' she sighs. 'He has a lot of work.'

There is a chorus of insincere sympathy from the group.

The Brigadier clears his throat. 'Where's LN?' he demands gruffly. 'No kot-piece today?'

'Uncle!' Anjini sees him and flies gracefully to her feet, her pink chikankari draperies fluttering about, showcasing delicious glimpses of dimpled flesh. She hugs the Brigadier. 'How nice to see you! How *are* you?'

Dylan, watching this effusive display, is positive she doesn't remember his father's name.

'Er, he's Brigadier Shekhawat,' he puts in.

Anjini turns to him, her eyes sparkling with mischief.

'Of course I know who he is!' she says archly. 'Do you think I make a habit of hugging men whose names I don't know?'

'Do you?' Dylan grins. 'I won't tell you my name then.'

Anjini giggles.

'Okay.'

It's one little softly uttered word but she manages to infuse it with a world of intimacy.

'I'm Dylan,' he tells her hastily. 'And you're A for Anjini. Pleased to meet you. I'll go find uncle.'

As he strides towards the house, he encounters a sporty-looking young girl rolling a gas cylinder down the driveway and into the annexe of Number 16, a lanky twelve-year-old child trailing in her wake. This is really meet-the-family day for me, Dylan thinks resignedly as he reaches down and grabs the cylinder by the neck.

'Here, lemme get that,' he says. 'I'm –'

'Dyllllan.'

He nods, taken aback. She stands back and looks him over, assessing him with big black eyes. Dylan resists the urge to suck in his stomach and puff out his chest. But he can't stop himself from swinging the heavy cylinder a little, casually, so she knows how strong he is. 'Where do you want me to put it?'

'Upstairs.' She gestures vaguely. Then she gives him an impudent snub-nosed grin. 'I'm Eshwari. You're sucking up to me, aren't you?'

Whoa, that's direct. These Thakur sisters clearly don't mess about.

'Now why would I do that?' he asks smoothly.

'Because you're so pretty,' is Samar's explanation.

Dylan looks down at him, impressed. 'You've got a good eye, young Thakur.'

Samar doesn't say anything. Nobody knows it yet, but he has plans for Eshwari. She is only five years older than him. It feels like a lot now, but when he's twenty-one and she's twenty-six, it won't mean a thing. He's almost as tall as her now, and luckily she's short – and he *thinks* she's stopped growing.

'I'm a Singh,' he clarifies. 'Samar Vir Singh.'

Eshwari chuckles. 'You *know* why.'

'Yes, I am sucking up to you,' Dylan confesses. 'Is it working?'

'I'll let you know,' she replies airily. 'Walk ahead of me.'

He obeys and Eshwari falls back a little, crossing her arms across her chest and squinting.

'What?' Samar nudges her. 'Where are you looking? Is there a stain on his pants, Eshu?'

'Eshu *mausi*,' Eshwari whispers in reply. 'And shhushh!' And then to Dylan, who has turned around and is looking at her enquiringly, 'C'mon, you've got to take it up that flight of stairs.'

'So how'd I do last night?' Dylan asks as he hauls the cylinder up the narrow steps. 'Did I feature in your girlie bedtime conversation at all?'

'Not really.' Eshwari grins amiably. 'We were too busy discussing if Anji didi would look like Kenny G if she got her hair permed.'

'Ah,' Dylan replies ironically. 'That puts me in my place.'

Eshwari smiles at him, turns around and goes back downstairs. Dylan puts down the gas cylinder for a moment and looks at Samar, who is watching him intently.

'I like her hair as it is,' Samar says.

Dylan nods, panting just a little. The cylinder's heavy.

'How many more flights of stairs?' he asks.

'Just one more,' Samar replies. 'You're lucky. In the main house there are three – the toppest one is where the Pushkarni fell from when she died.'

'Who?' Dylan asks, confused.

Samar sits down on the steps. 'The Pushkarni. My grandmother. Or rather,' he clarifies conscientiously, 'my *step*-grandmother. She went to the terrace to pick up the clothes from the washing line because it was storming, but then the storm became so strong that the lights went out. The terrace became dark, so she just stood there and started screaming, *Pushkar... Pushkar...*'

'Who's Pushkar?' Dylan struggles to stay with the plot.

'Her husband. And then she heard footsteps behind her and she relaxed... and then he said (here Samar assumes a horrid, giggly sort of voice), Here I am! And she was so relieved, she said, Pushkar! And then he grabbed her shoulders and said (Samar's voice goes all high and giggly again), *You* only said push kar – and he pushed her right off the roof!'

Dylan's jaw drops. 'That is a horrible story!'

Samar grins. 'Isn't it? I think it may even be true.' He hesitates, then lowers his voice. 'But I'm not sure about all the other things Chachiji says. I think she could be imagining all that. Do you believe in ghosts?'

They have reached the top of the stairs. Dylan puts down the cylinder and stares at the lanky lad seriously.

'No,' he says with finality. 'There's no such things as ghosts.'

Samar looks philosophical.

'Thought so,' he says laconically. 'Namaste, Chachiji.'

Dylan looks up to see a bulldoggy lady sitting in the semi-darkness, staring blankly out of the window.

'Hello, ma'am,' he says courteously.

'Hello, hello,' she replies, her chins wobbling. 'You are Steesh, no?'

'I'm Dylan. Nice to meet you.'

Then he turns to Samar. 'Any more stuff to be brought up? Four-poster beds? Suits of armour? Dead bodies?'

Samar shakes his head seriously. 'Gulgul bhaisaab did all that.'

'I wish I could offer you some tea,' Chachiji frets. 'But there is no milk...' Her jowls start to quiver. 'No cheeni... no leaves...'

'It's okay, ma'am,' Dylan assures her hastily. 'I'll be downstairs, all right?'

Running down the narrow stairs, he encounters Debjani hurrying up, hugging a stack of lurid green-and-yellow striped curtains. He places his palms along both walls, blocking her path, leaning down and smiling at her, his dark eyes warm.

'Hey,' he whispers.

'What are you doing here?' She stops, startled.

But Dylan doesn't reply. He just stares at her, staggered by the impact this sudden, delayed sighting of her is having on him. She glows, he thinks helplessly. Her hair is loosely twisted into a wet fragrant rope along one shoulder, trailing water droplets onto her white cotton kurti. He wants to reach out and touch it.

'Ingratiating myself with your family,' he says finally, lightly. 'For reasons I am not yet ready to divulge. How pretty you look. You'd look even prettier if you didn't,' he reaches out and touches her chin gently, 'insist on painting that fake dot on your chin every day. That...' he purses his lips and shakes a finger reprovingly, 'is actually kinda cheesy.'

Debjani gasps in outrage and pushes at him with her armload of curtains. He buckles over, laughing, but then, as she stumbles too, he straightens up and steadies them both, gripping her upper arms. Her breath catches. Her eyes lock into his, twin pools of Pears darkening.

'God curse you, A.N. Thakur!' Chachiji wails from upstairs. 'Bringing me to live in this wretched servants' quarter! I wish I were *dead*!'

Dylan's eyes widen comically. Debjani gives an involuntary snort and pulls away.

'Don't make *fun*,' she says. 'My aunt's suffered quite a sadma today.'

'Okay.'

His voice is very deep. Debjani realizes she's feeling nervous, which is stupid.

'Hey, guess what,' she says. 'They called from DD. I get to read again this Friday. So it wasn't such a disaster, after all.'

'That's great,' he replies, still holding her.

Silence.

Then, 'Go down to the garden,' she tells him. 'The table's all set up and your dad is waiting.'

'Aren't you coming?' he asks, not letting her go. 'I mean, your sister's nice and all, but she doesn't say hukum – the soul of Balkishen Bau may take offence.'

'There's no running water in this hovel,' Chachiji moans from upstairs. 'How will I even wash?'

'Go downstairs, Dylan,' Debjani, too shy to meet his eyes, firmly orders the collar of his shirt. Looking down at her lashes curled against her cheeks, he realizes, with a surge of happiness that is clearly disproportionate, that this is the first time she has said his name out loud. His arms tighten about her, curtains and everything.

'Say that again.'

'What? Go downstairs?'

He shakes his head. 'My name.'

Colour floods her cheeks.

'Why?'

'Because,' he says simply. His eyes slide down to her mouth. 'Say it.'

She looks away. Warning bells, straight out of the climactic temple scene in a Hindi movie, are ringing madly inside her head. But she ignores them. After all, it's just a name. What's the big deal about getting her lips to shape two simple syllables?

'*Say* it.'

This is ridiculous.

'Dylan.' She says it with her cheeks mortifyingly red but her head erect. As his eyes rise to meet hers again, his gaze warm and quickening, she adds, 'Singh Shekhawat. See? Was that supposed to be some kind of test? I can say behenchod too. And maadarchod. And She Sells, Sea Shells. Shall I?'

'You were right,' he says, his lips twisting wryly. 'You really don't know how to flirt.'

'Now go *downstairs*.'

'I'm going,' he replies, still holding her fast.

'Um...' Debjani talks to his shirt again. 'You're still here.'

'Yeah... What shampoo is that?'

She starts to say that it's Halo – because, excuse me, what other shampoo is available in this country – but before she can, he lowers his dark head and kisses her, very softly, on the place where her wet cotton kurti falls away to reveal the delicate skin at her collarbone.

Debjani freezes.

Dylan pulls back.

His eyes are closed. As she notices, numbly, how long and thick his lashes are, he opens them and looks at her. His eyes are curiously alight.

'You can't just... kiss me like that,' she manages to say.

'No?' he asks, his gaze now on her mouth. 'Why, exactly?'

'Because...' She falters, hardly knowing what she's saying. 'Because it's wron –' She stops short. 'Because I don't *want* you to!'

'Really?' He is murmuring into her ear now, his arms sliding down to wrap themselves smoothly around her slim body. 'Are you sure? Besides, it was such a little kiss. Too little to count, surely? Maybe you imagined it.'

Her eyes widen in outrage. 'I did *not*.'

She spits this out so vehemently that he releases her, raising his hands and moving backwards, leaving her path free.

'I'm sorry,' he says, consternation in his voice.

'It's okay,' she returns, her cheeks flaming.

The curtains have fallen from her grasp. As she bends down to pick them up, he bends too.

'Lemme carry those,' he offers. 'They're heavy.'

'Oh, please,' Dabbu flares up. 'I haven't exactly gone weak in the knees, you know.'

'But you dropped the curtains,' he points out, totally straight-faced. 'Surely that's something.'

'Oh, get out of my way,' Debjani says, confused, red-cheeked and totally fed up.

'Okay, okay,' Dylan returns peaceably. She can feel him piling the last of the curtains into her arms. 'I'm going.' His voice comes closer, becomes a whisper, becomes cockier – she can tell he's smiling. 'I'll save you some Maggi.'

His footsteps sound lightly down the stairs, and then Dabbu sinks down on the steps, her heart thumping wildly. Chachiji appears on the landing.

'Curtains?' She sniffs morosely. 'Of course. Shut me in. Block me out. Seeing my face in her window like a gaand ka tukda will give your mother a bellyache, I know.'

⋅⋅⋅⋅⋅⋅⋅⋅

'Dabbu, tell me *all* about you and that delish son of Shekhawat uncle. Now!'

Thus, Anjini on the terrace, flinging herself down on the mattress between her two younger sisters and casting her arms around Debjani's neck.

'There's nothing to tell.' Debjani's cheeks are fiery red. She has just spent a harrowing evening not looking at Dylan across the kot-piece table.

'Oh, but he stared at you all evening. I know, because I stared at *him* all evening. And he didn't even notice me. Even when I yanked the neck of my dress as far down as it would go. Should've worn a kurta, actually. Then I could've popped open a couple of buttons. Anyway, he's got it bad for you.'

'I cannot believe,' Debjani says primly, 'that you're talking like this when you're thirty years old.'

'I'm thirty – not dead,' Anji replies candidly. 'Or in the convent like *you*. Sister Dabbu. The nun who has no fun – ooh, he's Christian, isn't he? That's kind of...' her voice grows deep and purring, 'kinky.'

'No, it isn't!' Dabbu, totally appalled at how she let Dylan kiss her after meeting him barely six times, bursts out. 'Anji didi, you really talk such rubbish. Eshu, *say* something.'

'He's got an awesome butt,' says Eshwari unhelpfully. 'I fully checked it out. And I know he likes you. I accused him of currying favour with me and he admitted it.'

'What!' Debjani's toes curl in squirmy horror. Oh god, so Dylan knows she's been having girlish little chats about him with her sisters! No wonder he was so cocky when he met her on the stairs. She *hates* cocky men – although she has to admit he hadn't looked so cocky afterwards, during the kot-piece session. He had looked shaken, even confused. And he had played *very* badly. The Judge, who had drawn him as a partner, harangued him all evening. Wow, kissing her was *so* awful it had totally put him off his game.

'What did you tell him, Eshu?'

'Oh, how does it matter.' Anji comes quickly to Eshu's defence. 'You like him, don't you?'

'I don't,' Debjani insists. 'He just took me by surprise, that's all –' She stops abruptly.

'How?' Anji pricks up her ears. 'What did little Dillu do? He looks like a total harami. That kind always falls for a Vestal Virgin. Did he corner you against a wall and smoulder at you, Dabbu? Is your supta vastha officially over now?'

'Mind your own business!' Debjani, goaded beyond endurance, finally lashes out. 'I don't ask you what you're doing here, or why Antu bhaiyya never phones you, do I?'

Eshwari gasps.

Anji goes very still.

'I'm sorry, Anji didi.' Debjani's voice is a wretched whisper.

'It's okay.' Anji has gone rather pale. 'You're right. I should respect your privacy. Like you do mine.'

'Anji didi...' It is Eshwari who speaks now.

'You girls sleep,' Anji says. 'I have to check on Samar anyway. Goodnight.'

There is a shocked silence on the terrace after she leaves.

'You'll get chhaalas in your mouth,' Eshwari says with certainty. 'Big, painful blisters. Talking like such a kutiya. Why did you have to twig her about Antu bhaiyya?'

Dabbu shakes her head, stricken. 'I don't know where that came from. It was horrible of me. I'm just... really stressed today. Should I go downstairs and grovel?'

Eshwari shakes her head. 'No point. She's in martyr mode now. Which basically means we're screwed. The only thing worse than a bubbly Anji didi is a hurt and dignified Anji didi. Thanks a lot, Dubz.'

Hey there, Georgy girl...

'Wake up, Georgy girl.' Eshu, back from her early morning run, chucks her sneakers across the terrace with such force that Debjani sits up, blinking. 'She's been singing that like a maniac for the last hour. Samar had to hear it as he chugged down his Bournvita, and as he sat on the pot. It's being sung in your honour, you know.'

'When did you last wash those socks?' Debjani wrinkles up her nose.

'Did you *hear* what I said?'

'Yes.' Dabbu burrows under the sheets again. 'I'm not deaf. She wants to tart me up for the newscast... Just kill me now.'

The enthusiastic warbling continues relentlessly from below stairs.

'Just go down and get it over with,' Eshwari prods her. 'You totally owe it to her after last night. And she knows it.'

Dabbu straightens up with a groan, pushes her feet into her chappals and makes her way down the stairs warily. Anji is sitting in the verandah, sharpening her nail file with the happy air of an executioner readying his blade for a ritual slaughter.

'*There* you are!' she beams. 'Good morning! I thought we'd begin with a nice manicure-pedicure. Dip your fingers in this basin.'

And so it starts.

'Your nails may not show on TV, but you'll know they're pretty and that will give you confidence,' Anji says. 'Just look at this dead skin – gross! Now show me your underwear... Uff, I know you don't plan to flash it but it has to be *sassy*!'

The family gets no eggs for breakfast that day, and no banana shake either, as Anji sticks the entire ration of both these items into making a 'bouncy banana eggnog' for Dabbu's head. She also throws henna powder, tea leaves and coffee beans rather haphazardly into the mix, which gives Dabbu the uneasy feeling that she is being guinea-pigged with. Her head has to be covered in a plastic Gambhir Stores packet before she can wander about the house, as the Judge and his grandson protest that they are in danger of asphyxiating from the odour emanating from her hair.

'Sissies,' Anji scoffs as she herds Dabbu into the bathroom and soaps her head vigorously with reetha suds. 'Men have no *concept*. Arrey, let them get their threading done just once and then we'll see! You don't worry, Dabbu, it'll all wash off – and anyway, people can't *smell* you through the TV, can they?'

Eshwari, perched on the edge of the clothes-laden bed, is watching the action with keen interest. 'Abroad, there is apparently a company called Wella that makes hair colour,' she pipes up after a while. 'You can get any shade you want, I saw the ad in *Woman and Home* magazine.'

Anjini emerges from the cupboard, where she has been burrowing terrier-like for over half an hour, her pretty hair all dishevelled. 'Fat lot of good that'll do *you*, Chubs, your hair is so black it will take no colour. And don't you ever get your threading done? Your eyebrows look like caterpillars smooching. Now, Dabbu, *this* petticoat, it's satin, it'll make you feel like a queen. And this nice, light sari, wear it and show – not now, stupid, you'll wet it!'

As the afternoon draws to a close, the smells are vanquished, the sari tried on and the effect declared airy and bright. Debjani, who knows there is no stopping her eldest sister when she is on a mission, submits quietly, voicing objection only when Anjini produces her trusty hairdrier and a set of twenty-four pink sponge-rollers.

'I don't want sausage curls,' Debjani wards her off firmly. 'You might enjoy going around looking like you're wearing a judge's wig, Anji didi, but I don't. I have to tie my hair up to read, it helps me concentrate.'

'Fine, whatever.' Anji, intent on 'goodness', heroically ignores the red rag that is the judge's wig crack. 'But at least plait it loosely, like so.' Her quick fingers braid Dabbu's hair and bring it over to lie along one shoulder. She tousles the crown, letting some curls escape and fall loosely around Dabbu's face, and purses her lips. 'You need something more. Dangly earrings?'

'No!' Dabbu wails. 'I could be reading about train crashes. Or plagues. Or earthquakes. How can I do that wearing dangly earrings?'

But Anjini, humming 'Georgy Girl' under her breath again, isn't listening.

'There's got to be something... something unique... Oh, I know! *Hah!* Thank me for changing your life forever, Debjani Thakur!' And Anji, extracting a single white rose from the vase Mrs Mamta has placed on the dressing table, bites off most of the stalk with her teeth and sticks it ceremoniously into Dabbu's plait, settling it in the nape of her neck. 'A rose for a rose. You're perfect now, baby! And Anji didi made you so!'

She marches Debjani through the aangan and into the drawing room. 'Ma, Bauji, how does she look?'

'D for dazzling,' the Judge says with an encouraging smile.

Could he be more fake? Dabbu thinks, exasperated. He doesn't even have his glasses on.

'But it's not about how you look,' the Judge continues, much to Anjini's disgust. 'It's about *self-belief*. Remember how you took on the Vunderful Vladimir, while all the others cowered!'

'Oh, please,' Anji scoffs. 'We didn't *cower*. We were just smart enough to know that Vladimir wasn't actually going to skewer you to death inside that box, Bauji!'

'I love the rose!' Mrs Mamta Thakur puts in hurriedly. 'Well done, Anji! And Dabbu, smile a little more when you read. You have such a lovely smile, baba!'

'Don't let the laindi dogs jump on you!' Anji agonizes as Debjani heads for the door. 'They'll spoil your clothes... Uff, who's phoning *now*?'

Debjani, who is right next to the phone in the passageway, grabs it and holds it to the non-rose-festooned side of her neck. 'Hello?'

'All the best.'

His voice sounds toe-curlingly hot on the phone. Still, this is a little too high-handed for Debjani.

'How are you so sure it's me?'

'How are *you* so sure it's me?' he replies and she can hear laughter in his voice.

Debbie flushes. Flirt. Harami. Kiss grabber. Also, autocue coacher, she remembers guiltily. But the autocue coaching was probably just preparatory to the subsequent kiss grabbing. *Cunning* kiss grabber.

'Thank you,' she says with bad grace.

'I'll be watching,' he says, his voice a caress. 'Blow them away.'

And that evening, Debjani does 'blow them away'. She greets the camera without any self-consciousness, reads naturally and doesn't falter once. Dylan, watching in his living room with his mother and brothers, finds it hard to take his eyes off her.

'She's pretty,' Ethan declares. 'Prettier than the rose in her hair.' His eyes slide slyly towards his big brother. 'No, Dyl? See, Mamma, how *hard* he's hugging the cushion while watching her!'

Dylan chucks the cushion at him and enquires mildly if he wants a kick in the goolies.

'The question is not what *I* want,' says the incorrigible Ethan, 'but what *you* want.'

'I want to listen to the news,' Dylan answers pleasantly. 'So keep your trap shut or I'll shut it for you.'

Debjani talks in dulcet tones about the President's visit to a medical college in Maharashtra. She speaks of the inauguration of an art exhibition in Pragati Maidan by the Minister for Culture. And at the fag end of the main news, she mentions that '*the Special Investigation Commission appointed to investigate the incidents following the assassination of the late Prime Minister in New Delhi submitted its findings today. It recommended no criminal prosecution of any individual and cleared Member of Parliament Shri Hardik Motla of directing the riots*'.

Then she smiles her pretty, lopsided smile. '*And now for the sports news. England continued to dominate on the fourth day of play against India in Calcutta...*

Dylan stares at the television screen in bewilderment. No criminal prosecution of any individual? What about fucking Hardik Motla and his gang of goons? What about all the eyewitness accounts? What about *my* eyewitness account, for heaven's sake? He gets to his feet and as his mother watches uneasily, walks up to the TV and switches it off. Debjani, now wrapping up the news bulletin, her skin more dewy than the rose in her hair, vanishes with a little *blipp*. Dylan stalks out of the room, picks up the phone and dials the *India Post* office, very white around the mouth.

'Yeah, it's me. I want to speak to VO. He's in Delhi? Oh, board meetings. What? Really? Okay, I'll give him a call then.'

⊷┉◉┉⊷

A tall, thin, fair man with a dyed goatee and a beatific Hindu-god smile is listening to somebody speak, his eyes half closed, his body language elaborately attentive. His arms are crossed, his fingertips, tapping gently against his arms, are slim and pale and twitchy. Somehow they manage to give the impression that they spend a lot of time up his thin nostrils, like worms seeking out their hidey-holes.

'Mr Motla, would you like to share your reaction to the findings of the Special Investigation Commission with the viewers of *Viewstrack*?'

The voice is Mitali Dutta's. The camera cuts to her briefly as she speaks. She is looking rather warrior-like in a peacock blue kurta and bright red lipstick.

Hardik Motla opens hooded, watery eyes. 'I feel vindicated.'

He has a trick of tilting his eyes upwards as he speaks, until only the whites show, like a prophet seeing visions. '*Vindicated.* A lot of things have been alleged about me, and I am very happy to get this clean chit from such an apex body. Yes. Also,' he clears his throat, his smile staying miraculously intact, 'my heart goes out to the families of all those who died in that dark time. I pray for the souls of...'

'How the fuck does he manage to smile and speak at the same time?' Varun Ohri asks, fascinated. 'His cheeks must be as steely as Jane Fonda's thighs.'

But Dylan is too disgusted to theorize on thighs.

'I can't believe they gave him a clean chit.' He shakes his head. 'This SIC is like some sick joke.'

'He's obviously got friends in high places,' murmurs editor-in-chief Hiranandani suavely, his silver hair gleaming above his thin, sad-clown face in the afternoon sunlight that is filtering in through the windows of the *India Post's* Delhi office. 'Or he's got dirt on people in high places.'

On the TV, Mitali narrows her eyes and pushes the mic closer to Motla's face.

'Sir, what about the statement of one of the officers who was in the briefing room with you on the night of 30 October, that you said – and I quote – "Get people to vent their anger. It's much better that way. Keeping anger, rage, violence pent up inside is unhealthy. It can give you cancers."'

Motla leans forward.

'Who was this officer? What is his name?'

Mitali looks discomforted.

'We both know, Mr Motla, that the statement was made anonymously. The officer said he feared for his life.'

Motla sits back in his chair, spreads out his pale palms and rolls his eyeballs upward. 'Only cowards are anonymous.'

'But he said you said – and again I quote – "Ask any good psychiatrist, keeping anger inside is bad. It can give you ulcers, giltees, cysts and cancers. So if you don't get the poison out in small-small controlled bloodlettings, it will build up and build up and one day it will explode."'

'Nice story.' Motla smirks. 'Only, it's not true.'

'You went on to give examples from history. You said,' she bends down to consult her notes, '"The anger of the German people was not allowed to be vented after the First World War. They had to keep it all inside so their resentment just kept building and building and building, and then what happened? Hitler happened! Second World War happened! This is history – let us prevent it from being repeated."'

Hardik Motla wraps his arms around himself and massages his upper arms rhythmically.

'Look, Mitaji, I have been very patient. I have sat here and listened to all your questions. Because you are from a video news magazine and everybody wants to encourage these new, so-modern video news magazines filled with pretty young journalists. But ten officers have testified that this so-called cancers speech of mine never happened. It is made up! Untrue! Rubbish!'

'So you deny it entirely?'

'Yes! These Sikhs, they only have themselves to blame. Arrey, if you distribute sweets and laddoos and sing and dance to celebrate the assassination of a beloved Prime Minister, you are asking for trouble, na! Every action has an equal and opposite reaction! That is physics.' He smiles at her, trying for charming and achieving distinctly creepy.

Varun Ohri snorts. 'Fucker used to be a high school teacher or what? First history, then physics.'

Mitali doesn't smile back. 'What about the reports that you supplied party workers with voting lists so they could zoom into Sikh households and torch them with kerosene *you* provided?'

'Find me one party worker who says I did this! The SIC hasn't been able to. Maybe *you*, being a modern video news magazine, can do it!'

She ignores the sarcasm and ploughs ahead. 'Sikh people have testified that they heard you incite the Hindu crowd from the back of a truck in Tirathpuri. They say you were the one who started the chanting of the slogans *Blood for Blood!* and *A Life for a Life!* which spread like wildfire to the rest of the country.'

'That is all *rubbish*,' Motla snaps testily, his smile wearing and tearing. 'These are faceless and baseless accusations made up by that half mad reporter Shekhwati.'

'You mean, Shekhawat?' Mitali corrects him, looking taken aback. 'From the *India Post*?'

'Yes!' Motla nods. 'See, this Shekhwati and other people are just doing name-calling, but when I ask them to supply proof, they slink away like shadows!' His eyelids stop flickering suddenly, and his eyes lock into camera. His smile grows steadier, wider, more assured. 'I *tell* you what, *I* tell you *what*!'

'What?' Mitali prompts, moving a little closer.

'Let me issue a challenge to the Indian media today, on *your* programme! You people give big talks about my briefings to ten-ten civil service officers, to an army of party workers, to a colony full of common people! Yes ki no?'

'Yes,' she says.

'So if you can find even *one* civil service officer, *one* party worker

and *one* common people to testify against me, I will myself walk
to the closest police station and surrender humbly. Bas!'

Mitali looks startled but makes a quick recovery. She says, with
the satisfied air of somebody who's got their scoop, 'Well, that's
fair enough. A defiant challenge being issued here on *Viewstrack*
today by MP Hardik Mot –'

Varun waddles forward and punches the pause button on the
VCR. Dylan pushes his hair off his forehead and shakes his head.

'Well, Shekhwati, what do you make of that?' Hira raises an
eyebrow. 'We've just had a direct challenge made to us.'

'I know,' says Dylan, still reeling.

Hira steeples his fingers. 'So have you dug up anything new
here in Delhi that we could use for this? Or has DeshDarpan
become your new whipping boy?'

Dylan acknowledges this thrust with a faint grin. 'You should've
written that piece yourself, Hira.'

'Oh, I agree.' Hira nods. 'As it stands, you've made me look a
right monkey.'

'What I said was justified,' Dylan maintains.

'Mostly,' Hira concedes. 'I'm not sure why you took off on that
sweet newsreader though. I wouldn't have done that – that was
just mean. Poor Ms Mathur.'

'Thakur,' Dylan corrects him, flushing.

'Thakur.' Hira's keen eyes gleam with sudden, speculative
interest. Dylan gets the feeling he wants to pursue the topic but
all Hira says is, 'So, what about Motla? And the non-findings of
the SIC? Should we make a hoo-ha about it? Or will the Prime
Minister's Office have a coronary?'

'You have the answer to that,' VO says heavily. 'You're the Fop,
not us.'

'What a revolting word.' Hira grimaces. 'I'm assuming it means Friend of PM?'

'Yeah,' Varun nods stolidly. 'So you tell us.'

'Let's *go* for it!' The words burst out of Dylan before Hiranandani can speak. 'It was all so clear from what he said – all we need are three unshakable, unbreakable witnesses. People who won't back down, who will be willing to reveal their identities.'

'But people are too scared to talk, Dylan,' Hira says. 'That's why the SIC failed. Motla knows that, that's why he issued such an arrogant challenge!'

Dylan shakes his head. 'That's all eyewash. The SIC failed because somebody high up muzzled it. People *want* to talk. How about we just print our interviews directly in the paper?'

'We'll ruffle too many feathers...' begins Varun, looking uncomfortable.

'Ah, but what are ruffled feathers,' Hira murmurs, 'before people who have lost their lives, that too in such a sickeningly barbaric fashion? And he's named us personally! If we don't take up this fight, our motto *Truth. Balance. Courage.* will become a complete joke.'

The trouble with bloody Hiranandani, Varun thinks in disgust, is that I never know when he's serious and when he's just being facetious. Sarci fucker.

'Let the Sikh associations fight it,' he suggests warily. 'It's their war, not ours. God knows they're rich enough.'

'It *is* our war,' Dylan says, his eyes blazing. 'Don't back out at this point, VO!'

There he goes again, Varun thinks resentfully, channelling Bade-papaji. It's like *he's* the official grandson, not me.

'Taking him on will push up our circulation figures too,' Hiranandani says thoughtfully.

'See?' Dylan grins. 'Circulation! It's a *good* idea, VO!'

Silence. Except for Varun Ohri doing a gulping fish imitation. Bloody Stephenians, he thinks, feeling harassed. It's like the mafia around here.

'One IAS officer, one party worker, one common man,' Dylan says, leaping lithely to his feet and counting off on his fingers. 'With testimonies that no legalese can shake. And who won't go hostile on us. That's enough to nail him. And after this character certificate Motla's just handed me, people in Tirathpuri will be falling over themselves to tell me stuff!'

'I approve it.' Hiranandani nods with sudden decisiveness. 'Go get 'em, tiger.'

'Don't mind me,' Varun says lightly. 'My granddad just owns the paper. Now can we watch that interview again? Fast-forward that ugly bugger Motla's bits and linger on Dutta. She's hot. That nose ring sends shock vibrations straight down to my jaded loins. Weren't you two an item not so long ago, huh, Dhillon meri jaan?'

'We were in college together,' Dylan says matter-of-factly. 'And we sort of keep in touch.'

'Ah,' Varun murmurs. '*College* and all.'

'The family business does a gross disservice to your vast talents, VO,' Hiranandani says resignedly. 'You should run a gossip magazine. That's your true calling.'

6

'So what do you make of that Shekhawat boy?' Mrs Mamta asks the Judge in the privacy of their bedroom.

The Judge looks up, immediately interested. 'His name starts with D,' he says. 'Don't think I haven't noticed.'

She snorts, picks up her maroon comb and starts to work it through her long rippling hair. 'Well, thank you for not bringing *that* up. I didn't think you could be so subtle.'

'She read better after he coached her. Looked better too.'

His wife sniffs. 'Anjini spent all day getting her look right. I don't think you can give him credit for that.'

'And when we play, he keeps looking at her. With stupid, mooncalf eyes. And when he carries in the table, he uses it as an excuse to hang around like a bad smell.'

'You're very observant,' his wife says drily.

The Judge looks at her curiously. 'Do you like him, Mamtaji?'

'I like him,' she says. 'And I know what you're thinking, but the Shekhawats are a good Jaipur family, everybody knows that – and Christians aren't Muslims, you know. Besides, after the whole scandal with Chandu, we can't afford to be too choosy.'

The Judge throws back his head. 'Don't take that girl's name in my presence! And what rubbish! We can be as choosy as we like!'

'Do you think he earns well?'

'I could ask old Shekhawat,' the Judge says dubiously. 'Should I? Does Debjani even like him?'

'Eshwari seems to think so,' his wife says. 'Find out, LN. But do it subtly. And if it isn't much – his salary, that is – please don't snigger.'

Her husband looks injured.

'Am I a bloody lala?' he demands. 'Or trading class trash to go grubbing for salary slips? The lad's a journalist, isn't he? I'll go to the club library and take a look at his articles. See if he's got an intelligent head on his shoulders.'

'Do that then,' Mrs Mamta says. 'But first...' She hesitates.

'What?'

'Well, he's from Bombay,' Mrs Mamta says slowly. 'Things are different there. He could just be... amusing himself with our Dabbu. I've heard he has quite a reputation. Juliet has told me herself, many times. She says she has no control over him.'

'Arrey, how can parents not have control?' the Judge demands, forgetting for the moment that his third-born ran away with an unknown Estonian on the eve of her wedding. 'What kind of world are we living in?'

'The *real* one,' she replies crossly. 'And handle this carefully, or you'll end up losing your last kot-piece crony.'

'That's true!' the Judge says, much struck. 'How horrible! Should we just let it go, Mamtaji?'

'No no, sound out the Brigadier,' Mrs Mamta decrees. 'But *subtly*. And if the boy is not serious, he should stop coming over to our house at once.'

And so, the very next evening, when Dylan enters the living room after a long, sweaty, discouraging day digging up leads in

Tirathpuri, he finds both his parents sitting on the couch, eyeing him solemnly.

'Are you serious about Dabbu?'

For a moment, Dylan has no idea what they're talking about. Then, 'What's all this?' he enquires, not very pleasantly. 'A court martial?'

'Because if you're not, you're not to go over there to play cards any more!'

Dylan absorbs this. So the ball-squeezer has told her parents that he kissed her. Well, she's a newsreader – he ought to be grateful she didn't announce it on DD's national network last night, just as cheerfully as she announced the 'findings' of the Special Investigative Commission. And now they've all made the faster-than-lightning leap from kissing to love to marriage. Typical.

He allows himself to flashback to the encounter upon the stairs for the first time since it happened, and his stomach promptly goes so Russian ballerina that he staggers against the wall weakly, a movement his mother doesn't miss.

Oh, please. You haven't exactly made me go weak in the knees.

Why the hell had he kissed her? God knows he hadn't planned it. He hadn't planned any of it. He just wanted her to stop looking so damn shattered about that write-up in the *IP*, that's all. But his parents are making it sound like she's embroidering pillowcases with a D&D monogram – all on the basis of one kiss!

'And what a punishment that'll be,' he drawls, very sardonic. 'Playing kot-piece and eating Maggi is the current high point of my life.'

The Brigadier makes a hasty gesture. 'You're not to mess around with my friends' daughters, sir! This is not some Bombay floozie we're talking about.'

Dylan shakes his head in disbelief. 'Bombay girls aren't floozies, Dadda. You can't just make sweeping generalizations like that.'

'Bobby!' The Brigadier bristles. 'Explain to him!'

'Sonna, listen,' Juliet Bai says placatingly. 'Her father has noticed that you seem interested. He has enquired whether this interest is serious. If it is, fine, we can take things further. If it isn't, you can't meet her again.'

'But how can I decide if I'm serious about her if they won't even let me meet her?'

'You've met her seven times,' the Brigadier points out. 'Once, for an entire day. That's enough.'

'What is this, the fifteenth century?' Dylan demands. 'And did he happen to mention if *she* likes me? If she's serious about me?'

The Brigadier is at a loss. 'No, he didn't mention that, actually,' he admits. 'He said, Find out if your boy is interested, then I'll ask my girl if she's interested.'

'Mujhe Jesu, what a fellow!' Juliet Bai claps a hand to her forehead. 'Try and use your *brains*, Bobby. Laxmi Thakur is experienced, he has married off three girls. He knows how to play this game, how to hide his own cards while coaxing others to show theirs. You, it's only your first time, but you have to try to be cunning too! Sonna, do you like the girl? Tell me honestly now.'

But an entirely new thought has entered Dylan's mind.

'Bobby and Bobby,' he asks suspiciously, looking from one to the other. 'Did you guys set this up?'

'Of course not!' the Brigadier snorts. 'And talk to us respectfully!'

But Juliet Bai isn't listening.

'See how he's avoiding answering?' She nudges her husband. 'He likes her. I know. She's just his type. Angelic. Her face reminds me of the Madonna in the grotto in my mother's garden. He used to light candles before it, remember?'

'And I smashed it with a cricket ball, remember?' Dylan snaps.

'That was an accident.'

'Whatever,' he says, suddenly furious. 'Can't I ever come to Delhi without you guys trying to arrange my marriage? I don't have time for this. And I'll be damned if I'm interested if *she* isn't interested.'

--><--

Dylan spends the next three days digging up the whereabouts of the ten civil service officers who were present at Motla's 'cancers' briefing. Most of them have been transferred outside Delhi, three are posted abroad. Every single one, he discovers after three days of spadework, has been promoted. Except one, who has been shunted sideways and transferred to the wilds of rural Karnataka. Bingo, Dylan thinks and sets about trying to get hold of his phone number.

When he gets home, hungry but energized, his mother serves him cold shoulder for dinner, while his father makes it a point to bring up the Thakurs, mentioning how the Judge is sulking, how Mrs Mamta has enquired after him, and how there are shadows as purple as jamuns under Debjani's eyes. But Dylan doesn't want to think about Debjani's eyes.

She stands for everything I despise, he tells himself, shovelling rice onto his plate. She doesn't give a rat's ass about the news she reads, all she cares about is looking pretty and getting the pronunciations right.

Later in the night, moodily crunching coconut kalkals straight from the box, he decides that perhaps he owes her, if not an apology, then at least an explanation. With the result that when Eshwari trips down to Gambhir Stores to do her mother's shopping the next evening, she finds a gawky young boy leaning against the worn wooden counter, winking at her in a familiar fashion.

'Do I know you?' she asks with her usual friendly smile.

'No,' he says with a grin, his voice wavering peculiarly between squeaky and deep. 'But I know you.'

Eshwari crosses her arms across her chest. 'Okay...?'

'I'm Ethan,' the mysterious stranger says meaningfully. 'E for Ethan. I believe your dad's into the karma of first letters, *Eee*shwari?'

'How old are you?' she asks good-naturedly. 'Four?'

'... teen,' he says defensively. 'And I have a girlfriend, so don't get any ideas.'

'Listen, pipsqueak –'

'Let's talk business,' he interrupts cockily. 'Is your sister going out anywhere tomorrow? Far from Hailey Road?'

Eshwari stares at him. He stares back, his grin widening, and she can dimly see the promise of future hotness through the pimples and fuzz on his face.

'Ethan Singh *Shekhawat*!' she exclaims.

'That's right. So, is she going anywhere? What time? And how mad is she at my brother?'

Eshwari, much relieved, sings like a canary. Now all I need to do is supervise what she wears tomorrow, she tells herself as she hurries home excitedly. White chikan salwar kameez, I think, with that pink and firoza dupatta, yes, that's very princess-in-the-towerish... And I have to ensure she washes her hair tonight, not with Anji didi's smelly concoction, though.

And so, when the appropriately attired but completely clueless Debjani alights hunchingly from a DTC bus in front of the AIR studios the next morning, she finds the tall lithe figure of Dylan Singh Shekhawat lounging against the Shalimar Pan Bhandaar kiosk, waiting for her.

Debjani instantly unhunches. Her chin shoots up into the air, she tosses her dupatta in a regal gesture over her shoulder, and stalks right past the lounging Shekhawat, totally ignoring his half-sardonic, half-goofy smile.

'Hey!' Dylan demands as he scrambles to fall in step with her. 'Didn't you see me?'

Debjani whirls to look at him.

'I did, but as your father said you'd gone back to Bombay on some urgent work, I assumed it was an unpleasant hallucination brought upon by indigestion.'

Damn, Dylan thinks. So Dadda fed them some bullshit story to cover for my absence. Why hadn't Ethan found this out yesterday?

Aloud he says, 'Uh, I did go to Bombay. But now I'm back. Hi.'

'That was quick,' Debjani says ironically. 'As far as I know, Air India flies to Bombay only once a week.'

He looks caught out. She smirks and starts walking faster, files clutched to her chest. Dylan gives chase.

'Dabbu, wait!' he pleads. 'Listen, I've come especially to meet you. Can't we talk?'

'What about?' She walks even faster.

'I want to apologize,' he says. 'For... you know...' His voice falters and drops as she stops and looks at him '... for kissing you.'

Her eyes widen. 'When?'

Dylan comes to a halt, giving a short, disbelieving laugh. 'You're going with amnesia? Wow, *that's* mature.'

She stops too.

'Uff, of course I know when,' she admits crossly. 'Just why exactly did you kiss me, anyway?'

Because I'm a horny bastard. Because I couldn't help myself. Because your face is the face of the Madonna in my dead grandmother's garden.

He shrugs. 'It seemed like a good idea at the time.' His eyes lock into hers. 'Whyn't you stop me?'

'I did,' she says at once.

'Liar.'

There is a long pause.

Finally Debjani says, 'Ya, okay, so I didn't. Big deal. Why are you apologizing? It wasn't *such* a dead loss as kisses go, you know.'

He raises his eyebrows.

'Quite the little kiss connoisseur, aren't you?'

Debjani, whose only long lingering kisses have been from Moti, Voti and their offspring, manages to look convincingly worldly-wise. 'Oh, one gets around... you know how it is.'

Dylan, who has always believed in gender equality and in girls having their fair share of fun, immediately wants to line up everybody who has ever touched her and shoot them dead.

'Well, that's kind of a relief,' he says casually. 'Then you understand... that it was just a kiss.'

She gives him a withering look, throws her dupatta over her shoulder and starts walking again. Dylan strides alongside, his long legs easily keeping pace with hers.

'Still, no matter how many people you've allegedly kissed, I realize that your value system is slightly different from mine.(This had sounded far less glib when he rehearsed it at home!) So I just wanted to say that I'm sorry if my actions led you to think there was some, er... (why is this so damn *difficult*?) serious intention behind that kiss... because there wasn't. At least, not yet.'

'Is that it?' she says in a small, tight voice.

Dylan reminds himself that he has important work to do. He has to get on a train to rural Karnataka tonight and interview an IAS officer about a closed door briefing from his rabid ex-boss. He really has no time for this.

'Yeah, pretty much. That's about it. Sorry again.'

What a smooth, snaky little speech, Debjani thinks savagely. I wonder how many times he's made it. Well, it's his loss. *His* loss. She draws a long, ragged breath. His. Fucking. Loss. I don't care for him, I don't even know him, and this feeling of being emptied of all my stuffing and having the daylights kicked out of the limp shell that remains is just my ego taking a beating.

'Oh, that's fine,' she assures him steadily. 'I've no use for a man whose own father admits he's a fickle, striped insect flitting from flower to flower, dipping his proboscis into every sticky stigma that's stupid enough to open up for him.'

Dylan's eyes widen. 'Dadda said that?'

Debjani looks a little shifty. 'More or less.'

'He... my... *proboscis*?'

Debjani looks even shiftier. The truth is that she is grossly exaggerating the overheard conversation. It was conducted in the drawing room after the kot-piece session. It ended with the Judge asking his friend what the devil he meant by introducing a Casanova into his home. To which the Brigadier replied that the Judge was the one who had come galloping to the gate, flagged down the car and virtually handed his good-for-nothing son a total access pass. Eventually they both agreed that the entire blame was to be laid at the late Balkishen Bau's door, and parted friends.

'Yes,' she says sweetly. 'He said so. And I like my proboscises pure and committed and exclusive, thank you very much.'

There is a long silence. Two girls in burqas bang almost right into them, then circle around them and walk on, tittering.

Debjani looks up at Dylan, her arms crossed across her chest. She has made things pretty clear. So why is he still standing there, looking at her hungrily, like he's Moti and she's a stack of milk-soaked rotis?

Dylan is wrestling with a sense of anticlimax. Somehow this is not how he expected the conversation to go, he realizes with a surge of emotion that feels dangerously close to consternation. He had assumed she would do what girls invariably do when he tells them he isn't serious, 'at least not yet'. They assure him that they aren't serious either, and then the two of them go on to have a happy (for him, anyway) no-rings-attached relationship.

I should never have tried to seek her out and explain myself, he thinks in disgust. What a bloody waste of time. I should cut my losses right *now*, say something smooth, and bring down the curtain on this whole, messy episode.

'But there's no reason we can't be friends.' The words almost burst out of him.

'Friends who kiss?'

'Yeah,' he persists doggedly, hardly knowing what he's saying. 'Why do all girls talk like that sign in the Giggles Gift Shoppe, anyway? *Nice to look at, nicer to hold, if you break it consider it sold*?'

'You've just given away how *cheap* your thinking is with that obnoxious remark. Is that how you and Justin and Nathan talk in your chauvinistic all-boys house?'

'Jason and Ethan actually,' he replies, stung. 'At least I remember all your sisters' names – Apple, Ball, Cat and Elephant.'

She glares at him. He glares back. A machine-ka-thanda-paani cart hovers next to them hopefully.

'I'm not into *friendships* that lead nowhere, Dylan,' she says at last. There is no shy faltering over his name now, he notices with a pang, no looking at his shirt collar instead of his eyes. 'I told you I don't flirt.'

'And I'm not into pretty mouthpieces who read out the news without thinking twice about what they're reading!' he snaps back. 'How could you *smile* after saying the SIC has cleared Hardik Motla of all charges? How *could* you?'

'Wh-who's Hardik Motla?' Debjani falters, confused.

Dylan makes a hasty movement towards her, his eyes blazing with such fury that, for a moment, she is almost scared. Then he steps back, taking a deep breath, and slides his hands into the pockets of his jeans.

'Never mind,' he says. 'Leave it. Look, I have a lot of work to do, you know. A lot.'

Debjani shrugs. 'So, go do it.'

'Oh, I'm going,' he assures her, blocking her path, rooted to the road.

She stares at him for almost an entire minute, but all he does is stare back like he's incapable of moving. People inside the AIR building start to nudge and point. Finally, Debjani makes an infuriated little noise, steps around him and walks away, blinking back tears, furious with herself, swearing she will never, *ever* speak to him again.

'At least he was a straightforward snake,' Eshwari tells Dabbu on the terrace that night. 'I mean, he came out and said don't expect anything from me. Better than being a two-faced snake.'

'A one-faced snake is bad enough,' Dabbu replies candidly. 'I should have trusted my gut instead of being dazzled by his butt. He was kicking Moti the first time we met. He tried to give me some smooth story about protecting a kitten but now I think he just made that up.'

And so Debjani repeats her 'his loss' litany and sheds a few tears under the slowly fading amaltas. Dylan stays awake well past midnight, hunched over his Mac, moodily crunching kalkals. The Judge and the Brigadier talk extra-politely across the kot-piece table, urging Maggi and tea upon each other, playing games of seven-eights and heaping silent curses upon the heads of their offspring. Only Juliet Bai watches Debjani read the news every Friday with calm, proprietary pride. She knows something is Up. Just give him time, she tells the Brigadier, he'll come around, this one's different. And every night she sends up a fervent supplication to Mamma Mary that Debjani's heart stays both unbesieged and unwon. The summer waxes, then wanes.

But Juliet Bai's prayers seem to have lost their potency. Because as monsoon clouds gather overhead, Binni resurfaces from Bhopal in a blaze of glory, bearing news of a brilliant rishta for Debjani.

The arrival of her contingent is typically dramatic. Debjani and Eshwari are up on the terrace, peacefully watering the plants, when Samar Vir Singh clambers noisily up the stairs, taking them three at a time, his usual poise displaced by an expression of sheer panic.

'Hide me, hide me!' he yells, wild-eyed, hair askew. 'She's here! She's here!'

'Who, baba?' Eshwari asks, spraying him idly with the water hose.

Samar, always so nice to Eshwari, shakes the water off himself and frowns at her awfully. 'That bloody Bonu!' he pants, his voice squeaky. 'Keep her AWAY from me!'

Footsteps sound on the stairs. Samar, cornered, grabs the hose from Eshwari and braces himself with the air of a wet rat making its last stand. As Eshwari and Debjani watch, mildly intrigued, a scrawny little figure bursts onto the terrace, its short spiky hair standing up like cherry-and-cheese-festooned toothpicks speared into a whole cabbage at a birthday party. It is clad in acid-washed denim shorts and a muddy pink blouse, from the yoke of which dangles a demoralized-looking pink organza rose. It is brandishing a Kissan jam bottle in its hand.

'It's my *susu*!' warbles the figure gleefully as it capers about, shaking the bottle and making the yellow liquid inside it froth. 'Watch out, Samar! I'm going to throw it on you!'

Debjani reaches out, grabs this monstrous aggressor around its waist and lifts it off its feet even as Samar turns the full force of the hose upon them, drenching them both. They gasp, the water is cold.

'How dare you, Bonu Singh!' Debjani says, spluttering. 'That is *no way* for a young lady to behave!'

'Dabbu mausi!' Bonu casts both her arms ecstatically around Debjani's neck. 'I love you! You were on TV! I told everybody!'

'Yes, yes,' Dabbu replies warily, eyeing the bottle the little girl is still clutching in her hand. 'Put that down, Bones. Gross.'

Bonu giggles conspiratorially. 'It's just Dettol with a little water,' she whispers in Debjani's ear. 'But don't tell him, okay?'

Samar, still clutching the hose, points a shaking finger at Bonu. 'Stay. Away. From. Me.'

Bonu pulls a fierce face and makes as if to unscrew the lid of the Kissan jam bottle. Samar shudders, throws down the hose and hurtles down the steps. Eshwari scoops Bonu up and kisses her resoundingly.

'Dirty girl, where's your mummy?'

Bonu points, and all three girls walk over to the terrace wall and look down. A pot-bellied yellow and black taxi is parked in the Hailey Road driveway, and is busy disgorging, in order of appearance, two thin, bullied-looking young Oriya ayahs, six attaché cases, Bonu's fair, serene and sleeping twin Monu, and finally Binni didi, who emerges from the front seat beaming and gleaming (it is a hot day), her polka-dotted pallu crumpled to a thin, inadequate strip across her ample frame. Mrs Mamta eyes the contingent with a sinking heart – five more mouths to feed, and these Oriya girls, it's not nice to say, but they are each capable of putting away a kilo of rice a day. Besides, Binni never offers to help financially when she visits, unlike Anji, who is always sashaying down to Gambhir Stores to buy groceries and flirt with young Mr Gambhir, one of her oldest and most faithful swains.

'I'm from Delhi only,' Binni tells the cabbie. 'I know what the rates are. This is all you're going to get. Now go.'

Only then does she turn to greet the family, who have by now lined up neatly to receive her. The Judge first, she bends to touch his feet; then Mrs Mamta Thakur, she bends again; and then the rank and file that are Debjani, Eshwari and the cringing Samar Vir.

'Hello, Dabbu-Chabbu!' Binodini pats her sisters' cheeks carelessly. 'Hello, Samar Vir Singh, visiting *again*? And so thin!

You must eat more – here, I got you some chocolate éclairs. Vickyji has started a new business in confectionaries, you know!'

'These are not Cadbury's.' Samar, restored to equilibrium now that he is far away from the dreaded Bonu, examines the éclair label carefully. 'They are *Catburies*. What's Catburies, Binni mausi?'

But Binni mausi is busy making sure that Monu has touched his grandparents' feet.

'Whatever happened to the pharmacy business?' the Judge enquires mildly, while Samar bites gingerly into the chocolate éclair.

Binni's round face goes pink. 'It didn't *go*, Bauji,' she admits. 'People in Bhopal are too healthy. There was no real gap in the market. But,' her face brightens, 'they all have a sweet tooth so this confectionary factory will go well.'

They all troop into the house, Samar looking a little bemused. The label said chocolate éclair, but he hasn't found the chocolate yet. He bites into it a little harder, but is seems to be toffee through and through. Rather muddy toffee, too.

'He is an engineer in the merchant navy,' Binni announces after the twins have been bathed and fed and deposited into the drawing room for the night. 'Earning in dollars, spending in rupees. Tall, fair, handsome. Only son. His grandfather was a Rai Bahadur. Over the last two years, he has rejected every single Rajput girl between eighteen and twenty-five in UP-Delhi-MP. That's how eligible he is!'

'That's how *gay* he is,' Eshwari murmurs, giggling.

Mrs Mamta looks harassed. 'Bhai, I don't want a boy who has turned down all my friends' daughters! It makes things very awkward on Hailey Road. As it is, after Anji married Anant, everybody became so formal with me – they only warmed up again after Chandu ran away.'

Binni bridles instantly. The Judge, relieved that she seems to have got over the shall-I-explain-it-to-you-again-in-Hindi crack, forgets to thunder his usual 'No talking about Chandu' admonition. Instead, he hurries in to express the gratitude Binodini clearly thinks is due. 'Well done, Binni! Mamtaji, we shouldn't look a gift groom in the mouth – let's at least meet him, hmm?'

'He really fancies Dabbu,' Binni says. 'He got off the ship, saw her reading the news and fell in love with her that very night. He said her accent was excellent.'

'What's his name?' Mrs Mamta asks uneasily.

'Dev Pawar. His aunt knows Vickyji's mamaji, that's how they contacted me. See!'

She has two photographs: a full-length picture of the boy in a formal suit and a mid-shot where he is smiling, wearing a sporty, hooded Nike jacket, standing on the deck of his last ship with the ocean gleaming azure behind him.

'See how fair he is?' Binni says triumphantly.

'I think the picture's overexposed.' Anji squints critically. 'Look, his hands aren't the same colour as his face.'

'He seems nice,' Eshwari allows, after a tentative glance at Dabbu. 'He'll shower you with Juicy Fruit chewing gum and BASF tapes and French perfume. And I think that hoodie jacket is really cool.'

'It's the *same* boy,' Mrs Mamta says. 'He turned down Gayatri's Anju. Said her gums were too big. Like a chimpanzee's. (Which, to be honest, they are.) And Manno bhabhi's Meera – because she's a doctor and wouldn't have time for him. Gayatri and Manno bhabhi still aren't talking.'

'He sounds *horrible*.' Debjani's voice trembles. The Judge shoots her a keen look. 'Thinking he's such a fat fish, thinking everybody's out to land him, going around rejecting girl after girl! I don't want to meet him!'

'Meet him and turn him down,' Anji advises. 'Good for your ego and good for his soul. Tab se girls reject kar raha hai, he has it coming. You can do it with a clean conscience.'

'Arrey, but he says he likes her already!' Binni avers. 'From his side it's a yes!'

'He said that for Gayatri's Anju too,' Mrs Mamta says soberly. 'After he saw her photo. But when they met and she smiled – though her mother had warned her not to – just one flash of her purple masoodas was enough to make him run backward out of the house and onto a ship bound for Dar es Salaam.'

'You just don't want to meet him because *I* got the rishta,' Binni huffs, her eyes filling with tears. 'You think ki I don't know any people worth knowing. That I only know Hindi medium types.'

'But there's nothing wrong with Hindi medium types!' Eshwari protests.

'Oh god, Binni didi!' Dabbu looks upset. 'I just don't... never mind... uff! I'll meet him, if you insist – but no sulking if I turn him down, okay?'

'Okay, okay.' Binni face turns sunny instantly. 'I'll phone and let them know tomorrow. That's settled then! Ma, what's for dinner? My maids eat early.'

Mrs Mamta sighs. The house is bursting at the seams. Monu-Bonu drink three litres of full-cream milk between them every day. Voti has just had another litter of ugly puppies and needs daily calcium supplements. Add to that Samar's prodigious appetite and Anji's penchant for putting the week's ration of eggs into her hair, and it has become impossible for her to balance her budget.

Later, in the privacy of their bedroom, she tells the Judge that she isn't *too* averse to the Dev Pawar rishta. The boy seems nice and keen, the family is good, and as Debjani's gums are exactly what gums should be, things should go smoothly.

'It'll be worth it just to see the expression on Saahas Singh Shekhawat's face,' the Judge muses. 'He'll know then how much in demand my girls are!'

'Don't be childish, LN,' Mrs Mamta cautions. 'It's a question of Debjani's entire life.'

'And in return for getting us this grand rishta for Dabbu, I suppose Binni expects us to forget that she's actually filed a case against me in court,' the Judge says. 'When are we going to talk about that, I would like to know?'

'I thought of bringing it up,' Mrs Mamta admits. 'But then I thought, she's here for quite a few days, we'll discuss it by and by. Why rush these things?'

'That's what you said when your precious SIL number two swallowed up all the money from the sale of the Kanpur plot,' the Judge says gloomily. 'That money should have gone to all five girls. Instead, he talked us into *loaning* it all to him to invest in his wretched business. Now if we ask about it, she shouts and screams and gets an asthma attack. And now she wants her one-sixth hissa! That girl, I tell you, she's turning out to be just like her uncle Ashok.'

Mrs Mamta touches his shoulder. 'Don't say things like that. You know it's her husband who pressurizes her. We'll just have to deduct that Kanpur money out of her one-sixth share in this house. That's the simplest way.'

'Why couldn't Shekhawat's son have been less of a harami?' the Judge grumbles. 'I actually liked the fellow. Even though he took so long to choose which house was trumps, and ate up *all* the peas in the Maggi. But I suppose we have to open ourselves up to the idea of this Dev Pawar. Oh, well. D for Dabbu, D for Dev.'

He gets up, pulls on his kurta and starts to shuffle out of the bedroom.

'Where are you going *now*, LN?' his wife asks, surprised. 'It's so late.'

'Oh, just for a little stroll,' he replies offhandedly. 'I want to clear my head.'

<hr />

'He said, let them have a good time tonight.
But the party ends at dawn.'

In the little town of Puttur in South Kanara, behind a shiny plywood desk in a tiny, clean white-washed office, I finally find Anandam Dhas, a man I have been searching for, for several months.

A native of Jamshedpur and a rank holder in the IAS entrance exam, Dhas used to be a high-profile officer serving in Delhi and poised for bigger things. Why is he now cooling his heels in the interiors of Karnataka?

'You know the answer as well I as do.' Dhas shrugs as we sit down to glasses of chilled buttermilk and a plate of sliced apple. 'I was unfortunate enough to be present at Hardik Motla's infamous briefing to his officers on 1 November – and stupid enough to talk to the press about it afterwards.'

Why did you choose to give the interview anonymously?

Another fatalistic shrug.

'To protect my job and my family. And I was hoping that

my speaking up would motivate my other colleagues to also come forward.' He smiles wryly. 'Safety in numbers, you know.'

So what did Motla say exactly?

Dhas shakes one leg restlessly, shuffles the papers on his desk. Then he turns to me suddenly, and his words come out in short bursts, like rounds of machine-gunfire.

'He said the whole piece. Everything that's been reported in the press. Everything. Get the anger out, it is required, it will prove cathartic – keeping it inside is unhealthy in the long term. We listened quietly, agreed to take no steps to stop what was basically state-sponsored genocide, but finally somebody asked him how long the pogrom would be allowed to continue. He said, after thinking about it for a while, 'Let them have a good time tonight. But the party ends at dawn.'

He described it as a party?

'Oh, yes. Absolutely. Those were his words. Ten people heard him. Eight men, two women.'

Did you speak to your colleagues privately? Ask them to come forward?

'Yes.' Dhas looks whimsical. 'But they chose to move forward instead. Everyone's been promoted. Need I say more?'

So why haven't you been promoted? You haven't come forward with this testimony either?

'Somehow word got out that I was the anonymous source. Maybe I have some of my colleagues – the ones I was trying to convince to testify to the press along with me – to thank for that.'

Why have you decided to speak to us openly today?

'Well, I had high hopes from the Special Investigation Commission. I suppose I was hoping the truth would come out without my having to get involved in the outing. But it didn't. So now I'm telling it like it *is*. Openly.'

Is this revenge? Because your career has languished?

'Oh, no.' Anandam's smile, earlier so wry, now bursts out wide and cheerful. I get the sense that some massive weight has been lifted off his shoulders. He looks like a mischievous boy. 'This is just self-preservation. You see, if I keep my anger and my bitterness and my disappointment with the system inside me any longer, it may give me cancers.'

DSS

7

'Six eggs and one bread please, Gambhir uncle.'

Old Mr Gambhir is hunched over the *India Post*, his forehead furrowed, his index finger slowly moving between the lines of text, his lips forming each word of Dylan's article laboriously. Young Mr Gambhir is nowhere in sight.

'Er, Gambhir uncle?'

The old man looks up, his eyes glazed. 'Kya?' he demands querulously, no hint of recognition in his eyes.

'Namaste.' Eshwari grins amiably. 'Six eggs, one bread. So sorry to disturb you.'

He stares at her for almost a minute, then nods, folds up the newspaper carefully and dodders away to the back of the store.

One of his grumpier days, Eshwari thinks, leaning against the white Kwality ice cream refrigerator, drumming her fingers against it lightly.

'Oh, hey, Steesh!'

'Hello,' Satish growls as he shuffles up, dragging his chappals. 'There oughtta be a law against parents. Who the hell kicks you out of bed this early on Sunday to fetch... shit! What did she want?'

What an unlovely, unwashed sight, Eshwari thinks, looking

him over with a shudder. If only the class eight chicks with brand-new tits could see him now. They'd get over crushing on him instantly. That reminds her.

'I wanted to ask you something.'

But Satish is busy having a crisis. 'Shit, help me, Bihari, I can't remember what Amma asked me to get. Coffee? Condoms? Cockroach killer?'

'Soap maybe?' Eshwari hazards pointedly. 'Deodorant? Nose plugs for herself?'

'I'll walk back with you and ask her again,' he says. 'Here, lemme carry your stuff. What did you want to ask me?'

Eshwari tosses her bouncy ponytail and assumes a mysterious expression. 'Nothing important.'

She has heard that one Gitika Govil, a class nine lovely, confessed during a party game of Truth and Dare that she has hormonal stirrings for Satish Sridhar. This Gitika is hot stuff – she is known as GG amongst the class twelve boys, which stands not for her name but for her Golden Globes which bloomed suddenly and spectacularly halfway through class seven. Half the graffiti in the girls' toilets in Modern School is dedicated to her. The Bihari and Manipuri hostellers, whose life's ambition it is to one day hold the coveted Golden Globes award, duck into this forbidden zone the moment school empties out and scribble heartfelt sonnets to her in scratchy ballpoint pen.

Gitika Govil ke mammay mahaan
Unpe tika hai Hindustan
Young fold mountains, world's most high
I will climb them by and by!

'Must be *something*, I know that look,' Satish says, raising his voice to be heard above the manic *khatakhatakhata* of several portable generators. 'Phew, all I can breathe are diesel fumes! Ask me, I'll tell you the truth, promise.'

Eshwari gives him a sidelong glance. 'Had fun at the weekend party?'

He looks at her curiously. 'Yeah, it was funnish, I guess. Bunch of girls with shoulder pads and plastic earrings singing along to "Like a Virgin", desperately trying to act like they aren't virgins.'

'I heard you found someone *special* there.'

He goes still, in a very filmi, over-the-top way. His eyes start to dance. 'Whoooooo?'

'Gitika Govil. Are you guys going out?'

Satish immediately assumes an air of self-important nonchalance. 'I don't know. Let's see.'

'There's still something left to see?' Eshwari says incredulously. 'Knowing you, you must have seen *everything* she's got by now.'

'Don't be crude,' he replies primly. 'You girls think south Indians can't think of anything but *that*.'

'Don't lump half the country with your personal randiness,' Eshwari replies tartly. '*You* can't think of anything but that.'

Satish sobers up. 'I know you think I'm an animal, Bihari, but I'm not. I'll take it slow with GG. She's a sweet little thing.'

'So you *are* going out with her.'

'Uh huh.'

'And you're in love with her?'

'Uh huh.'

The electricity comes back just then, and the generators quit throbbing. Things are suddenly very quiet.

'Well, this *is* a turnaround,' Eshwari marvels. 'The beast has acquired a heart. Rather than just a private part.'

Satish's eyes gleam. 'And if she gets me *so* turned on that I lose my head and am in danger of surrendering my all to her, I'll cool myself down by thinking of *you*. You'll be my very own visual cold shower. Good plan, huh?'

Eshwari's eyes widen in outrage.

Satish grins.

'Actually, I think it's a really good match,' she says. 'I mean, she's what – twelve?'

'Fourteen,' he growls.

'And your mental age is ten. So you should suit each other perfectly. Of course *some* people might say she's too old for you, but I'm not one of them.'

Satish comes to a dead halt, slapping his hand against his forehead. '*Of course!* I was supposed to buy Green Label chai. Thanks for reminding me, Bihari.'

'How?' she asks, puzzled.

Satish's face splits into a huge grin. 'By turning green.'

She continues to look at him, still confused.

He snickers. 'Must be envy.'

*

'Babejani, did you hear last night's bulletin?' says Amitabh Bose as they both sit in high chairs getting their make-up done. 'The one read by Sameep and yours truly? Wasn't it shocking?'

'Well, yes,' Debjani agrees. 'It was terrible.'

'It was the stuff of horror films,' he shudders. 'Harrowing! Really, standards have fallen so *low* in this country. Of course, I don't mean you, darling.'

A little puzzled, Debjani tilts her head. *(Don't moving, madum.)* 'You mean the report on the earthquake in Manipur, right?'

He beams. 'Exactly. *(Don't moving, sir.)* So you noticed too?'

'Well, it was kind of hard to miss. The footage was so graphic. Over 1,000 dead – and 300 villages annihilated, I believe.'

'Only,' he leans in close and she can smell mint on his breath, laced with cigarettes and hunger, 'that clown Sameep said *aanhylated*. And then he went on to say that rescue operations were under*vay*. Under*vay*! And one had to keep a straight face while listening to him say this. He *has* to know someone big in the ministry – that's the only explanation for a Neanderthal like him reading prime-time English bulletins. But contacts or no contacts, if he keeps this up, he'll be shunted down to Parliament News. *Aan*hylated indeed!'

And Dabbu realizes that, for Amitabh Bose, the bigger tragedy is not the death of a thousand Manipuris but the mauling of the English language. No wonder Dylan was practically grinding his teeth at me that day, she thinks suddenly.

'Really, my dear, the trials of this job! One deserves a hardship allowance to compensate for sitting under those hot lights listening to Sameep Chaddha speak. *Ob*original! *Yoo*rope! *Pidi*gree! And once there was a devastating avalanch*ay* and over 3,000 people *piri*shed. Luckily one wasn't reading along with him that night – one would have died laughing.'

'Haha,' she says weakly.

'Also,' his tone grows conspiratorial, 'his natural voice is a reedy treble. That baritone is entirely assumed. It slips sometimes, like a loose pair of knickers.'

'Really?'

Amitabh Bose nods.

'Now, when *yours truly* was born,' he says, throwing back his shoulders. 'And yours truly cried, as babies are wont to do, yours truly's grandmother, who was seated in the next room, enquired of the nurses why heavy furniture was being dragged about. *That's* how deep yours truly's baritone was!'

'My sisters love your voice,' is the only thing Debjani can think to say in reply. 'They think you sound like Cliff Richard.'

Amitabh Bose nods, accepting this tribute like it is only his due. 'A word of advice to you, darling,' he says. 'Your smiles are getting to be a little – now what would be a good word to use here – *gratuitous*. Never show too much teeth. Newsreading is serious business. You don't want to come across as frivolous. We should look like we *care*. Ah, I'm done, thank you, dada.'

The old make-up dada, moving on to a line-up of muscular young women who are there to sing a rousingly patriotic Hindi song, smothers a thin smile. So AB is getting insecure about little Debjani Thakur. The make-up dada wants to tell Debjani to smile as much as she likes, that the nation loves her smile, but he doesn't. The nation will make its wishes known soon enough, he thinks.

And the nation does. Mrs Mamta is peeling a large green lauki in the drawing room when it happens. The monthly viewer's feedback show *Aap aur Hum* is on. A popular announcer reads out letters from all over India to a senior DD director and he answers them at length. The first letter, from Pritam Rawal, Saharanpur, Uttar Pradesh, bemoans the fact that the late-night Western music programme *Hot Tracks* is damaging Indian culture and is a bad influence on the youth. The director replies by assuring her that Indian culture is extremely robust and that in any case all objectionable portions of songs – kisses, displays of bare thighs, underarms, navels and immodest dance movements – are rigorously censored. The second letter from Shahid Imtiaz, Hyderabad, says that the serial *Ramayana* is communalizing the country, to which he smoothly replies that the Ramayana is not religion but culture, and provides archetypes of the ideal husband, the ideal wife, the ideal brother and the ideal friend, which are instructive to everybody, regardless of their religion. And then she reads out the third letter, from one Satinder Singh, Bokaro Steel City, which says: *Congratulations on discovering the talented and beautiful newsreader Debjani Thakur. She is a breath of fresh air in the newsroom. Her English is too good, her smile is like warm sunshine, she is so modest, and I am a deewana of the mole on her chin and the rose in her hair. Please give her more opportunities to read, why only Fridays?* To which the DD director smiles and starts to make some reply, but Mrs Mamta doesn't hear it, she jumps to her feet, scattering lauki peels everywhere, and runs to get the Judge, to get Gulgul, to get everybody, the dhobi, the chowkidar, the chinkie Mother Dairy token-wallah, and tell them how famous her Dabbu has become.

'Promise me you and Steesh didn't write that letter,' Debjani tells Eshwari as they get ready for bed that night.

'It was from *Bokaro Steel City*,' Eshwari replies, rolling her eyes. 'I'm not even sure where that is. Anyway, it's not like you got *one* fan letter. You must've got loads, so they read one out, kind of representative of all fifty. Why can't you just be happy?'

'Oh, I am happy,' Debjani assures her. 'Only, it feels so unreal. In a nice way, though. In a *really* nice way. Oh, Eshu, d'you think *he* would have seen it?'

'Who?' Eshwari grins. 'Satinder Singh from Bokaro Steel City? Hundred per cent. Maybe he's young and juicy and a millionaire and next month he'll propose to you via *Aap aur Hum*. That'll show Amitabh Bose.'

At which Debjani hits her on the head with a pillow.

'Ow-ow-ow!' Eshu groans. 'You meant the one-faced snake? How was I to know? I thought you were done with him!'

—◆——◆—

'*And*... the next school to come on stage is... Modern School, Barakhamba Road! Give them a big hand, everyone!'

'What the hell does that mean, give them a *big hand*?' Satish grumbles as he slides behind the drum set to tepid applause on the darkened stage of Kamani Auditorium. 'Are they going to present us with a giant Godzilla hand wrapped up in red wrapping paper? This compère's such a penis.'

'Shhh!' Eshwari nudges him hard. 'The mics are on.'

Satish is wearing a martyred look today – he always looks martyred at school events where he has to play 'wimpy nursery rhymes by sissy bands like Cool and the Gang and that crown prince of gay dorks, Eric Clapton.

'Eric Clapton isn't gay,' Eshwari had told him as they walked back together from Gambhir Stores last night.

'His songs are,' Satish had replied doggedly. 'The lyrics are so... so *basic*. What *is* all that moaning about her looking so *wonderful tonight*? And if she's looking so wonderful, how come at the end the fucker gets an aching head and she helps him to bed? Is he *impotent*?'

'Steesh,' Eshwari had sighed. 'Just let it go, okay? Do it for the school.'

'Why can't we ever play heavy metal at these school events?' he had grumbled. 'You're a big shot in school, why can't you make it happen? Why is it always sissy shit like Rod Stewart and A-ha? Why not Megadeth? They have deadly drum solos. I tell you, Bihari, I've *had* it. I can't sit behind you giggly, lipglossed chicks and tap out "She's So Fresh" any more. My dick will fall off.'

Now he scowls down at the crowd, perking up slightly at the sight of his newest girlfriend – the second one since GG and he broke up a while ago – sitting in the front aisle with her cute little friends. They're sitting in the middle of the large, banker-blue Modern contingent, cheering wildly in order to drown out the boos of the big jhund of Delhi Public School, Mathura Road students sitting right behind them. Satish acknowledges the Modernites with a half-hearted wave as Mohit Razdan, Modern's fair and handsome lead guitarist-cum-vocalist, loosens his school tie and addresses the crowd. 'Hey there, people,' he calls out. 'We're gonna start with our solo, Eric Clapton's "Wonderful Tonight".'

The Dipsites boo, Satish's new girlfriend and her buddies scream and cheer. Mohit strikes up the opening chords and Satish joins in dutifully, rolling his eyes and making covert gagging gestures at Eshwari with his free drumstick at the same time.

Mohit's voice is deep and melodious, he has all the chords down pat (they're dead easy, Satish has assured Eshwari) and the song is a hot favourite with the crowd.

As Eshwari joins in on 'You look wonderful tonight', she realizes that every time he hits the chorus, Mohit is turning to look right at her. His hazel eyes (he is Kashmiri) bore right into hers, and a couple of times she's actually scared he'll fumble the chords.

The duet and group song go off well and soon they're all bowing to the usual mix of cheers and boos. As they troop backstage Mohit comes up to her and grabs her hand urgently.

'Eshwari.'

Eshwari turns around.

'Hey, Mohit. Good job. You sang really well.'

'You sang well too,' he says, his voice sounding strangled.

That's overstating it, she thinks, she's just one of three backup singers who join in the choruses now and then. Satish has told her (often) that the school band only picks her because, for some reason, audiences tend to boo less when she's on stage. *Basically you scare the crowd shitless, Bihari.*

Mohit's hand is warm and clammy, his eyes are bulging slightly and he is looking all pent up, like he is about to burst. Eshwari wonders if he's going to ask her where the bathroom is.

'I like you,' he says suddenly. 'I've liked you for ages. Can we go to the school farewell together?'

Huh? What? He likes me? Okay. Wow. Well, he's nice enough, Mohit Razdan, he's popular and everything, but he reminds Eshwari, just a little, of boiled white channa. The kind her mother has stopped cooking because BJ says they give him gas.

'Let me think about it, okay?' she tells him kindly, because she is basically a kind girl. 'I have to go home early today. Can't even wait for the results to be announced.'

Mohit's face falls. Behind her, she is aware of Satish Sridhar's girlfriend jumping up and down, yanking at his tie and kissing his neck. She's acting like a groupie, Eshwari thinks. So wannabe. Like this isn't Kamani Auditorium in freaking New Delhi but Madison Square Garden in freaking New York City. She realizes Mohit is talking to her.

'I thought you and Sridhar were an item. But clearly you aren't. So I thought...'

Eshwari leans around him and clicks her fingers at Satish.

'Steesh, you have to drop me home. You promised. C'mon, can we go?'

Satish disengages himself from the sticky little number's arms and lopes up to them.

'You're such a bloody coitus interruptus, Bihari,' he says good-naturedly. (His girlfriend giggles loudly behind them.) Then he turns to Mohit. 'Kya gaaya, man. You had the dames all stoked.' Then back to Eshwari, 'Okay, let's go.'

Mohit, not very sure if he's being mocked, smiles uncertainly and lets Eshwari's hand go. She smiles back at him, a strictly perfunctory smile, and walks towards Satish's bike.

'Did the terrorist ask you out?' Satish asks in a conversational voice.

'Yes, he did. Did you have any clue he liked me?'

Satish snorts. 'He's been turning to look at you soulfully every time he says "Wonderful Tonight" for the last two months. Haven't you noticed?'

'No,' Eshwari admits. 'But I noticed today. Don't call him a terrorist just because he's Kashmiri, Steesh; seriously, you are *so* messed up.'

'He's just so... wet,' Satish says, handing her a helmet. 'Like Maggi without Tastemaker. Are you gonna say yes? What about milord's no-dating-till-you're-twenty-one rule?'

His tone is casual but his eyes are searing. Eshwari swallows hard and sits down on the bike, cradling the helmet in her lap.

'I don't know. He's cute.' She looks up at him. 'What do you think I should do?'

He hesitates for a moment and then shrugs. 'Go ahead,' he says lightly. 'He's a nice guy. Give him a try.'

'Princess Elizabeth of England,' says the Judge, sitting on the terrace parapet early on a thunderously brewing Sunday morning, 'woke up one morning and found she was queen.'

'Huh?' Dabbu sits up, blinking, and gives a little scream when she spots her father. 'You'll fall over, BJ!'

'You are queen,' he says smugly. 'Everybody wants to marry you. You can pick and choose.'

She looks at him, confused. Of course, she knows she has become popular. People recognize her wherever she goes now. Is that what BJ means?

'The phone's been ringing non-stop. Rishtas are pouring in – it's a *monsoon* of rishtas! I've never seen anything like it before, even in the reign of princess Anji.'

Dabbu's eyes light up. 'Really? *More* than Anji didi?'

'It's the TV, of course,' he says. 'In all fairness, Anji never read the nation the news with a white rose in her hair. So, do you want to see them all – or only the ones your mother and I shortlist?'

'I want to see *everything*,' Debjani says, rising lithely from her bed, feeling better than she has felt in weeks. 'Let's go.'

⁂

In the Parliament Street office of the *India Post*, the editor-in-chief pops his head into Dylan's cubicle, a big smile on his face.

'The phones are ringing non-stop,' he announces. 'Compliments – and information. It's a *monsoon* of information! Everybody's talking about how the *India Post* has risen to the challenge issued by Hardik Motla! One down two to go, they're saying. We're getting a lot of leads for the other two witness stories too! Do you want to see them all, or just the stuff the team shortlists?'

'I want to see *everything*,' Dylan says, rising lithely from his chair, feeling better than he has felt in weeks. 'Let's go.'

⊷⊶◉⊷⊶

Dabbu's list of reasons for turning down perfectly nice, healthy, decently earning incomepoops under thirty
(compiled by Anjini Singh and Eshu Thakur)

He said 'intrusting' instead of interesting.

He said Moti looks like he is in great pain and the kindest thing to do is to put him to sleep.

He said Mandakini was his favourite actress.

He said a lot of the brave children in the 26 Jan parade exaggerate their brave deeds to win the award.

He said, 'What a good system! We will also name our children alphabetically!'

He didn't know who Hardik Motla was. (Who IS he, anyway?)

He said, *seven* times in one evening that 'we don't believe in dowry'.

He said, 'Nothing can be done with this country.'

He had hairy ears. Like Yoda.

He asked, 'Are you sure you are the *real* Debjani Thakur? I don't want to meet any fakes.'

He came first in *every* exam, *all* his life, from nursery to IIT to IIM.

He had an uncool bum.

He waggled his tongue at Eshwari when he thought no one was looking.

His mother wore a spondylitis collar, his sister's arm was in a cast and his bhabhi was on crutches.

But the *real* reasons for turning down every single incomepoop, Debjani admits to herself, as she selects her attire for yet another lunch date, are these:

He didn't have long dimples in his lean cheeks.

He wouldn't stealthily drop a large clean handkerchief into her lap if he saw her weeping.

Her life wasn't on hold till he kissed her again.

He wasn't Dylan Singh Shekhawat.

Dylan stares in exasperation at the pudgy young Sardar in the blue shirt. He had sounded promising on the phone – a native of Tirathpuri and an eyewitness to the rioting. But now he's not even sure this Sardar *is* a Sardar. There is something distinctly impermanent about his long, bushy beard. And his turban is very inexpertly tied.

'So you were *there*?' he asks again. 'In Tirathpuri? You *saw* what happened?'

The Sardar(?) nods. 'Oh, yes, I saw everything. You'll put my pikchurr in the paper, no? Nice big one?'

'Most people,' Dylan says sardonically, 'want to retain their anonymity. They're worried about the safety of their families.'

'Oh, I have no problems, ji.' The Sardar shakes his head. 'Why to be afraid? Of whom to be afraid? You didn't bring a camera?'

What a publicity hound. The man, Dylan thinks in disgust, probably wasn't even in Delhi, let alone Tirathpuri, on the first of November. I have a good mind to lean over and yank at his beard.

'Like I said,' he says, 'sources generally prefer to remain anonymous.'

'I want my pikchurr,' his guest says doggedly. 'Or I will take my story to another paper.'

'I think you'll find that we're the only ones who'll print it,'

Dylan tells him pleasantly. 'And we *will* check up on you, you know. This isn't sensationalism. It's responsible reporting.'

But the Sardar isn't listening.

'I'll have Amreekan Chop Suey,' he tells the waiter. 'The one with the fried egg on top. Haan. And a Campa. And afterwards lychee with ice cream. Now Dhillonji, where do I begin?'

'Why don't you begin at the beginning,' Dylan suggests, feeling rather like Alice in Wonderland. 'Go on till you reach the end, then stop.'

'Vul!' His source aligns his cutlery neatly in front of him and assumes a lugubrious expression. 'I woke up in the morning and heard shouting and screaming, *ladies* shouting and screaming. So I ran down, shirtless – you can click my photo shirtless, it will be more authentic – and kicking and swearing and abusing, pushed over this big crowd of mens all holding lathis and swords, and saved the izzat of three ladies, one-after-the-other.'

'Wow,' Dylan replies, pushing his tape recorder a little closer. 'That's, um, cool. Can you give me more details?'

'Of course. The first lady was an older lady. Two men were voilitting her. The first one I gave a punch on the neck, he fell at once, the second one I kicked in the backside, he also fell. Then I knelt by the side of the lady and said, Don't cry, bebe, I am here, your son is here (not that she was my mother, you know, Dhillonji, but I meant ki she was *like* my mother). Three fellows came up from the backside then, but I tripped them by sticking out my foot. Then with a roar I moved to the second lady –'

'Yes, yes.' Dylan has got the man's measure now. 'Uh, look, Sardar saab, this is a recording device, why don't you continue speaking all your testimony into it, while I go finish off some other work I have to do?'

The Sardar nods obligingly, Dylan gets to his feet and strides out to the corridor outside Berco's Chinese restaurant. It is drizzling, the air is clean and fresh and Connaught Circle, washed clean of dust and grime, gleams in the filtering sunshine like a large white Polo mint. Dylan stretches out, breathing in a great gulp of wet, fragrant air, and sighs. The hunt for his three key eyewitnesses, in spite of the occasional attention-seeker like the one demolishing *IP*-funded Chop Suey inside, is going well. The pressure on the government to do something about Motla is building. Things are looking up. Dylan feels optimism surge through his veins. Maybe I'll take a little walk and buy some green guavas and have a chat with the shoeshine guy about life in general, he thinks. And just as he is setting off to do so, who should come walking down the road, past the vibrant background of balloon sellers and watch-repair men and aggressive Gujarati ladies selling cushion covers embroidered with elephants, her cream dupatta billowing in the breeze, her curling walnut hair likewise, but Debjani Thakur, lover of losers, who wouldn't be friends-who-kiss with him.

She is with somebody, he realizes, even as he automatically ducks behind a pillar. A tall, smug young man, who looks, Dylan thinks uncharitably, rather like Clark Kent. Big glasses, bigger head. And he doesn't even turn into a superhero at night, which really is the *only* redeeming thing about Clark Kent. And who the hell wears a suit in Delhi, in the afternoon, in the *monsoon*?

Clark Kent and Debjani go into Berco's. Dylan immediately loses all interest in chatting with shoeshine boys. I'll go in and share the questionable Surd's Chop Suey, he decides. After all, I'm paying for it.

And so, as the questionable Surd tells tales of his bare-chested derring-do, Dylan tunes him out and tunes into the couple at the next table.

CK: Can I take this seat? More leg room. I am, by god's grace, more than six feet tall.

DT: Of course.

CK: So I was saying, if you have not seen the sun set on an endless expanse of rolling ocean, you have seen nothing! Nothing!

DT: Really?

CK: It makes you realize how insignificant you are – an ant, a worm, a mere mosquito. Whenever I have the midnight watch, I look out at the ocean and tell myself that Dev Pawar, just because by god's grace you earn (pause, modest laugh) 25,000 rupees a month, don't think you are very great! The ocean is much bigger than you!

DT: That's true.

CK: I can see the ocean from my 2BHK flat in Cuffe Parade too, by god's grace.

DT: How nice. So you can feel humble there also.

CK: Yes. Waise, people tend to resent you when you have so much, but by god's grace my friends never minded when I paid off my flat at age twenty-eight only. They jokingly said, yaar, we will take twenty years more to pay off our home loans, you are making us all look bad, we're going to paint your face black. So I said, go ahead, yaar, by god's grace I am *too* fair, so a little blacking will improve my complexion!

DT: You're so right.

CK: It's a little hot in here – the AC isn't very effective – I hope I'm not sweating? Half my batchmates don't get affected by the heat any more – the benefits of balding, you know! But I, by god's grace, still have a full head of hair! No man in my family has ever gone bald. You can say that, by god's grace, good hair genes are my *inheritance*! Along with my family home built on a 4,000 gaj plot in the best part of Bhopal, of course. But we are only talking about me. I want to talk about *you*. Tell me all about yourself, Debjani!

DT: Um, okay. Well I'm –

CK: Oh, look, the washroom is free. I'll just freshen up. Please order whatever you like. By god's grace, money is no object.

The oppressive aroma of aftershave lifts as he walks away. Debjani sits at the table, studying the menu, her face a carefully controlled mask. The minutes tick by and still no Dev Pawar emerges from the toilet.

'Maybe he has the runs,' a deep voice sounds in her ear. 'Maybe, by god's grace, he'll die of 'em.'

Debjani gives an involuntary snort of laughter, lowers the menu and sees an unshaven and rather scruffy Dylan Singh Shekhawat looking across at her, his eyes gleaming with huge enjoyment.

The Brigadier's son. Here. In Berco's Chinese restaurant. Hope rises wildly in her chest. Is he following her? Then she takes in the pudgy man in the slipping turban sitting beside him. He isn't. He's here for Talumein Soup and American Chop Suey, like everybody else.

'Hey,' he says.

'Hi!' she replies, her cheeks pink. 'How are you?'

'You should marry him.' He grins. 'D for Dev. He's perfect for you. You're a loser-lover and he's a loser. It's a match made in heaven.'

'He *isn't* a loser,' Debjani retorts. 'Didn't you hear? He earns twenty –'

'– five thousand rupees a month,' Dylan finishes. 'I think the whole restaurant heard.'

'That's quite good,' the questionable Surd puts in, nodding wisely. 'Has his own flat also. Suna maine – 2BHK in Tuff Parade. Waise, you must also be earning quite well, Dhillonji?'

Dylan shoots him an irate look. 'Would you just continue with your recording?' he snaps. 'The battery in that contraption is about to die.'

The Sardar looks injured. 'Okay, okay, no need to be a rude,' he says austerely. He picks up the recorder, then turns to Debjani again. 'But didi, you better clarify ki twenty-five grands is before tax or after tax.'

Dabbu nods faintly. She hardly knows what she's doing. It is just so... incredible to see Dylan again. Just sitting there, radiating awesomeness. He makes all the men I've been meeting look like round, soft little atta dough boys, she thinks helplessly. Should I tell him I've been reading up those riots he's so obsessed with? Why is he looking so unkempt? He needs a haircut and a shave. And is he wearing *chappals*? How lean and sinewy his feet look. They match his hands. Well, *obviously* they match his hands. It would be weird if they matched somebody else's hands. How am I ever going to marry some Pawar when I could have had *that*?

'So is he honest and kind and brave enough for you?' Dylan enquires, jerking his head in the direction of the toilet. 'Or have you given up on that too, just like you've given up reading news that's even remotely accurate?'

'You've been watching me read,' she manages to remark, quite composedly. 'Thank you. I'm flattered.'

Dylan's lean cheeks redden. Of course he's been watching her read. Every Friday night without fail. He dims the lights, locks the doors (he lives alone in Bombay, but why take a chance?) and glares at her moodily. Watching her lips move, her lashes flutter, checking obsessively for the appearance of more rings on her fingers besides the silver ladybird he know so well. Waiting for that moment at the end when she'll look up, tilt her head slightly, flash the lopsided street-urchin smile that India loves, the one that always turns his stomach into a tutu-wearing ballerina, and say, '*That's all from the news desk tonight. Goodnight.*'

But I *have* to watch her, he reminds himself quickly, because it's important to keep track of the bullshit the government is feeding the people. They hire sweet-faced people like Debjani Thakur and make them say that the deaths of almost 4,000 Sikhs were caused by a spontaneous outpouring of grief. It's sick.

'You didn't answer my question,' he presses, his gaze half sarcastic, half ardent. 'Are you going to marry him? That supposedly god-fearing, constantly self-congratulating, smug ass?'

Their eyes lock. Staring into those twin pools of Pears, he wonders how he will ever be able to look away.

'That's really none of your business, is it?' Debjani says finally, sweetly. 'You'd better eat your Chop Suey before it gets soggy.'

He starts to reply, but just then Dev Pawar comes back to the table.

He's been primping, Dylan thinks, checking out Dev in disgust. He's slicked back his hair, straightened his collar, tucked his shirt in tighter and – although Dylan can't be hundred per cent sure of this – applied moisturizer. What a chick.

Dylan's hands ball into fists, he deliberately turns his back on the now conversing couple and gives the questionable Surd his full attention.

'Continue,' he says.

But the Surd only looks at him out of shrewd gooseberry eyes.
'You two had some chakkar?' he asks sympathetically. 'She left
you, hain? And now she's with Mr Tuff Parade? My Sunita left me
too, but when she sees my photo in the *IP* and reads how brave I
was, she'll take me back. It's a good plan. *You* better think of some
good plan too.'

⋯⋯⋯

Juliet Bai and the Brigadier have discovered Pac-Man. They spend
entire evenings in front of Dylan's Apple Mac, bathed in a ghostly,
tubelighty glow, taking turns at chasing and gobbling up Blinky,
Pinky, Inky and Clyde, the four foul Japanese ghosts who have
taken the civilized world by storm.

'Get the banana, get the banana, *get* the banana, Bobby, uff,
you died. My turn now – move,' Juliet Bai tells her husband as she
elbows him away and takes possession of the arrow keys.

'You jostled my arm,' he accuses her. 'You're *cheating*, Bobby!'

'I didn't,' she replies, not quite looking him in the eye. 'Now
shush, let me concentrate.'

She has progressed to the third level, playing smoothly and
surely, with the Brigadier watching her every move, when Dylan
saunters into the room. He is impeccably dressed. Dark trousers,
a light shirt, a narrow tie. His hair is cut and slicked back, his jaw
smooth after months. Nobody looks at him.

'Cherries! There are cherries! Get the cherries!' the Brigadier
cries, leaping up and down.

'I'll *die* if I go chasing cherries now,' Juliet Bai replies tersely.
'You just want me to die, I know.'

'Um, hello, you guys,' Dylan says.

But Juliet Bai is hearing only beeps, boinnnggs and bleeps. She continues to work the arrow keys. The Brigadier looks around and gives a surprised grunt.

'Bobby, look, some stranger just wandered into the house.'

She ignores him. She is leaning forward, going for the kill, she has just reached the next level. The Brigadier is impressed.

'Wah! Level four! Pinky's on your tail – run, Bobby, run – you can *do* it – careful now!'

Abruptly, the *tunu tunu tunu tunu tunu waaown* death knell sounds. Juliet Bai slumps back in her chair, her eyes suddenly blank.

'Dead! And that too on the fourth level.'

'Mamma,' Dylan says plaintively.

She rubs her eyes and looks around.

'Hoh! You shaved! Looking so handsome. Where are you going, sonna?'

'Nowhere,' he replies lightly. 'I just wanted to talk to you guys.'

'Most honoured, I'm sure,' mutters the Brig as he pauses the Pac-Man.

'I make 8,000 rupees a month,' Dylan announces, ignoring this snide aside. 'I'm not sure if you know.'

'So much?' Juliet Bai says in awe.

'Don't look so impressed, it's all inflation,' the Brigadier snorts. 'Eight thousand doesn't buy what 800 could a few years ago.'

'I also get a small company flat, a petrol allowance, a medical allowance, a leave travel allowance and a month off a year,' Dylan continues, ignoring both these remarks. 'If I switch to another paper – which I don't want to coz I like the *IP*, they have the only decent editorial content in the country, Hiranandani notwithstanding – I'm guessing I could jump to twelve a month, easy.'

They look at him, confused.

'The media industry is poised at the brink of a major breakthrough. The government has started dismantling the Licence Raj, all kinds of new multinational brands are poised to be launched and the subsequent jump in advertising spends will see both television and print journalism boom.'

His parents gape at him. Dylan never talks to them about his work. He snaps if they so much as comment on any of his writing.

'I'd also like to point out that, post-liberalization, many jobs that seem lucrative now will turn into dead-enders. Like, for example, nothing personal against it of course, the merchant navy.'

There is silence. Dylan appears to have said his piece.

'Why,' demands the Brigadier, 'are you telling us this?'

Dylan squares his shoulders and meets his father's eyes.

'So you can go over to Hailey Road and tell Justice Laxmi Thakur that I want to marry his daughter Debjani.'

8

All hell breaks loose the next morning when Chachiji, after brushing her beautiful silver payals carefully with toothpaste just like Anjini has advised her to, leaves them drying in the sun and stumps silently into the annexe kitchen to find the Hot Dulari seated in A.N. Thakur's lap, tenderly being fed cucumber slices. She launches herself upon him with a bloodcurdling yell that awakens half of Hailey Road.

'Now I know why you said never take them off!' she screams. 'Hai! You sick bastard! I am going to *kill* you – give me that cucumber knife!'

Ashok Narayan Thakur is a handsome man: tall, well built, always flamboyantly dressed. Growing up, his nieces idolized him. They loved the summer vacations they spent at Number 13 while their own house was under renovation. There was always something exciting going on. Sometimes Chachaji would summon a whole ice cream thela into the aangan and command the thela-wallah to hand out ice cream after ice cream till the girls cried enough. Sometimes it was chaat. On one memorable winter night, it was a charcoal tandoor full of juicy, red hot chicken tikkas. Of course they had no idea then that the bill for these extravagances was invariably picked up by their father. They hung onto their dashing Ashok chacha's arms, letting him pick them up two at a time as part of his morning workout, blushed at his compliments and laughed at his pug-faced wife. It wasn't till much, much later, when the whole sordid truth about his debts and his rumoured relationship with the Hot Dulari came out, that the girls realized that they'd been, to put it rather crudely, *had*.

Now they watch wide-eyed from the kitchen window of the main house as Chachiji pushes her husband out of the annexe, screaming abuses at his face and hurling bottles of aftershave after him, to burst upon the cemented drive (like so many shattered dreams, Dabbu thinks fancifully).

'You've ruined my life, A.N. Thakur!' Chachiji cries while he begs her to keep her voice down. 'May your soul rot in hell, you sick bastard! May you be eaten by worms! May termites gnaw at your...'

'Anus,' Eshwari completes with a grin. 'She's in full flow, isn't she?'

'Do you think this is the ghost of the Pushkarni taking possession of her?' Anjini asks, leaning against the window frame interestedly. 'Or is she doing this all by herself? Either way, it's better than *Buniyaad*.'

But Dabbu looks stricken. 'It's soo sad,' she mourns. 'I mean, poor Chachiji, married to a handsome but essentially cold man, starved of love and unable to have children. It's...'

(just like my life, thinks Anji, slightly horrified)

'... *horrible*.'

This is a new angle for Eshwari. She has always regarded her uncle and aunt in the same light as *Tom and Jerry* cartoons. The fact that they might actually have feelings is something that has never occurred to her. She wraps her mind around this new thought, frowning.

Finally, she says, 'I think it's really mean of Ma not to let the Ant and Chachiji live in the main house. I mean, just for a few months. The annexe is almost like a servants' quarter.'

'There's nothing wrong with the annexe,' Mrs Mamta says, coming up behind them with the morning tea. 'We could rent it out for 1,000 rupees a month tomorrow. It's just the Ant's antics that belong in a servants' quarter.'

Eshwari chuckles, but Debjani frowns.

'Servants have morals too, Ma,' she says. As her mother bristles at this reproving tone, she quickly adds, 'The sad truth is that Ashok chacha is a bit of a saanp.'

Mrs Mamta Thakur sighs. 'That's true. But you know, girls, your father's entire family is like that only. My mother used to say he's the white sheep of his family.'

Privately though, she can't help wondering if there is any truth in Bhudevi's constant insinuations that the Judge is having an affair too. Why else would he sneak off to Gambhir Stores to make phone calls? She has even asked him about it, but all she has received in reply is a blank look and a testy 'I don't know what you're talking about, Mamtaji'.

'Why doesn't he talk to Ashok chacha?' Debjani asks. 'Drill some sense into his head?'

Mrs Mamta shakes her head. 'That toh is out of the question.' She sighs. 'He won't even *talk* to AN.'

'That's really mature,' Anjini says scornfully. 'And what are we supposed to do if we see him? Or if he talks to us? Pretend he doesn't exist?'

'I don't think that's going to be an issue, actually,' Mrs Mamta says. 'AN will go scurrying off behind that Dulari, wait and see.'

Sure enough, the scene outside the annexe plays out exactly

as Mrs Mamta predicts. The Hot Dulari emerges, beating her breast, protesting her innocence, accusing Chachiji of being a dirty-minded, insecure woman who thinks everybody wants to sleep with her husband and son. When Chachiji asks her why, if she is so pure, had she been sitting in another woman's husband's lap eating cucumbers, she raises a mighty ruckus, weeps noisily, invokes the gods to bear witness to her purity, and marches out of the back gate, calling down curses upon Chachiji's head and utterly delighting the denizens of the lane behind Hailey Road. Ashok Narayan Thakur slinks off behind her a couple of hours later.

Chachiji is granted her wish: she is shifted into the main house, administered warm, sweetened doodh-double-roti and two Calmposes. She is just falling asleep, emitting little hiccupping sobs, her hand firmly grasping Debjani's, when the phone rings. Eshwari enters the bedroom a little later.

'Ma, where's BJ, there's a call for him. It's the Brig.'

'He isn't home, Eshu, take a message,' Mrs Mamta replies shortly. It has been an exhausting twenty-four hours and the Brigadier isn't exactly her favourite person nowadays.

Eshwari vanishes, and then pops her head into the room again, her black eyes very round.

'Ma, he wants to speak to you. He says it's *urgent*.'

Debjani's hand twitches inside Chachiji's grasp. Chachiji's lids flutter open instantly to reveal beadily, glittering eyes. What's all this?' she demands woozily. 'He comes over every day, what does he need to say that can't wait till evening?'

'I'm coming,' Mrs Mamta says, getting to her feet. 'Dabbu, make sure Chachiji rests. I'll go see what Saahas Shekhawat wants.'

The pretty floral-themed drawing room – Mrs Mamta Thakur's pride and joy – is having to do double duty as a makeshift dormitory for her three grandchildren. By ten in the night, the children sit, freshly bathed and brushed, before the pot-bellied Weston colour TV, picking out all the nutritious vegetables from their Nirula's cheese-onion-capsicum-tomato pizzas and flicking them through the window into the flowerbeds outside.

'Anant mausa got me this doll from America,' Bonu says importantly as she chews. 'Look, she actually has a grown-up *chest*.'

A non-stop stream of little girls has been trooping into the house all day, wanting to look at Bonu's new doll. Nobody has ever seen anything like it. It has two quite clearly defined breasts and the longest, thinnest legs in the world. Samar will never admit it, but even he is intimidated by its perfect, plasticky pulchritude.

'What a stupid doll,' he says. 'It can't even stand on its own feet.'

'*You're* stupid,' Bonu retorts. 'She's smart. She's a doctor Barbie. See her white coat? It can come off – all her clothes can come off, actually. Want to see?'

The boys shake their heads hastily. Bonu, slightly deflated, sits her Barbie upon her lap, leans forward and whispers impressively: 'Dabbu mausi is getting married.'

'*Really?*' Monu's eyes swivel to meet Samar's questioningly.

'Children should be seen and not heard,' Samar replies smartly to cover for the fact that he doesn't really know.

Bonu snorts. 'If you're so *grown up*, you should be in the adults-only meeting discussing Dabbu mausi's shaadi. Why are you eating peeza with *us*?'

'It's not *peeza*,' he tells her loftily. 'It's peedza.'

'I like to pronounce things wrong on purpose,' she tells him defiantly. 'It's my *style*.'

Samar's long thin face creases into a disbelieving smirk. He reaches for another slice of pizza.

'Who's she marrying?' Monu wants to know.

'Nobody knows for sure, yet,' Bonu explains knowledgably. 'She has so many rishtas. Because she's so famous, na. But it may be a...' she lowers her voice, '*love marriage*.'

'Ho ji!' Monu is horrified. 'Is she going to have a baby?'

'You're such a crack, Monu,' his twin tells him pityingly. 'Isn't he, Samar?'

'Samar *bhaisaab*.'

Bonu tosses her spiky head. 'You're no relation of mine,' she says. 'Not by blood, anyway. So I don't have to call you bhaisaab.'

'Are love marriages allowed?' Monu wants to know.

'Of course,' Samar says confidently.

'If only the poor Pushkarni had had a love marriage,' Bonu says, shifting tracks slightly. 'Her life might have been happier, no?'

They all look at each other. They have arrived at the topic they discus hotly every night, with the zeal of convent inmates reciting their bedtime rosary. The Death (and rumoured Resurrection) of the Pushkarni.

'Does the Pushkarni really *take over* Chachiji?' Monu asks Samar for the nth time.

Samar nods. 'That's what she says.'

'Have you actually *seen* it happen?' Bonu presses.

Samar purses his lips. 'Not really,' he replies doubtfully.

The twins stare at him, their eyes as large as dinner plates below their identical spiky mushroom haircuts.

'What happens when the bhoot comes?'

'Her eyes roll back,' says Samar, ticking the manifestations off on his fingers. 'She shakes her head a lot. And there is a smell. A very horrible smell that fills the room.'

This is met with a slight sense of anticlimax. Monu-Bonu look at each other doubtfully.

'Like a fart?' Bonu asks.

'Worse,' says Samar, deciding that if a story is worth telling, then it's worth telling well. 'Much worse. Like the fart of a hundred snakes that have eaten mooli. Like the fart of a dead pig who ate the hundred snakes that ate mooli. Like the fart of a dead pig who died in the Union Carbide gas tragedy after eating the hundred snakes that ate mooli.'

'Dead pigs don't fart,' Monu points out. 'And snakes don't eat mooli.'

Samar quells him with a withering look. 'And then she *speaks* like the Pushkarni,' he says. 'Her voice becomes low and growly. Like a bear's. I've heard her.'

The twins look at each other again. Samar is five years older to them, and they often get the feeling that he's just messing with them.

'What does she *say*?' they ask cautiously.

Samar shrugs. 'Stuff about how she was murdered, mostly. And how she came back for badla on her husband. And how she'll never let the building in Number 13 be completed – she'll kill the labourers off one by one.'

'Cool,' the twins breathe in awe.

'I don't know about that,' Samar says. 'Seems a bit unfair to the labourers. What did *they* do?'

'You're just boring,' Bonu tells him. 'I think it will be so fun if she starts killing people – okay, listen, should we put on the scary movie?'

They have a choice of two films to feed into the jaws of the shiny new VCR Anji has bought her parents: *Nightmare on Elm Street* or *Masoom*. Monu is keen on *Masoom* as everybody tells him he looks just like the little kid in the film. This is precisely the reason why Bonu would rather watch *Nightmare*. She thinks the kid in *Masoom* is a whiny loser – fair and green-eyed and weeping about his dead mummy and letting himself be bullied by a bunch of girls.

'Put this one,' Monu says, waving *Masoom* under Samar's disgusted nose.

'I want to see the scary movie,' Bonu says.

'Mummy said no scary movies.' Monu frowns.

'Mummy ka chamcha,' his twin returns scornfully.

'*My* mother bought the VCR,' Samar says firmly. 'And I'm older. So *I* get to pick the movie. And I say *Nightmare*.'

'Yeah,' Bonu agrees with him quickly.

But Monu is feeling mutinous. 'No,' he says, a look of stubborn stolidity settling on his face.

'My VCR, my choice,' Samar says.

But Monu comes back strongly. 'The VCR may be yours but the house is mine. So you *don't* get to choose.'

Samar, who is in the middle of wolfing down the last of his pizza, is so surprised to meet strong contradiction from this unlikely quarter that he stops chewing for a moment. 'I'm the eldest grandson,' he replies. 'What do you mean the house belongs to you, you bloody Monu? It's mine as much as yours.'

'No, it isn't,' Monu lisps stoutly. '*I'm* Justice Laxmi Thakur's eldest grandson. When I grow up this house will be *mine*.'

'And *mine*,' Bonu chimes in.

'No, it won't,' Samar responds, swivelling to look at her in astonishment.

'It's *our* house,' Bonu says, crossing her arms across her skinny chest. 'Mine and Monu's. Mummy told us. You won't get it because Anji mausi isn't really your mother, but,' she smiles encouragingly, 'I'm sure you'll get something nice from your real mother's family, so don't feel too bad, okay.'

Samar considers this. It sounds like it could be true, but it doesn't factor in the fact that he is Bauji's clear favourite.

'What about the other mausis?' he asks.

Monu shrugs. 'Mummy says they all have a hissa. Not Chandu mausi, though, because she ran away.'

A tight knot forms in Samar Vir's stomach. It must be all that pizza he has eaten.

He says, his voice shaking slightly, 'BJ loves me *best*. And Anji-ma's the eldest. Why would BJ leave his house only to you two channas, huh? Because your papa looks just like a bhatura?'

On screen Freddy Krueger gibbers manically in his green-and-red striped jersey. In the living room Monu-Bonu, behaving in a manner the angelic child actor from *Masoom* would definitely have disapproved of, jump Samar Vir Singh, who sidesteps them smartly and grabs them by the scruff of their collars and thunders: 'Say sorry!'

'Sorry,' Monu says immediately.

'*You* say sorry!' Bonu flares, baring her little teeth. 'How *dare* you call my papa a bhatura?' She struggles out of his grasp, spits on the floor and runs out of the room.

'All in favour of First Officer Dev Pawar, raise your hands!' cries out Binni's husband Vickyji, getting to his feet and thumping the dining table with vigour. 'Majority wins.'

The Brigadier's phone call last evening, in which he placed his eldest son's proposal before Mrs Mamta, has led to a high-level conference at 16 Hailey Road. The whole family is gathered in the drawing room to discuss the 'situation'. The arrival of two sons-in-law – one from Bhopal, the other from the US – has only added to the war-room like atmosphere.

'That's just silly,' Eshwari remarks. 'Majority has nothing to do with it. What Dabbu says goes.'

'You be quiet,' Binni snaps. 'Ma, she should be in the drawing room with Monu-Bonu and Samar. Chabbu, *go.*'

'*No,*' Eshwari says combatively, tossing her spiky fringe out of her eyes.

Binni scowls. She has never really forgiven Eshwari for thumbs-downing Vickyji outright when his rishta came for Binni, five years ago. Eshwari, then only twelve, had taken one look at his photograph, drawn a horrified gasp and blurted out, 'Don't do it, Binni didi! He can't even shut his mouth – you'll spend your whole life keeping him from swallowing flies!'

Which was a slight exaggeration. But it can't be denied that Vickyji's teeth radiate out wondrously, like the rays of a cartoon sun. They are also nicely spaced – like modern housing – with a half-inch gap between each tooth. This causes his spit to sometimes spray out. Add to that his short stature, wispy curls and sing-song nasal voice, and one can understand why his wife avers that looks are nothing, it is *character* that is of supreme importance.

And Vickyji's character is top ka, declares Binni loyally. See how much guts he has! Doing his own business instead of being a salary slave like that boring Anant Singh.

Basically, I've got a dud set of brothers-in-law, Eshwari muses gloomily. The first is a handsome bore, the second is a thook-spraying loan solicitor and the third is so persona non grata that I'm not even allowed to mention him. I *have* to get Dylan into this family.

'Of course this can't be settled by a show of hands,' the Judge says testily. 'Sit *down*, Vickyji.'

Vickyji sits down, not at all abashed.

'Either way, it's a problem of plenty,' Anant smiles gravely. 'Which is great news. You've become such a star, Dabbu. Well done.'

'I'm a little surprised, ekchully!' Vickyji admits. 'Because theek hai, she is reading the news and all, but it's not like she's very beaut – I mean,' he amends hastily, with an apologetic glance at Debjani, 'she's no Binni, let's just say.'

He looks at his fair, buxom, bold-eyed wife with proprietary pride. Binni blushes.

'B for beautiful,' Eshwari murmurs, nudging Debjani. 'D for dowdy. E for, um, excruciatingly ugly.'

Anjini waits for Antu to jump in and extol her virtues too. But he doesn't. He isn't speaking to her at all. Why has he even bothered to come? she wonders petulantly. If all he's going to do is ignore me! I've a good mind to sleep on the terrace with the girls tonight. Shrugging her shoulders, she says, 'Dabbu likes Dylan. And we know the family.'

'*I* know the Pawars,' Binni chimes in.

'The mother's Christian, no?' Vickyji enquires. 'And before that, what was she? Matlab, her family couldn't have converted more than 300 years ago. *Must* have been some scheduled caste before.'

'They weren't any schedules 300 years ago,' the Judge says, looking distinctly thunderous.

Mrs Mamta hurries in to fill the breach. 'Dev is nice too. Earning so well.'

'And the Pawars don't have any demands.' Binni throws down her trump card.

But the Judge just snorts ungratefully. 'They'd better not – or they'll end up in jail! "Demands" (he makes exaggerated inverted commas in the air) are against the law! Why do people always say "we have no demands" like it's so very noble of them? Demands indeed!'

He glares at Vickyji. The bugger has got his wife to move the court, demanding the division and sale of the very house we're sitting in, he thinks with a strong sense of ill-usage. Bloody hypocrite.

'Besides, a *lot* of people,' he continues meaningfully, 'pretend to have no demands at the time of the wedding, but later they sit on top of your chest and never stop demanding!'

There is an awkward silence. The Judge glowers at Vickyji. Binni blushes. Mrs Mamta makes soothing sounds. Then Vickyji gets up, mutters something and hurries out of the room.

'My friend Saahas has no "demands" either,' the Judge informs the room in a calmer voice.

'Ya, but I'm just saying, Bauji, that for such an educated, fair, well-to-do and eligible boy to have no demands is unusual. But for a dark, ordinary fellow, and a half-Christian at that,' Binni curls her generous lower lip, 'it's not such a big thing, after all.'

'Dev Pawar is butt ugly,' says the incorrigible Eshwari. 'He looks like he's wearing diapers.'

'Eshwari!' her mother says, shocked.

'This child is spoilt,' Binni declares. 'Ashleel. Shameless. Aur bhejo Modern School.'

'And he isn't a nice person either,' Eshwari continues doggedly. 'He turns down girls because their gums are too big.'

'*You* want to turn him down because his *bum* is too big!' Binni glares at her. 'What *is* it, Vickyji?'

Her husband has just popped his head into the room and is looking at her meaningfully.

'I want to talk to you, Binni,' Vickyji says, winking now. 'Privately.'

Binni gets up, tosses her dupatta over her shoulder and walks out. Probably for a quickie, Anjini thinks morosely. Lucky girl.

Mrs Mamta turns towards her fourth-born.

'So, Dabbu, what do you say?'

'Well, his butt *is* rather well padded, by god's grace,' Debjani admits.

'Not about his backside,' the Judge says patiently, wondering for the millionth time why the Almighty had thought it fit to bestow him with so many daughters and not even one single uncomplicated son. 'About whether you want to marry him.'

Debjani hunches up and hugs herself, her hair obscuring her face. *Why* has Dylan done this sudden about-turn? Because he saw her at Berco's and realized he couldn't live without her? Seriously? Does she still want him? If only she could speak to him.

'Bauji, I'd just like to understand, it isn't a Dev-versus-Dylan situation, is it?' Anant asks in his low, pleasant voice. 'I mean, there *are* other rishtas.'

'Well, she refuses to consider NRIs,' Anji says. 'And of all the other offers, these are the only two she hasn't rejected outright.'

'I don't see what the rush is,' Anant persists. 'She's only twenty-three.'

'Antu, good boys go like *that*!' Anjini snaps her fingers. 'We can have a long engagement, of course.'

'Do Antu others as you would have them do Antu you,' the Judge pipes up, looking mighty pleased with his pun.

'He means,' Eshwari says helpfully to Anant, 'that you and Anji didi got married when she was twenty-three too.'

'I *got* that, Eshwari,' Anant says patiently. 'Still...'

'Arrey, what is the need for a long engagement?' Binni demands breathlessly as she re-enters the room. 'Vickyji has explained everything to me. You follow your heart, Dabbu. *I* won't put any emotional pressure. We don't want you running away like that crack Chandu did! And don't worry if you don't choose Dev, I will give some excuse to the Pawars and manage everything!'

Dabbu stares at her sister, stunned. 'Really, Binni didi?'

Binni nods vigorously. 'Really.'

'So that's settled,' the Judge says, his tone satisfied. 'So now, Dabbu, what do you say?'

The entire clan turns to Debjani. She looks around the room, her eyes going from Eshwari to her father to finally settle on Mrs Mamta Thakur, who smiles at her encouragingly.

She throws back her head and sits up straighter, her cheeks flush a delicate shade of pink.

'I choose Dylan,' she says composedly.

⊷•⊛•⊶

'Hello, could I speak to Debjani please?'

Mrs Mamta Thakur smiles. The Shekhawat boy sounds a little nervous, which is just as it should be.

'Hello, Dylan,' she says warmly, mentally adding this new name to the roster of 'her' boys. 'I'll fetch her, just hold for a moment, all right?'

She walks out to the verandah, bouncing a little with suppressed excitement, and beams at the gaggle of pretty sisters sitting there shelling peas. They look back at her questioningly.

'It's Dyllllan,' she bursts out, trilling roguishly over the 'l's, her eyes dancing.

Everybody instantly starts jumping up and down and squealing with excitement – so loudly that the dogs starts to bark in the sand pile outside. Mother and sisters push the stunned Debjani to her feet. She runs into the drawing room to get the phone, then races back to the door, very red-faced, and slams it shut behind her. They hear the sound of a latch being drawn.

'Cow!' Eshwari gasps. 'Ma, I keep telling you we need to get an extension line!'

But her mother isn't listening. Sudden tears have risen to her eyes. She leans against a verandah pillar.

'And so another one flies the nest,' she reflects. 'Enjoy these days, Dabbu.'

Inside, Debjani picks up the receiver, her heart slamming madly against her ribs.

'Hello?'

'Hi,' Dylan says, his voice unusually hesitant. 'So, how are you?'

She laughs. 'I'm fine, I guess. And you?'

'Oh, I'm good,' he replies, sounding rather rueful. 'I'm the laughing stock of my whole family, but that goes with the territory, I guess.'

She doesn't ask why. That would be coy, and Debjani doesn't do coy. Instead she says, 'This feels kind of weird.'

'What?' There is a hint of laughter in his voice, he is clearly starting to feel more confident. 'That somebody wants to marry you?'

He wants to marry me, Debjani repeats dazedly to herself. Dylan Singh Shekhawat. Writer of scathing editorials, owner of a dirty reputation, a strong, shadowed jaw and that perfect, *perfect* butt.

'Not somebody,' she replies honestly. 'Just you. I mean, what happened? Don't you want to flit from flower to flower and sip, without ever paying nectar tax?'

'No,' he replies, his voice warm and disturbingly intimate. 'I want to make my proboscis exclusive to you.'

Debjani determinedly ignores the curling effect these words have on her toes.

'But *why*?' she asks sensibly.

He sighs. How much this girl can talk.

'What kind of ring would you like? A ladybird? What are male ladybirds called, by the way? God, they must be messed-up creatures. Talk about gender confusion.'

A ring.

But that sounds so... final. Panic grips her belly, causing her toes to uncurl.

'What made you change your mind?' she asks again, her voice squeaky.

Dylan realizes there is no dodging this question.

'Well, it's kind of hard to articulate, but I'll try – I do these things much better non-verbally, actually.'

'You'll explain by getting physical with me?' she asks suspiciously.

'You have a mind like a sink,' he replies candidly. 'You know that big green mailbox you have hanging outside your gate? Just check it tomorrow morning.'

'Okay,' she says, a surge of happiness making her almost dizzy. 'I will. Goodnight then.'

'Goodnight, Debjani.' His voice is a caress. 'Sleep well.'

⊷∙◈∙⊷

'Where are you going?'

Anant's voice is grave as always. And very distant. Anji blinks back sudden stupid tears.

'To sleep on the chhat with my sisters,' she replies tightly. 'You can sleep down here with your son.'

There is silence. Then, 'Samar will be happier sleeping with Monu-Bonu in the drawing room.'

'And I will be happier sleeping with Dabbu-Chabbu on the terrace. She could be getting engaged tomorrow – we have tons of stuff to discuss.'

'Fine,' Anant says. 'If you don't need me here, I'll leave in the morning. I came because I thought your parents would think it odd if I didn't stop at Delhi before taking the train to Allahabad.'

'So you came only because you were worried about what other people would think.'

'Well.' There's a faint hint of humour in his voice. '*Somebody* has to worry about what other people think. You clearly don't.'

'You find this funny?'

'No,' Anant says steadily, 'I find this exhausting. I've worked like a dog all week, done large amounts of gift shopping for the kids, travelled twenty-six hours non-stop, participated in a three-hour-long war council about how to lasso another poor bakra into marriage with yet another one of your princessy sisters, and now I'm terribly jet-lagged and I just want to sleep.'

'So you're a bakra?' Anji's voice trembles. 'And I lassoed you?'

Anant sighs. 'I'm tired, Anjini.'

'Fine.' She walks up to the door. 'Sleep well and have lovely dreams about your office.'

'Come away from the door, Anjini,' he says, his voice curt. 'People can hear you.'

'So *what*?' Anji snaps at him. But she does come away from the door and sits down on the edge of the bed in a whirl of sulky, scented satin.

'So I lassoed, na,' she says, her chest heaving. 'Fine then, I'll unlasso you.'

Anant's face is white. 'What exactly do you mean by that?'

She looks away. 'Just that as you're *so* deeply unhappy with me, I should maybe just,' she shrugs, 'let you go.'

There is a long silence.

Finally Anant looks up. His eyes seem blind, opaque.

'Fine,' he says, his voice very low.

He wants to leave me, Anji thinks wretchedly. Because I can't have a baby, I suppose. How humiliating. And after all my attempts at goodness! I've done *weeks* of volunteer work at the Muskaan School for Mentally Challenged Children. I've stopped caring about being thinner than my sisters. I haven't flirted at all. Well, barely. I've worn fully body-covering clothes. Well, most of the time. I've even fed Dabbu's hideous, khujli-covered dogs! And it was all pointless. I didn't chalk up any brownie points on that giant scoreboard in the sky. God didn't hear my prayer. Anyway, that settles it, I *will* get my hair permed, after all.

'And what about Samar?' she demands, her voice shaking a little. 'Have you thought about him? How will he feel?'

'He'll recover,' Anant says evenly. 'And anyway, we can share custody.'

Custody. The word lies out in the open between them, like a dirty diaper nobody wants to pick up. Then Anjini raises her chin. Anant must never know that the ten days she has spent here have been so agonizing that at times she thought the pain may drive her mad. That she spent more than an hour getting ready in Eshu's bathroom for him today, that her hair has been freshly shampooed and set using her twenty-four faithful pink sponge-rollers, that her négligée is new.

'Fine,' she says. 'Just stay here till tomorrow. Brigadier Shekhawat's family is coming to tea and Ma and Bauji would like you to be there.'

Anant nods. His face is a mask, devoid of all emotion. 'I'll leave day after morning then.'

Anji shrugs indifferently.

'Okay.'

―――・◆・―――

The next evening, on Dylan's last day in Delhi, the Shekhawats drive down in their trusty Maruti 800 to meet the Thakurs. It is an extremely distinguished looking, though nervous little party. It is their 'first time' after all, something Juliet Bai has repeated ad nauseam.

'Stop saying that, Bobby, you sound like Ethan trying to get laid,' her husband says. 'And Jason, stopping kicking me with your bloody long legs!'

'Don't swear on such an auspicious day, Bobby,' his wife

entreats. 'How much I tried to stop this wretched boy from eating when he was younger. Just grew and grew and grew and now he doesn't fit anywhere!'

Jason subsides, muttering. Ethan, on the other side of his mother, fusses with his shoes and smooths down his hair. The Brig shoots a disapproving look at his Bruce Lee T-shirt. One fellow looks like a giraffe and another fellow looks like a thug.

'Why are you carrying a Swiss Army knife to your brother's rishta?' he demands. 'Going to stir your tea with it? Fool!'

'I want to make a good impression,' Ethan explains. 'It's my coolest thing.'

Then he pulls a solemn face, clears his throat and says ponderously: 'Dearly beloved, we are gathered here to mourn the sad demise of Dylan Shekhawat, a lusty, full-blooded player whose passing will be lamented in lacy boudoirs across the land...'

'Shut up, rat.' Dylan twists Ethan's ear amiably.

'Ethan, did you call your math tutor and cancel today's class?' his mother asks from the front seat.

'No,' Ethan mutters, rubbing his ear. 'But don't blame me, blame your malgado. He's been prowling around the phone the whole day, waiting for it to ring, but the newsreader never called. If I fail in math it'll be her fault.'

'She didn't call?' their mother asks worriedly. 'Isn't that bad, Dylan?'

'No, it's good,' Dylan replies serenely.

Juliet Bai fidgets with her pallu. Ek toh this Dylan also! So much fuss to make up his mind... First saying no and huffing off. Then, when the girl's family moves on and gets a good rishta from someplace else, rushing back and saying yes. And expecting her and Saahas to sort out everything double quick! Thank god the Judge and Mrs Mamta were still open to the rishta, though Mrs Mamta hadn't been able to resist mentioning the merchant navy officer's salary to the Brigadier when he had called. Oh Lord, let this tea party go off well, with no unpleasant surprises from either side.

Dylan, unaware of his mother's interior monologue, is keeping up one of his own out loud. He is starting to feel a little sick and his palms are clammy.

'Okay, here we are – Number 16. Lord, just look at the number of women in that family! One can only pray we get out of this unscathed. Mamma, wait, let me get your door for you. You don't want Moti and family to destroy your sari.'

But Moti and co. have been banished today. 16 Hailey Road is looking its finest. Eshwari has picked masses of sunflowers and jasmine and set them about in vases all over the verandah and living room. Anjini has baked a Dundee cake. Binodini has laid a plate of Catburies èclairs upon the table. There are freshly fried namak-paras and little Monaco biscuits topped with baked beans, boiled egg and tiny florets of coriander. Not a bowl of Maggi in sight. The Judge is hovering over the gramophone in the drawing room and Debjani is pacing up and down the kitchen garden at the back of the house, dressed in her bootcut jeans and a pastel Kashmiri kurti, trampling Mrs Mamta's painstakingly grown pudina plants to pulp.

Debjani is in a state of complete panic. She had run down to the mailbox early in the morning expecting a long love letter (her first) and found a gift-wrapped package containing a bottle of Anais Anais and a note that reads *Keep smelling good* in terribly untidy, cramped handwriting. Which is romantic, of course, but not very enlightening. What happened, she had wondered, staring blankly at the bottle, to all that talk about Pears soap? How come he's switched to perfume? And the note is definitely corny – so corny, in fact, that she hasn't told her sisters about it.

For a moment, everything Dylan has done so far seems suspect. Kicking her dog, kissing her in that high-handed fashion, telling her his intentions aren't serious and then wanting to marry her. And as an explanation for this weird see-sawing behaviour: a bottle of (admittedly expensive) perfume.

I should have talked to him more and marvelled at the squareness of his jaw less. Oh god, I don't know anything about him! Suppose he's mean with money? Suppose he's a wife-beater or an alcoholic and has a debauched lifestyle in Bombay? After all, his own father said he doesn't offer any guarantee for him. Suppose this wanting to be engaged is just an elaborate ploy to get me to kiss him some more and then dump me?

Inside the house, the Thakurs and the Shekhawats are sizing each other up. Things aren't too awkward, because the two husbands have been fast friends for over ten years. Even Juliet Bai and Mrs Mamta Thakur, though not intimate, have nothing but goodwill towards each other. So it's really Dylan, the rogue son from Bombay, who gets the full force of the Thakur clan's Critical Evaluation Scanner and reels under the impact.

That fat chick is definitely wishing me dead, he thinks wryly as he smiles vaguely around the room and sits down on a flowery couch between his brothers. She must be sister number two, B-something, the bearer of the Pawar rishta. No wonder she looks hostile. Anjini looks as temptingly like a pastry as ever. The hubby doesn't look like he has much of a sweet tooth, though, pity that. Samar and Eshwari have done a bunk just when I needed them – and where in god's name is Debjani?

'So what kind of writing do you do?' Anant is asking.

'Editorials,' the Judge answers before Dylan can even open his mouth. 'This Sunday he said that all this excitement around the opening up of the economy is misplaced, that it's going to split the country even more sharply, the rich will get richer and the poor poorer, and in ten years' time, we will end up with two entirely separate Indias – a tiny one that will be a clone of the first world and a massive one that will be sitting in the gutters. It was well argued.' He nods encouragingly at Dylan, who feels touched and, knowing the Judge's intellectual prowess, gratified.

'I don't know.' Anji pulls a face. 'I'm all for opening up. We'll get Coke again in India, imagine that!'

'How old are you, Dylan?' Mrs Mamta asks with her sweet smile.

'He's twenty-eight,' Ethan promptly replies. 'Jason is twenty-five. And I'm fourteen.'

Why isn't anybody letting me speak? Dylan thinks, frustrated. How will I slay them with my killer charm if they don't let me get in a word edgeways? He smiles at one of the B-sister's cherubic infants. It takes its fingers out of its mouth long enough to say, 'I'm fairer than you,' and then subsides.

And that, Dylan thinks resignedly, is that.

'Is there a lot of money in journalism nowadays?' asks B-sister's husband, a man whose teeth remind Dylan of the coconut scrapers everybody uses back in Mangalore.

'Well,' Dylan says slowly, not very sure if Vickyji expects him to whip out his salary slip. 'There's a –'

'Because I'm a businessman, you see,' Vickyji informs him. 'I'm thinking ki maybe, if it is profitable, I could start a magazine-shagazine? Not boring news and views, but something pataka – with pictures of foreign models and all. We could be partners.'

'I do volunteer work at Muskaan School for Mentally Challenged Children,' Anji says hastily, obviously feeling his remark needs to be compensated for somehow.

'Where's Debjani?' Juliet Bai asks.

'Just coming,' Mrs Mamta says serenely, as if she is completely unaware of the panicked trampling of the pudina plants in the back garden. 'Eshwari's gone to get her.'

If she comes in with a tea tray, Dylan thinks, looking down at his meticulously polished shoes, I'll stab myself in the head with Ethan's Swiss Army knife and end the pain. This whole situation is too medieval for words.

But it is Eshwari who brings in the tea. Debjani wanders in a little later, holding Samar's hand and looking decidedly pale.

'Debjani!' ejaculates the Brigadier, a little too loudly and heartily, revealing his 'first time' status for all to see and pity. 'Come, beta, sit with Dylan. Move from there, you duffers.'

'Hello, uncle.' Debjani flashes a ghost of her street-urchin grin and folds up obediently next to her suitor.

An odd silence follows. Ethan fiddles with his Swiss Army knife and clears his throat meaningfully, looking at Eshwari. She gives a start. 'Hi there,' she grins. His entire face turns as pink as the tips of his pimples.

'Do you go to Modern also, beta?' Mrs Mamta asks kindly.

Ethan shakes his head gloomily. 'St Columba's. It's a convent school. No girls.'

Meanwhile Samar looks dreamily out of the window and Binni smiles politely around the room, thinking how hard-faced the half-Isayee fellow is. His hands are huge, she frets. And we know what *that* means. Kha jaayega hamari Dabbu ko. He'll eat her up in the bedroom only.

And then everybody starts to talk at once. Anjini asks Dylan what he makes of the Shah Bano case. The Judge immediately answers for him. Ethan asks Samar Vir how old he is. Vickyji asks Jason how tall he is. Anant tells Juliet Bai he considers Goa a lovely holiday spot. She replies that she isn't from Goa but from Mangalore. The Brigadier smiles foolishly at Mrs Mamta and tells her how lovely she is looking. And then Juliet Bai exclaims rapturously, 'What a lovely beauty spot, ba!'

Debjani stiffens at once, but it is Anjini who answers with a sparkling laugh:

'Isn't it? When it first appeared, she was six, you know, aunty. We thought she'd drawn it on, because she was a big fan of Dabbu – Randhir Kapoor, you know – and some of his heroines had a mole just like that!'

Debjani rolls her eyes. Dylan's light up with amusement.

'It's lovely,' Juliet Bai says.

'That reminds me of a family joke,' the Judge says affably, as he passes around the Monaco biscuits. 'When I went on a foreign trip to Malaysia, my wife insisted we get passports made for the whole family – in case they all decided to accompany me on the trip, you know. Well, the trip didn't materialize, but we did get a new family surname in the bargain – the Molons. Tell them, Debjani.'

He nods encouragingly at his fourth daughter, his eyes full of affectionate pride.

Debjani is mortified. What is the need for BJ to bring up Malaysia like it's something great? She knows the Brigadier has been on several foreign postings – probably the boys have travelled abroad too – besides, the Molon joke is not very funny at all.

'Tell no, Debjani!' Juliet Bai entreats her.

'Well...' Debjani begins reluctantly. 'Passports have this "distinguishing marks" column, you must be knowing that, of course. And we noticed that the officials had put mole-on-lip, mole-on-chin, mole-on-nose, mole-on-cheek for all of us. So Eshwari, who was ten at the time, said it was like we were a Chinese family. The Molons. She was Molonneck, the other girls were Molonnose and Moloneye, BJ and Ma were Moloncheek and I, of course,' she concludes, red-faced, 'was Molonchin.'

'Haha!' The Judge beams around the room. Everyone laughs politely.

Kill me somebody, Debjani thinks, looking down at her hands.

'I would be a Ziton,' Ethan pipes up after a pause. 'But my last name would keep changing – one day Zitonnose, one day Zitoncheek, one day Zitonnose*and*cheek. And Dyl would be a Scaron. Scaronchest, you know...'

'Ethan, shut up,' Dylan growls as Eshwari instantly goes *oooh* and throws him a naughtily speculative glance. He then realizes that these are the first words he has spoken so far. Way to go, he thinks resignedly and reaches for some Dundee cake.

Ethan and Eshwari reach for the last piece of baked-beans-on-Monaco together. 'Same pinch,' he grins.

'You take it,' she says.

'No, I meant same pinch because we're both the youngest. Youngest are coolest, don't you agree?'

'What rubbish!' Anji instantly pretends to look offended. 'Eldest is best, no, Dylan?'

Dylan, who is chewing on cake, can only nod.

'But in the Bible, youngest is best,' says the irrepressible Ethan, thrilled to be talking to the hottest woman in the room. 'David was the youngest of his brothers. So was Joseph. So was Jacob.'

But Anji waves away Joseph and Jacob. 'In the Ramayana, Ram is eldest and best.'

'And he inherited the whole kingdom,' Samar speaks up suddenly, glaring at the twins from within the safety of his father's arms. 'He didn't give anybody one-sixth hissa! And if you're the eldest of the eldest of the eldest, that makes you even more special, right?'

Anji and Anant look at Samar, horrified. Binni's face is like thunder. The twins, sensing a storm, squirm uneasily. Then the Brigadier laughs. 'Of course. Being eldest is a huge responsibility. Right, Dyl?'

Dylan nods. He turns to Samar and says seriously, 'The eldest has to be *first* in all the responsibilities and *last* in all the fun stuff.'

Just like me, Anjini thinks sentimentally. I'm always having to do that. You know, I really *like* this Dylan Singh Shekhawat!

Juliet Bai smiles around the room.

'It's our thirtieth wedding anniversary this year,' she says brightly. 'How many years have you and LN been married, Mamta?'

'Thirty-three,' says Mrs Mamta.

'Thirty-four,' says the Judge at the same time.

They get into a little argument. Juliet Bai keeps going.

'In our community, we usually have a big celebration on the twenty-fifth anniversary. But Saahas had a surgery that year, so we couldn't celebrate. The boys are planning a big thirtieth for us now, I believe.'

The boys look shifty. Eyeing them, Dabbu doubts that they've planned anything at all yet.

'It has always been my fondest hope,' Juliet Bai confides, now in full form, 'that our grandchildren walk down the aisle in front of us scattering flowers at our thirtieth anniversary Mass.' Her eyes twinkle. 'There won't be enough time for *that* to be arranged, unfortunately! Not even if we marry you both off today!'

Debjani closes her eyes, feeling like a prize cow. This is the stuff of nightmares. She wonders if the nice Mrs Shekhawat is next going to ask if her periods are regular.

But Juliet Bai is pursuing another chain of thought.

'How well matched these two are,' she muses, half closing her eyes and looking at the hapless couple upon the couch with artistic pleasure. 'Dylan, of course, is tall and sinewy and muscular – his veins actually *show*, you know, that's a sign of extreme fitness.' She starts pointing out fine details the Thakurs might have missed. 'Notice his strongly corded neck, leading up to the jaw of a cowboy, to the mouth of an angel, and to eyes that –'

'Mamma, this isn't an art appreciation class,' Dylan's angelic mouth mutters through gritted teeth.

Juliet Bai starts. 'Sorry,' she says apologetically. 'And Dabbu is so pretty too! That hair, and those long, curling lashes! They always look so pretty when girls drop or raise them. So innocent! Some people say it's a flirtatious habit, but I don't know. My mother always said, never trust a person who doesn't blink. Who just *stares* and *stares*. Like a snake, you know?'

'Bobby, now you've set everybody blinking,' the Brigadier chuckles. And everybody does blink for a while. Except Debjani, for whom these words have touched a forgotten chord. She frowns, puzzled. She has heard this particular theory before. But where?

While she is puzzling over this, she realizes that the moment she has been dreading has arrived. Dylan is addressing her directly.

'Debjani,' he says formally, and his voice is as toe-tinglingly deep and warm as she remembers, not at all the voice of a wife-beater or a miser-drunkard. 'Are you sure you're okay with the –'

And that's when it clicks.

My grandmother always said, never trust a person who doesn't blink.

Debjani gasps.

'You!'

He raises an eyebrow, amused.

'Uh, yes, me. I'm sorry, were you expecting somebody else?'

Everybody laughs, like this is a bit of a good joke. The Brigadier and Mrs Shekhawat turn away and start speaking to the elder girls, looking more relaxed.

But Debjani has turned pale. She says, her voice unsteady, 'It was you – you wrote that article, you're Roving Eye!'

Dylan frowns. 'Yes, but –'

'Not that article again,' the Judge mutters. 'I thought we had moved on from that.'

'Oh my god.' Debjani shakes her head. 'I'm so *stupid*... Of course it was you!'

Mrs Mamta leans forward. 'Dabbu, relax, all that is behind you now, you stress too much about that arti –'

'No, Ma, BJ. You guys don't understand. He *wrote* it.' She whirls to look at Dylan. 'Didn't you?'

His dark eyes look apprehensive. 'Uh, you want to go into this now?' he asks. 'I mean, here? Can't we do this later?'

'*Later*? When? After we're engaged?'

'Dabbu.' The Judge's voice is perplexed. 'There must be some confusion. And if he wrote it before he met you, what difference does it make?'

'But he deliberately *lied...*' Her voice has risen sharply. She stops, trying to calm herself. 'He misled me.'

'That's true enough,' Dylan admits swiftly. 'But then I explained...' He frowns. 'Didn't you check your mailbox?'

She stares at him, stunned. 'You think *that* makes up for it?'

Dylan goes rather white about the mouth.

'Well, yes,' he says, his deep voice growing perceptibly cooler. He is speaking now in the dangerously neutral tone that everybody in the *India Post* office recognizes and does their damnedest to avoid. 'But obviously you don't agree.'

The room full of people suddenly goes very quiet. Juliet Bai, who was talking to Anjini and Binni, stops and looks around. The Brigadier puts down his quarter plate of baked-beans-on-Monaco and asks uneasily, 'What's all this?'

'It's our first time,' adds his wife.

'Leave it, Dadda,' Dylan says testily. 'It's nothing.'

'Then why is Debjani asking if you have a roving eye, sir?' demands his father. 'Explain!'

'Uncle, it's just a column in the *India Post*,' Eshwari hurries to explain. 'Nothing cheap.'

'Well, that's quite a good joke, then!' the Judge ploughs ahead valiantly. 'And by the way, I told Dabbu the critique there was only fair. On *all* counts. So, do you write this column on a regular basis?'

'No, sir,' Dylan replies. 'It's my boss's column. But he was tied up that day so he told me to write it, which is irregular but not illegal, because it isn't his own byline but that of a created entity called Roving Eye.' He shoots an uneasy glance at Debjani.

But Debjani has turned to ice. Her brain has started reciting a well-remembered litany. *Wide-eyed. Breathless. Naïvely overwhelmed.*

She says, her voice high and thready, 'I don't want to do this any more.'

'I think you two should talk alone,' Mrs Mamta Thakur says hastily.

'Yes, good suggestion, Mamta.' Juliet Bai nods in relief.

'I don't want to talk to him!' Debjani bursts out.

There is a stunned silence in the room. Nobody quite knows what to say, the break with all known social etiquette is so complete. The Judge makes a heroic effort.

'Now, Debjani, don't D for dither, hehe...'

'Bhaisaab,' Mrs Mamta cuts in, touching the Brigadier gently on the elbow. 'Come, let us step outside for a bit.'

Everybody backs out of the room, the children reluctantly leaving last. Debjani's mother shuts the door on the two of them, her face impassive.

'I assume this is your warped notion of revenge?' Dylan says quietly.

Debjani stares at him in disbelief. 'You're calling *me* warped?'

'Well, you've got your money's worth, that's for sure,' Dylan continues in the same, oddly quiet voice. 'You've managed to insult me thoroughly, turning me down in front of both our families – my mother, my little brothers. Rather a personal revenge for what was, at best, a purely professional attack.'

'I don't know what you're talking about,' Debjani replies, plunging her fingers into her hair and massaging her throbbing head. 'All I know is that you lied to me. Clearly we know *nothing* about each other.'

'I thought I knew you,' he says heavily.

Debjani turns towards him involuntarily, but his eyes stop her. They are suddenly as blind and impersonal as TV static.

'But obviously that *you* was some idealized bullshit I made up inside my own head. I should have realized that someone who doesn't bat an eyelid when reading about the deaths of thousands of human beings but cries when a pie dog dies must necessarily be petty and small-minded.'

'I *do* care about people!' Debjani replies, stung. 'And animals can't speak up for themselves. And *what* did you just call me?'

'You heard.'

Debjani feels sick. Like there is a stone in her stomach. Her cheeks are hot, her throat is tight and dry. But he's the one in the wrong, she thinks confusedly. So why does it feel like I'm in the dock?

Dylan laughs. 'I just realized something.'

'*What?*'

'I couldn't quite put a finger on it till now. But I finally get it. Why you like dressing up and sitting inside a box and talking at people who can't talk back at you.'

'I do *not* –'

'Because you live in a bubble of smug superiority. You never take emotional risks or go out a limb for anyone. The deepest emotion you're capable of is pity – perfect for dogs and losers.'

'That's not true! You're the liar here, you're the pretender – why aren't we talking about that?'

'Goodbye, Debjani,' he says dismissively. 'Have a nice life telling yourself every day of your married life that you're better than the poor D for dumbass you're sure to end up with. And now if you don't mind, sir,' he strides up to the door, opens it and addresses the Judge, who is standing just outside, 'my family and I would like to take your leave.'

9

Three months later

'Did Dabbu like the boy, Bhabhiji?'

Mrs Mamta shakes her head. 'I don't think so,' she says shortly. 'She said he was a ball of atta.'

'Hai. But he was an engineer, na? From IIT! And tall also.'

'This girl won't be getting married anytime soon, Bhudevi.' Mrs Mamta sips her tea. 'Which is good, I suppose – how could we have a wedding with so much construction going on next door?'

The noise from the construction site at Number 13 is certainly deafening. Cement mixers spin busily all day. Brick-red bajri lies about in huge mounds, like burst pimples upon the road. Dust sits thickly on the leaves of the amaltas trees. The ranks of snot-nosed urchins in the back lane have swelled exponentially, as have the number of Modernites who squat in the sand every day to teach the children their ka-kha-ga as part of their SUPW curriculum. And at the crossroad of Hailey and Barakhamba roads, a giant, red-faced Raavan in a stiff, multi-coloured anarkali kurta stands glowering at passers-by; a grim, dependable promise of more cacophony to come.

'Aur... what about Bombay? Any news?'

'None,' says Mrs Mamta. 'And frankly, I don't think there ever will be.'

She had phoned Juliet Bai the day after the disastrous tea party at Hailey Road to apologize for Dabbu's volte face and to somehow close the whole ugly mess with a neatly tied, civilized bow. Juliet Bai had told her (in a rather airy, off-hand manner, Mrs Mamta felt) that Dylan was back at work and very busy and that of course the Brigadier would remain friends with Justice Laxmi Narayan. That went without saying. But the doctor had advised him to do something more active in the evenings, so please not to misunderstand if he didn't show up for cards. It was only because, Juliet Bai had explained earnestly, he was taking up squash.

'So they just squashed us and went off!' Chachiji says gloomily. 'And half the community knows our girl has been rejected. What sad days for the Thakurs of Hailey Road! First girl is Banjjar, second girl is a Khanjjar – she has filed a court case against her own father! Third girl ka toh what-to-say, and fourth girl has been rejected by a Christian! And fifth girl wears such short-short skirts and plays basketball with boys. Hundred per cent she will blacken our faces one day. And,' she adds fairly, 'in the younger brother's family, the father has gambled away his inheritance and run away with the cook while his son has failed his law exams for the third time. Someone has done jaadu-tona on our family, Bhabhiji. We had better do a Satyanarayan ki puja.'

'Don't be silly, Bhudevi,' Mrs Mamta says wearily. 'He didn't reject her, she rejected *him*.'

Chachiji sniffs. 'That's what everybody thinks,' she says. 'You can keep saying what you like till your face is blue.'

Which is true enough, Mrs Mamta has to admit.

'Waise, I toh think ki he hadn't made up his mind properly

only,' Chachiji says frankly. 'He was still doubting. Must have started sweating when he saw the tea tray and the snacks and the whole family all dressed up and thought ki we were about to put a ring through his nose. So when she shouted at him just a little bit, he jumped on that excuse, pretended to be offended and ran away. Boys panic like that sometimes.'

'Let's not talk about it.' Mrs Mamta looks around. 'I wonder where Dabbu is. Nobody tells me anything any more.'

'Respected judges, honourable principal sir, members of the staff and my dear friends. This house believes that *there is power in honesty but no honesty in power* and I am strongly against the motion...'

What a tongue-twister of a topic, Debjani thinks as she fiddles with her JUDGE place card and smiles encouragingly at the young speaker, Jai Kakkar. He is a tall, handsome boy from Eshu's class and she remembers him from her last year in school as a skinny, stammering class six squirt. He's definitely licked the stammer, she thinks. Good for him.

The crowd cheers for Jai: he is clearly popular, and he looks earnest and well combed as he plunges into his argument with the usual quotations and self-consciously outrageous statements.

'They say power corrupts, absolute power corrupts absolutely... great men are almost always bad men. Our principal Mr Bakshi wields a great amount of power in this school. Is he then a bad man?'

I'll give him five on five for expression, Debjani decides as the students applaud this sally. But only two for content. I mean, he's totally mixed up and *very* stale.

But then Jai says something that makes her look up.

'Today's *India Post* tells us that Anandam Dhas, the only civil services officer to testify to Hardik Motla's infamous cancers speech, has been accused of embezzling and has been dishonourably discharged from service. He is to get no pension after thirty years of service and could even be imprisoned. The journalist who wrote this story, a Delhi boy called Dylan Shekhawat, is on a sticky wicket too, with MPs calling for his immediate sacking. Where then is the power in honesty?'

That bloody Eshu, Debjani thinks as her heart gives a lurch. She's been blabbing about me in school. Why else would Kakkar bring up Dylan in his debate? He's hardly *that* famous.

An hour later, the motion is sustained and Jai Kakkar ends up coming second overall. Eshwari and Debjani discuss the verdict as they walk home together.

'I can't believe the other judges loved that invertebrate,' Eshwari snorts. 'He hasn't stopped talking since he lost his stammer. He's even become some sort of stud. And he has no beliefs at *all*, you know, Dubz, he'd have argued just as passionately against the motion.'

'He'd make a good lawyer then,' Debjani points out. 'BJ would love him.'

'I'm glad I got to show you off in school, though,' Eshwari says, moving onto a more interesting topic. 'You're so famous! The English teachers go gaga over your diction and all the boys think you're hot.'

This is indeed the national opinion on Debjani. Her popularity has sky-rocketed over the last few months – she is recognized wherever she goes, her dentist on Pusa Road has stuck a picture of her wearing braces at fourteen in his shop window and a very famous star son has officially declared in *Stardust* that he is crushing on her.

My supta vastha really *is* over, Debjani thinks, giving her glossy waves of hair a complacent pat. Just then a shower of wet cement falls from the construction site at Number 13, peppering her thoroughly. Eshwari chuckles.

'I wish this stupid building would just hurry up and complete itself,' Debjani huffs. 'I'm sick of their hammering!'

She is also sick of her elder sisters' visits. They are both back, kids in tow, and are sitting around sipping tea when Eshu and she walk into the kitchen. Chachiji isn't there, mercifully.

'Ma, is it really true, what Chachiji keeps saying about Dadaji pushing Dadiji off the terrace?' Binni is asking. 'I thought she fell because it was dark.'

'What?' Mrs Mamta Thakur's head snaps around. 'What rubbish! Who told you that?'

Binni looks uneasy. 'Chachiji only. She said the Pushkarni was murdered by her husband after she had a big fight with him about selling off one more house.'

'That's nonsense, Binni,' Mrs Mamta says firmly.

But Binni is in full flow.

'And now Chachiji says she's haunting the construction site, spooking the labourers, causing accidents and delays, and she will never let the building be built.'

'All this wet cement fell on Dabbu just now,' Eshwari exclaims, hugely thrilled. 'You think that could be...?'

'*No,*' her mother snaps. 'And please don't repeat any of this in front of your father, girls. He'll get extremely upset.'

'He's *already* extremely upset,' Anji says gloomily. 'How long is he planning on sulking at Ashok chacha? It's so immature.'

'It's understandable,' Binni says with a sympathetic air. 'Life has been rough on him ever since he retired. First Chandu ran off, then Ashok chacha and he fought, then Balkishen Bau died, and then Dabbu caused a fight between him and his best friend.'

Debjani stays quiet – her father hasn't been talking to her of late.

'Maybe you should withdraw the case you've filed against him, Binni,' Anji says bluntly. 'That might cheer him up.'

But that Binni will not do. Vickyji needs the money from her hissa to consolidate his business. What she's asking for, she insists, is well within her rights. And that's that.

Everybody sips their tea.

'Let's go to the tailor,' Eshwari says suddenly. 'I've borrowed a really good sample from a friend of mine. They're Levi's – actual *Levi's*, imagine – with a skinny fit and a cinched-in waist. We'll get Amreek tailor of Up-To-Date boutique to rip it off in light blue denim for all of us!'

The borrowed Levi's jeans are tried on by everybody, and even though they sag on Debjani and strain on Binni, they decide that Amreek tailor will surely be able to adjust that much. A search is launched for the cranking handle and soon Anjini drives the old Ambassador to the buzzing tailoring block that is CP's Mohan Singh Place.

Inside Up-To-Date boutique, Amreek tailor himself greets them with a cordiality that borders on obsequiousness. As he is an extremely sought-after personage and actually has tattered posters of Farrah Fawcett and Brooke Shields to testify to his Up-To-Dateness upon his plywood walls, this is extremely gratifying.

'Kuch cold drink vaghera?' Amreek offers, smiling coyly at Debjani as he motions to a minion to turn the revolving ceiling fan towards her. 'Campa ya Frooti?'

Eshwari giggles. Anji, who has always been Amreek's muse amongst the Thakur sisters, looks surprised. Debjani shakes her head quickly. 'Oh, no. Bas, yeh sample hai, please will you copy it for us?'

Amreek accepts the Levi's from her outstretched hand. 'Amreekan hai,' he says knowledgably as he turns them inside out, pinching the rivets and fingering the double seams. 'Yes, I can do it. When your friends ask, say ki your jeans are also Amreekan.' He winks. 'Because *Amreek* tailor made them!'

Debjani laughs dutifully at this well-worn joke and allows him to slip his yellow measuring tape around her slim waist. He notes down the measurements quickly, discreetly covering his notations with one hand – too many slanging matches have started in his shop because the sisters sniggered at the size of one another's hips, waist or thighs.

Debjani sits down on a little revolving stool at the back of the shop and twirls on it idly. In front, Mrs Mamta and Amreek bicker about the delivery date for the jeans (*Diwali season hai, Bhabhiji, at least two weeks it will take!*). Suddenly she sees Juliet Bai, who has just entered the shop, bearing a bulging plastic bag.

Juliet Bai spots the Thakurs and utters a surprised squawk. For a moment it looks like she's about to turn tail and run out, but then she squares her shoulders and steps up with dignity.

'Hello, Mamta,' she says, and nods graciously at the gaggle of girls. 'How are you all?'

'We're well, thank you, Juliet,' Mrs Mamta replies with equal politeness. 'And all of you?'

'Fine.' Juliet Bai's voice is a little high. She puts her plastic bag down on Amreek's counter top. 'Alteration karana hai.'

Amreek nods majestically. 'When I am finished with these ladies, I will see to it, ji.'

'Of course, of course,' Juliet Bai says gracefully.

'What are you getting altered, aunty?' Anji asks.

'An old jacket of my husband's,' she replies. 'He's put on a little weight but he wants to wear it for our thirtieth anniversary party.'

There is an awkward silence as everybody recalls the last time Juliet Bai and the Brigadier's thirtieth wedding anniversary was discussed with them.

'And also some old shirts of the boys that I'm getting cut down to my size – I like to wear them when I'm painting.'

Debjani stares down at the plastic packet. It has *Vaz Bakery, Mangalore* emblazoned along one side. Some of the shirts inside could be Dylan's, she thinks with a weird, forlorn pang.

'What a clever idea,' Anji exclaims. 'I must do that with some of my husband's shirts!'

'I started doing it when I first got pregnant,' Juliet Bai confides and Anji's face falls.

Cow, thinks Debjani, not very fairly.

'He makes nice jeans,' Juliet Bai continues. 'My boys come here usually, but this year, as Dylan is travelling to Canada and all, Amreek here,' she turns to him and smiles, 'has lost out on some business!'

'Is he travelling on work?' Mrs Mamta asks politely.

Juliet Bai nods, her eyes shining with pride. 'For an interview,' she explains. 'Waise, you must have seen his articles in the *India Post*? With his byline? And photo also?'

They politely assure her that her firstborn has become world famous. Juliet Bai smiles a little uncertainly and says, 'We will be sending you the invitation for the thirtieth anniversary party, of course.' She looks Debjani straight in the eye. 'You *must* come.'

And so Debjani has to listen to Anjini and Eshwari eulogize about Dylan all the way home. They have clearly taken the sighting of Mrs Shekhawat as a licence to gush upon the hitherto taboo subject of her son.

'He's doing so well, just see! Travelling to Canada and all. He's like an avenging *crusader* fighting for... for whatever it is he's fighting for. It's that mouth that makes him so hot – what did his mother say that day? Notice the strongly corded neck, leading up to the jaw of a cowboy, to the mouth of an angel! Waise, I like his eyes too. Dabbu, I really think you overreacted about that stupid article, so what if he wrote it, he must have felt bad, no, that's why he coached you afterwards. Juliet aunty clearly still likes you. And you would have looked so pretty in church – in wispy cream lace, with lots of flowers. Not everyone can carry off cream, you know, Ma, but Dabbu can. Because she looks just like me.'

Mrs Mamta sighs. 'Girls, let's talk about something else. Why are you here again, Anji? And how's your goodness project going?'

Anji, who has no happy answers to give to any of these questions, promptly shuts up. But she has made her point.

'I wish I could lobotomize myself or something,' Debjani mutters to herself as she combs her hair agitatedly in her room that night. 'Cut out great fat chunks of my brain and just throw them away. I might forget all the GK I mugged up for the DD job, but at least I won't have these bloody *memories*.'

The comb snags upon a knot, jerking sudden, stinging tears out of her eyes.

But it was such a little kiss. Too little to count, surely. Maybe you imagined it?

She dashes her knuckles into her eyes savagely, blows her nose, banishes all thoughts of a blue checked handkerchief from her mind, pulls her Jaipuri razai over her head and goes determinedly to sleep.

⊷⊶◉⊷⊶

'You were aiming for three solid witnesses, weren't you?' Hira asks Dylan in the *IP* office in Ballard Estate. 'One civil services officer, one party worker and one common man? How's that going? You managed the officer but the poor sod's been totally discredited now. Do better with the other two, tiger.'

'Surely you haven't swallowed that trumped-up embezzlement charge?' Dylan swivels around in his office chair, dishevelled and stubbly, and stares at his boss out of grimy, reddened eyes. 'You know it's fake, right?'

The freshly washed, shaved and delicately scented Hiranandani looks down at his young protégé and sighs. 'When did you last go home to bathe and sleep?'

'He'll go,' Varun Ohri steps in hastily. 'He's got some stuff he's got to wrap up. And why should he doll up for us, anyway? We're not chicks.'

Dylan looks around, taking in the unlovely sight of the *IP* newsroom, full of paunchy, crumpled men drinking tea and eating batata vada. His eyes light up with genuine affection. 'You're better than chicks,' he says sincerely.

Everyone beams. Varun hands Dylan a steaming glass and a batata vada placed upon a greasy newspaper square. Dylan bites into it.

'Waise, you'll kill all of us, working so hard, behenchod,' Varun grumbles as Dylan chews. 'Take it a little easy.'

But Dylan can't help himself. The tapping of typewriter keys is the only sound that focuses him nowadays. He feels at peace only when the words are leaping out of his fingers in a white heat, marching in orderly black rows across the screen, spilling onto the edit page and creating havoc in the body politic.

'You've got everybody all stirred up,' Hira tries to explain to him. 'People are clamouring for something to be *done*. We need to get all three witnesses out there – boldly saying stuff that can put Motla and gang into prison – or the readers will turn against us.'

'You didn't answer my question,' Dylan says thickly to Hira through a mouthful of batata vada. 'You know the embezzlement charges are fixed, right?'

'Immaterial,' Hira replies lightly. 'This paper is interested in getting Motla his just desserts. Anandam Dhas's charges won't stick. So, what's your plan?'

'You *know*,' says Dylan, stretching out in his chair, 'that ex-party worker in Canada. He's promised complete disclosure.'

'Good,' Hira says. 'Let's hope he doesn't do a bunk on you too, like so many others have. And what about the third witness? Somebody who actually lived in Tirathpuri, and was there that night?'

'I'm working on it.' Dylan crumples up the greasy newspaper and chucks it into a bin across the room. 'I've sent out feelers all over Tirathpuri. They know I'm sympathetic. Somebody will bite.'

Hira nods. 'Okay, go get the interview. And get a little R&R too. The ladies are complaining that you're starting to lose your looks – and you know that's the only reason we keep you around.'

Dylan grins, not looking too worried about this feedback. He knows he blotted his copybook with the *IP* girls last Saturday night, when he took the prettiest one of them to the International

Film Festival of India, made her sit through two rather sordid films – one Iranian, one Korean – and dropped her home, unloved and mystified, five hours later.

'Fine.' He gets to his feet. 'I got all that. Now will the two of you stop clucking over me like a pair of maiden aunts?'

'We used voting lists to figure out where the Sikhs lived. Hardik Motla gave us kerosene and iron rods.'

The government of India has famously stated that 'when a giant tree falls, the earth shakes'. But Kailash Tomar, an ex-party worker now settled in Canada and working in a gurudwara to 'atone for his sins', remembers those three dark days following the death of the then PM rather differently.

'The news broke on AIR first, that it was Sardars who had murdered the PM. It made us very angry, because we loved her like a mother. Then we heard that Sardar families were distributing sweets and dancing to celebrate her death. That made me furious. But my wife said, let it go, jaane do, what can you do now? So I just prayed for my leader's soul, wept and went to sleep.'

'But later that night, the bulawa came. We were picked up in jeeps and driven to the residence of our leader, Motla saab. He was heartbroken too – his kurta was torn, his hair uncombed, there were tears spilling from his eyes. He came to the front gate and addressed us. There were no mics, but we could hear him clearly. He said, 'An eye for an eye – a life for a life.' He repeated it two-three times, louder and louder, till everybody became quiet. Then he said, 'Here are the voting lists for my whole constituency. It will help you track down every single Sikh family – find them and make them wish they had never been born.'

As his people handed out bottles of liquor and jerry cans of kerosene, we took up the chant: *Blood for Blood! A Life for a Life!* They distributed hockey sticks and iron rods too. Then we got back into our jeeps and, drinking and chanting, drove down to the trans-Yamuna area. The Sikh colony of Tirathpuri was very quiet, too quiet. They were hiding, of course, by then they knew we were coming and that we would seek them out.

Rest all what to tell you, saab, it was like there was a fever upon us. I did things that night that I never want to think of again. I became a demon, a haivaan. Men, women, children, old people, I spared no one. My shirt was soaked in blood, petrol and alcohol. We had been told that the army would be called the next day, so when the sky grew lighter, we got back into our jeeps and drove away. When I got home I just slunk quietly into my bed and slept for two days. My wife said nothing.

Nobody came looking for me later. Nobody at all. Motla saab kept his promise.

But Karma came looking. Karma took away my son, he was only ten years old – he got polio and died. My daughter died in her husband's home in a kitchen fire. My wife got sick at heart. She only lies in bed and stares.

And so now, to seek forgiveness for my sins, I clean the shoes of devotees in this gurudwara. None of the people here knows what I have done in India. If they find out, god knows what they will do to me. But even that I am willing to face.

You can print my name, photo, everything. I hope, once I have done this, Karma will release its hold on my wife and she will become well.

DSS

⋯⋯⋯

'Hey, who's that downstairs in the *schwoonng-schwoonng* car?' asks a gangly intern, leaning out of the window of the *India Post* office in Ballard Estate. 'Looks like a big shot. Do you think he's coming up here?'

Nobody replies. The intern scoops up his table tennis ball and goes back to his game, while downstairs, the door of the gleaming white Ambassador slams shut, seemingly extinguishing the swirling red and blue VIP light. Guards armed with walkie-talkies race ahead deferentially and commandeer the rattling elevator. Two minutes later, Hardik Motla glides out onto the second floor, steely smile well in place, a rolled up *India Post* in his hand, passes through the double glass doors emblazoned *Truth. Balance. Courage.* and endeavours to make eye contact with the thin Parsi receptionist.

'I want to meet Shri Purshottam Ohri.'

'Bade-papaji doesn't sit in office any more,' she replies, her carrying, high-pitched voice dismissive.

Motla's smile doesn't falter. 'Then, that...' His long thin fingers twitch and snatch a name out of the air. 'That Hiranandani chap will do.'

'Do you have an appointment? Ya aise hi?'

He smiles even wider and starts to reply, but before he can, the phone on her desk rings. She picks it up.

'Is that Hardik Motla?' Hira asks gleefully.

'I don't know.' The receptionist looks the man standing before her up and down dubiously. Then she cocks one deep purple-tipped finger at him. 'You are Molta?'

'Motla,' he corrects her.

'He's *saying* he is,' the receptionist reports back to Hira, her voice redolent of doubt.

'Send him in!' Hira's voice practically purrs down the line. 'I haven't had lunch yet. What happy happenstance!'

The receptionist puts down the phone.

'You can go, Mr Minolta,' she says, managing somehow to convey the impression that he has barely made it in by the skin of his teeth. 'Just walk right down the corridor. It's the last door...'

Dylan is playing carrom with the guys in the production room when he is summoned to Hira's room half an hour later. He strides in, a little wary. Word has got around that Motla is in the office.

'You wanted to see me, Hira?' he asks in his deep, pleasant voice.

'Come, come, Dylan,' Hira says hospitably. 'Mr Motla was asking for you.'

Dylan crosses his arms across his chest and nods. 'Hello.'

Motla, sitting next to Varun Ohri on Hira's low sofa and thus at a slight height disadvantage, puts down his Shiv Sagar mausambi juice glass and gives Dylan the full blast of his creepy rictus.

'Mr Motla had some questions,' Hira says, assuming a sombre expression. 'He was wondering how, um, reliable our sources are. How accurate.'

Dylan glances briefly at Motla, and back at Hira.

'Just our sources, generally? Or...?'

Hira's eyes seem to twinkle. But his voice is very grave.

'Specifically, he's anxious to know about those two interviews you conducted. In response to his, er, suggestion, shall we say.'

'Well, he is uniquely placed to vouch for them,' Dylan says lightly. 'He can judge their accuracy better than anybody else in this room, surely?'

Motla's smile grows a little fixed, but he ignores this jab.

'That's just it,' Varun comes in smoothly. 'He says they're, er, rubbish.'

'The sign on the door says *Balance*,' Motla smiles persuasively at Dylan. 'But your stories are unbalanced. Why don't you ever print *my* side of things?'

'Because...' Varun begins.

'Print it now.' Motla smiles inexorably. 'Explain how that IAS fellow is an embezzler and a liar. And this poor chap from Canada, I did not want to make this public because it is so sad, but the truth is that the deaths of his children have driven him mad. His mind has become completely... what is that word? It has become...'

'Unbalanced,' Hira supplies, his eyes twinkling quite openly now. 'Like our stories.'

Motla eyes him suspiciously.

'That's right,' he says grudgingly.

Dylan realizes that everybody is looking expectantly at him.

'What?'

Varun Ohri mops his forehead.

'I'm sorry, I must be very stupid,' Dylan continues, his voice carefully neutral, 'but I don't understand what you want. What *do* you want?'

'I want you to leave me alone,' hisses Motla. 'I have been given a clean chit by the Special Investigation Commission – you cannot put me on trial again in your newspaper like this.'

'Or?' Hira prompts.

'Or...' Motla spreads out his hands. His smile grows even more distressed. 'Or things will get nasty. Licences may be revoked. And your paper may have to be shut down.'

Whoa, this cat doesn't pull his punches, Dylan thinks. Talk about unsubtle.

'Try to understand,' Motla continues. 'Outside forces are trying to destabilize our country, weaken it from within. They would love to see us fail. And so, putting doubts in the minds of loyal citizens, making them suspicious of senior leaders like myself – that is an irresponsible and unpatriotic act.'

What crap, Dylan thinks, disgusted. But I should check out the insanity angle on that guy from Canada, see if it has any factual basis.

'And I did not expect this from you, Shri Hiranandani,' Motla continues smoothly. 'You are, after all, a friend of the PM. Have you no consideration for his party?'

Hira gets to his feet and draws himself up to his full height.

'This newspaper does not compromise, Mr Motla,' he says loftily. 'We print the truth, wherever we find it, no matter who it incriminates – and we suffer the consequences without flinching.'

Silence.

'Well, it's a free country.' Motla smiles, getting to his feet too. 'I had just hoped you would see things from my point of view. But it is all right. The juice is sour, by the way, so I apologize for not finishing it. Goodbye!'

He glides out of the room, teeth still bared in that death-defeating smile, leaving them staring after him in stunned silence. Presently, the *schwoonng-schwoonng* of his VIP siren floats up to their ears.

Hiranandani gives a crow of delight. 'Wasn't that fun! *That's* why I left England to work in Bombay. Sleazy politicians storming into my office, cajoling and threatening, giving me the chance to look heroic and act incorruptible. Thanks for giving me this opportunity to make such a noble, my-paper-is-not-for-sale speech, tiger. Now go out and keep writing your soul-stirring, shit-stirring little pieces. Fancy going out for lunch, VO? How about we hit Copper Chimney?'

'I'm not hungry,' Varun replies weakly.

Dylan pauses awkwardly by the door. 'Hira. Thanks.'

'All in a day's work.' Hiranandani makes a dismissive gesture. 'I never could stand that philistine. He studied in a kendriya vidyalaya, you know, an actual *kendriya vidyalaya*. Can you credit it?'

'That's really not the poin –' Dylan starts to say but Hira has already put on his spiffy little jacket and is heading out of the door.

'Just get me one last eyewitness now, Dylan baby,' he sings out as he exits, 'and we'll nail the Motla.'

<hr />

'Can't we take a holiday?' the Judge asks his wife wistfully in their bedroom one morning, as the winter sun coaxes the harshringar tree into blossom outside. 'Just you and me. We'll run away for a week – go to Gulmarg, ride those little tattu horses, hire fur coats and eat cherry buns.'

'Those cherries always get stuck in my teeth,' Mrs Mamta replies as she combs her rippling hair.

'And make a little F for Falguni,' he continues. 'How about *that*, huh, Mamtaji?'

She laughs. 'I'm fifty-six years old, LN!'

'I want to make you happy,' he says restlessly. 'There was a time when I could. Now you want things I can't give – like happy marriages for your daughters and babies for Anji and god alone knows what else.'

'I don't want anything,' she replies, giving his hand a squeeze. 'Don't stress, LN. What's got into you?'

'This mess with Dabbu, I suppose,' the Judge says gloomily. 'And the not talking to Ashok, and the constant thuk-thuk and dust and drilling going on next door. When will that wretched building be completed?'

According to Chachiji, the answer is never. She is convinced that the Pushkarni will never let a building block – gracious looking though it is, and rich with plaster of Paris detailing and many curlicues and pillars – replace the old bungalow where she lived and died.

'She haunts it,' she tells the wide-eyed children, who hang on to her every word, in the drawing room late at night. 'She walks there after midnight. You know that labourer who fell off the scaffolding and broke his leg last week? She pushed him. And she's going to push many, many more.'

'How do you know?' Samar asks her in a hushed whisper, even though he knows the answer.

Chachiji strokes his hair off his forehead and gives the weirdest little cackle.

'Because she told me,' she says. 'She comes upon me sometimes, you know. She gets into my body and suddenly I crave food I don't like, and sing songs I've never heard, and know things that haven't happened yet.'

Monu takes his thumb out of his mouth.

'Do you know what questions will come in the class two final exam?'

Chachiji nods nonchalantly. 'Ya, of course. Just bring me the books, I'll close my eyes, invite the Pushkarni into me, and she'll tick the questions you need to study.'

The twins are thrilled. Samar, however, is concerned that the old lady is losing it.

'I think you should move with the times,' he counsels her sleepily. 'Anji-ma says a small flat will be easier for you to keep clean, one desert cooler will be enough to keep it cool, and you'll have so many nice new neighbours to play with!'

Chachiji sniffs. Ashok Narayan has been singing the praises of the new flat too, rabbiting on about Italian marble and built-in teak woodwork and fancy bathroom fixtures. But Chachiji would rather squat over an Indian-style potty in a bungalow than perch elegantly upon an English-style WC in a matchbox-sized flat.

'Over my dead body,' she tells Samar fiercely. 'I'll never step foot in that tiny flat! A.N. Thakur can just move in there alone and hire a cook to cook for him!' She shoves the hapless Samar's head hard into his pillow. 'Go to sleep now!'

Mrs Mamta, petrified that she may have Chachiji living in her annexe forever, starts to extol the many virtues of the flats every day. Anjini and Eshwari go over to scout around and come back with glowing reports of the genuine teak shelving in the kitchen and the dazzling light that comes in through the French windows. Chachiji takes in all this rhapsodizing quietly, an inscrutable expression on her bulldog face. And one week later, when Samar rushes into the annexe to tell her that his kite has got cut over the construction site and the workers are refusing to hand it back to him, she gets to her feet and announces abruptly that she will go over and retrieve it.

When she returns, a whole hour later, she is head over heels in love with 'Hailey Court', which is the proposed name of the building complex. She stumps into Mrs Mamta's kitchen, asks for a cup of tea and starts to list the many glorious features of her new home.

'The floor is like mirror! The doors are white! There's a slit in the front door for letters, can you imagine? The servants' quarter is bigger than our old master bedroom! And the kitchen sink is made of *steel* – actual stainless steel – I saw the sticker, it says twenty-year guarantee!'

'So lucky,' Mrs Mamta murmurs, sliding a cup of piping hot, sweet tea across the table. '*My* sink is old and cracked and made of cement, I have to clean it with a toothbrush every day...'

And so Chachiji starts to believe that the social ignominy of having to sell the family home can perhaps be lived down, and that she may have landed on her feet after all. She perks up enough to go over every day and watch the labourers as they do the 'finishing' at Hailey Court. Many a skinny brown construction worker, clad in vest and striped underwear, whistling to the music on his transistor, has looked up to find Chachiji's beady gaze fixed upon him. 'Properly do, you!' she says sternly. 'You missed a spot there. See, the marble isn't sparkling as it should.'

The Judge and Mrs Mamta start to hope that the A.N. Thakurs will be out of their annexe in two months' time.

'And about time too,' says the Judge in the privacy of his bedroom. 'Why is that Eshwari always stuck to the phone nowadays, Mamtaji? Doesn't she get enough time to chat with her girlfriends in school?'

'It's boys, LN,' his wife replies. 'Though, of course, it's always a girl when I pick up the phone. *Aunty, can I talk to Eshu please?* And right after saying that, they hand the phone over to their brother. I can't believe they think I don't know. I wasn't born yesterday.'

'Why don't you stop it, then?' the Judge demands.

Mrs Mamta shrugs. 'Eshu is a sensible girl.'

The Judge doesn't reply, but privately he decides to 'take Eshwari in hand'.

The next morning, an article on the science page of the *India Post* catches his eye. He reads out the headline.

'Sex during the teenage years can make you stupid and depressed.'
Eshu blinks and puts down her cornflakes spoon. 'What?'

'A study was conducted on 800 hamsters,' her father continues matter-of-factly. 'Where forty-day-old male hamsters (equivalent in age to human teenagers) were made to mate with adult female hamsters in heat. After mating, when put into a pool of water, the hamsters showed no inclination to swim vigorously, which is a sign of depression. The dendrites of their brain showed less complexity too. The hamsters that did not have sex, however, swam vigorously in the water and had very complex dendrites.' He looks up at Eshwari meaningfully. 'See!'

'See what?' she demands.

'You know what!' He frowns intimidatingly.

Eshwari sighs. 'BJ, you're being gross. And what kind of sickos carry out these experiments, anyway? Sitting around in lab coats, egging on hamsters to copulate – I mean, get a life, right?'

'That is not the point. The point is –'

'I *got* the point, BJ.' Eshwari rolls her eyes. 'And I'm a really vigorous swimmer. I even have some Delhi state swimming medals. Why don't you trust me?'

'Oh, he trusts you,' says Mrs Mamta moving in smoothly to sit at her husband's side. 'He was just reading this article aloud because... because we should all read the news and be aware of what's happening around us, no, Dabbu?'

'Hmm?' Debjani, who has been staring vacantly into space, says blankly.

'Nothing,' Mrs Mamta sighs. 'Where are you off to, Eshwari? It's Saturday.'

'Interact Club work,' she replies. 'Bye, you guys.'

The Judge frowns. 'You're always going out,' he says austerely. 'Something or the other all the time. Basketball, Western music, Interact...'

But Eshwari is already out of the room and in the corridor.

The room suddenly feels very silent. The Judge still isn't speaking to Debjani.

'And you, Dabbu?' her mother asks. 'What are *you* doing today, beta?'

But before Debjani can reply, Eshwari sticks her head back into the room. 'Oh, BJ, Old Mr Gambhir said to tell you that his phone bill has come. He said you would understand.'

'Oh... ah!' the Judge nods. 'Fine, I'll, um, talk to him about it. You better hurry, Eshu.'

'Okay. Bye!'

Mrs Mamta turns back to Debjani. 'Well?'

'Oh, nothing much.' She shrugs. 'I've already read the news twice this week, so I'm free. If you guys are done with that newspaper, can I have it?'

'Why don't you get a job, Dabbu?' Mrs Mamta asks gently.

'I don't need it,' she points out, sensibly enough. 'I'm making 4,000 a month just reading the news. It's more than enough. And I do voiceover work. Besides, I don't feel like going anywhere nowadays.'

'It's not right to cut yourself off from the world like this,' her mother says worriedly.

'I'm not cut off,' she replies shortly. 'Just give me the newspaper.'

'There are some interesting news articles in there nowadays,' the Judge says to the teapot.

'Don't I know it?' Debjani addresses the fruit bowl. 'Old Mr

Gambhir shakes them under my nose every time I go there to buy even a Rin ki tikia. He clearly thinks Dylan Shekhawat is some kind of hero. He'd award him with an honorary Sikh turban if he could.'

'Really?' her father grunts, still talking to the teapot. 'And what do *you* think?'

'I think it's disgusting that even the kirana shop owner knows what goes on inside our drawing room!' she flares up. 'Gossiping is rampant up and down this road. It's ridiculous!'

Mrs Mamta hurriedly hands her the newspaper and starts to sift through her mail. Debjani pursues the headlines. Presently, Mrs Mamta gives a low exclamation. Debjani and the Judge both look up.

'I'm sure Old Mr Gambhir doesn't know about *this*,' Mrs Mamta says, producing an elegant cream and gold envelope and placing it on the dining table. 'At least not yet.'

Debjani picks up the envelope, addressed in neat type to *Justice Laxmi Narayan Thakur, Mrs Mamta Thakur and Fly*. She opens it and slides out a pale gold card with cream lettering, upon which is painted a single white champa flower.

A Mangalorean lass and a Rajput knight
Eloped one day on an Enfield bike
There was no celebration
Which is an abomination
Thirty years later, please help us put that right!

'It's the invite,' Debjani says unnecessarily, suddenly feeling like she's about to burst into tears. 'It's on Friday the twenty-seventh. And it's not just for you and BJ, Ma. The envelope says *and Fly*.'

'Will you step into my parlour, said the spider to the fly,' the Judge murmurs, only half whimsically. Then he nods at the teapot. 'So, do you want to go?'

'Call for you on line two, darling!' The high-pitched voice of the thin Parsi receptionist pierces through glass and wood partitions alike, reverberating through the office. 'Pick it up!'

Dylan immediately stops his frenetic typing and reaches for the phone. Varun Ohri looks up.

'How do you know she was talking to you, bastard?' he demands aggrievedly. 'You're the only darling in office or what?'

Dylan grins, motioning for him to be quiet. 'Yes, hello... speaking.' His expression changes, becomes intent. 'Yes, ma'am, this is the real Dylan Singh Shekhawat. You're calling from? Delhi! No no no, actually that happens to be perfect – I'm travelling to Delhi tomorrow.'

Varun, intrigued by the edge of excitement that has crept into Dylan's voice, listens in shamelessly.

'Day after tomorrow, one o'clock. At the United Coffee House in CP. Yes, I know it. I'll be there.'

He puts down the phone and turns to Varun. His eyes are blazing.

'This could be it! She's twenty-two – which makes her eighteen during the time of the riots – an adult witness. And a genuine resident of Tirathpuri! She lived in Block 32 she says, Room Number 12. My god, I know that room! It's on the first floor, right above the area where the rioting was thickest. She saw everything but her father wouldn't let her testify before the SIC.

But he just died – so she can come clean. She'll speak only to me, she says. I have a good feeling about this, VO!'

'Good for you,' Varun responds. 'Though she sounds a bit of a cold-blooded little cow calling you before her father's ashes have even cooled. Did she talk about money?'

Dylan shakes his head. 'No, but she's the real deal, I can tell!'

'Whatever,' Varun grunts. 'Just be careful. Hira might have acted all chilled out when Motla paid us his flying visit, but there's pressure from marketing to close down your little party. So keep the mess-making sanitary, okay?'

'Okay, okay.' Dylan nods vigorously. 'I'll be meeting her in the afternoon at a public place. She said she's thin and fair, with long hair.'

'Sounds promising.' Varun's voice is sour. 'Have fun, darling.'

10

Dylan has the strangest sense of déjà vu when he enters United Coffee House. There is an all pervading smell of sambar and masala dosai, but he's suddenly back in Berco's Chinese restaurant, face to face with the questionable Sardar. Think positive, he mutters to himself, and notices a thin girl in a floral salwar kameez eyeing him furtively. He walks up to her.

'Hello, I'm Dylan. Are you Kamaljeet?'

'Preet,' she corrects him. 'Kamalpreet. Yes, I am she.'

She has a clear, sweet voice. Dylan pulls up a chair, sits down next to her and quickly switches languages.

'You've come alone, Kamalpreet?' he asks her in Hindi.

She nods, looking at him out of huge, brandy-coloured eyes, rimmed with fine, pale lashes. She is thin, too thin. He wants to squeeze her hand, tell her everything will be all right and feed her a good nourishing meal.

'My condolences for your father's death. I trust everybody at home is coping well?'

Kamalpreet's chin starts to wobble alarmingly. Her eyes well up and she lets out a convulsive little sob. People at the other tables stare at Dylan accusingly.

He flushes and reaches into his jacket and drops a clean handkerchief onto the table.

'Here,' he says awkwardly. 'We can do this later, you know. There's no hurry.'

'Oh, yes there *is*,' she says fiercely, her huge eyes burning in her tiny bit of face. 'I've been wanting to say this out loud for years. Have you got a pen?'

'I've got a cassette recorder,' Dylan says. 'But don't you want to eat something first?'

Kamalpreet shakes her head. A lock of curly brown hair escapes her guth and falls on her forehead. 'No!' she says vehemently, twisting his handkerchief between her fair, bony fingers. Then, realizing she's being rude, she adds in careful English, 'Thank you, but I am not hungry.'

Dylan's heart turns over. He says lightly, 'Here, take my card. You should check that I am who I claim to be, you know. What if I'm not?'

She smiles at him. 'Oh, I know ki you are Dhillon only,' she says confidingly. 'Aapki picture dekhi hai na, paper mein.'

He looks at her warmly. 'You're being very brave doing this. Does your mother know?' He sounds absurdly like an Abba song, he thinks irrelevantly.

'Mummy toh wahin khatam ho gayee thi ji,' she replies matter-of-factly. 'She died in the rioting only. Myself all alone.'

He frowns. 'You might get a lot of attention after the story breaks. Unwanted attention. Where will you go? Have you got anything planned?'

She squares her thin shoulders. 'You don't worry about all that, Dhillonji,' she tells him, almost comfortingly. 'You just take your recording.'

He nods, privately resolving to keep an eye on her for a while in case the story starts to spiral out of control. 'I'll just order my coffee and then you can start talking. It's okay to record you, right?'

Kamalpreet nods. Her brandy-brown eyes grow huge as he loads a new cassette into the recorder. She sits up straight and pulls her chair in a little closer.

'Should I pick it up?' she asks, reaching eagerly for the gadget.

'Just let it lie there between us,' he says quickly. 'And now it's... *on.*'

English transcription of the conversation between Dylan Singh Shekhawat and Sardarni Kamalpreet Kaur

DSS: You are Kamalpreet Kaur?

KK: Lai, I just now told you that!

DSS: Answer yes or no, please.

KK: Yes.

DSS: Erstwhile resident of Room Number 12 of Block 32, Tirathpuri?

KK: Yes.

DSS: And you were present in this house on the entire night of 1 November 1984?

KK (muttering): I already told all this, why is he asking everything two-two times?

DSS (patiently): I have to, Kamalpreet, this is the proper official way.

KK (slightly mollified): All right.

DSS: So, can you tell me, in your own words, what happened that night?

Pause.

DSS (gently): Kamalpreet?

KK (in a tightly wound up voice, that seems to belong to a

much younger girl): Mummy-Papa were scared. Very scared.
They locked up the door, put off the lights and turned on
the radio. We listened very softly to All India Radio.

AIR was reporting from the funeral of the PM. Who-
who had come. What-what they were saying. People
were singing holy songs. There were crowds at the funeral
chanting *Blood for Blood! A Life for a Life!*

Suddenly, shouts and cries came from outside our
house. Papa rolled me up inside a mattress and carried
me out to the balcony and dumped me down with the
other mattresses. I was very thin in those days, na.

Pause.

DSS (teasingly): You're still very thin. What happened
then?

KK: Jeeps. Full of men with fire torches and sticks. They
stopped in the chauraha – the crossroad below our room
– started banging on the doors, cursing all Sardars and
telling them to come out.

They banged on our door, broke it down... Mummy
ko worry thi ki they would find me, so she ran out,
without her dupatta, I think-so to distract them... She
was a beautiful woman, my mummy.

Pause.

DSS: Then?

KK: I never saw her again, though we searched and searched
all the hospitals, all the rubbish heaps, and later, all the mass
graves. Papa remained hidden in the cupboard... He got
scared, I think-so... He saved himself, but since that day he
was just... broken inside.

Pause.

DSS (very gently): Kamalpreet, think and answer – could
you recognize any of these men if you saw them now?
Have you ever seen any of them again?

KK (voice chattering slightly): I can recognize the man who was in the first jeep, the leader. In a black kurta and jeans. He had a fire torch in his hand and he kept shouting, Reward! Reward! Whoever kills the most Sardars will get a reward! He is always on TV now, wearing white. My father just sat down and died when he heard he had been clean-chitted.

Sobbing.

DSS (gently): Would you like us to stop?

Sound of nose being blown vigorously, followed by sniffing.

KK: But maybe it's good that he died, because I am freed from the promise I made to him, and can now testify against this man.

DSS: Who is this man, Kamalpreet?

Pause.

KK (very quietly and clearly): That madarchod Hardik Motla. Murderer. Khooni. I'll never forgive him. God will never forgive him. He'll go to hell, you'll see. Rats will eat his eyes.

Long pause. Just the humming of the tape rolling.

KK (with a little tinkling laugh): Aur lo ji, here is your coffee. Lai, are you going to drink it without any milk or sugar? Isn't it kauda?

DSS: I like it kauda. No no, it's okay, you can keep that handkerchief.

<hr />

'You've got that smitten look again,' Ethan tells his brother as they lean against the bar in the Jasmine Garden at the Gymkhana Club. 'Who have you met *today*?'

'Shut up, rat,' Dylan says lazily. He is feeling quite at peace with the world. He has sent off the transcript of the Kamalpreet

Kaur interview to Bombay and reached the club well in time for the party. 'And straighten your tie. Have you been scraping your pimples again? You've got all these red scabs on your face.'

Ethan, looking rather dapper in his very first suit (Jason's, altered by Amreek tailor to his height and skinniness), pulls a face. 'Probably an allergic reaction to meeting all the Rics from Balmatta, Mangalore.' He grimaces. 'Can you believe they've *all* shown up?'

Dylan grins. 'Cedric, Ulrich, Derek, Eric, Patrick, Scooter Rick and Auto Rick?'

Ethan nods. 'The seven sons of Prick. Not to mention their lovely sisters Cecilia, Camellia and Cordelia, the daughters of Genitalia.'

'Lord, it's a circus, isn't it?' Dylan says, not without pride, as he looks around and sees how very full the Jasmine Garden is. Fairy lights twinkle in the neem trees, lending an intimate air to the gathering of over 300 people. The old wooden dance floor, highly polished and sprinkled lightly with talcum powder, glitters like a sugar-dusted chocolate brownie begging to be bitten into. The bearers, smart in their white, silver-buttoned uniforms, eye the frisky crowd, pick up their trays and throw back their shoulders, like soldiers readying for war. 'I never thought *everybody* we invited would show up.'

But everybody has. The Mangaloreans, thrilled that the party is in October, when the weather in Delhi is actually pleasant, booked an entire bogey on the Konkan–Delhi express and have turned up in full strength, bearing kilos of frozen shrimp, shellfish, baangday, taarlay and koobays packed in ice-boxes as gifts. The prettiest Mangy daughters have arrived with their mammas, eager to interact with the handsome Shekhawat boys who, despite the Rajput taint, are still a prized matrimonial catch. The only problem, the mothers say darkly, is *catching* them. Still, it can't be denied that they know how to make a girl feel both weightless and adored on the dance floor.

The Rajus are here in full strength too. Most of them have driven down in jeeps from Jodhpur, Jaipur and Mount Abu, and arrived with their handlebar moustaches windblown and flashing eyes red-rimmed, carelessly crumpling the numerous challans they've picked up along the way, shouting for garma-garam tea and double-fried eggs even before they have got out of their vehicles. Their wives, bright and bovine in their crushed, floor-sweeping georgette poshaaks, hurry to comply, all the while cracking lewd jokes at their husbands' expense.

There has been a perfunctory puja in the morning and an emotionally charged church ceremony at five in the evening. And now, Brigadier Shekhawat's old Commanding Officer, dug out from his soggy, rundown estate in Coorg, is about to raise a toast to Saahas and Juliet. After this the party (and the bar) will officially be declared open.

'The Lobster looks lovely,' Ethan says, rather pleased with himself for noticing this. 'I rather like that butter chicken sari.'

The sari has been named thus as it is soft, butter-coloured mul mul, thick with cream chikan embroidery. Juliet Bai has teamed it with tiny white pearls around her still slim throat and wrists. A riot of champa flowers cascade down the bridal bouquet in her arms, teamed with feathery fern. Her cheeks are as flushed as a young bride's.

'Well, I hope she's happy,' Dylan says. 'If I hear the words champa and champagne one more time, I might go stark, staring mad.'

Juliet Bai, deprived of a wedding, has turned the full force of her artistic genius into the planning of this party. 'I was saving champa and champagne as a theme for *you*,' she had told Dylan bitterly, 'but as that won't happen till our Prime Minister takes us into the twenty-first century, I might as well use it for Saahas and me.'

And so at the centre of each of the circular tables swathed in lace tablecloths is an empty champagne bottle holding a bunch of white champa flowers with a sprinkling of fern foliage. The labels of the bottles have been peeled off painstakingly and replaced with antique cream labels upon which Juliet Bai has handpainted, in beautiful golden calligraphy, *Saahas & Juliet 1958*. The Rajput contingent, used to bright pinks and vibrant oranges, doesn't quite know what to make of this pale showing and hopes the champagne theme doesn't mean the bar won't be serving Black Label. As for the old Mangalorean ladies, they whisper that that Juliet was always crack, running away with a Rajput and painting her own living room walls, and remember how she turned up her nose at the decorations at Prince Charles' and Lady Diana's wedding? Naturally, roses and lilies and chrysanthemums must have seemed too boring to her – or *maybe*, they add snidely, they were too expensive. Must have got her trio of rowdy boys to swarm up trees and pluck the champas. And the bottles must be from the kabadiwallah only.

But Juliet Bai doesn't care. The decorations have turned out exactly as she visualized them, and her artistic soul is quite satisfied. If only, she thinks, her lower lip trembling imperceptibly, the labels could have read *Dylan & Debjani* instead.

As everybody shuffles ahead to stand around the dance floor for the speeches, Dylan's great-grandaunt Philomina Bai, who is seated in a place of honour next to the Brigadier's mother, points at somebody with her quavering finger.

'Who is that plump pigeon, ba?'

Dylan turns to see.

The taloned finger is pointed unerringly at Jason's simpering girlfriend. She is hovering around the trolley bearing the beautifully iced thirtieth anniversary cake, proprietarily holding a matchbox.

'Why?' Dylan counters.

'Don't you backtalk me,' the old lady snaps. 'She's trying to smarm up to us, that's why. Rubbed off all my rouge with her kisses and then dived so hard for your Dadi-sa's feet that we thought she'd dropped dead of a stroke.'

'It's nobody, Aunty Philo.'

The old lady snorts.

'Nobody who is hoping to become somebody, obviously. And I think her blouse is padded. That body type is always flat-chested with a big, jiggling bum.'

'Maneater,' says Dadi-sa hoarsely, her kohled eyes snapping in her hawk-like face. 'He's a fool. Who is taller – you or him?'

'He's the tallest, Dadi-sa,' Dylan replies, hoping this will make the old ladies more favourably disposed to the luckless Jason. 'Six feet four.'

'And therefore the stupidest,' Dadi-sa pronounces. 'The tallest boys are *always* the stupidest – the blood doesn't reach their brains, you know.'

'Only their balls,' Philomina Bai agrees.

Dylan doesn't quite know what to say to this.

The two old ladies regard him beady dissatisfaction.

'What?' he says uneasily.

'Where's *your* girl?' Philomina Bai barks. 'That pretty newsreader? Or was that just some story your mother made up?'

'I don't have any girl,' Dylan replies shortly.

'Just *many* many girls?' Dadi-sa sniffs. 'It's your Christian upbringing, I suppose. You've grown up surrounded by loose-charactered Anglo-Indians.'

'We *aren't* Anglo-Indians!' Philomina Bai retorts, grossly insulted. 'We're very high caste Brahmins –'

'Nothing wrong with Anglo-Indians,' Dylan puts in fair-mindedly.

'We're *Brahmins,*' Philomina Bai continues hotly, taking no notice of this mild interjection, 'who were ex-communicated 200 years ago for eating fish! And *you* shouldn't talk. I watch Hindi movies – I know Rajputs are always driving about in jeeps looking for village girls to rape.'

Dylan is rendered speechless. But Dadi-sa has no such problem.

'And have you seen *Julie*?' she asks sweetly. 'Waise, what a coincidence ki baat – Julie sounds just like Juliet, na?'

Dylan, thoroughly alarmed at the direction this conversation is taking, is relieved to see that the Colonel from Coorg has finally located his speech. Leaving the sparring matriarchs behind, he strides over to the mics and taps on one for silence. Philomina Bai and Dadi-sa have no choice but to lower the fingers they're waggling under each other's noses and subside.

'Good evening, everybody,' Dylan says, his deep voice lazily pleasant. 'Thank you so much for coming, bearing gifts and looking so glamorous for our parents' thirtieth anniversary celebrations. This is a big day for the Lobo-Shekhawats and we're delighted to share it with you...'

Why does he have to sound so *nice*? Dabbu, cowering behind her parents, thinks despairingly. And look so handsome? I don't remember him being *so* handsome. It isn't fair.

She is standing with Anjini, who has nobly restrained her lovely hair into a tight bun and swathed herself in a large brown dupatta so Dabbu can 'shine'. But maybe I should just open my hair and lose the dupatta, she thinks, looking at her little sister with satisfaction, because she's shining *anyway*.

Shining and pining is how Dabbu would put it. The situation, she thinks, drinking in the sight of Dylan Singh Shekhawat in his dark suit, cream shirt and striped tie, is as bad as ever. Thank god the Butt is hidden beneath the jacket. The sight of it encased in those fitted dark trousers might have made her weep. His hair is longer, curling crisply at the edge of his collar. It makes his jaw look stronger somehow. And she doesn't even want to get into the extremely sexy way in which his lips are almost grazing the mic. She watches as the crowd heckles him good-naturedly, demanding he sing, and when he demurs, asking when he's getting married and giving Juliet Bai grandchildren.

'Keep it clean, people,' Dylan rebukes the hecklers mock-sternly. 'Now, Romeo and Juliet had a nurse as their go-between, but Rajput and Juliet had someone brawnier. I'd like to invite Colonel Rammiah from Coorg, who acted as coach, catalyst and matchmaker in *l'affaire* Lobo-Shekhawat, to give us a blow-by-blow account of their infamous elopement. Sir, the floor is yours!'

He hands the mic to the Colonel from Coorg and steps back into the crowd. The Colonel smiles around shortsightedly, opens a thick sheaf of papers and begins to read.

Well, that wasn't so bad, Dabbu thinks shakily. I survived him talking on the mic and everything. But when is he going to come up and talk to *me*? Oh my god, supposing he doesn't come up to me *at all*? Supposing he *ignores me completely*? Why didn't I think of that before – *that's* what he's going to do! I am going to be completely and absolutely *humiliated*! Why did I even come to this stupid party?

Her head starts to spin, she takes a staggering step backward and a hand comes up to steady her.

'Do take this chair, dear,' a smooth voice entreats. 'You look a little faint, like.'

Dabbu turns around. An older gentleman with silver hair and a striking resemblance to Humphrey Bogart is smiling at her gently. There is an unlit cigar between his fingers. He is wearing a dark coat, a rakish paisley silk scarf and exuding expensive aftershave and an indefinable aura of romance. Dabbu blinks, feeling hypnotized.

He puts his hands on her shoulders. 'Sit,' he says in a caressing voice.

Dabbu sits.

On the dance floor, the Colonel's speech is going well. Under cover of the laughs he is getting, Dylan whispers to his brother, 'What have you done with the church contingent? Father Charlie and Father Vaz? Are they okay?'

'I left them talking to that hot sister of your newsreader's,' Ethan replies. 'She's gushing on and on at them about her favourite book – something called *The Thornbirds*. There are priests in it, apparently. They seemed pretty happy.'

Dylan goes very still. He knows that Ethan, though his expression is noncommittal, is waiting for him to ask if Debjani is here too. But he can't. The words won't come out of his mouth. So he just stands there, head slightly averted, pretending to hang onto the Colonel's every word like he hasn't heard the story of how Saahas met Juliet a hundred times before. He raises his glass of red wine when everybody does, drinks when everybody does and then claps as his father gets to his feet to reply to the toast.

The Brigadier has spent a lot of time writing his speech and delivers it straight from the heart, but Dylan barely hears a word – he is too busy *not* wondering where Debjani is. With the result that by the time the speech ends, he is extremely annoyed with her.

Presently, the cake is wheeled out. The plump pigeonesque girlfriend has been vanquished, Philomina Bai and Dadi-sa are flanking Jason and have firm possession of the matchbox. They light the thirty candles, beaming benignly at the 'young' couple, and as the Brig stands to one side, his nose suspiciously red, Juliet Bai blows them out with tears in her eyes and a very full heart.

'Mujhe Jesu, look you after my boys,' she prays fervently. 'Keep Saahas healthy, cure Ethan's acne, give Jason brains and make my Dylan happy again.'

There are cheers and clapping and the bearers step forward with beautifully packed plum cake slices for everybody. Dylan shoves his untasted into his coat pocket.

'Is she also here?' he asks casually.

Ethan, chewing steadily, is sensitive enough not to ask *who*. Instead, he says, with a slight tilt of his head, 'Yeah, there, look.'

Dylan looks. Through the gay throng of people cheering and clapping around the dance floor, beyond the huddle of mandatory ayahs clutching the mandatory wailing babies, past the glowing candles and fern fronds and the delicately fragrant champas. And espies Debjani Thakur, lover of losers, at the other end of the lawn, standing with her side profile turned charmingly towards him, smiling up at that old goat Donny Noronha, who is holding one of her slim hands between his two sweaty palms and talking up an oily storm.

She is wearing a diaphanous leaf green and silver sari, and her hair, pinned back on one side with a single white rose, is like a dusky cloud about her shoulders. As she raises her wine glass, sips the deep red liquid and flashes that entrancing street-urchin grin, Dylan finds that his belly has rediscovered its talent for ballet. It raises itself up, flips over gracefully and then swoons over backward in an attitude of abject surrender.

'Yeah, it's her all right,' he says indifferently. 'Prise her away from Donny soon, will you? He looks like he's about to ejaculate in his pants.'

Ethan snorts. 'Prise her away yourself,' he says, reaching for a chilled beer. 'Are you man or mouse?'

Dylan plucks the beer from his grasp. 'No drinking till you're twenty-five,' he says smartly. 'Here, have a Campa.'

Presently, he sips the beer he has confiscated and moodily watches Debjani across the garden. Donny Noronha and she are now sitting side by side. They look amazingly intimate. The white rose drops from its place behind her ear and lands on the grassy ground. Donny pounces to retrieve it – like a famished mongrel after a dead rat, thinks Dylan irately. Rising, red-faced from the effort, he smiles and seems to be offering to pin it back for her.

Dylan swears and gets to his feet. He strides halfway across the garden, then checks himself abruptly, executes a right turn and approaches a circle of girls chattering brightly, sipping from their glasses of Rasna orange and beer.

'Ladies.' He smiles, looking the prettiest one straight in the eye. 'It's time to start dancing!'

And just like that, the party explodes onto the dance floor. The band kicks off with the latest chart-topper, UB 40's 'Red Red Wine'. Dylan's partner is light on her feet and channelling the latest Madonna moves and soon all eyes are on her smoothly undulating, shoulder-padded black jumpsuit.

Anjini takes one look at her, drops her muddy brown dupatta, shakes out her hair and smiles encouragingly at a gangly young man hovering around the next table. He is at her side in an instant. Before heading off to the dance floor, she pokes Debjani in the ribs.

'Stop *hunching*! Smile! And for heaven's sake, *dance*!'

It's all very well to say, Debjani thinks crossly, but somebody has to ask me!

'My sister isn't at all a snob,' Anjini leans over and assures a handsome young man sipping a drink at the edge of the dance floor. 'She likes people who aren't overawed by how famous she is. And she loves this song!'

And soon Debjani is on the floor too, swinging somewhat unwillingly to 'Get outta My Dreams, Get into My Car', inches away from the girl in the clingy black jumpsuit.

It seems to Debjani that Dylan goes off the floor the moment she steps onto it. He escorts Jumpsuit back to her gaggle of friends and then goes over to Mrs Mamta to say hello even as Dabbu watches, outraged. They talk cozily for what seems like ages, until the Brigadier breaks it up by asking Mrs Mamta to dance. Left all to himself, Dylan loses no time in finding another partner and leading her to the dance floor.

'Bastard,' Debjani mutters under her breath as she sees them approach.

'Sorry?' says her partner.

'I'm hot.' She fans herself. 'I'd like to sit down now.'

And she exits the floor, her pallu practically trailing across Dylan's chest as she walks past him with her nose in the air.

And so it continues. Juliet Bai, closely observing this immature class seven type behaviour, starts to feel extremely frustrated. Until finally the band strikes up Phil Collins' plaintive 'Groovy Kind of Love' and Dylan moves away from the bunch of cousins he has been chatting with at the bar and walks across the garden towards the Thakur sisters.

About time, Debjani thinks crossly as her heart leaps into her mouth, hits the back of her teeth and then sinks down to her chest to pulsate alarmingly between her ribs. I have sat through a never-ending church service that was *way* longer than anything we Hindus can ever be accused of, and Anji didi's tied the naada of the petticoat so tightly it's about to saw my body into two, and corns are burgeoning between my toes from these horrible too-small shoes, and my cheeks are aching from smiling at people I don't know, and my mole has been mauled by about thirty strangers – but now all of that shouldn't matter, should it, because Dylan Singh Shekhawat has finally deigned to saunter over and talk to me. Well, I'm *not* going to dance with him. Pompous little shit. I'll say no. I won't go. I'll pretend I twisted my ank –

'Shall we?' Dylan smiles at Anjini.

Anjini gives an appreciative, throaty giggle. Dylan, who seems to have eyes for no one but her, leads her gracefully to the dance floor.

'I assume you want to know the weather report?' she asks him as they begin to dance. 'It's stormy and getting stormier.'

He raises his brows. 'Oh, no,' he says blandly. 'It's nothing like that. Just...' He grins. 'Age before beauty.'

'Horrible boy,' she says without rancour. 'Don't bullshit me.'

'Well, I did want to ask her to dance, but she looked so snooty I thought, screw it.'

'You mean you chickened out,' Anjini says.

Dylan's eyes kindle with sudden rage. 'This isn't funny.'

'No?' Anjini shakes with suppressed mirth. 'Okay.'

They dance the rest of the song in silence and when it's over, he escorts her back to her table. Debjani is sitting there, deep in conversation with Donny Noronha.

'I hope you're enjoying the party?'

His voice is distinctly surly. Debjani responds by looking left and right ostentatiously, as if to be sure he is indeed speaking to her. Her hair swirls beautifully with every move, the curls thick and glossy.

Surly and Curly. Anji stifles a smile. So *cute*.

'Me?' Debjani asks, her eyes wide. 'Are you actually speaking to *me*?'

Dylan's lips tighten. 'Yes,' he says tersely.

Debjani smiles. 'Yes, I'm quite enjoying myself. It's a very nice party.'

'Yes, lovely party,' chimes in Donny Noronha suavely. He is sitting next to Debjani, a proprietorial arm around the back of her chair. 'Er... shouldn't you circulate, like? You're the host, after all.'

Dylan just glares at him. Donny Noronha smiles back blandly and points at somebody behind Dylan with one negligent hand.

'I think those people are looking for you.'

Dylan doesn't turn around. Instead, he leans in, eyeballs Noronha, and says in a clear, level voice: 'Daisy Duck.'

Debjani gasps. Anjini looks mystified.

Donny flushes a dull red.

'You really are a very odd boy,' he says with dignity. Then he looks at the girls. 'My dears, your glasses are empty! Let me replenish them, like.'

Saying which, he plucks their glasses out of their hands and scurries away, leaving a grimly satisfied Dylan glowering at the table, in clear possession of the field.

'*That* was *rude*!' Debjani exclaims.

'No no,' says Dylan coolly. 'He's used to it.'

Very quietly, Anjini gets up and walks away too.

There is silence, well, except for the band, now performing a soulful rendition of Cutting Crew's 'I Just Died in Your Arms Tonight'.

'Was he *the* Donny Noronha?' Debjani asks finally. 'The one your mother told us about? Heart-breaker, hymen-breaker?'

'Yeah,' Dylan replies, smiling faintly. '*The*.'

She giggles.

He grins.

'So what were the two of you discussing so animatedly, anyway?'

This is Dabbu's chance to show off just a little.

'Oh, just the HDW submarine deal scandal,' she replies airily. 'And if the government really is as blameless as it's making itself out to be. And then we talked about the Bofors gun scam.'

He was nodding, his eyes on the dance floor, giving the overall in-charge ones, like he has drinks to refill and aunties to kiss, but at this his eyes come around to lock into hers. Debjani's heart gives a weird little bump.

'Excuse me?' His eyebrows rise.

She nods, doggedly maintaining eye contact. 'You heard me.'

'So you've been reading the newspapers,' he says witheringly.

'How sweet. But a little knowledge is a dangerous thing. Remember that.'

Which is a pretty D for devastating remark, but Debjani is a full-blooded Rajput. No wimpy Mangalorean blood thins *her* veins.

She raises her chin.

'You're *such* a pseudo,' she tells him sweetly. 'I'm pretty, so I must be stupid. Thank god I didn't marry you.'

Dylan immediately wants to marry her on the spot. Father Charlie and Father Vaz can perform the ceremony – they're sitting right there, eating prawn-pao and payasam.

He crosses his arms across his chest.

'So now you *know* you're pretty,' he notes regretfully. 'There goes your nicest quality.'

'Only a complete MCP would like a girl because she has no self-confidence,' Debjani flashes. 'But I guess that's a perfect description of *you*.'

Dylan stares at her uncomprehendingly. She got male chauvinism out of his behaviour? What *is* this girl? And why can't he get her out of his head?

'Look, Dabbu, I don't want to perform a post-mortem here. What's past is past. I was foolish enough to let my parents brainwash me. They gabbed on and on about grandchildren and how well they know your family, etc. And you are, as you have just stated, pretty. Quite pretty, actually. It was a lethal combination of emotional blackmail plus a gun to the groin. Today I thank you for saying no to what would clearly have been a hugely incompatible match.'

It is a prepared speech and it sounds like one – any impartial observer would suss that out immediately. But Debjani isn't impartial.

'Don't call me Dabbu!'

'What? Okay.' Suddenly, he winces. 'Damn, the Mangys have got hold of the mic.'

Debjani looks over his shoulder. A large contingent of old Mangalorean uncles have mounted the stage and are now thanking everybody who has flown in from out-of-town for the function. The list is a very, very long one, since Mangys take wedding anniversaries extremely seriously. Then they start talking in slow quavering voices about the dreadful things the Shekhawat boys got up to in their grandmother's house in Mangalore when they were little. This goes on for so long that the Rajus, out of sheer self-defence, start heckling them rudely on another mic. Which, of course, goads the Mangys to debate the ancient historical question regarding the origin of the Rajputs, right there on the stage, into the microphones.

Rajput,

Tu maha choot,

Tu kahan se aaya re?

'Get up there before they hit the second verse,' Juliet Bai hisses into Ethan's ear. But

Golkund

Meri ma-ki-bhund

Mein wahan se aaya re!

has already been belted out triumphantly before he can clamber onto the stage, strap on a base guitar and hit some mean chords. 'Sing, Ethan, sing!' scream the girls in the crowd, immediately diverted. Ethan grins and proceeds to give the people what they want, which is the UB40 version of 'I Can't Help Falling in Love with You'.

'Wise men say!' exclaims old Donny Noronha, materializing suddenly at Dabbu's elbow. 'Would you like to *rush in* with me, my dear?'

He leans forward, hand outstretched.

Debjani, moving without any thought, puts out her hand – and finds it, not in Donny Noronha's clammy grip but in an entirely different, cool, firm grasp.

'Shall we?'

She looks up at Dylan. His eyes are intense, not at all like the eyes of somebody who claims to be entirely indifferent. But that's probably just the fairy lights, she thinks bitterly. After all, emotional blackmail and a gun to the groin are what got him to propose to me. She tries to pull her hand away. He doesn't let go.

'This song's too slow,' she mutters.

He holds fast to her hand, tilts his head and smiles. It's not a very nice smile. 'So we'll take it slow.'

He pulls her to him with a sharp tug and soon they are whirling around on the dance floor. One hand grips the small of her back while the other holds fast to her right hand. It's the closest they've ever been physically. Thank god the music is so loud, she thinks. Nobody but I can hear my stupid heartbeat.

'So how's the kot-piece?' Dylan, clearly used to such close proximities, asks lightly. 'Do you guys still play?'

Why is he making pc? she thinks darkly, not bothering to answer. Like he gives a damn – he only ever came to play because there was a *gun* to his *groin*.

'Are you sulking?' He sounds amused. 'You know, most people would consider me the wronged party here.'

Up comes her head. 'Oh, yeah? Everybody on the Raju circuit thinks *you* turned me down.'

'But you're so famous and all,' he points out reasonably. 'How could they think so?'

'Well they *do*,' she says. 'I'm a girl. You're a guy. So.'

He tilts his head.

'Now who's talking like an MCP?'

'My father still isn't speaking to me,' she says, her eyes almost welling over with tears.

'Debjani.' He sounds a little bored. 'Get over it. Worse things happen in this world every day. I've just met a girl whose mother was raped and murdered in the anti-Sikh riots. She saw it happen but her father made her promise never to go to the police about it. *Those* are real father-daughter issues.'

'There you go again, giving the big picture ones,' Debjani says crossly. 'Three thousand people died in a riot, so it's silly to weep over one puny street mongrel! Typical!'

'Are you calling yourself a street mongrel?'

'Shut up,' she snaps, tossing her hair. 'I *hate* you.'

It's that hair, he decides, staring down at her. Angel hair. And those collarbones... and that crunchy little grin. They combine to create an illusion, and that's all it is – an illusion. In reality, she is both vain and self-centred. His arms tighten around her, drawing her closer.

'Suppose I kissed you now?' he says, his voice husky. 'Would that make them think I was hopelessly in love with you, and it was you who did the dumping?'

'I guess so,' she replies with credible nonchalance, even though her cheeks are flaming. 'It would work even better if I slapped you afterwards.'

'You might not *want* to slap me afterwards,' he murmurs, his spikily lashed eyes glittering.

Debjani gives a hollow laugh.

'Ha.'

'Ha or haan?'

She looks around the Jasmine Garden. The dance floor is full of gently twirling couples, the lawn is dotted with people conversing, eating, laughing. Anjini is a few feet away from her, dancing with a smitten uncleji. Just looking at her stiffens Debjani's spine. She turns her eyes to Dylan.

'I don't want to kiss you,' she tells him politely, like he is a waiter and she's declining an offer of Rasna orange.

This clear, categorical statement and the look of rebuking scorn that accompanies it make him feel suddenly cheap. He flushes.

'You still don't know how to flirt.'

'Oh, I do,' she assures him. 'I've learnt. I just don't want to flirt with *you*.'

'You really hate my guts, don't you. But why? Just because of that one article?'

'Yes,' she replies tightly. 'And also because, though you profess to be all concerned about human tragedy, you're just a cold professional hack, chasing a big fat story. You don't have any *feelings*.'

'What crap!'

'Because if you *did*,' she continues passionately, 'you would have told me about the article yourself, you would have explained – you wouldn't have tried to brush it under the carpet and then tried to bribe me with a big fat bottle of expensive perfume.'

Dylan stares at her uncomprehendingly.

'What perfume?'

'The Anais Anais, obviously,' she says crossly.

'Debjani, I didn't give you any perfume.'

She looks up. 'What?'

He nods. 'I wrote you a letter. And put it in your letter box. This androgynous-looking little kid on a tricycle with very short, spiky hair and gold stud earrings...?'

'Bonu,' Debjani supplies automatically.

'Yeah, Bonu then, this kid Bonu saw me do it.'

Debjani looks up at him doubtfully. Behind them, on the bandstand, Ethan winds up the song. The music stops.

'Then who gave me the perfume?'

'I have no idea,' Dylan says, his arms dropping away from around her body, making her realize how chilly the night air has grown. 'Ask Bonu. What a foul name, by the way. *Bonu.*'

'They were expecting just Monu,' Debjani explains, her mind spinning crazily, trying to internalize what he has just told her. 'So when they had twins, they said she was a bonus and named her Bonu.'

But Dylan isn't interested in the story of how-Bonu-was-named-Bonu.

'So now you're telling me you never got the letter I wrote you the day before we came over for tea? How do I know you're not lying?'

'I'm *not* lying! I didn't get it! Why would I lie?'

The lean dimples flash in a rueful smile. 'Maybe because you're regretting letting me go, now that I'm so famous and all.'

'I'm famous too,' she snaps. 'Anyway, I don't believe there ever *was* such a letter. I think you're lying. Like you lied about the cat.'

'I lied about the *cat*?'

'Well, I've never seen a cat in that sand pile. *Ever.*'

Dylan stands back and says, 'Look, I don't have to prove anything to you. Ask Bonu about it if you like – and if you *don't* like, don't.'

Then, as she stares up at him, all doubt and confusion, he leans in and flicks the tip of her nose with one careless finger.

'One caveat, though. The sentiments expressed in the letter are a bit dated. *Quite* dated, actually. Remember that. And now, goodnight. Thank you for the dance.'

11

'Bonu Singh?'

She is crouching in the verandah, an aluminium paper clamp clipped to her chin, a Natraj pencil clenched between her nose and upper lip, Mrs Mamta Thakur's floral nightgown wound about her head like a turban.

'I'm a Sardar,' she whispers, spraying spit and promptly dropping the moustache-pencil. 'It's a disguise, so Samar can't find me.'

Debjani unclips the paper clamp. 'You'll cut your chin with that, silly girl,' she says, massaging the reddened skin. 'And why are you hiding from Samar?'

Bony wrinkles her forehead. 'I teased him about his crush on Eshu. What do you want, Dabbu mausi?'

'How d'you know I want anything?' Debjani counters.

'Arrey, you never talk to me any more. Mummy says it's because you've become famous.'

'It's because I've become *stupid*,' Debjani says, hugging Bonu's thin body hard. 'Uff, look at your cheeks. You should put cream – winter's coming, you'll get all scaly.'

'Only if you give me your Nivea cream, from the blue tin. I don't like Mummy's Charmis. It's sticky.'

'Listen, Bones, you're right, I do want something. Well, actually, I wanted to ask you something.'

Bonu's eyes, large and long-lashed under her absurd floral turban, gaze up at Debjani's face trustingly. 'What?'

'Did you see that Dylan bhaiyya – the one I was going to marry – did you see him put a letter in our mailbox the day before he came here with his family?'

Bonu's eyes skitter away. She starts to play with the nightgown wound around her head. 'N-nooo,' she says slowly.

Debjani's heart plummets with absurd disappointment. 'You didn't?'

'Noooyess.'

'Noooyess?'

Bonu's thin fingers pluck at Debjani's shirt. Her words come out in a rush. 'Dabbu mausi, that Dylan bhaiyya is a *Christian* – one of those people who go to church every Sunday and stick their tongues out at the priest.'

'So what, baba?' Debjani pats the rapidly unravelling turban.

'If you marry him, you won't have a hissa in the house. Because of Hindu Undivided Family Law. And I want you to have a hissa in the house. You're my favourite mausi!'

'Who told you that, Bones?'

Bonu yanks down her grandmother's nightgown till her face and body are completely covered in floral cloth. Her voice drops so low, Debjani has to strain to hear it. 'Papa. I heard him. On the night all the adults were discussing who you should marry, I fought with the boys and hid in the passage. Papa's lawyer phoned him and told him – and then Papa called Mummy out and told her.'

Debjani stares at the small veiled figure before her, feeling sick. So *that's* why Binni had done such a volte-face in favour of Dylan that night... and I had been so pathetically touched. But she's my sister, how could she? It's that bloody Vickyji, she concludes fiercely. Creep. He's got her completely under his thumb.

Aloud she says, 'Did you hide the letter?'

The veiled figure nods.

'Could you give it to me?'

The floral nightgown tumbles off. Bonu's eyes are all concern. 'But your *hissa*, Dabbu mausi!'

'Never mind my freaking hissa.' Debjani gives her a little shake. 'Life is not about hissas. Earn your own money when you grow up, instead of waiting around for your parents to die. Mercenary little ghoul! Now go get my letter – and *where* did you get that expensive bottle of perfume?'

'Oh, Steesh got that.' Bonu, now that she is confessing, seems to be quite happy to make a clean breast of things. 'For Eshu mausi. He gave it to me to give to her. I put it in the mailbox – because I know you don't like perfume – and the next day, I just looked sad and told Steesh I dropped it and it broke.'

'Bonu, you shouldn't tell lies.' Debjani looks at her, appalled. 'It's not right.'

'Mummy lies,' Bonu says blithely. 'She says it's okay if you're doing it for the right reasons.'

'It's *never* righ – oh, never mind, just give me the letter. Where have you hidden it?'

But the little girl is looking stricken.

'Are you going to tell everybody I hid it?'

Debjani, in a fever of impatience, scoops her up and kisses her on both cheeks. 'No. And nobody will ever know, I promise. Now where's my letter? *Give* it no, Bonu Singh... *Please*, Bonu Singh, it's my *vewy fwerst* lurrrve letter, Bonu!'

Bonu giggles. 'You're funny!' She jumps out of Debjani's lap and runs from the verandah. Then she scampers back in complete panic. 'I forgot my disguise! Samar will recognize me. Put my beard on again, quick!'

—⊷❀⊶—

Darling Debjani,

May I call you that? It's alliterative, so your father will definitely approve, but then so are dear and dearest, but somehow for me, dearest doesn't even begin to cover how I feel about you.

Do forgive the fact that this isn't handwritten – not very romantic, I know, I should be wearing a floppy white shirt and writing with a feather quill if I must write at all – but feathers are messy and floppy shirts sissy and hammering things out on a keyboard is how I express myself best.

My parents ran away and got married when he was twenty-one and she was eighteen. The whole affair was madly spontaneous and barely legal. Their families had two coronaries apiece, of course. My folks didn't care, though. Apparently they saw each other across a crowded parade ground and just knew this was it.

When I saw you at the gate that first evening, I knew too. I didn't want to accept it at first, but I knew.

There, isn't that romantic? Better than a floppy shirt, surely? All my life I've dreamed of meeting a girl who is lovely without knowing she is lovely, who is fierce and sweet and as straight as a die.

And so I must be straight with you. Because you don't actually want somebody romantic, do you? You want somebody honest and kind and brave – a very tall order, that, but let me try for honesty at least.

I admit I've had a few relationships, which have gone nowhere because that's precisely where I wanted them to go. My mother would say it's because I suffered a 'broken heart' at seventeen, but I won't hide behind that excuse. For years now, it's just suited me to be selfish with women. The only defence I offer is that I've never made any false 'forever' promises to anyone.

When I was in class eight, I stole ten rupees from another boy's pencil box and spent it on cigarettes. I once spent an entire summer watching porn film videos. I've got pissed drunk a few times – not in the last two years, though.

I guess I can be said to have 'corrupted' my brothers... my parents certainly think so.

I'm ruthless, professionally. I'd do most anything to get a story.

And one more thing: I wrote an anonymous column in the *IP* recently.

Yes, that Roving Eye article. About you. That was me.

What can I say? I've had issues with DD's style of reportage for years, and it got worse when I personally witnessed the immediate aftermath of the riots in Tirathpuri. I'm not very rational on that subject, but I do realize now that I can't expect people who haven't seen what I've seen to feel as I do. Also, I was mad at my boss for making me write the column without giving me any credit for it, so I used it as an opportunity to make him look bad – as he was one of the PM's main advisors on the 'new' DeshDarpan. So basically, I used the column to score petty points. And ended up mounting a totally personal attack on you.

And so, my apology is two-fold. Firstly, I'm sorry for all the snide, unwarranted things I said in the piece. And secondly,

I'm sorry for not coming clean about it afterwards. But how could I have? The moment I saw the real you – and not the doll that DD demands – I started plotting how to make you like me. Telling you I was Roving Eye definitely wouldn't have helped my cause! Besides, you're such a star now (even Dev Pawar wants to marry you!), how does one disgruntled print journalist's criticism even matter, anyway?

That's it, really. Glad to get it off my chest at last. Lately I've been dreaming that you've found out all this stuff through some other source and given me my marching orders.

What do you say? Am I forgiven?

If all this is too glib and quick for you, as I suspect it may be, and you need more time to think post these 'revelations', do ask your parents to phone mine and let me know. I'm willing to wait as long as it takes. Otherwise – and I hope with all my heart it will be otherwise – I'll see you in the evening.

All my love,
Always,
Dylan

'Why didn't you ever tell me about the perfume?' Eshwari demands of Satish in school the next day. '*Why*, Steesh?'

He shrugs, looking uncomfortable. 'What would I have said? Hey-hey, Bihari, I got you a big-ass perfume bottle but your retarded niece broke it? What would be the point?'

'She's not retarded,' Eshwari says crossly. '*You* are.'

They are heading down to the common hall for a meeting of the Interact Club of which Eshwari is president. They are wearing their usual blue uniform, a shade reminiscent of nightsuits or banker's shirts, him in pleated trousers, her in a short, swingy, box-pleated skirt. Eshwari wears a pin on her dark blue blazer, proclaiming her to be Gandhi House Captain, and the scrunchie that secures her ponytail is bright red, which is against school regulations but does amazing things for her black hair and creamy skin. Satish's attempt at being sartorial begins and ends with his blazer collar, which is turned up jauntily.

'Sorry for not telling, but you also never told me that Dillu gifted Dabbu the very same perfume, on the very same day. I would've made the connection then, maybe. Anyway, now spill, ya. What did his letter say? What did *Dabbu* say?'

Eshwari draws a long, deep, heartfelt breath and turns to him. Her eyes are shining under her spiky fringe. 'It was *so* romantic, Steesh, you've no idea. I think *I* have a little crush on him too, after reading his letter. And his ass toh I told you, na...' She exhales gustily.

'Yes, yes, his ass should be awarded the Bharat Ratna, you've told me that before,' he says testily. 'And stop banging into people, look where you're going. So he wrote this romantic masterpiece and what did your sister say?'

'It wasn't just romantic,' Eshwari muses dreamily, and draws another deep breath. 'It was –'

'Hello, leave some air for the rest of us,' Satish tells her hastily, shooting dirty looks at a couple of class eleven boys who are staring mesmerized at how magically Eshwari's chest is swelling every time she inhales.

Eshwari turns to looks at him. 'It was *honest*,' she says. 'And like he thought she was, I don't know, a *higher* thing than just a girl somehow... It was the sort of stuff I imagine Christians say in confession.'

'Sounds kinky to me,' Satish says sapiently. 'And now you're lusting after your would-be brother-in-law? You're sick, Bihari.'

Eshwari glares at him. 'Stupid. That's not what I meant. You don't know anything at all.'

'Because you're not telling me. What was Dabbu's reaction?'

'Well, she cried. And then she cried some more. And when I left home, Ma and she were blubbering over the letter together and talking about how best to bring it up with BJ.'

'It'll sort itself out, don't worry,' he tells her as they emerge on the second floor. 'Dabbu and Dillu sound like they are made for each other. Now when do I get a treat for doing your sister's setting?'

'Excuse me?' Eshwari's eyes widen. She says, with a toss of her ponytail, 'All you did was mess things up! If your stupid perfume bottle hadn't replaced his romantic letter, everything would've been fine!'

'But thanks to me and the retar – I mean, the little kid, there's all this highly gratifying Romeo-Juliet action happening,' he points out. 'Drama, misunderstandings, reconciliations!' He leans in really close and sniffs her thoroughly. Eshwari feels like she is being inspected for narcotics by a large hairy beast. 'Whyn't you wear the perfume though, Bihari? Don't tell me Dabbu used it all up in three months?'

Eshwari turns a little pink. 'You shouldn't have given me that. It's too expensive.'

He cocks his head to one side, looking absurdly like a German Shepherd that wants to play. 'But I told you,' he says, 'I won it at a hoopla stall. Full fluke. And it isn't the real thing, anyway, just a fake from Gaffar Market.'

Yeah, right, Eshwari thinks darkly. She had showed it to Anji didi – who knows about this stuff – and she had declared it the real thing, bought from that big shop in South Extension, no less.

Meanwhile, Satish is peering into her face, grinning. 'Unless you're suggesting I actually blew, what, a *grand* on genuine perfume? For *you*? Wow, I must think you seriously stink.'

Eshwari pushes him away. 'Don't talk crap, Steesh. Now get out of my way. I have to go call this meeting to order and you need to go sit in the back and look at porn with your ugly friends.'

The Interact Club is a community service initiative whose manifesto vows to 'work for the upliftment of the blind, the aged, the orphaned and the sick'. Students participate in large numbers, mostly to swell the application forms they send to foreign universities. There are cleanliness drives, educational outreach programmes in the slums and blood donation camps. The only decent thing about the Interact Club, according to Satish, is that they organize the annual Modern School Diwali Mela, which is really *the* place to meet hot dames in Delhi.

This quarter's blood donation camps, Eshwari tells the assembled students, are going to be held close to different places of worship, so as to underline the secular beliefs so dear to the club. The first one has been organized at the Sacred Heart Cathedral at Gol Dak Khana, the second at the Idgah on Rani Jhansi Road and the third at Gurudwara Bangla Sahib on Baba Kharak Singh Marg.

'I'll go to the Gurudwara one,' decides one of Satish's back-row buddies. 'We'll get *deadly* grub there – hot-hot suji ka halwa and kala channa and puris. The Catholics are damn stingy – they don't let anybody eat that thin wafer thingie.'

A thin, bespectacled Malayali turns around earnestly to explain the concept of the body and blood of Christ to this ignoramus but Eshwari hastily interrupts, knowing that members, if diverted, are capable of not letting her get a word in till the period is over.

'Contributions to blood banks have slowed to a trickle because everybody is shit scared of getting AIDS,' she says, sitting down atop the desk, knowing the sight of her smooth, muscular legs will secure the attention of the rowdiest of the boys. 'We'll need to design and print some educational pamphlets.'

'Let's put your legs on the posters, Bihari,' somebody calls out and the entire crowd lets out a cheeky, musical woahhhhhhh.

'Chup, chutiyon.' Eshwari frowns around the room. 'Now somebody will have to go around to all the shops in the neighbourhood requesting permission to put up posters. I need volunteers...'

'We'll need auto money,' somebody says and immediately has to put up with good-natured accusations about embezzlement and cooking of books. School stud and ex-stammerer Jai Kakkar puts up a hand and politely enquires if the esteemed president has considered organizing a sperm donation drive instead.

Eshwari looks at him witheringly.

'I did think of it,' she says, black eyes very cool. 'But then I thought it was better to organize something to which *you* could actually contribute, Kakkar.'

Another lilting woahhhh bursts out from the crowd. Jai sits down, looking slapped and smitten. The meeting ends. The hall empties and Eshwari is picking up her papers when Satish comes up to her again.

'I want to talk to you,' he says. '*Alone.*'

'Isn't this alone enough?' she asks as she leans around him to show the middle finger to a gang of stragglers who are sniggering at how close Satish and she are standing. They snigger even louder and scurry away, and Eshwari turns back to Satish.

'Talk.'

'Why do you give that ass Kakkar so much patta?'

Eshwari's eyes kindle. 'Excuse me?'

'Scratch that,' he says hastily. 'I'll start over. I'm not very good at this.'

'You're not good at most things besides calculus. What is it?'

But Satish is looking oddly hesitant.

'You liked it when Dillu was honest with Dabbu, right?'

'Right.'

'Okay.' He nods, and takes a deep breath. 'So, I know I asked you out last year and you said no, but I just wanted to double-check again this year, because sometimes...' He pauses and looks away towards the crowded corridor full of sweaty, recessing Modernites. Then he looks back at her, his eyes searching. 'Sometimes I get the vibe that maybe... maybe you want me to ask you again. So I'm asking.'

Eshwari is appalled to feel her heartbeat quicken. Because this, after all, is only Steesh. He may have topped the year and scored a few match-winning centuries and silly girls like Gitika Govil may be swooning over him, but it is still only stupid, stinky-after-cricket Steesh.

'*What* are you asking exactly?'

He shoots her an exasperated *I know you're doing humanities but apply yourself a little, will you* look.

'Go with me to the farewell,' he spells it out for her. 'Be my chick.'

At which unpoetic utterance Eshwari's heart, fresh from reading Dylan's eloquent outpourings for Debjani, instantly goes back to beating normally again.

'No, thank you!' she declares, tossing her glossy black head. 'I told you I'm not allowed boyfriends till I'm twenty-one.'

He looks at her for a while. She looks right back.

'And what am I supposed to do till then, huh?' he says finally, bluntly. 'Jerk off to pictures of you at your sister's wedding?'

Eshwari chokes.

'You are an *animal*,' she spits out. 'Just... never, *ever* talk to me again, okay?'

⋅⊱────⊰⋅

'So now the princess has changed her mind?' The Judge throws up his hands in disgust. 'And she wants to marry him, after all? Is she *sure*? Suppose we invite him home and she heaps insults on him again?'

'LN, I *explained*,' Mrs Mamta says patiently. 'There was a mix-up with the mail...'

'What does that Sridhar pup mean by gifting Eshu perfume, I'd like to know!' the Judge continues agitatedly. 'Insolent young hound. This house is turning into a bloody Majnu ka tilla, Romeos crawling out of the damn woodwork – damn this thing!'

This, because the drawstring of the pyjamas he is attempting to climb into has slipped inside the seam at one end. He sticks a finger inside and rummages around for the submerged string in a helpless sort of way.

Mrs Mamta Thakur takes the pyjamas from him.

'Can we just talk about Dabbu?'

'Why?' the Judge demands, taking long strides around the room, his white kurta flapping. '*Why* should we talk about her? Did *she* talk to us before throwing a tantrum in a drawing room full of people and insulting my oldest friend? He's not even speaking to me any more! Thankless! They're all thankless!'

'They are good girls.' Mrs Mamta's voice trembles. 'And don't you start on about poor Chandu again! I think it's high time we started speaking to her, just imagine, her baby is crawling now. Antu met them on his trip to the US. He looks just like you, apparently, only with blond hair and blue eyes. Antu said,' her voice catches, something that doesn't happen very often, 'that he has a little hammer, *just* like a judge's gavel, and that he frowns and shouts and bangs it about,' she gives a great gulp, blinking back tears, '*just* like you! And his name is *Hendrik*!'

'Yes, I agree it's a dreadful name but there's no need to cry,' the Judge says impatiently. 'Little Hendrik Narayan Lippik. Fine name for a grandson of the Thakurs of Hailey Road to have!'

'I was thinking we could invite them to Dabbu's wedding,' Mrs Mamta says, dabbing dolefully at her eyes with the Judge's pyjamas.

But this is too much. The Judge whirls around furiously, kurta flying, knobby knees flashing.

'Dabbu's wedding to *whom*?' he demands, making frustrated snatching hand gestures in the air. 'You are living in a dream world, Mamtaji. With what face can I go back and speak to the Shekhawats?'

'Just read the letter,' Mrs Mamta, more composed now, says as she hand him back his pyjamas, slightly damp now and with both ends of the drawstring easily accessible. 'Please.'

He glowers at her and slowly starts to climb into them, one bony leg at a time. 'What's the use of getting these girls married, anyway?' he grumbles. 'They never leave the house – Binni is always here, whining about her hissa, Anji seems to have dug herself in too, not to mention those three young tapeworms Samar, Monu and Bonu, devourers of everything they see.'

'Anji's having some problems,' Mrs Mamta says. 'She won't talk about it, though.'

'She doesn't deserve that nice Anant,' the Judge replies. 'He is a decent man and she's driving him crazy. Poor fool.' He pauses. 'And that Vickyji deserves one kick in the backside.'

Mrs Mamta doesn't reply.

Presently the Judge says, almost pleadingly, 'The Shekhawats will want to bring up the grandchildren as Catholics. Pour water on their heads and other outlandish things like that. And the boy is trouble – likes to charge at windmills. And he's had so many girlfriends! Good riddance, I say. Let's just wipe that slate clean and look for a nice new boy for Debjani – she's become so well known now! Can't you talk her out of this, Mamtaji?'

But Mrs Mamta, now combing her rippling hair with her large maroon comb, looks unconvinced.

'He is the correct boy for her. Read the letter, you'll see.'

'Fine!' The Judge slaps his palms together. 'I'll *read* it. But even if it reads smoother than a Shakespearean sonnet I won't speak to Saahas immediately. Debjani needs to think this through carefully. Marriage isn't a joke.'

'Isn't it?' his wife asks wearily.

'I never thought she would behave like this,' he says, shaking his head as he climbs into bed. 'Not *Dabbu*. My favourite!'

'Serves you right for having favourites,' sniffs his wife, rolling over and going to sleep.

⊷⊶◦⊷⊶

Ethan wakes up for school at six a.m. on the Monday after the thirtieth anniversary party. As he shambles down the corridor to the bathroom, rubbing his gummy eyes, he trips over a phone cord stretched taut across the corridor at a height of about two feet and lands on the floor with a thud. Looking up, he observes that the cord is leading inside Dylan's room, the door of which is shut.

'Mamma!' he shouts, rubbing his sore backside. 'Dylan's trying to kill me.'

The phone is still in Dylan's room at ten a.m. and Debjani hasn't yet called. Perhaps she couldn't track down that Bonus kid, he rationalizes, staring at the dumb instrument. Because Bonus doesn't live with them, right? She just comes down for the holidays. Maybe she took the letter back with her to wherever she comes from. Bhatinda? Bhopal? Something with B. Should he just call her himself? It's been almost two days since they spoke at the party. No, better wait for her to call – or maybe not?

He is staring down at the phone, willing it to ring, when suddenly it does. He scrambles for it.

'Hello!'

'Is that Dylan Shekhawat? The journalist?'

'Yes, this is he,' Dylan replies, swallowing his disappointment.

'Mr Hardik Motla, MP, would like to speak to you. Hold the line, please.'

What the...? Dylan thinks.

And then Motla's voice comes oiling down the line. 'That girl is making a fool of you.'

What? Dylan thinks, feeling disoriented. She is? And how on earth does he know?

'That Kamalpreet Kaur. She is ek number ki fraud. It is in a spirit of mutual cooperation that we are telling you, my boy – because journalists and netas must cooperate with one another – that you had better not believe anything she says.'

'How do *you* know about my story?' Dylan asks. 'I haven't even written it out yet. It's just a transcript on an audio tape.'

'For which you should be grateful,' Motla replies. His voice picks up both menace and urgency. 'No harm has been done – *yet*. But if you publish it, we will sue you. You will lose both your accreditation and your reputation, and maybe even your health.'

'How do you know about Kamalpreet Kaur?' Dylan asks, mystified. 'Are you having me followed?'

Motla clicks his tongue dismissively. 'We *know*. That is enough. Consider this a friendly warning.'

'I'm recording this,' Dylan says quickly. 'I put on my recorder the moment your secretary put you through. You better watch out, Mr Motla.'

There is a short pause.

'You're bluffing,' Motla chuckles. 'Besides, I haven't said *anything* incriminating! Now you listen to me...'

He's scared, Dylan thinks exultantly, his pulse quickening. I've touched a raw nerve this time. This cat is shitting bricks.

'You *listen* to me, Shekhawat! Are you listening?'

'I'm listening.'

'Print that kahani and it will be the last one you write. Got it?'

'Got it,' Dylan says crisply and cuts the connection.

He is staring at the phone, his head reeling at the sheer unreality of what has just happened, when it rings again.

'Motla's on the war path,' Hiranandani's voice purrs gleefully down the line. 'Well done, tiger.'

Dylan grins. 'He called you too?'

'Called and threatened to shut me down. Called Bade-papaji too – tried to get me sacked.'

'And?'

'And what, bastard? Are you implying that this newspaper can be bullied or bought?'

Dylan laughs. 'So we won't be suppressing it?'

'Of course not!' Hira chuckles. '*Truth. Balance. Courage.* And by a happy coincidence, tomorrow is the first of November, the fourth anniversary of the massacre. It's the perfect day to print the story. Just hammer the damn thing out and send it to me. You'll make the top half of tomorrow's front page. With your byline and picture and everything.'

'Great!' Dylan says, pleased. 'I'll get down to it immediately. I did want to do a little more on Kamalpreet first. Show her photographs around Tirathpuri, talk to the neighbours, get their take on her.'

Hira makes impatient clicking noises.

'Dylan, if you spent another day dicking about Tirathpuri, we'll miss the anniversary.'

'You're right,' Dylan says. 'Okay, I'll sit down to write it right away then.'

It takes him quite a while. Late in the evening, he drops off the finished story in the dispatch room of the *India Post* office and drives home, tired but satisfied. He had struggled with the piece – not wanting to come across as shrill or tear-jerking or sensationalistic – and finally settled for a simple, factual account that will nevertheless ensure that Hardik Motla spends the next few years behind bars. But writing it has got him a little worried about Kamalpreet. She *is* his responsibility, in a way. And he doesn't even have her contact number. He has no way of getting through to her at all.

When he gets home Juliet Bai tells him that some Punjabi girl has called for him thrice and will call again in a bit. Dylan wolfs down dinner, staring at the phone, while Ethan makes snide remarks and Jason sulks. Dylan isn't letting anybody make any calls and his girlfriend's been sulking ever since the old biddies were rude to her at the party.

The phone rings at five in the morning. Dylan lunges for it.

'Kamalpreet? Are you okay?'

'Haanji, okay,' she replies in her clear, sweet voice. 'Good morning.'

Phew. It is only now as he relaxes that Dylan realizes how tense he had actually been.

'You should have given me a number for you! Why have you been calling so many times?'

'Oh,' she says. 'Pata nahin, maybe it my veham only, but last two-three days there seem to be strange men looking at me.'

'That's because you're so pretty,' he tells her, still a little light-headed with relief.

'You are joking, of course. Being jolly. But these are not the usual roadside cheapies. These are *different*. Apne kaha tha na, that maybe Motla will try to finish us off? I think-so these are *those* types of men. The finishing-off types.'

Dylan sits up. 'Are you serious?'

'Cent per cent serious, ji,' she says, the sweet voice wobbling just a little.

Dylan curses under his breath. He knows better than to suggest she go to the police. He knows what the people of Tirathpuri think of the police.

'Should I come there?'

'No no,' she says half-heartedly. 'Why would you...?'

'I'm coming,' he says, suddenly decisive. 'Tell me where.'

Without further protest, she gives him the address. 'But just till the evening. I am catching a five o'clock train to my native place. If you could be with me till then, and see me off at the station.'

'I'm leaving now,' Dylan assures her as he gets to his feet. 'Stay inside the house. And I'll bring you a copy of today's *India Post*. It may cheer you up – your story's on the front page!'

―◦―

Over at Hailey Road, Eshwari is sneakily rifling through her sister's cupboard looking for the wispy cream net chunni that Debjani has spent months embroidering all over with tiny pink rosebuds. She wants to wear it to the blood donation camp at Gurudwara Bangla Sahib today.

She tries not to think about the fact that Dabbu hasn't worn it yet, that she had probably hoped to inaugurate it on some sunny winter's afternoon, when she would throw it on like a scarf over a floral dress and go on a long drive with Dylan through the little villages just beyond Qutub Minar and drink chai in a dhaba and perhaps buy wild chrysanthemums and green guavas from cute looking village children.

And you *will* do all that, Dabbu, she thinks fiercely, looking at her sleeping sister. Just not today. Today I want to wear it, because we're going to the gurudwara and because... Uff. Just because. Sorry, okay?

Most of the members of the Interact Club are already at the Gurudwara gate when Eshu rattles up in a black and yellow autorickshaw. It is a misty morning and everybody is in a good mood, especially Satish, who has a big black camera hanging around his neck.

'For the winter issue of *Sandesh*,' he explains. 'I want a big fat picture of me giving blood right there in the centrespread. You click me, Bihari, I've been working out with Gulgul bhaisaab – I'm gonna flex my muscles and all.'

She stares at him, surprised and more than a little irritated. 'Oh, so now you're talking to me again? Why couldn't you tell me this earlier? I could have taken a lift with you on the bike instead of rattling up here in a bloody auto!'

'Arrey, *you're* the one who said never talk to me again,' he comments as he fishes out a Megadeth bandanna and starts to tie it around his head. 'You called me an animal. Forgot or what?'

But Eshwari is just gawping at him.

'What?' Satish demands.

'You can't wear *that* inside a gurudwara! There are skulls on it – it's blasphemous!'

Satish considers this. Then he turns to the one Sikh in their group.

'Hey, Kakkar, is my bandanna cool?'

Jai Kakkar shrugs. 'Yeah, it's cool.'

'See?'

Eshu rolls her eyes. 'Fat lot *he* knows,' she mutters. 'He's a Cut Surd, anyway.'

But Jai Kakkar now feels he should pass verdict on everybody's headgear. 'You're good, you're fine, that's okay, and...' He goes a little pink as he looks at Eshwari. 'You look *really* pretty with your head covered.'

Woahhhhhh! choruses the Interact Club. Eshwari blushes and swears. Satish glowers.

They surrender their shoes, walk through the little channel of running water and climb up the cool marble steps to the main part of the gurudwara. There is a lovely scent of fresh flowers and halwa frying. Everybody sniffs appreciatively and has a collective epiphany.

They do a quick dive into the main worship area, then come out looking virtuous and queue up for the kada prasad. The man doling it out is fiery-eyed and just a little scary looking, but the Interacters shamelessly hold out their cupped palms at him till he loads them up quite full. It is extremely hot and they have to blow on their hands frantically as they run down the steps to eat near the water tank.

'No swimming, washing or wringing of clothes by this tank,' Satish reads out the rules solemnly. 'No vigorous rubbing or soaping of armpits or other body parts either – and definitely no gargling. Got it, you lot?'

Jai Kakkar comes up to Eshwari as she sits, feet dangling in water as smooth as a sheeted mirror, entranced by the beauty of the place.

'Eshwari.'

'Boo,' she replies idly without looking at him. That's all it takes to get rid of Jai, usually.

'Are you and Satish going around?'

She turns around, surprised. He is still there, sitting beside her.

'I'm not scared of you, you know,' he says conversationally. 'Not any more. I'm taller, and my hair doesn't curl girlishly now – gone are the days when you could spill red ink on my shorts and tell the whole class I had got my period.'

Eshwari winces. 'I did that?'

He nods. 'Yes, you did. But I didn't mind. You were the only one who made fun of my hair, not my stammer.'

'I was evil,' she says, conscience-stricken. 'Evil Eshwari. I'm so sorry.'

'Are you guys going around?'

This phrase always makes Eshwari think of BJ. Going Around indeed, he is wont to snort whenever he hears this with-it lingo. What an image that conjures up! A daughter of mine hand-in-hand with some chinless, gulping fellow, going around and around *what*, exactly? A mulberry bush? The Dhaula Kuan roundabout? A sacred fire?

'No,' she says baldly. 'We're not.'

'But he's picking you up for the farewell party?'

'Yeah, but that doesn't really mean anything,' she explains. 'It's only because he lives next door to me.'

Jai rolls up his pants till just below the knees and lowers his legs into the water.

'That's good,' he says finally.

'Oh?'

'Yeah. I don't think we should complicate school friendships with this "going around" nonsense. We're too young. You don't want to screw up your board results, do you?'

Eshwari pulls back in mock horror. 'Who *are* you?' she demands. 'And what have you done with stud boy Jai Kakkar?'

He gives her an odd, twisted smile.

'Can we just be friends?' he asks. 'I'm a nice guy. Really.'

'Okay, okay. Don't be so *filmi*,' she mutters, suddenly self-conscious. 'Chalo, we're friends now, you and me. Jai and Veeru. I mean, Jai and Eshu. Happy?'

He nods, the sunshine dancing on the water reflecting in his eyes, gets up and walks away. As he does so, she notices that his butt is definitely Dylanesque. She has always thought she is way too cool to fall for anybody as obvious as the school stud, but at this moment, she's not too sure. As she gets to her feet slowly, Satish comes up from behind her.

'Don't listen to that choot,' he hisses. 'He's got sex on the brain. Yesterday in bio class, he *twice* said orgasm instead of organism.'

'Oh, shut up, Steesh.' She pushes him.

'Pushy fucker.' Satish shakes his head. 'And after I *told* him you're not allowed boyfriends till you're twenty-one!'

'You what?' she says, startled. 'No wonder...'

'And he's not the only one,' Satish grumbles. 'They've *all* suddenly discovered you – even that ass Mohit, who started playing the guitar because none of the girls would look at him otherwise. You're a little Assamese oil trickle and everybody's a white guy shouting Digboi-Digboi. It's because all the hot twelfthies have passed out, I suppose. And because this north Indian cloth you've wound around your head is making you look all goody-goody.'

'I hate you,' she says with feeling. 'Let's get the camp started now, okay?'

The polyclinic in the gurudwara compound has put up a banner announcing the blood camp, and two stern Malayali nurses are already in place behind the makeshift counters. They hand the Interacters a set of questions to ask every would-be donor and sit down on their shiny, round-with-a-hole-in-the-middle steel stools, cross their white nylon stocking-encased legs and exude a spirit of pessimism. AIDS has really put a dent in blood donations recently.

The questions to be asked are pretty simple.

Name?

Age?

Please stand on the weighing machine.

Any alcohol intake in the past twenty-four hours? If yes, please do not donate.

Do you have multiple sex partners? If yes, please do not donate.

This last question is the cause of much sniggering and nudging and ribbing amongst the Modernites. Everybody tsk-tsks and regrets the fact that unfortunately, in spite of *really* wanting to, they won't be able to donate, because they're sexually so active, don't you know. Eshwari, disgusted by this juvenile behaviour and stressed out by the fact that there seem to be hardly any donors in sight, sets out on a little walk, intent on commandeering people towards the camp.

'Please save a life!' she sings out as she hands pamphlets to everybody she encounters – families, couples, old ladies, single, hopeful looking men. 'It's for the Red Cross – please save a life!'

But it's slow going. People take the pamphlets from her happily enough but then hurry off to the parking lot, eyes lowered. It's just like the first two camps, she thinks, disheartened – and this, when they're showing all those films on DD every day, explaining exactly how AIDS spreads.

'We use disposable syringes,' she tells people. 'It's perfectly safe.'

But it's no use. Finally, discouraged by the heat, the mugginess and the glare of the sun bouncing off the golden dome of the gurudwara, she sits down under the Red Cross sign.

You'd think, wouldn't you, she rages silently, that people who have come all this way to *pray* would be willing to give a little blood to save somebody's life? That's why I thought holding these camps in places of worship was such a good idea! But obviously I hadn't a clue.

'Eshu puttar?'

She looks up and beholds Old Mr Gambhir, all dressed in white, smiling from ear to ear, the dome of the gurudwara forming a halo behind his head.

'Namaste, Gambhir uncle,' she says without much enthusiasm,

thinking, oh, what's the use? He's about a hundred years old. If he donates 470 ml blood he might keel over and die.

But Old Mr Gambhir has enthusiasm enough for both of them.

'Seen the paper, puttar? Dhillon ne toh aj kamal kar diya! He is wonderful. All his stories were good, but today's is the best. It is *top* ka!'

'Really? What is it?'

Old Mr Gambhir, who is apparently so delighted with Dylan's piece that he is carrying the *India Post* around with him, produces it immediately.

'Today is the anniversary of the Sikh massacre, na, that is why I have come to Bangla Sahib to pray. See, see the story, puttar, this will put that butcher behind bars for sure, don't you think? See what guts this girl has? God bless her!'

'Front page,' Eshwari says, impressed. '*I saw Hardik Motla with my own eyes – he was leading the massacre, promising rewards to whoever killed the most Sikhs.* Wow, this is explosive stuff, Gambhir uncle. Conclusive too.'

Several people hurrying past hear her and ask to read the paper. A small, excited crowd starts to form at the Red Cross station. When the Modernites sidle up and ask the swirling masses if they would like to donate blood and save a life, they pause for just a moment before they roll up their sleeves. The Malayali nurses get busy, sticking in their needles and pumping out large amounts of Punjabi blood with gusto.

In the midst of this spontaneous celebration and fluid extraction, old Mr Gambhir's eyes suddenly brim over with tears. 'Justice at last!' he says, his voice trembling, and bows reverentially before the Bangla Sahib. Then he turns to Eshwari and raises his hand, a saint making a benediction. 'Tell your mother, if Debjani marries this boy, I will supply all the Campa Cola and Gold Spot at the wedding for free! *Free.*'

'That's, um, really generous,' Eshwari says, stunned.

'*And* I will give, ten – no, twenty per cent discount on all the ghee, sugar, atta and dry fruits. But *only* if she marries this boy!'

'Don't you worry, Gambhir uncle,' Eshwari assures him. 'I think she will marry *only* this boy.'

New Delhi Railway Station is teeming with travellers, coolies and beggars. Noise and flies sit thickly on everything. Dylan, shouldering Kamalpreet's pink Rexine duffel bag, cuts through the crowd, taller than most, as she trots behind him, looking docile but determinedly pulling a trolley suitcase.

Who the hell brings a trolley suitcase to a railway platform, he thinks in disgust. Doesn't she know this place is full of stairs?

'Lemme get that,' he tells her but she shakes her head.

'I am fine,' she says. 'You walk ahead. What platform number is it?'

He stops and looks at her. There are dark circles under her eyes and she looks terribly distracted.

'Are you okay?' he asks gently. 'Spotted any strange men yet? *Looking* at you?'

'Make fun,' she says bitterly. '*You* are not on the front page today.'

'Actually, I am, and unlike you, even my photo has been printed.'

'You're used to it,' she says dismissively. Her eyes skitter around the platform.

'Would you like something to eat?'

She shakes her head.

'Waiting for someone to show up? A boyfriend, perhaps?'

'Ho-hai, don't be silly,' she responds, looking a little scandalized.

Dylan studies her face critically. 'Have you been dreaming about your mummy-papa or something?'

'I'm fine!' she snaps suddenly. 'Please hurry, I think maybe we have missed the train.'

Okay, whatever, Dylan thinks resignedly.

They descend onto platform Number 11 and find the train already standing there, emitting steam and stink, its whistle blowing. Dylan busies himself with looking for her name in the second class unreserved coach. She stands back, still clutching her prized trolley suitcase, looking around the platform nervously.

'Here you are!' he tells her, tapping a finger on the printed list triumphantly. '12 C. C'mon, let's get you on board.'

She hangs back. 'There must be some mistake. My ticket says 22 F. Look.'

He takes the ticket from her and studies it. The lean dimples flash and are quickly suppressed. 'That's not your seat number, Kamalpreet,' he tells her, carefully controlling his voice so that no laughter leaks through. 'That's your age and sex.'

Kamalpreet looks caught out and then gives a delighted little peal of laughter. What a nut job, Dylan thinks indulgently.

'Do you have water and everything?'

'Oh, yes,' she nods, and looks down at her HMT watch. 'Come, it's time I boarded, na?'

She drags her trolley suitcase to the train and manages to clamber on somehow. Then she turns to face him, her face sombre.

'Bye bye,' she says.

'Bye bye,' he replies, aware of a strange pang at parting from this vulnerable girl. Then he realizes he has forgotten something.

'Here, take this,' he says, handing her the pink Rexine duffel bag.

She reaches for it slowly, very slowly.

'Thank you so much,' she says, and there is an edge to her clear, sweet voice that he hasn't heard before. 'You are too generous – this money will change my life.'

'What?' Dylan says, confused, still holding out the bag. The train whistle has started to blow and he can't hear her properly.

Kamalpreet raises her voice.

'I will keep our agreement,' she continues, her gaze suddenly impersonal, looking no longer at him but somehow *through* him. 'I will never tell anybody about our deal, and never ask you for more money. What is inside this bag is my full and final payment.'

As he stares at her, bafflement and consternation writ large across his face, she reaches out and plucks the pink Rexine bag from his grasp. Immediately, a heavy hand lands on Dylan's shoulder.

'Check the bag.'

Dylan watches like a man in a dream as khaki-clad policemen force Kamalpreet off the train. The pink Rexine bag is quickly unzipped to reveal stack upon stack of stapled hundred-rupee notes.

'You are under arrest,' the plump senior officer tells Dylan. 'For bribery, witness-tampering, falsification of evidence, rumour-mongering and slander. Take him away.'

12

'I *told* you, na,' Binni says smugly, 'ki that Isayee is *not* okay. See what he's been up to – cooking up ganda-ganda stories of rape and murder! Chhi, I can't even think about it, it's too dirty. And you wanted Dabbu to marry him. He would have been in jail before the mehendi faded from her hands!'

The defeated silence that often greets her utterances prevails yet again.

'Say something, Ma!' Binni prods. 'Don't you agree?'

But Mrs Mamta is too overwrought to speak. Binni looks at her father.

'You're right, Binni,' the Judge admits with a sigh. 'It's quite likely the boy did cook up some stories. He sounded frustrated about not making any breakthroughs even in that letter he wrote Dabbu. He says he's not very rational on the subject of the riots and then goes on to admit that he is ruthless professionally and will do almost anything to get a story.'

'He was being *honest*, BJ!' Dabbu flashes. 'Because I kept going on about being honest and kind and brave. Stop treating every word he wrote as court evidence. You shouldn't have let him read my letter, Ma!'

As Debjani herself pressed her mother to show the letter to the Judge, this a little unfair. But Mrs Mamta lets it pass.

'And he watches porn.' Binni prims up her mouth. 'And he stole ten rupees once.'

Dabbu whirls to look at her mother with huge, betrayed eyes. 'You let *Binni didi* read my letter?'

'And why not?' Binni bridles up huffily. 'They read it, Eshu read it, why not me?'

'Because...' Debjani starts to say, then goes quiet.

'I found it on your dressing table,' Binni tells Debjani. 'So I read it.'

'Don't you know it's *very very* rude to read other people's letters?' Debjani demands.

'Bhai, *I* went to an old-fashioned Hindi medium school.' Binni tosses her head. 'Not to modern-fashioned Modern School. So I don't know these modern manners.'

Dabbu makes a strangled sound. Binni continues, 'And he drinks also. And sex record toh his own mother has told us. And now police record also. Chhi chhi chhi.'

'How can you!' Dabbu is almost white. 'How *can* you talk like that about somebody when they're down and out? I mean, Dylan's in *prison*. It's like kicking an injured animal.'

The Judge and his wife exchange glances. It's pretty clear to them what's happening. Saahas Shekhawat's son is about to swell the ranks of Moti the hairless dog, flop actor Randhir Kapoor, least popular Beatle Ringo Starr and the West Indies cricket team. They have to veer Debjani away before she takes it in her head to adopt him, defend him and never let him go. Because the boy is trouble, pure and simple.

'I don't think the situation is *that* bad, Dabbu,' Mrs Mamta says soothingly. 'He's not in prison, only in lock-up, and he's sure to get bail or something.'

'Vickyji says he'll be locked up for years under TADA,' Binni says smugly. 'And I think-so jail is the right place for him. Thinking up imaginary ganda-ganda rapes and killings. Must have got the idea from all the porn he watched.'

'But one thing is really confusing me, Binni didi,' Debjani says tightly, knowing she may regret saying this, that she may get chhaalas in her mouth, but unable to keep it locked up inside her any more. 'Last time I checked, you *approved* of this boy and you *wanted* me to marry him – on the basis of some legal advice your lawyer gave Vickyji. What happened? Did the advice turn out to be incorrect?'

Binni's plump cheeks suddenly sag. She swallows hard. 'I-I don't know what you're talking about, Dabbu. You're mad or what?'

'No,' Debjani replies. 'Because I checked with Gulgul bhaisaab too, and he told me your lawyer had got hold of the wrong end of the stick completely.'

'What are you two talking about?' the Judge asks, mystified.

'Girlie stuff, BJ,' Debjani answers as Binni seems incapable of speech. 'Oh, and Binni didi, in case you were wondering, the same law applies to girls who marry American-Estonian Christians too.'

'Silly Dabbu,' says Binni, turning to face her father with a laugh. 'I don't know what she's saying. I *really* have no idea – but she's right, maybe we're being too hard on this Shekhawat. After all, he *could* have been framed. No, Bauji? What do you say?'

'I think I have a very good idea of what just happened here,' the Judge says, his nostrils white and pinched. 'So let me make one thing very clear. I'll say it only once, so listen carefully, all of you. Binodini, this house belongs to *all* my daughters, no matter who they marry or whether they have any biological children. And tell your husband that unless he returns the "loan" I gave him three years ago – you know damn well what I mean, so don't look so blank – I'll carve it out from your share of this house, so that when we sell it, everybody will get a hissa except you. Understood?'

Binni gasps, starts to her feet, throws an anguished glance at her mother and stumbles out of the room. Mrs Mamta shoots the Judge a furious look and follows her out.

The Judge glares at the swinging door, looking grimly satisfied.

'Oh, isn't that *typical.*'

The whisper is low and furious. The Judge looks around, startled.

'You don't give a damn about me.' Debjani's voice is trembling. 'All you care about it is your stupid *house* and your stupid *money* and Binni didi's *court case* and Anji didi not being able to have any *babies*. My life isn't worth even a fifteen-minute conversation.'

'That's not true, Dabbu,' the Judge protests.

But she has already stood up. 'I'm going to DD,' she says curtly. 'Bye.'

<hr>

'Now look here, Hijranandini –'

'Bade-papaji, *please*,' Varun interjects in an agonized whisper. 'It's *Hira*nandani.'

'You don't interrupt, duffer. Tum dono ke dono incompetents ho, out to dubao the newspaper I built with these two bare hands. Can't you see what is right in front of your nose?'

You are, Varun thinks resentfully. A short, bald, chubby hobbit of a man, with bulbous eyes, twin rows of broken teeth and nostril hair so long and bristly they actually cast a shadow.

The Fat Old Man of Indian Publishing has summoned the two newsmen to his poolside for an emergency meeting. They have had to watch him swim eight laborious laps (one for each decade he has spent on the planet, his yoga teacher has instructed him) and then clamber out, practically catatonic, wheezing and snorting, exuding a strong odour of chlorine. A solemn ritual followed, where he hopped first on one foot and then the other, his flabby bits jiggling importantly above his tight red chaddis, till the water cleared out of his ears. Then he donned a loose white towelling robe, knotted it tightly right below his massive paunch and sat down to his evening naashta. Now, spraying watermelon seeds in every direction (he needs to eat one whole watermelon to keep his bowels in good nick, his yoga teacher says), he wants to know what the newspaper is doing about the fact that 'Motla put on a bra and harem pants, batted his lashes, wriggled his bum and led all you chutiyas up the garden path'.

'*What's* in front of our eyes, Ohri saab?' Hira asks patiently.

But Purshottam Ohri is not in the mood to answer questions. He leans forward, flashing slivers of wrinkly hairy thigh on either side, and glares balefully at his editor-in-chief.

'It's a conspiracy,' he states, breathing hard. 'It's the Emergency all over again.'

Both Varun and Hira give simultaneous silent groans. If

Bade-papaji were ever to wear a bonnet, the Emergency would be the bee in it. He is obsessed with the Emergency – with the clamping down on free speech, the gagging of the press, the enforced vasectomy of an entire generation in return for a square meal and pocket transistors. *India Post* was a major hero during the Emergency and sometimes Varun thinks his grandfather just misses the buzz of those good old days.

'Why do you say that, Ohri saab?' Hira asks respectfully.

The old man smirks. 'You're humouring me, aren't you, Hira?' he asks. 'You think I'm being paranoid. I can tell you're planning to forget this conversation as soon as you're out of my house, but you would do better to listen to me – because you have *no idea* what's happening in Delhi.'

'What is?' Varun demands abruptly.

The old man leans back. Water drips from his red swimming trunks. 'This government,' he says expansively, 'emboldened no doubt by the brute majority we were stupid and sentimental enough to give them after the old lady got assassinated, is about to introduce an anti-defamation bill into Parliament.'

'What's that?'

'It's an anti-press bill,' the old man elaborates. 'It means that if you write a negative story about some politician or the other, he can claim it isn't true and have you thrown into jail immediately, no questions asked, for defaming him. And then it's up to *you* to prove your story's true and that you're innocent. Which could take months or years – and you'd probably be sodomized and half dead by then. Get it?'

'No.' Varun shakes his head. 'I mean, yes, I suppose so. But how do you know this is happening? And why?'

The old man gives him a beady look. 'It's happening because

we've all been writing such complimentary stories about the government, *that's* why,' he says sarcastically. 'We've exposed a sixty-four crore gun scam, a submarine scam, a story about offshore accounts in St Kitts, several stories about the government's botched attempts at sucking up to the Muslim voter in the Shah Bano case, and of course, a slew of blistering reports on how they're protecting that mass murderer Hardik Motla. *That's* why. The government has a brute majority, so it's acting like a brute, amending the law and going for our jugular.'

'How do you know all this?' Hira asks, fascinated.

Purshottam Ohri snorts.

'I'm not dead yet,' he says shortly. And dives into another massive slice of watermelon.

'Don't you think you're being just a little paranoid, Bade-papaji?' Varun suggests diffidently. 'And anyway, how does this tie up with the Shekhawat case?'

'Pass the kala namak, duffer. I think Shekhawat's case will be cited as a prime example of an irresponsible press running amok. Don't you see? The timing's perfect. Shekhawat will be the government's opening gambit, their example of how low the press can sink if it isn't accountable to anybody. They'll use that fake Punjabi witness and the bribe of lakhs of rupees, which they themselves have set up, to push the bill through.'

The two newsmen look unconvinced.

'It's an interesting theory,' Varun says cautiously.

'First time I've heard of an anti-defamation bill,' Hira remarks, shrugging.

Purshottam Ohri bangs his fist on the little table. Watermelon seeds fly everywhere.

'They're keeping it quiet! They'll sneak it through both Houses of Parliament in just one day! Journalists will become too scared to report freely and fairly on *anything* – they could be locked up otherwise!'

'Okay,' Hira says cautiously. 'So, what do you want us to do about it, Ohri saab?'

The old man sits back. 'I am going to Calcutta to meet with some other publishing houses. They share my low opinion of the "goborment". We'll organize a protest march. You two concentrate on getting Shekhawat out of prison, theek hai?'

'He's only in the hawalat,' Hira hastens to say. 'Not actually in jail, per se.'

'Haan haan, let's not quibble,' the old man replies irascibly. 'Now tell me what *you* think. Do you think Shekhawat bribed that laundiya?'

'I don't know what to think,' Hira admits. 'The police statement says that Dylan bribed the girl with five lakh rupees –'

'Where would Dylan get five lakh rupees?' Varun throws up his hands. 'We all know what his salary is.'

'From the Akal Takth apparently,' Hira says wearily. 'At least, that's the theory the police are espousing. That he met up with separatist Sikh leaders when he went to Canada and *they* provided the money. To bribe witnesses, destabilize the government at the centre and inject new enthusiasm into the movement for an independent Khalistan.'

Purshottam Ohri snorts. 'They're all jealous. Because he's so handsome and dashing. Same thing used to happen to me when I was young.'

Varun and Hira maintain a polite silence.

'The *Post* is losing credibility as we speak,' Purshottam Ohri continues, pronging plump red bits of fruit and shovelling them into his mouth. 'Everybody I meet in Calcutta and Delhi will want a statement from me. Do I defend Shekhawat? Wash my hands off him? What? What are the facts of the case?'

Telling the old man that they will get back to him very soon, the two men hightail it out of Ohri Mansion and head for the Press Club, a seedy, barrack-like building in the Fort area, hung with so many windows that the city politicians refer to it as the Glasshouse. (Those who drink in Glasshouses shouldn't throw stones, they often say.)

Sipping tepid whiskey sodas in the smoky buzzing bar, Varun and Hira face each other over a bowl of soggy masala peanuts.

'Everybody's looking at us,' Varun says gloomily. 'We're the whatchumacallit of all eyes.'

'I've written an editorial saying we're behind our correspondent, of course,' Hira says. 'That we support him fully, that this whole thing is a set-up and a gross abuse of power. But quite frankly, I don't know if I have the balls to print it.'

'So you *do* think Dylan's been influencing the witnesses,' Varun says.

Hira's face sags a little. He spreads out his hands. 'I don't know what to think, frankly. You know I'm fond of Shekhawat. He's the best we've got. But these young firebrands, they tend to get impatient. Sometimes they take shortcuts. The justification usually is: I know it's true but I don't have proof, so let me fake it. They think the end justifies the means.'

A long silence follows. They sip their drinks morosely.

'I can't believe the old man is going on a protest march,' Varun says presently. 'He'll have a coronary within the first hundred metres.'

Hira smiles a small smile.

'D'you think his theory could be correct?'

Hira averts his eyes. 'I have the greatest respect for your grandfather, Varun. But...'

'You think he's imagining things.'

Hiranandani shrugs. 'He was jailed during the Emergency, wasn't he? I missed all that action, working in London. But I think it made all the press people who lived through it a little prone to conspiracy theories.'

'How serious is the case against Shekhawat, anyway?' Varun asks after a pause. 'Why don't you speak to the PM about it?'

Hiranandani leans forward. 'The PM,' he says emphatically, 'is pals with me precisely because I never ask him for any favours. Besides, I need to be absolutely sure of my facts before I bring it up with him.'

'Speak to Dylan then,' Varun tells him suddenly. 'Go down to Delhi, hear his version of how the whole thing happened. Maybe that'll give us some leads, tell us something that can connect this wretched girl to Motla. You could do a little digging on this anti-defamation bill too. Meanwhile, I'll put a team on it here.'

Hiranandani stares into space for a moment and then nods and gets to his feet. 'Good idea,' he says crisply. 'So let's hold the fire-breathing editorial for a couple of days, till we find out how many cubic feet of shit we're actually in. You muzzle your Bade-papaji somehow. Got it?'

Varun looks around the crowded bar in a panic. 'You're just gonna walk out and leave me alone *here*? With everybody looking at me and sniggering?'

A wry smile spreads across Hiranandani's thin, sad-clown face. 'That lass from *Viewstrack* just walked in.' He points discreetly.

'The one you fancy. Shall I introduce you? She's from College too, you know.'

And fifteen minutes later (maybe because it is be-nice-to-short-fat-men day, Varun tells himself) Mitali and he are sitting together and talking animatedly. At least, Mitali is.

'So you actually think Dylan bribed that chick? *Dylan?*'

Varun is mesmerized by the way her nose ring hovers so tantalizing above her red lips. He nods automatically, and then realizing what she's just said, shakes his head quickly.

'No no,' he says, with some vehemence. 'Of course not. He's been framed. By that Motla.'

'By that *lordu* Motla,' Mitali agrees with passion and knocks back the last of her Romanov and Limca. 'You're right, of course, Varun Ohri. Hey, you're an Ohri – that means you're the owner of the *India Post*, right?'

'*One* of the,' Varun corrects her despondently. 'It's a very large family. I own about half a page of the paper – probably the comic strips. Or the obits. Haha.'

'Now don't put yourself down like that!' She smiles at him. 'Listen, why don't we team up and crack this thing right open? You guys cover it for the print media and I'll cover it for *Viewstrack*. What do you say?'

'I say a cautious okay,' Varun replies, thrilled at the prospect of spending more time with her. 'Provided you don't double-cross us and break the story first, of course.'

'That'll never happen. We move way slower than you print types. Processing, edit, sound. And then two days for the no-objection certificate from the censors. *Then* we get the tapes out.'

'Well, in that case, Mitali Dutta,' he says (unwittingly revealing that he knows her last name and therefore knows exactly who she

is, though he's been feigning ignorance for the last half hour),
'let's shake on it.'

When Debjani gets to Akashvani Bhavan she finds it buzzing.
The Information & Broadcasting Minister visited the studios in
the morning so everything is spic and span. The cigarette butts in
the potted plants have been scooped up and the pots themselves
are gleaming bright orange with a fresh application of powdered
brick. In the green room, Amitabh Bose is sitting on a high chair,
reeling from a just-met-the-minister high.

'He knew me *immediately*,' he crows. 'The DG tried to
introduce me, but he said, no need for introduction, inhe toh
sab jaante hain. Everybody knows him! And then he asked me if
everything was okay and I said it was all good.'

'But you're always saying ki everything *isn't* okay,' Debjani
points out. 'That there are flies in the studio – one showed up
clearly that day when Sameep was interviewing Cliff Richard!'

'Yeah, well, I think Sameep attracts flies, frankly,' Amitabh
Bose says testily. 'I wouldn't have bothered the I&B minister with
such a small thing.'

'And the loos?' Dabbu demands. 'You keep saying they could
be cleaner. And the autocue breaks down all the time. And...'

But Amitabh Bose is having his face powdered and cannot
reply. The make-up dada smirks, thinking that this the first
time Bose babu has turned up so early. He has been prowling
around the building all day, hoping to meet the minister. While
the minister was prowling around the building all day hoping
to meet the pretty lady readers – he heard him enquire after
Debjaniji *twice*.

'What was the purpose of the visit, anyway?' she asks him presently, as they take their seats in the studio.

'The special broadcast for Independence Day,' he replies. 'The PM's address. And also,' he adds, his voice sinking to a whisper, 'how DD's become too anti-government lately.'

'Huh?' Debjani says, bewildered. Her mind goes back to Dylan's blistering piece in the *IP*. 'But I thought we suck up to the government too much!'

'Not enough, apparently,' Amitabh Bose murmurs. 'Operation Credibility was all well and good for the time being, but now there is an election looming and we need to grab our pompoms and break into a bust-thrusting, butt-wriggling cheerleader routine in favour of the ruling party.'

Debjani unconsciously crumples the scripts Young-Uday has just handed them, starting to feel vaguely mutinous. Amitabh Bose continues, 'And he also said the new lot of newsreaders needs to pull up their socks. That they aren't as, ahem, *polished* as us oldies. That they fumble and mumble and look panicky. He said DD should bump them down to reading Parliament news only. But I defended you lot bravely. Thank me!'

Dabbu listens, feeling more indignant by the minute.

'Debbie, you haven't read through your script,' Young-Uday says hesitantly. 'Don't you think you should? You always do.'

'It's okay,' she says shortly. 'I can handle it.'

But when it is time for her to read the last paragraph of her section of the bulletin, she wishes she *had* read through it. Because then she could have swapped it with Amitabh Bose. Or pleaded sick. Or fainted. Or something. Anything to avoid reading out loud, to the whole country, even as a wretched feeling settles in the pit of her stomach:

'Human Rights organizations have condemned the actions of India Post *journalist Dylan Singh Shekhawat, saying that the bribing and coaching of witnesses in the anti-Sikh riots case has done the cause of justice irreparable harm. They observed that such actions undermine the capability of civil society to have any imprimatur of impartiality in investigating Human Rights violations and urged that Shekhawat be punished severely.'*

'How much money can you make being a journalist, waise? Matlab ki, wot is thee starting celery?'

'Not much,' Dylan says wearily. 'Five hundred bucks.'

The three policemen absorb this information. They are all sitting around cozily in the warm chowki hawalat. There is a cement bench built into the wall. Sour smelling iron bars. A few dead tubelights do nothing to illuminate the faces of the law-keepers whose yellowish khaki uniforms blend seamlessly with their yellowish khaki complexion, not to mention with the yellowish khaki beedis clutched between their yellowish khaki teeth.

'You have to do some special course-worse?' they ask next. 'Ya bas, graduation is enough?'

Dylan is starting to wonder if any of this is really happening. 'A course helps,' he replies. 'I did a two-year diploma at the IIMC in Delhi.'

'Expensive hoga,' the cops say dismissively. 'Out of our league. Bhai, our starting celery is only fifty rupees a month. *But*,' one of them adds, balling his hand into a fist, 'we have *pow*-ur.'

Bit of an over-statement that, Dylan thinks, glancing at the cold, grey bars of the electric heater in the corner. We haven't had any power in the what, sixteen, hours since I've been here.

'We get kung fu karate training also,' says the fattest one. 'The nunchaku is an Indian invention, did you know? In my village of Doondahera, we use two short dandas with a rope in the middle to herd the buffaloes.'

Dylan's conviction that none of this is actually happening grows stronger by the minute.

'You also have a really efficient investigative system going here,' he manages to say. 'I mean, the way you moved in to arrest me just as I was handing over the bribe. Caught me in the act. Impressive. How did you figure that out?'

The policemen look at each other and smirk.

'Trying to pump us,' one of them remarks sapiently. The other two promptly turn to glower threateningly at Dylan.

'We can kill you, you know,' the fattest one says, pinching the lobe of Dylan's ear lovingly. 'We can do anything we like – no one will ask even one qwoshun.'

'Not today, though,' objects the third conscientiously. 'I can't do any voilent acts today – my son's mundan ceremony is at five o'clock – I have to stay holy and pure.'

I wish they'd just leave me alone so I can *think*, Dylan thinks exhaustedly. Try and make sense of what the hell just happened. That girl was obviously a plant, a set-up to discredit me and the paper. But whose stooge was she? Motla's? That's why he called me up to say don't print the story. And I, like a damned fool, got all excited, walked straight into his trap and printed it. But is that all there is to it? Or is there more?

'We can still *beat* you,' the first cop is saying dreamily. 'But very cleverly, pyar se, without any scars or fractures. So that even if you get bail somehow – you bastards always do – you won't be able to write a story on police brutality the moment you get back to work. What do you say to that, my dear? Want some kambal pitai, hain? Some tender loving cane?'

'No, thanks,' Dylan tells them sincerely. 'And if I get out, I'd rather do a story on your outrageously low salaries. Try and get you guys a raise.'

The cops look at each other and chuckle fatly. 'Oh, we get by,' winks the one who has sworn off all 'voilence' today. 'Fifty rupees is only our *basic*, you could say.'

'The perks of *pow*-ur.' Dylan balls his hand into a fist and grins. 'Cool.'

'But day-to-day life is expensive, you know. Ab, take this mundan only. Three thousand rupees it is costing!' The cop repeats the figure with gloomy pride, '*Three* thousand rupees!'

'You could earn it back by gambling,' his fat colleague suggests slyly. 'Diwali season hai – what about a quick round of teen patti? Ho jaye?'

But the first cop holds his ears and shakes his head virtuously. 'I have given my zubaan on the head of my three-year-old daughter. No more teen patti for me. No flash. No blackjack. No poker.'

'We could play kot-piece,' Dylan hears himself say. 'There are four of us, and it's a game for four. Gimme the cards, I'll show you.'

For a moment, the cops look at him in surprise. Then they nod indulgently.

'Here, take,' they say as they surrender the cards to Dylan. 'Enjoy the pleasure of our company while you can. When they shift you to Tihar you won't find the surroundings half as friendly.'

'And in how many days will that be?' Dylan asks as he starts to deal out the cards. But before they can reply, the tubelights flicker on and the dead heater starts to glow a slow, dark orange. The little TV blips on and Debjani's face stares down at all of them from the top of a dirty refrigerator.

'*Human Rights organizations have condemned the actions of* India Post *journalist Dylan Singh Shekhawat, saying that the bribing and coaching of witnesses in the anti-Sikh riots case has done the cause of justice irreparable harm. They observed that such actions undermine the capability of civil society to have any imprimatur of impartiality in investigating Human Rights violations and urged that Shekhawat be punished severely.*'

⟶◦◦◦◦⟵

'The call came from a working women's hostel in Paharganj,' Mitali tells Varun over the phone excitedly.

'Is that a hill station?' he asks, slightly at a loss.

'No, stupid! It's a sort of market in Delhi, near the railway station.'

'Are you sure it's the right number?'

'Yes! See, I got a friend of mine from College – who's in the IAS now – to dig out the details of all the calls your receptionist received that morning. It came through around eleven, lasted only three minutes and is from a Delhi number. It *has* to be the one!'

'And this IAS, he gave you the address too? Isn't that illegal?'

She clicks her tongue impatiently. 'He's really fond of Dylan. Besides, *College* connection, you know.'

Varun, who finds it really irritating that Stephenians call their college just 'College' with a capital C, like there are no other colleges on the planet, ignores this. 'So should I book our tickets?' he asks instead. 'Let's get to this working women's hostel and rent you a room there?'

'Yes, let's,' says Mitali and cuts the line.

The next afternoon finds the two of them at the Yuvati Niwas in Paharganj, talking to a nun with a moustache. The nun tells them that they are usually always full up, but luckily for Mitali, one of their girls has just done a bunk. Her room is empty and Mitali is welcome to have it if she can make the necessary payments and provide a certificate of good character from her employer. Varun, posing as Mitali's elder brother, provides the three months' advance rent and helps her move in.

'Now remember, this is a shared scoop,' he tells her as he attempts to lug her stuff upstairs. 'Equal credits to *IP* and *Viewstrack*.'

'But I've done all the digging,' she objects, scooping up her duffel bag.

'And I've paid for the train tickets and provided your rent,' he points out. 'Call me tomorrow at ten if you have any leads – or even if you have nothing. Okay?'

Mitali giggles. 'I don't think she believed me when I said you were my brother.'

Varun shoots her an austere look. 'I wonder why.'

He fixes up to meet with Dylan's parents the next morning, and when he gets to their house he is greeted by Juliet Bai, depressed and loquacious in equal measure.

'It's all my fault,' she informs Varun dolefully as she opens the door. 'I was too proud of him – of his height and his handsomeness and his lovely deep voice and his athlete-of-the-year trophies, and yes, even his girlfriends. It was wicked of me. I used to look at all the other mothers on sports day – so excited about the single measly bronze medal their child had won – and feel superior and pity them. *How* I wish now that Dylan was short and podgy and ugly and came last in all the races, at least then nobody would have put nazar on him like this!'

'No no, aunty,' Varun murmurs as he sits down to the breakfast she has laid out. 'Hello, uncle, boys.'

'*We're* very proud of Dyl,' Ethan pipes up before the Brig can get a word in. 'His battle for justice has clearly got the government rattled. It is the sacred duty of all Rajputs to be battering rams in battle and brave in bed, you see. Or is it brave in battle and battering rams in bed?'

The Brigadier smacks him on the back sharply. Ethan emits an outraged squawk and shuts up. Juliet Bai gives a huge gulping shudder. Tears splash into her teacup. She stirs it, and as she sips, some very unworthy thoughts about Debjani's family cross her mind.

'Mamta's sister-in-law Bhudevi does a lot of voodoo and tantric witchcraft. She's even been claiming to be possessed by the soul of her dead mother-in-law! Do you think – after the scene in their house that day – she put some sort of hex on Dylan, Bobby?'

'That's rubbish, Bobby,' the Brigadier says shortly. 'Varun, you tell us, what exactly is the situation? Have you come to get Dylan out? He has done so much for the newspaper – what are you doing for *him*?'

'Take more cornflakes,' Juliet Bai urges. 'You're not eating anything.'

'Uh, yes, thank you, aunty,' Varun says, red and flustered. 'My editor-in-chief is meeting Dylan in the hawalat today. And I'm investigating that so-called Kamalpreet's background. Trying to nail the link between her and Hardik Motla.'

'He was quite taken by her,' Ethan volunteers in a subdued voice. 'Said she was a lovely girl – so vulnerable yet so brave.'

Juliet Bai snorts. 'Dylan is a fool about these so-called vulnerable girls. But this Kamalpreet makes the Judge's daughter look like an angel, *that's* for sure.'

'Never mind all that, how will you prove this whole thing was a set-up?' the Brigadier asks, frowning repressively at his wife. 'And who will believe you? That's if you even have the guts to print the story?'

'We'll get the proof,' Varun assures them. 'Chief Editor Hiranandani – he's a close friend of the PM – has managed to wrangle a meeting with your son today. You'll have news of Dylan quite soon.'

━━◆━━

'Somebody is here to meet you.'

Dylan, sprawled on the cement bench and staring at the grubby wall opposite, looks around, squinting against the light.

'Hira?'

'What's up, tiger?'

The voice is low, and shaking with emotion. Dylan sits up and smiles.

'The fastidious Mr Hiranandani!' he says lightly. 'How tragic to see you in such insalubrious, boorish environs.'

Hira's sad-clown face splits into a grin. 'Don't let's get into all that. Stand up and let me look at you properly – are you quite all right?'

'I'm fine.' Dylan gets to his feet and stretches lazily. But he doesn't walk up to the bars or take Hira's outstretched hand. 'Sorry to disappoint you.'

'Yeah,' Hira says ruefully. 'Now, we don't have much time, so listen carefully to what I'm going to say...'

Dylan raises his eyebrows. 'I'm not sure I want to,' he says and there is a peculiar edge to his voice.

Though he hadn't got much time to think initially, around

midnight the thaana had settled down to a marathon porn watching session. In the ensuing quiet that followed, punctuated only by the occasional grunt or moan, Dylan has managed to figure out some stuff. A whole lot of stuff, actually.

'What?' Hira looks confused. Then he shakes his head. 'Never mind, just pay attention. I've cut through all the red tape and assured the PM of what a good journalist you are, vouched for you personally – and so has old man Ohri. And we've worked out quite a good deal. So listen – you *are* listening, right?'

'Oh, I'm listening.' Dylan nods, his eyes glittering strangely.

'Admit to the bribery charge and I'll have you out on bail, pronto. Immediately. Deny it and you could be in here for years.' He holds up a hand as Dylan starts to speak. 'I know what you're about to say – that you didn't do anything – but that's a battle we can fight later, once we've got you out.'

But Dylan shakes his head. Once, very gently.

'Why did you do it, Hira?' he asks.

The older man stares back at him, his eyes perplexed. 'What?'

'Was it because I insulted your new, improved DD in your own column? That made you look like a bit of a fool, I suppose. Or was it because Bade-papaji is so fond of me? Or was it something else – your pal the PM piling up the pressure... What was it?'

'I don't know what you're talking about.' Hira's voice is bewildered. 'Why did I do *what*?'

'Get into cahoots with Motla. It happened when he came to meet you in office, didn't it? You were pissed off with me about the anti-DD piece, but you pretended you weren't. Instead, you gave me a nice long rope to hang myself with. My own byline, a photograph to accompany my pieces, lots of fame. But you were just fattening me up for the kill. Kamalpreet – or whatever her real name is – was the bait. That's why you urged me to print that piece so quickly – you said we'd miss the anniversary of the riots if we bothered to get background colour on her from Tirathpuri. You knew she was a fake, didn't you?'

'Have they been hitting you on the head or something?' Hira asks, looking deeply concerned. 'Could it have affected your memory? Because I clearly recall telling you to check up on her thoroughly before we printed her story – the motto of our paper is *Truth. Balance. Courage.*, for heaven's sake! I never said anything about missing any anniversary.'

'You're such a smooth bastard,' Dylan says with quiet disbelief. 'I can't believe I couldn't see it earlier.'

'They *have* been hitting you.' Hira's smile is distinctly sinister now. 'You've forgotten that you called me up and assured me that the Kamalpreet story had checked out, that it had been thoroughly double-checked and verified.'

Dylan leans in close.

'We both know I didn't.'

'Yes,' Hira agrees, thrusting his hands into his pockets and rocking on his heels. 'We both know you didn't. And we both know you've been getting too big for your boots. You cheeky little bastard, how *dare* you trash me in my own column? You think that because that senile old man thinks you're such a hotshot, you can get away with *anything*? Well, you can't. Tonight, with a heavy heart, I am going to write a prize-winning, introspective editorial about how tragic it is when young journalists stray from the straight and narrow. I'm going to say you're a liar, a bribe-eater *and* a bribe-giver. I'm going to take full personal responsibility for hiring you, and with profound sorrow, I'm going to offer to resign. Of course, the Ohris won't accept my resignation.'

Dylan stares at him, wondering how he could ever have idolized this man, considered him a mentor, or even a worthy boss. He's just a weedy, insecure ass, he thinks. I was totally wrong about him. What else have I been totally wrong about?

'But *why?*' he asks finally. 'Just because of the DD piece?'

He is met with silence.

'But you went to College!'

Hira winces at this.

'Oh, please,' he says irascibly. 'This whole College connection is so overrated. The truth of the matter is that the PM is trying to get a piece of legislation through Parliament – a little something called the anti-defamation bill. I'm just trying to help him do it. For a certain, er, fee.'

'The *what* bill?' Dylan looks at him in blank incomprehension.

But Hira is already backing away from the bars.

'I'd think about confessing to the bribery and witness-tampering charges if I were you,' he says. 'They'll book you under TADA otherwise – for conspiring with Canadian terrorist organizations and fomenting unrest – and stick you into Tihar till you're an old man. Your Gregory Pecker will wilt away unused. So consider confessing. Now goodbye, I have an editorial to write.'

❦

'Can you please explain what we are doing here?' Varun asks Mitali plaintively. 'The suspense is killing me.'

She doesn't so much as glance at him. 'Wait wait wait,' she murmurs, eyes glued to the tiny TV monitor before her. 'I'm looking for something...'

'But *what?*' Varun knows he is sounding petulant but he

can't help it. They've been cooped up inside a tiny edit studio in Safdurjang Enclave for hours now, in a tiny six-by-six-foot basement that reeks strongly of naphthalene balls and damp. 'I would like to warn you at this point, Mitali Dutta, that my crush on you is in danger of languishing away entirely due to lack of nourishment.'

'Silly,' she says, glancing at him briefly. 'You don't have a crush on me – you're just programmed to think that all career girls who smoke and put kajal and wear nose rings are hot.'

'That's rubbish,' Varun returns stoutly. 'I've seen beyond your smoke-screen of oxidized silver and carbon monoxide. I know you're worthy of deep emotion.'

'Do you want to hear what I'm looking for?' she asks hastily.

Varun grins. 'Yes, please.'

Mitali presses pause on the footage she has been watching and turns to face him. 'So, basically, I chatted up all the girls and the old nuns in there to find out about this girl who's gone missing. Nobody knew much about her. "Kept to herself" was the general verdict. But then somebody happened to show me a picture of a bunch of the girls on the porch of the Yuvati Niwas. And she's in the background talking to a wrinkly old guy who used to come over to meet her often. Their records have him listed as her maternal uncle. I took a picture of the register. Look!'

She hands Varun two photographs. Varun peers at the first, his forehead crinkling. 'What an unlovely sight. And this wrinkly old man is...?'

'Somebody I've seen before,' Mitali says, banging on the console hard. 'I wish I knew where – I know it's in some old footage, so I'm checking all the stories I've done, but no sign of him so far...'

'We're trying to link her with Motla, aren't we?' Varun points out. 'So why don't you look through the footage of your interview with him?'

Mitali looks mildly surprised. 'You're right. I should have thought of that myself.'

Varun shrugs. 'It's only common sense,' he says modestly. But Mitali doesn't hear him, she is already burrowing through the box of dusty tapes at her feet. She straightens up, her face red with excitement, adjusting the neckline of her kaftanesque kurta which has slipped deliciously low.

'Got it,' she says breathlessly. 'Let's check it out.'

They spot him about halfway through the recording. Motla requests a break, holding up his palm horizontally and sticking a finger below it in the time-out sign. He wipes his face with a hanky and then – as Mitali and Varun watch with bated breath in the smelly edit studio – the wrinkly old man from the Yuvati Niwas photograph steps into the frame bearing a packet of Pan Parag. He opens it, extracts a spoonful with a tiny tin spoon and upends it onto Motla's extended palm. The whole manoeuvre takes only about five seconds. The two players do it with the ease of long practice.

'Of course!' Mitali says ecstatically as she freezes the image. 'That's why I remember him. We played this shot again and again when we were fine-tuning the edit. This wrinkly old guy kept getting into the shot. He's clearly Motla's Man Friday, isn't he?'

'Yes, he is.' Varun nods emphatically. 'Now all we need to do is print both these pictures in the paper – the one of him with Motla and the one of him with Kamalpreet. Along with an 800-word piece that I will personally write. And we're *home*.'

She gives him an impulsive hug. 'And so is Dylan,' she says, her eyes alight with happiness. 'This is fantastic.'

Varun shoots her a wistful look. 'Yeah, that'll make you happy, huh? I thought you were just doing this because it's such a big story.'

'Oh, it's a huge story,' she agrees fervently.

'I know. Bade-papaji and Hira will be thrilled.'

<hr>

Journalist still in lock-up.
Verdict expected soon.

Villain Singh Shekhawat, as Hardik Motla's spin doctors have dubbed the *India Post* journalist who has been accused of bribing and coaching witnesses, continues to languish in the lock-up. The editor and owners of the newspaper remain tight-lipped on the issue and have issued no statement.

<hr>

Chachiji is a happy woman. The flat is almost ready. A big artistic signboard spelling out *Hailey Court* in gorgeously curvy and curling type, has gone atop the six-storied building. The builder has been most obliging, fawning over her gratifyingly and carrying out all her little changes and special demands. The workmen are polishing the marble now, their massive machines grinding late into the night. The sound is music to Chachiji's ears as she sits at the window in the annexe, her tongue between her teeth, making laborious drawings on green graph paper of how she will arrange her furniture in the flat. 'The navy-blue sofa set will go here,' she has told Mrs Mamta. 'The glass-topped driftwood table over there. My cupboard full of porcelain dogs just here. And of course my carpet with the two Chinese dragons will go in the lowbie. There is a lowbie also, did I tell you?'

Mrs Mamta puts up with this effusiveness bravely, telling the girls that they have weathered the worst of it, and soon Chachiji will be ensconced in her own home, busy and happy.

Anjini is of the opinion that her mother is being way too optimistic. 'She'll need somebody to hate, Ma,' she warns her. 'She's got nobody to bitch and moan and carp on about ever since she sent the Hot Dulari packing. Watch out she doesn't promote you to the status of Enemy Number 1.'

Mrs Mamta looks harassed. 'Now, girls,' she says feebly.

'I agree,' says Binni. 'Every time she goes out to water the plants in her tiny balcony, she'll see your big spacious garden below and hate you. And she'll come over and make fun of your marble chip floors and your plywood kitchen shutters and the Indian-style toilet in the terrace loo.'

'And she'll tell everybody Eshu's having an affair with the Mother Dairy booth ka chinkie,' Anji adds.

'I wish,' Eshwari sighs. 'But I think he's got some hot Mandakini type hidden away in the hills. Still, you don't want Chachiji zooming in on you as her primary hate target, Ma. Let's dig up the Hot Dulari, wherever she is, and bring her back.'

But Ashok Narayan Thakur does this before they can. Resurfacing after a fortnight of 'work', he drops by to airily inform Chachiji that he ran into the Hot Dulari while on his travels, and because she looked so broken and bereft and starved, he apologized to her on Chachiji's behalf for dismissing her so unfairly, and (out of pure, disinterested human kindness) offered to re-instate her as cook-cum-housekeeper in the new Hailey Court establishment. And she accepted. He then summons Gulab and slaps him twice and tells him to forget about opening any gym-shim. He finishes by telling Chachiji that if she doesn't like the Hot-Dulari-in-the-kitchen arrangement she can continue to live in the annexe at her brother-in-law's mercy or return to her father's village in UP.

And so Chachiji heads for Mrs Mamta's kitchen, wailing, beating her breast and gnashing her teeth. The Judge, hearing her approach, gathers his newspapers and beats a hasty retreat, ignoring the bitterly reproachful glance his wife shoots at him. Mrs Mamta sighs, puts the saucepan on the gas, and gets ready to dish out tea and sympathy.

'Over my dead body,' fumes Chachiji as she sips her tea, to a sympathetic circle of Number 16 ladies. 'AN's father murdered his wife and that is exactly what AN will have to do if he wants to get that woman inside my flat!'

'That's not true, Bhudevi,' Mrs Mamta rebukes her gently. 'Don't say things like that – the children are here.'

'Oh, we know already,' Bonu assures her. 'Samar told us the whole story. She was standing on the terrace, shouting *Pushkar, Pushkar*, so he came and pushed her.'

There is a shocked silence. Chachiji sips her tea, her eyes glittering. Bonu giggles.

'What nonsense!' Mrs Mamta manages to say finally, with a credible amount of vehemence.

'These children should be playing outside with a ball vaghera,' Binni declares. 'Not sitting in the kitchen drinking tea with the big people.' She slaps Bonu's wrist. 'Don't drink tea! When children drink tea it makes them dark. Drink milk only.'

'So I'm going to follow family tradition and kill myself,' Chachiji reiterates loudly, nettled that the spotlight has shifted away from her. 'On the very day of the building inauguration next week. And *then* I'll come back for him. Like *she* did. The

Pushkarni. She gets inside me, you know, takes me over – she wants to do it now, I can tell.'

She throws back her head, rolls up her eyes and starts to rock back and forth. Debjani, curled up in a chair next to the kitchen window, wholly divorced from these proceedings, grits her teeth and resignedly starts to hum a little ditty inside her head. *I love my faamly, I love my faamly, I love my faamleee, I love them all...*

Just then, the Judge walks into the kitchen, holding a small brown packet of eggs.

'Why did *you* go to get the eggs?' Mrs Mamta asks suspiciously. 'You know that's Eshwari's job.'

'I wanted some fresh air,' he replies evasively. 'And I'm glad I went. I got talking with old Mr Gambhir, he's very upset about Dylan's arrest. Mamtaji, I think we should pay the Shekhawats a visit.'

Mrs Mamta Thakur casts a nervous glance towards Debjani, who has gone unnaturally still. 'Do you want me to come with you?'

'I'll come.' Debjani gets to her feet abruptly. 'Let's go, BJ.'

'I'll come too.' Bonu bounces up. 'I want to say sorry.'

'What for, stupid girl?' Binni frowns. 'Sit down and finish your tea.'

<hr>

'What happened at Juliet's house, LN?' Mrs Mamta asks her husband that night. 'Why has Dabbu come back looking like a limp dupatta somebody forgot to starch? Why isn't she saying anything?'

The Judge sighs and sits down on the bed, his chappals dangling dispiritedly from his toes. 'Ab what to say, Mamtaji,' he says, massaging his closed eyes. 'Basically, hamne der kar di. We were too late.'

'Matlab? He's not,' her breath catches fearfully, 'he's not *dead*, is he?'

The Judge shoots her an irate look. 'No,' he says. 'He's alive. But it appears he has moved on a bit since he wrote your daughter that eloquent epistle assuring her of his undying love.'

'Is he married?' she asks, confused. 'But when, how?'

'Neither dead nor married,' the Judge replies. '*Taken*, I believe, is the correct youthful phrase.'

When Debjani and the Judge arrived at the Shekhawats' home, they found the entire Shekhawat clan in a euphoric mood. A short, chubby man and a beautiful raven-haired, red-mouthed girl were sitting in pride of place in the drawing room, telling Dylan's family all about how they had just dug up evidence that would vindicate Dylan. The Judge and Debjani were given all the details, of course, but ended up feeling sort of redundant. Juliet Bai greeted them cordially enough, but she seemed distracted and very taken by the red-mouthed girl – Mitali, her name was – pressing tea and kalkals upon her, admiring her clothes, her guts, her brains.

'She's so *famous*, bhaisaab,' Juliet Bai told the Judge gushingly. 'She is a correspondent for *Viewstrack*. Everybody knows *Viewstrack*. Nowadays people don't even watch DD – it only mouths the government line, you see – but everybody watches *Viewstrack*.'

And Debjani knew at once that Juliet Bai had watched the bulletin in which she read out the Human Rights organization's adverse comments on Dylan.

Mitali and Dylan went to College together, they were told.

Mitali and Dylan used to run on the Worli seaface together every day, they were told. Mitali and Dylan had had some stupid fall-out early in the year, but in the last three months he had sought her out, and since then, they had been meeting almost every day, they were told.

'How nice,' Debjani said tightly. 'I'm so happy you've found all this evidence, Mitali. When will this story break?'

'In four days, I think,' Mitali replied, glowing happily. 'It's the end of the month, na, so we're going to fast-track it and shove it into the tape that's going out now. I've already written out the script and we have most of the footage already, so basically, one day to shoot, one day to edit, and then the whole tape will be sent off to the censors. You'll be able to pick it up from your local kirana store before the week is out.'

'That's awesome,' Debjani said wretchedly. 'I most definitely will.'

'And of course, the *IP* will carry it the very same day,' the short chubby man put in with a smile.

'Thank you so much, you have no idea what this means to all of us. Dylan – I mean, Saahas uncle is one of my father's oldest friends.'

'Oh, don't you know Dylan personally then?' the man enquired of Debjani.

'Well, I've met him a few times,' she replied. 'And of course we all read his columns.'

An uncomfortable silence followed. And then the chubby little man burst out laughing. 'Oh my god, I just realized, he wrote that anti-DD piece about *you*, didn't he? How come your families are still talking?'

Debjani shrugged, smiled and stood up to leave. Juliet Bai saw them to the door, hugged Debjani and thanked her sincerely for coming. The Brigadier shook his friend's hand hard and cautioned them that not a *word* must be said to anybody about what would soon be out on *Viewstrack* and in the *India Post*. Father and daughter responded by giving their solemn word.

'And then husband and wife shut the door in our faces and went to rejoin the happy-clappy circle around the beauteous Mitali,' the Judge concludes bitterly. 'And did I mention, she's highly eligible. Her father is a very senior IFS officer.'

Mrs Mamta extracts several long silver hairs that are clinging to her maroon comb, winds them into a tiny ball and throws them into a frilly cloth dustbin embroidered all over with cross-stitch pansies. The Judge gets the sense that she is consigning Dylan Singh Shekhawat to frilly oblivion. 'Thank god Dabbu's job is going well,' she says. 'It'll distract her from this whole mess. Still, it's sad – she was settling down so nicely and then that wretched letter came along and upset her all over again.'

'We shouldn't have taken her to the anniversary party,' the Judge says heavily. 'But she wanted to go. She said so.'

After a pause, Mrs Mamta says, 'Chalo, the good news is that your friend's son will be out of the hawalat soon. And if you think about it, LN, Dylan and this girl broke up in March, he came to Delhi and fell for Dabbu in April. Sounds like a rebound affair to me. Good thing it didn't work out. Let's just rally around Dabbu and cheer her up.'

13

Juliet Bai attends early morning Mass on Sunday. She leaves home before the *India Post* arrives, but on her way back she pauses at her kirana to pick up the latest issue of *Viewstrack*. She asks for it in a voice trembling with anticipation, hurries home and switches on the VCR. She doesn't have to alert the rest of the family – they are already lined up neatly on the sofa – two men and a boy who have just tumbled out of bed but are radiating the tense, focused energy of athletes poised on a racing track, waiting for the whistle to blow.

Juliet Bai inserts the cassette with a thumping heart and sinks down on the sofa between her boys.

'Please, god,' Ethan mutters.

The *Viewstrack* theme music kicks off with a flourish of keyboards and drums; slick graphics roll, images of India unfold, the screen freezes on a 3D *Viewstrack* super and then the camera cuts to the presenter – a beautiful Bombay film actress, now married and a mother of (reportedly drug-addicted) teenaged children.

'Hello, and welcome to *Viewstrack*. This month, our teams travel the length and breadth of the country to bring you political updates from Srinagar and Ayodhya, a report on the state of the rhino in Assam's Kaziranga National Park, a cosy tête-à-tête with delicious new debutant actor Aamir Khan, the star of the superhit film *QSQT*, and last but most definitely not the least, they discover that there is much more to the Kamalpreet Kaur bribery case than meets the eye.'

The Shekhawats bounce up from the sofa, clapping their hands and whooping hoarsely. Ethan does a little dance around the room, while Jason dives down to the VCR and fast-forwards it – past the wounded soldiers in Kashmir, past the screaming activists in Ayodhya, past the rhinos who are apparently being poached in large numbers for the aphrodisiac powers of their horns in Kaziranga, past delicious debutant actor Aamir Khan – and stops at a shot of the presenter looking into the camera with grim sincerity.

'And finally, a hot-off-the-press exclusive investigative story that links the prime accused in the anti-Sikh riots investigation with the very woman who allegedly received a bribe for giving false evidence against him. This story has wheels within wheels within wheels. Brace yourselves, ladies and gentlemen, for what is, in this year of exposés, perhaps the biggest exposé yet, brought to you by *India Post's* Varun Ohri and *Viewstrack* correspondent Mitali Dutta!'

Juliet Bai draws a long shuddering breath. The presenter fades out and an image of the porch of the Yuvati Niwas fills the screen.

Ethan turns to look at his parents, his eyes fever bright. 'This is it,' he crows, his grin triumphant. 'This is the point where Dylan Singh Shekhawat rises like a phoenix from the ashes and rubs Hardik Motla's nose into the dirt! Are you ready, people?'

They nod, eyes glued to the screen where the image of the Yuvati Niwas porch seems to have frozen.

Jason frowns.

He presses a few buttons on the VCR.

Nothing happens.

Jason presses down even harder. His father winces.

'You'll break it, Jase. Careful.'

Ethan leaps up and starts twiddling random knobs. 'I don't get it. Why isn't it moving?'

The screen goes black now, and a weird beeping noise fills the air. Words scroll across the screen. Well, only one word, actually.

Censored. Censored. Censored. Censored. Censored.
Censored. Censored. Censored. Censored. Censored.

'What the...?'

The screen remains black. 'Censored' keeps scrolling across it for a good six minutes – pretty much the full length of the Kamalpreet Kaur interview. And then the anchor is back.

'And that's all for this month's edition of *Viewstrack*,' she says with a smile. 'See you next month! Till then, take care and Jai Hind.'

The signature music kicks in again, the camera pulls out and away from the glittering set. The credits roll. Finally, static fills the screen.

And still the Shekhawats sit, dumbfounded and disbelieving, before the TV screen, unable to internalize what has just happened. Ethan suddenly races out of the room and returns a minute later clutching the morning newspapers.

'There's nothing in the *IP* either,' he says, his voice sounding suddenly very young, his face pale and anxious. 'I don't know... Mamma, Dadda... what could have happened?'

'What the fuck, Hira!'

Hira looks up, his sad-clown face slightly haggard. 'What?'

Varun glares at him, bewildered and angry. 'You *know* what. Why didn't you print my story?'

'Did the *Viewstrack* story come out?' Hira enquires back.

Varun's face clouds over. 'No,' he admits. 'It was censored. Motla must have pulled some strings. But that's not the point. Why didn't *our* story break?'

'Do you want to sit down?' Hira says mildly. 'Because what I'm going to tell you may come as a bit of a shock.'

'What?' Varun snaps.

Hira sighs and looks him right in the eye.

'I met Shekhawat in the lock-up,' he says. 'It was a rather unpleasant encounter. He admitted to bribing that young woman. Admitted it quite brazenly, actually. He said exactly what young journalists say in such situations – that the ends justified the means.'

'What?' Varun sits down rather suddenly. 'But then why – how – what about all that stuff we discovered in Delhi?'

'All that stuff *Mitali* discovered in Delhi,' Hira corrects him gently. 'She's always been a little unbalanced, that one. And madly obsessed with young Shekhawat. They were an item for quite a few years, I believe. She made up a pretty little tale to get him out. And you – because you care for your buddy so much – believed it.'

Varun stares at him, slack-jawed, his mind working overtime. Mitali telling him the call had come from the Yuvati Niwas. Mitali showing him the photo of the wrinkly old man. Mitali fast-forwarding the interview tapes. Mitali clutching his arm, smiling up at him.

'I – I can't believe it,' he says slowly. 'Mitali wouldn't... Dylan couldn't...' He leans in closer. 'He actually *admitted* to you that he bribed that woman?'

Hira looks directly at him.

'Yes.'

'And the money?'

Hira shrugs. 'Came from Canada. *Now* do you understand why I withheld your story?'

Varun nods shakily.

'I'm not sure exactly what Mitali's playing at,' Hira continues. 'What is true, what is concocted, if it's all personal ambition or just plain infatuation. But one thing I know – I'm not putting anything into my paper defending Dylan after what he told me in the lock-up.'

Varun sits up a little. 'Maybe...' he says hesitantly. 'They've been torturing him? And he said what he said under duress?'

Hiranandani gives a little bark of laughter. 'Don't be absurd, VO. I found him looking quite relaxed, and on first-name terms with all his captors.'

'Still.' Varun's expression grows mulish. 'I'd still like to get my story out. The wrinkly old man connects Motla and the prime witness testifying against him. That's definitely news. How about I run it past Bade-papaji?'

'Sure,' Hira says lightly as he gets to his feet and puts on his exquisitely tailored jacket. 'But he's in Delhi right now, marching to protest against the anti-defamation bill. He turned out to be right about *that*.'

'Yes,' Varun admits forlornly. 'He really *is* a newsman, isn't he? He has the nose, he can sniff out a story. Not like me – I should be running a fruit stall in Crawford Market or something.'

'Don't be silly.' Hiranandani smiles at him bracingly. 'I'm

headed to Delhi for the protest march too, as a matter of fact. How about we discuss your story with Bade-papaji together once I'm back? And then take a call? Okay?'

And Varun has no option but to say, 'Okay.'

◆

'Hello, and welcome to a special edition of *Face-2-Face*. With me in the studio today is editor-in-chief of the *India Post*, M. Hiranandani. Welcome to the Delhi DeshDarpan studio, sir.'

'Thank you.' Hira smiles, his face relaxed and disarming under the soft studio lights.

The interviewer, one of those syrupy women with the coy lips and kiss curls that DD loves, leans forward and looks at him intently. 'Mr Hiranandani, you participated in the march against the anti-defamation bill today. What were your thoughts as you marched down Bahadur Shah Zafar Marg all the way to the gates of Parliament?'

'Well,' says Hira thoughtfully. 'Naturally, I believe in a free press.'

'Naturally, naturally, we all do,' the interviewer neighs in immediate agreement.

'But at the same time,' Hira continues, 'we cannot escape the undeniable fact that something is rotten in the state of Denmark. I mean, we do take shortcuts sometimes. We do sensationalize. It happens.'

'It does, it does.' The interviewer nods fervently. She's such a suck-up, Debjani thinks, irritated, as she watches from the shadows. Agreeing with everything that man is saying. Cow.

'So *maybe*, a judicious amount of control is not such a bad thing. Not too much, of course, nothing that compromises freedom of speech, but just enough to keep us *responsible*.'

They go on to talk at length about the protest march – ruing the poor turnout, bemoaning the apathetic public which had not responded to the call of the Grand Old Men of Indian Publishing, and hinting, basically, that the government was not going to be particularly impressed.

'I think the bill will be passed,' Hira says in conclusion. 'Now all we can do, as conscientious newsmen, is to ensure that it is as toothless as possible.'

'Haha,' the interviewer twinkles coyly. 'It is bitter medicine perhaps, but the patient is in need of it. And on that healthy note, goodnight.'

The lights go off. Hiranandani and the interviewer walk out of the studio and back to the green rooms. When Hiranandani emerges a little later, he is alone and Debjani is waiting for him.

'Hello, sir.' She smiles. 'Such a pleasure to meet you.'

Hira nods, all suave, avuncular charm. 'Ah, hello, you're young Debjani Thakur, aren't you. Quite the celebrity. Didn't you go to College?'

'Well, yes,' she replies, slightly confused. 'You have to be a graduate to read the news.'

'But not to *the* College, clearly,' he continues smilingly. 'Well, you could've fooled me, you read so well. Very smoothly, with none of those dreadful rounded vowels favoured by the lesser DU colleges. Well done.'

What an ass, thinks Dabbu.

'Thank you, sir,' she says. 'Actually, I came to the studio today specially to ask you something.'

'Make it quick, young lady,' Hira says, glancing at his watch. 'I have a flight to catch.'

'Just if you had any news of Dylan Singh Shekhawat,' Debjani says, her cheeks very red. 'He's a – a family friend and I thought perhaps you might have some news of him?'

Hira's face softens. 'You poor child,' he says gently. 'I wouldn't say this on camera but I can tell you privately: Shekhawat turned out to be a sad disappointment. Able chap, but morally unsound. He's a disgrace to the profession, frankly, and deserves every bit of what's coming to him.'

Debjani stares at him, her brain spinning. 'But I thought *Viewstrack* and your paper had done a story...?'

'That was a *fake* story,' Hira says firmly. 'Made up by a silly girl who was in love with him. You aren't a silly girl too, are you?'

Debjani throws back her shoulders. 'Oh, no,' she says, her eyes flashing. 'I'm not silly.'

'Good.' Hira pats her shoulder. 'Forget him. He's going to be in Tihar for a long time. Move on. That's my advice.'

Even his boss says he's lying, Debjani thinks dispiritedly as she ties on her sari for her newscast that night. And his father told BJ that he offers no guarantee for his son. His own mother told me the story about the fake wedding invitation cards he got printed. He made up a fictitious cat to explain away the fact that he was cruelly kicking Moti the first time we met. He *is* a liar. And what kind of pathetic loser am I for refusing to let this go?

Valiantly, she tries to wrap her mind around the depressing fact of Dylan's essential dishonesty (D for dishonest) but her mind is reluctant to oblige. But Dabbu, who has managed to wrap her fingers even around Moti's loathsome balls by telling herself that you've gotta do what you've gotta do, is having none of that.

'He is a liar,' she tells herself firmly. 'Get this into your thick head, Debjani Thakur, *he is a liar*, and that poor Mitali deserves your pity, not your envy – so banish all filmi notions of visiting him in prison wearing that pretty net dupatta you embroidered all over with dainty little rosebuds...'

And that's when a horrible caterwauling sound floats to her ears, followed by hysterical barking and screams and squeals ripped from the throats of the three children lying in their makeshift beds in the drawing room. This is followed by her father calling out testily for someone to please go and see what that bloody racket is. Dabbu drops her sari pleats and walks out of her room.

'It's the ghost of the Pushkarni,' Monu quavers from below the bedcovers as another bloodcurdling yowl sounds from the gate. 'She's come to suck out my soul, like marrow from a bone.'

'Uff, what crap!' Debjani says and hurries out, hot on the heels of the intrepid Samar and closely pursued by the barefoot Bonu, down the drive and out through the gate. Moti and his family are on the ghostly silver sand pile, barking up a storm. She shushes them and such is her tone that they cower immediately, sidling backward into the sand. Debjani turns towards the house, her mind already back on her problems.

But Samar's hand tugs the end of her sari.

'Is that a baby leopard?'

Dabbu looks.

A tiny, mangy cat is crouching against the gate. Ragged, orangy-black fur, a horridly torn right ear, dirty rice-like teeth bared in a weedy, unconvincing hiss.

Debjani stares down at it like she's never seen a cat before.

'No, summervine,' she says, her voice shaking, a little tremulous, a little crazy. 'It's a cat. A tortoiseshell. Isn't it pretty?'

<hr>

The TV at the Connaught Place police chowki sits atop a weirdly hissing refrigerator, draped with an orange and white towel, like some fantastic electronic bride coyly doing ghunghat on the beach. At seven o'clock every evening, somebody lifts the towel, twiddles its twin brown knobs briskly and gets it going. Dylan can just about see it from the edge of his cell. He is careful not to let on, though, because then the policemen will push it out of his line of vision. It helps pass the time, especially late at night, when they watch raunchy movies featuring lovely large ladies whose rolling assets Dylan cannot help but appreciate.

When the TV crackles on this particular evening, his fourth in the lock-up, he realizes abruptly that it is Friday. With a pang of longing so sharp that the pain is almost physical, he recalls the scent of freshly cut grass in Justice Laxmi Thakur's lawn. The mouth-watering smell of fried onions atop the bowls of Maggi noodles, the pretty embroidered cheese-cloth napkins, the thrumm of the circulating fan as it turns its steely head to lift the little flyaway curls at the base of Debjani's neck and send in Dylan's direction the faint scent of Ponds Dreamflower talc.

He throws an arm over his eyes, rolls over on the cement bench, and mutters, his back to the TV, 'It really is high time this country privatized television.'

He dozes uneasily as the fat little TV beams out the Hindi news to the nose-picking policemen, following it up with the wildly popular filmi sitaron ka rangarang karikram, *Chitrahaar*, and an episode of the newly launched comedy show *Yeh Jo Hai Zindagi*, which has all the cops guffawing madly. But at nine o'clock, when the new theme music of the English news bulletin sounds, he sits up straight and stares through the bars at the little television with resentful slit eyes.

'*Hello, and welcome to the News at Nine! I'm Amitabh Bose!*' booms a familiar plummy voice and Dylan swears under his breath. Still, he can't help waiting, his heart in his mouth, for the camera to cut – which it does, right on cue – to Debjani, rose-bedecked and unusually pale as she twinkles gravely and adds, '*And I'm Debjani Thakur.*'

Amitabh has the lion's share of the news tonight. He drones on about the Prime Minister's visit to the North East, which cuts to visuals of the Prime Minister wandering about in jeans and T-shirt in some vaguely mountainous background, chucking babies under their chin, shaking a leg with some young ladies clad in black, red and silver, and gravely examining ears of grain in green terraced fields. Debjani comes in to talk about the celebration of some festival in the state of Gujarat, and then Amitabh talks about Mikhail Gorbachev's imminent visit and India's ties with the USSR for three whole minutes. And then it is Debjani's turn again. Dylan waits for her to fill everybody in on the happenings at the American Open, where Martina Navratilova and Boris Becker have had rather an eventful day. Instead, Debjani looks straight into the TV screen, draws a deep breath and goes abruptly, completely quiet.

It is just a moment's pause – probably a glitch with the autocue – but it feels somehow momentous. Maybe it's because the expression on her face is so strange. Oddly resolute and a little scared, but also like she might start giggling at any moment. Dylan gets the unnerving feeling that she can actually see him, that she is watching him watching her with unwilling eyes – unshaven, bloody and bedraggled – through the bars of the lock-up in the Connaught Place police chowki, nine kilometres away from the headquarters of DeshDarpan.

Don't be a fool, he tells himself savagely even as his belly plummets into a graceful swallow dive before rising again like the talented ballet star it is and pirouetting madly on its toes. Her eyes are just looking at the damn autocue, not searing into your stupid soul.

And as he continues, grudgingly, to drink in the sight of her, this new, seemingly omnispective Debjani squares her shoulders and looks straight into the camera, her eyes glowing with some inner resolution. So might a suicide bomber look before he presses the detonation button, Dylan thinks, then wonders if he's losing the plot entirely. She says, her voice as calm, as well-modulated and as matter-of-fact as always:

'*Meanwhile, in a startling development, video news magazine* Viewstrack *and the* India Post *conducted a joint investigation and discovered that the bribery and testimony tampering charges against journalist Dylan Singh Shekhawat are entirely false and were fabricated by MP Hardik Motla in a scurrilous bid to discredit the highly regarded journalist.*

'*Kamalpreet Kaur, the so-called eyewitness whom Shekhawat stands accused of bribing, turned out to be the niece of Motla's long-time employee and ex-driver.*

'*Our sources believe that the false case against Shekhawat is part of a larger conspiracy to make the press appear both immoral and incompetent in order to ease the passing of an anti-defamation bill through Parliament, which will give the government far-reaching powers to penalize any journalist that dares raise his voice against it.*

'Journalists of all publications gathered today at the capital's *Bahadur Shah Zafar Marg in a show of strength to urge the government to withdraw the bill. AIR and DeshDarpan too support them in this worthy endeavour.*'

She comes to a breathless halt and smiles the lopsided street-urchin smile that India loves.

'*That's all from our news desk for now. Goodnight.*'

14

The world didn't crash in on Debjani after she finished that evening's broadcast. Amitabh Bose, so quick to notice any minor mistakes in pronunciation, didn't even realize that his fellow newsreader had just read an entire paragraph of news that didn't feature on the autocue rolling before them, news that had been made up on the spot, that hadn't been carefully whetted by the I&B ministry. She was able to unclip her mic, walk calmly down the corridor and take the usual chartered cab home before the phones started ringing madly inside the DD offices.

Anjini didi and Antu bhaiyya have taken everybody out for jalebis at Bengali Market, Binni's Oriya maid tells her when she gets home. Does Dabbu didi want anything?

Debjani doesn't want anything – least of all to engage with the unfamiliar, panicked voice that hisses into her ear when she answers the telephone a little later, informing her that her services are no longer required at DeshDarpan. 'Don't expect a cheque from us for tonight's broadcast, either!' the voice wails hysterically. 'Instead, expect to be *fined*, expect to be *arrested*, expect to face a *criminal prosecution*!'

Whatever, she shrugs as she hangs up. She finds she isn't too concerned about her newsreader job right now, even though it's something she has worked so hard and so long to get. Instead, her palms are sweaty, her stomach is churning and her mind is totally occupied with how vulnerable she has made herself vis-à-vis Dylan.

He'll know I love him now, she thinks, mortified. How awful! What was I thinking? Suppose they let him out of jail on the basis of the evidence Mitali dug up and he shows up here with Mitali in tow to thank me, knowing all the time that I'm obsessed with him? Oh god, how do I cover up?

While she is agonizing over this, tossing and turning in bed, sunlight filters into the bedroom and the phone begins to ring. Mrs Mamta takes the calls, going from bemusement to straight out panic in about three interactions.

Is this Debjani Thakur? Oh, her mother? Vul, Mrs Mamta, how long did it take your daughter to infiltrate DeshDarpan? Is she part of any organization or is she working for the opposition? Are she and Shekhawat in a romantic relationship?

After a few hurried denials, Mrs Mamta puts the phone off the hook. Then she hustles Dabbu into the drawing room, summons the Judge, and demands to be told what's happening.

Dabbu, sulky at first, finally admits rather airily that she has become disgusted with the way the government keeps poking its nose into all of DD's doings. The anti-defamation bill was the last straw for her, and so, she had decided on the spot, all miked up and with the camera rolling, to do something about it.

'Anyway, what I said wasn't *too* bad,' she tells her parents. 'You guys must've heard me! It was the bit I read out right at the end.'

Her parents exchange guilty looks. To be very honest, watching Debjani reading the news has lost its novelty. Neither of them listened very carefully to the broadcast last night. They'd switched on the TV, watched the beginning, satisfied themselves that Dabbu was looking pretty, and then more or less let their minds wander. Mrs Mamta had knitted a sweater for Samar and brooded over Anjini's non-pregnancy and how grave and grey Anant looked all the time. The Judge had fretted over Chachiji's woes and his shameless younger brother's canoodling with the Hot Dulari. And then of course, they had all gone out for jalebis. And while they had been so criminally negligent, the Judge thinks bitterly, their fourth-born was busy scoring her most spectacular own goal yet. She had gone and messed about with an I&B ministry-approved script and destroyed a hansta-khelta career in less than three minutes.

'Hey bhagwan.' Mrs Mamta wrings her hands, looking uncharacteristically rattled. 'She read out something that wasn't approved, LN! To the entire country! At prime time! What does this mean? Will she have to go to jail?'

'Of course not,' the Judge says unconvincingly. 'At least, I don't think so. Calm down, Mamtaji!'

Mrs Mamta sinks into a chair and begins to fan herself.

'We should never have gone out to eat jalebis. But I was just so relieved to see that Anjini and Anant are getting along at last! I wanted to encourage them.'

The Judge privately thinks that far from 'getting along', Anjini and Anant have been softening up the family in order to break some big bad news to them, but this isn't the time to bring that up.

'Hai, isse better was that she stayed in supta vastha only! And does this mean she's still obsessed with that wretched boy?'

'I suppose so.' The Judge mops his brow.

'Ma, BJ, I'm *in* the room,' Debjani says, getting more panicked as she sees how panicked they are getting. 'Stop talking about me like I'm not here. And it's not *that* awful. Of course I won't get sent to prison. What an idea!'

'Why's Dabbu going to prison?' Eshwari, who has wandered into the room and is busy pulling on her sneakers, asks interestedly. 'To visit Dylan? That's kind of romantic. Like how Ba went to visit Mohan Das in Richard Attenborough's *Gandhi*.'

'Be quiet!' Mrs Mamta hisses so vehemently that Eshwari actually shuts up mid-word, her mouth open. 'Don't you *dare* go out or talk to anybody, either of you! Khabardaar! Sit inside the house and keep your lips buttoned or I'll break both your legs!'

Eshwari looks mildly astonished at this. Mrs Mamta doesn't usually subscribe to the Khabardaar school of mothering. Things must be serious.

'It's all your fault,' Mrs Mamta tells her husband. 'Going on about the Vunderful Vladimir. You've turned her head.'

'There's no point in being so dramatic,' the Judge says quietly. 'This is a serious issue. More serious than Debjani realized, obviously. Who knows what the repercussions could be.'

'They called from DD,' Debjani falters. 'Late last night. I didn't tell you guys. They said I was sacked and that I would be *fined* and that there would be a *criminal prosecution*.'

'Bas,' Mrs Mamta says fatalistically. 'The whole family will be clapped in irons.'

'Stop it, Mamtaji.' The Judge's voice is sharp. 'Debjani, if you can remember clearly, word by word, what exactly it was you said, I can prepare a statement for you to make.'

Debjani nods, her stomach churning. She had thought the worst was Dylan finding out she still had feelings for him. Going to prison hadn't even entered her mind. I could end up in a cell with Phoolan Devi, she thinks, breaking out in a cold sweat. And have to wear a bandanna and bell-bottoms and have my uterus removed. The loos will be filthy. And there will be mosquitoes and no electricity and AIDS lurking everywhere. Is that what Dylan is going through right now? Then I'm glad I did it. But oh god, I think I'm going to be sick.

'I can remember it all, I think,' she tells her father. 'I'll write it down and give it to you.'

'Good.' The Judge smiles at her encouragingly, the first time, she realizes, tears springing to her eyes, in almost three months. 'Now, everybody, please relax. If we could weather living with Chachiji for three whole months, we can surely weather *this*.'

And uttering these bracing words, he retires to his study alone, to face the fact that his favourite daughter is in very deep, very grave trouble.

––◆––

Late the next night, Varun Ohri is fast asleep when a sibilant whisper sounds in his ear.

'Sunn, Varun! Varun ke bacche! Arrey, sunn meri gal, lordu!'

Varun stirs, groans and sits up in bed, rubbing his eyes. A chunky silhouette, as wide as it is tall, hovers over him, breathing heavily. There is a strong scent of chamelis and chicken tikka.

'Bade-papaji? It's two in the morning!'

Purshottam Ohri bangs the floor with his metal-tipped walking stick. 'Read this!'

'Now?' Varun says, groping about for the light and switching it on.

The old man nods, his beady eyes glittering manically below his bushy brows.

'When else, duffer? It's a masterpiece penned by that overpaid idiot Hiranandani. He wrote it with my walking stick rammed down his chhakka throat, of course. Read it!'

'What?' Varun is thoroughly confused. 'What did you make him write?'

The old man hands him a sheaf of typed papers.

'Tomorrow's headlines.' He grins, flashing broken teeth. 'Every single word written in there is true. I have *made* it all come true.'

Varun quickly scans through to the end of the piece.

'I can't believe it,' he says, stunned. 'So Dylan didn't bribe that woman? And Hira *lied* to me about it?'

His grandfather looks at him with fond pity.

'Yes.'

'But how did you *do* it all, Bade-papaji? In just a day and a night? How many people did you have to kill?'

The old man gives a triumphant cackle.

'Nobody.' He wheezes. 'The poor sod was already screwed. That pretty little newsreader screwed him. She screwed them *all*. President Mikhail Gorbachev is coming to India in two days – the world's press will be here – the PM doesn't want all this filthy linen being washed in public. So I just talked some sense into Hijra and then *he* talked some sense into the PM. Listen, lordu, I said, this is an opportunity. Grab it with both hands. Come across as young and progressive and open – say that she read what *you* gave her to read – and throw that cockroach Motla to the wolves. Bas! They saw the dum in my logic in about fifteen minutes.'

'That's all it took?' Varun cannot believe his ears.

The old man shrugs his massive shoulders. 'Well, I think they'll yank Motla back before he's actually *eaten*. Maybe he'll come out of it missing a limb or two. And I promised their party some good press in the paper, going forward.' Then he grins. 'But that is a promise we can always break.'

'Wow,' says Varun, looking suddenly, boyishly carefree. 'Bade-papaji, you are truly an institution.'

The old man grunts, looking mighty pleased with himself. 'Take that laundiya out tomorrow,' he grunts. 'The one with the nathni. She likes you, I can tell. You make a good team.'

Varun's ears turn red as he mutters an okay. Then, as the old man pats him on the back and starts to stump away, he asks, 'Where are you going now?'

Purshottam Ohri turns and bares a ravaged row of broken yellow teeth in a cherubic grin.

'To the bathroom. I can tell, beta Varun, ki today there will be no sitting about and singing hymns on the pot! Aaj mujhe fatafat, bahut hi pyari tatti aayegi – I am going to finish my big job like this.' He snaps his fingers. 'Like *this*!'

❦

DeshDarpan Grows Up
Hats off to state broadcaster for ushering in an era of independent, fearless reporting
M. Hiranandani

All of last week the nation's premier publishing houses have been up in arms against the ruling party's attempt to force a devious bill that seeks to muzzle the free press through Parliament.

The bill's architects will try to convince you otherwise, by talking of national unity being jeopardized, security being compromised, governance being de-stabilized and so on. They will tell you that the bill is a necessary safeguard to ensure a strong, secure and united India. But I say to you that this bill is a beast that hides its teeth. It is no saviour of anything, except worthless political and bureaucratic necks.

Simply put, the single aim of the anti-defamation bill is to shackle the press. To render impotent the faithful watchdog that guards the interest of this nation of 800 million people.

Press stalwarts from all over India came together yesterday to stage a protest march against the bill. The government, however, remained unmoved.

Until last night.

Last night, DeshDarpan, in a move that showed true maturity, came out strongly in support of both the bill and detained *India Post* journalist Dylan Singh Shekhawat, who stands accused of bribery and testimony-tampering in cases clearly cooked up by MP Hardik Motla, a man whose hands are stained with the blood of the thousands who died in the anti-Sikh riots of 1984.

Pretty, fiery-eyed newscaster Debjani Thakur was the perfect choice to read out the statement that was clearly the new DeshDarpan's coming-out party.

In a special statement issued privately to this columnist, the Prime Minister declared: 'We want DD to be like the BBC – independent, mature, well-respected by the world as a source of news from the subcontinent. What has been done to Dylan Shekhawat is disgraceful. He is to be released with immediate effect. All cases against Hardik Motla stand re-opened. The anti-defamation bill, which the press has taken such a strong stand on, is henceforth withdrawn. This government is both progressive and responsive and seeks the support of a free, fearless and vigorous press to take us into the twenty-first century.'

⋆⊷●⊶⋆

'My life is over,' Eshwari says dejectedly. 'O-V-E-R *over*. What will I do with myself now?'

Debjani squints at the drooping figure lacing its shoes before the mirror.

'You'll get over it,' she says sleepily. 'Last day of school does not equal last day on the planet.'

'Cow,' Eshwari replies, fastening her ponytail. 'You're just saying that because you didn't exactly *shine* in school. But I'm so popular and all... suppose the best part of my life is already over?'

Debjani sits up and shakes back her hair.

'You're being silly,' she says firmly. 'And for heaven's sake, wear a slip under your uniform today. All the boys will write on your shirt – and you know that's just an excuse to grope.'

After dispensing this very valuable advice, she clambers out of bed and goes looking for the newspaper. It's been five days since DD's remarkable volte face, which the Thakurs had read about in the paper just like everybody else and breathed a massive sigh of relief. Mrs Mamta had immediately organized a Satyanarayan ki puja. The house is still reeking of havan samagri. All Debjani has to do now is maintain the fiction the creepy Hiranandani invented – that she simply read what she was given to read, and that is that.

'But start looking for a new job,' her father has advised her. 'Because, in a few months, when everybody's forgotten about all this, they'll sack you under some pretext or other.'

So Debjani scours the morning paper looking for jobs. She also waits, much to her own disgust. Waits for the phone to ring, waits for an electric-blue Maruti 800 to roll up outside the gate and set the dogs yapping, waits to be waylaid and jerked about and kissed as she walks to Gambhir Stores and back. Not that

I did any of it so he would show up here and fall on his knees. Or to prove I love him more than Mitali ever could. I did it for India, for Democracy, for Freedom of Speech, for Sexy Jaw and Awesome Butt. Oh god, please don't let me have to be the one who phones him. Let him phone me. Here's an opening for self-motivated sales people to sell Eureka Forbes's new range of vacuum cleaners. Must have good English and good complexion. Should I apply?

Panties should be red,
Films should be blue,
Mr Gaur should make babies
With Mrs Mattoo

'That is the lamest little verse I have ever seen,' Eshwari says, distressed. 'Who's written it so big on the blackboard? Think how upset Mrs Mattoo will be. Erase it immediately.'

'I don't think Gaur will be too thrilled about it either,' Satish remarks. 'And stop looking at me like that – I didn't write it. Anyway, nobody can find the duster.'

Eshwari looks around, hooking her thumbs into her school bag straps. The last bell has just rung, school is officially over and everybody is busy autographing everybody else's uniforms. There is pandemonium in Satish's classroom. A few people are crying. Cake crumbs and popcorn kernels dot the ground, which is sticky with spilt Campa Cola.

Eshwari sighs, mounts the teacher's desk and starts rubbing off the two objectionable lines with the palm of her hand. The chalk proves stubborn. She frowns. 'Is this *paint*?'

'Putai paint,' Satish says, peering at it. 'It's water based, thankfully. Here, use this.'

And with that he unbuttons his shirt, balls it up and hands it to her. Whoops and moans break out from the class immediately. Eshwari is on the verge of whooping herself. So the beast has a hot chest. Who knew? She shrugs, takes his shirt and busies herself with scrubbing off the paint.

Satish's gesture starts a trend. Boys who have never had one nice thing to say about Mrs Mattoo suddenly start stripping to save her distress. Eshwari, standing atop the teacher's desk, finds herself knee-deep in male nipples. As this is the engineering section, there are no girls in the class. Just despo, wanna-be IIT types, all of whom, she is sure, are busy looking up her skirt. She jumps off the desk and walks out of the classroom, her cheeks flaming.

'Hey, Bihari, wait up!'

Satish runs after her, buttoning his shirt. She notices with some satisfaction that the scrubbing has blurred the words 'PRIVATE PROPERTY NO TRESPASSING' his current girlfriend has doodled and then decorated with hearts all over the front of his shirt.

'Lemme write on you,' he says, producing a micro-tip pen and waggling it in the air above her shirt.

'No way.'

'But you've let everybody else do it,' he complains. 'There's practically no space left to write... no fair, Bihari.'

'Oh, shut up,' she says. 'You live next door, anyway. It's not like I won't see you any more once we're done with school.'

Satish's eyes widen. The wolf-puppy grin flashes, accompanied by a knowing glint that makes her want to slap him.

'You're asking if I'm gonna stay in touch with you after school,' he gloats.

'I'm not!' she snaps. 'I'm just trying to avoid being felt up by you, that's all. Bye now.'

And she walks away, feeling close to tears. She never expected to feel so emotional about leaving school. It's all so unsettling. Besides, she's not smart – like Satish, who will get into IIT for sure and therefore knows, more or less, where his life is going. Eshwari is clueless about what lies beyond the low red walls of the school she's queened for so long.

She wanders out to the bleachers, sits down and stares at the basketball court blindly.

Presently Satish sits down quietly beside her and slides a plate of steaming hot sambar vada under her nose.

'For the last time,' he says dramatically. 'Go for it, Bihari.'

And she does. It has never tasted as good as it does on this gorgeously cool but sunny, perfect February day. As she scoops up the last of the sambar, he grins at her companionably. 'Awesome, isn't it?' he says. 'Better than sex.'

'Like you would know,' Eshwari scoffs.

'Oh, but I do, Bihari, I do,' he says mysteriously. 'Can't get into the details of when and where and with whom, you know. Would be ungentlemanly.'

'Liar.'

'Oh, no.' He shakes his head. 'It's true. You said your folks won't let you go out with anyone till you're twenty-one, so I have to do *something* to pass the time till then, don't I? Keep my hand in, so to speak. Hone my skills. So that on that distant day, when we finally hook up, you'll be fully satishfied with my prowess. *Satish*-fied, get it, get it?'

'You're disgusting!' Eshwari slams the plastic plate down onto the bleachers. 'Talking about your girlfriend in such an obnoxious fashion! Sexist pig.'

He crosses his arms across his chest, which, now that she's seen bare, she doesn't want to dwell upon too much.

'There's sambar on your shirt,' he observes.

'Fuck you.'

'Why're you so mad?' he asks, rather amused.

'I'm not.'

'You are. Your nostrils are all flared. It's because you're jealous, I suppose.'

Eshwari tosses her head. 'Please. Far from being jealous, I've decided to follow your example. So gimme some good-friend advice – who do I pick, Mohit Razdan or Jai Kakkar?'

He goes very still. Then says, very casually, 'But I thought Milord's imposed a total cock-block till you turn twenty-one?'

'He has *not* imposed a –' She pauses, draws a deep breath, then continues in a cooler voice, 'That can be worked around.'

'No, it *can't*,' he responds with sudden violence. 'That's not *fair*. How come the rule applies to *me* but not to Kakkar or Razdan?'

He's jealous, she thinks with satisfaction. Good.

'Jai's nice and mature,' she replies steadily. 'And I love the way Mohit plays. It's so *sexy*. There's something incredibly hot about a guy who can make music with his fingers – unlike somebody who, you know, bangs like a bandar on the drums.'

Satish flinches, his eyes hardening, going from puppy to wolf in seconds.

'I get it,' he snarls. 'I'm being punished for taking you at your word and moving on with my life. For going out with other chicks after you turned me down. *Twice.* What was I supposed to do, huh, bubblewrap my dick and sit till your dad says you're old enough to go out with boys?'

Eshwari stares at him in frustration. 'Why do you talk like that? It's *gross!*'

'Like *what*?' he replies, genuinely bewildered. 'Honestly? I should lie?'

'You're doing this just to get to me,' she says. 'Going out with girlfriend after girlfriend. Giving me all the gross details. You think if you do this, I'll crack.'

He laughs. 'Is that what you've been telling yourself? That is just sad.'

'I *don't* want to go out with you,' Eshwari insists. 'Get that into your stupid head.'

'But you don't want me to go out with anyone else,' he says. 'You're just a dog in the manger. Bitch, rather.'

Eshwari gets to her feet, her face white, her eyes blazing, and stalks away. She is walking home when he catches up with her again.

'Well, at least Mattoo's modesty wasn't outraged,' he observes, his voice unsteady. 'We managed to clean the whole damn board before she showed up.'

There is a tense silence. Eshwari swallows but doesn't speak.

'Eshu?' His deep voice is almost pleading. And for the first time ever, he hasn't called her Bihari.

'Good.'

'Yeah,' Satish agrees, his relief palpable. 'But Gaur saw it. He pretended to be hassled but I could tell he was pretty happy.'

They walk in silence. Satish's house will come up in about three minutes. He walks as slowly as he can, hoping she won't notice that he's deliberately dawdling.

'So... you weren't serious about wanting my advice on picking between Razdan or Kakkar, were you? You were just kidding, right?'

Eshwari stops abruptly and turns to face him.

'Oh, no,' she says coolly. 'I was serious.'

Satish ducks his head. She can't see his face.

'So if you've got some proper, mature advice to give, *give* it.'

He mutters, still looking down, 'Why do girls always say that? How can I be mature at seventeen? Besides,' he looks up, and his voice hardens, 'why d'you have to pick? Make up for lost time and screw 'em both.'

Eshwari stops, shutting her eyes, gritting her teeth and counting till ten. Then she turns slowly. Traffic trundles up and down Hailey Road behind her. Seeing the expression in her eyes, he suddenly, fervently, wants for her just to stay quiet. It doesn't bode well – for him, for her, for everything. But it's too late.

'I never liked you, Steesh,' she says simply. 'Not that way. I made up that story about BJ saying I couldn't date till I was twenty-one so you wouldn't feel too bad about me turning you down. Sorry.'

'Liar.' It is Satish's turn to spit the word out now, and he does it with full vehemence and zero conviction.

Eshwari, not very sure herself if he is right or wrong, laughs scornfully. 'Oh, it's true. BJ never made any rule for me. He doesn't do stuff like that. And even if he did, do you really think I wouldn't have broken it if I liked a boy enough? If he was somebody romantic and charming, who knew how to *talk*, for heaven's sake, who didn't just walk up to a girl and say, "Duh. Be my chick."'

Three school buses laden with Modernites wheeze past them, blowing serious amounts of exhaust fumes into their faces.

The two of them stare at each other in silence.

'Good luck with the terrorist then,' Satish says lightly. 'Or with Kakkar. Or with both. Let 'em take you to the farewell. Have a nice life.'

This hurts. She is suddenly, painfully aware that for her, the entire excitement of the class twelve farewell was building up to that one critical moment – when stupid Satish Sridhar would ring the doorbell and she would open it looking all gorgeous and glowing in her emerald green georgette sari with the tiny ruby-red choli and (maybe, if she has the guts) a red rose stuck Dabbu-style behind her ear.

He would've fallen to his knees, raised his snout and *howled*, she thinks, furious. With sheer longing. Oh, I *hate* him. He's crass and rude and horny and immature. I never want to talk to him again.

She turns around, and with a swift, frustrated gesture, lets her bag drop off her shoulders. It reveals a square clean space at the back of her shirt – about ten inches by ten inches – entirely free of scrawled *All the best*s and *Collars up you're a Modernite*s and *Best friends forever*s and *xoxoxox*s and *See you in Harvard Business School*s.

'I saved that for you, asshole,' she says as she whirls around again, her voice low and furious. 'But now I think I like it just the way it is. Have a nice life too.'

And scooping up her bag, she walks away.

––⊙––

'Lord, what is this foul beast, VO?' Dylan demands, looking down with disfavour at a plump yellow-and-black body frisking unsteadily around Varun's chubby calves. 'And why has it just dipped its snout inside a jar of tar? What massive paws and ears and, um, private parts. Is it yours?'

'You should ask,' Varun replies bitterly. 'Its name is Hottie – because it's so *hot* and all.'

They are sitting out in the garden of the sprawling Ohri mansion on Sardar Patel Marg. It is a beautiful spring day and Bade-papaji has invited Dylan and his parents for brunch to celebrate his release. Seated under a pergola bedecked with fragrant chameli blossom, Bade-papaji is holding forth to the Brigadier and Juliet Bai on the future of journalism in India. 'The days of DD's hegemony are over,' he predicts as he wades steadily through the pomegranate juice and south Indian snacks. 'TV will open up now. No option. It has to. I'm thinking that we should also start a news channel. Varun and Dylan can run it together. We'll call it Purshottam Ohri Television – POTV.'

The Shekhawats, pinioned into place behind massive paper dosas, have no option but to sit and listen to him. Varun and Dylan, who are eating idli, are more mobile, and have managed to move out of Bade-papaji's direct booming range.

'Potty might've been a better name,' Dylan says critically, taking in the black-and-mustard colour scheme and generally lower-middle class demeanour of the mutt. 'It could have been the official mascot of POTV. And why shouldn't I ask?'

'Because it all happened in *your* parents' house only,' Varun returns feelingly. 'Mitali met this chick there who got talking disparagingly about pedigreed dogs – they keep having sex with their mothers and sisters, apparently, and are totally inbred and sickly and mind-fucked as a result. She spoke glowingly of what she called mixed breeds – by which she meant mongrels – claiming that they are hardy and loyal and so *honest* and so *kind* and so *brave*. Mits fell for it like a ton of bricks, of course. And that is why I am now the proud owner of this epitome of honesty and kindness and bravery that you see before you. So fuck *you* very much.'

Dylan goes very still.

'You met Debjani?'

'Yeah, the one who declared your innocence on DD – that's how the PM got to know about your case – you know that, surely?'

Dylan shrugs. 'She read out the news DD gave her to read,' he says curtly. 'What's so extraordinary about that?'

Varun looks at him in utter non-comprehension. 'They did *not* give her that news to read. You know how DD works. That's what they're claiming now, of course, but that's just some post-facto, face-saving bullshit Bade-papaji and Hiranandani helped them come up with. Why are you talking like such an ass?'

Dylan doesn't reply immediately. He bends down, picks Hottie up by the scruff of his neck and glares into his intelligent yellow-flecked eyes.

'I don't know,' he mutters.

Varun looks at him in concern. The last few days have seen an incredible turnaround for Dylan. And it's *all*, Varun thinks, getting rather worked up, a direct or indirect result of Debjani's broadcast that night.

'Why aren't you more grateful, fucker?' he demands. 'She said you guys were family friends. Why haven't you called and thanked her yet? What's the score?'

'There's no *score*,' Dylan says right back. 'Why're you being such a nosy choot?'

There is a short, confused silence.

'*I* know what happened!' Varun says finally. 'You hit on her and she turned you down. She *would*. She's that kind of girl – a good, sensible girl who'd have slapped away your oily coils and seen right through your harami charm.'

Dylan swears. A little too loudly. The dosa-eating trio turns and looks at him.

'Mamma,' Dylan manages to ask. 'Did Debjani come to see you while I was in lock-up?'

Juliet Bai looks distressed. 'Yes, sonna, she did. I wasn't very nice to her, I'm afraid.'

'Why didn't you *tell* me?'

'Because you got out of jail just three hours ago,' the Brigadier says. 'And then you spent one hour eating and one hour bathing. And then we came here. We haven't yet told you that the St Columba's principal came to see you, have we? Or that Miss Patsy called from Goa? Why this sudden interest in Dabbu all over again? Haven't you messed around with her enough?'

'Bhai, very pretty girl,' Bade-papaji says approvingly. 'Very soni kudi. And what guts! Like the girls in the Lahore of my youth – with bodies like lilies and hearts like lions. But then, this Dylan is just like me.'

Abruptly, Dylan gets to his feet and starts casting about for the car keys.

'Arrey, where are you going now?' his mother asks.

'To Hailey Road,' he replies shortly. 'VO, can you drop my folks home?'

'Of course,' VO says immediately. 'Not an issue.'

'Thanks for the meal, Ohri saab.' Dylan smiles as he shakes hands formally with the fat old man. 'And for all your support. Wish me luck.'

Purshottam Ohri flashes twin rows of broken yellow teeth in a happy grin.

'Luck!' he roars, thumping Dylan on the back approvingly. 'And tell your girl to quit DD and join my soon-to-be-launched-channel POTV. Theek hai?'

'Theek hai.' Dylan laughs as he runs lithely across the lawn towards the parked car. Hottie cavorts along with him companionably, tongue lolling, ears flapping. To Juliet Bai, misty-eyed with hope and happiness, it looks like a long line of her future grandchildren are racing across the grass with them, wearing nothing but white cloth diapers.

Let Dabbu not be too angry with the way I fussed over Mitali that day, ba, she prays. These wretched boys also, they don't say anything – who knows what goes on inside their stupid heads all the time...?

Then she frowns.

'Bobby, maybe Dyl should go there tomorrow. The Thakurs will be busy today – it's the day of the Hailey Court inauguration.'

But the electric-blue Maruti 800 has already reversed out of the gate and zoomed away.

15

The gracious Roman façade of Hailey Court is swathed in gainda phool and gladioli. A monstrous shamiana patterned with bright diamonds of red, green and yellow has been erected in the garden. A pink ribbon flutters across the fancy wrought-iron gate, stretching from the naked belly of a simpering stone cherub standing atop one gatepost to the bosom of a winged angel standing atop the second.

'Bhai, whatever you say, this building is ekko piece!' declares old Mr Gambhir, who is catering the boxes of veg patties and pineapple pastries that will be handed out after the ribbon cutting. 'Elegant. Sober. Matlab ki, *top ka!*'

Neighbours, vendors, dogs, cows and random passers-by caught in the jam caused by the general commotion nod in agreement.

'Suna hai, each and every flat is selling for one crore,' somebody whispers.

'Suna hai, each and every flat is cursed,' whispers somebody else. 'The ghost of the Pushkarni, na, she's angry they sold her house – the workers have heard her walking about at night, gnashing her teeth...'

Inside Number 16, the general feeling is one of being under

siege. 'First, non-stop construction for almost a year,' the Judge grumbles, pacing about the drawing room. 'Then all those journalists... and now this band-baaja-baraat! When will things get better, Mamtaji?'

'Soon,' she tells him soothingly. 'We've been through some rough patches this year, but things are looking up now. Dabbu didn't get arrested, AN and family will be back in Number 13 with all their debts paid off, Eshwari will finish school, Vickyji's business is showing profit, and best of all, Anant is here, finally, to take Anjini home.'

The Judge stares at her uncomprehendingly. 'What? In which world are you living? You *know* things are far from well! Anant looks like a dead man walking – and every time Anji laughs I worry that your bone china ice cream bowls will shatter inside their cabinets.'

'You just don't *like* Anjini,' Mrs Mamta says, her calm voice shaking slightly. 'And there's nothing wrong with their marriage that a good conversation won't fix.'

'Well, I hope you're right.' He purses his lips. 'But where are they going to have it in this house crawling with people? Have they gone out?'

Mrs Mamta nods.

'But only next door, to look at the Hailey Court flats,' she says. 'Ashok took them – Anant didn't look like he wanted to go, but Ashok insisted. I think he's hoping they'll buy one flat – the builder will give him a commission if they do.'

'It *would* be good if they bought here,' the Judge reflects. 'Imagine, if we could keep all the flats in the family. How happy my mother's ghost would be!'

Mrs Mamta shoots him a sour look.

'Joke, Mamtaji, joke,' he says hastily. 'There's no such thing as ghosts – somebody should tell Bhudevi that!'

But today the ghost of the Pushkarni seems to be lying quiescent. No dark clouds hover above Chachiji as she gets dressed in Debjani's and Eshwari's bedroom. Humming *Joh wada kiya woh nibhana padega*, making final adjustments to the folds of her fearsomely embroidered zardozi sari, she smiles benignly at Dabbu, who is hunched upon a stool at her feet, painting her horny toenails a shiny maroon.

'Your foot must look nice when you raise your sari and kick the genhu cup and enter the house,' she tells her aunt earnestly. 'Gulgul bhaisaab is going to click pictures. Don't fidget now, you'll smudge it.'

'Sorry, dear, sorry,' Chachiji says, her jowls creasing into a dreamy smile. 'I will be still as stone now, I won't move even *one* muscle, see! You will think ki I have died, so still will I be!'

'Good,' Dabbu says as she carefully paints the last hoofish toenail. 'Now don't jump just because I've finished, stay still. Let them dry properly.'

'Pass me that bowl of bhindi then,' Chachiji says with self-conscious martyrdom. 'I can at least do some work – I hate to sit idle, na.'

Dabbu passes her the bhindi and a long, wicked-looking knife. Chachiji starts to chop.

'Where's your uncle?' she asks offhandedly. 'Gone for his morning walk, I-suppose-so?'

It is almost eleven, way too late for a morning walk, but Dabbu doesn't point that out.

'I'll go look.' She smiles. 'You look really pretty, Chachiji!'

And she *does* look nice today – the colour of her sari makes her skin look brighter, her hair is secured in a neat bun and there is a soft, hopeful glow in her eyes.

'Thuttt!' she snorts, colouring up and waving her knife dismissively. 'Stop talking like Anjini – it won't make you look like her.'

And having re-established her no-nonsense credentials with this remark, she settles back in her stool to chop bhindi and wriggle her toes.

There's no *gratitude* in this world, thinks a deflated Dabbu as she walks out to the garden You can do anything for people – wax their chests, paint their toes, risk your job and defend them on live national television – and still they act like you did nothing at all. Like they got manicured feet and a prime-ministerial intervention all by themselves. Not that I want their gratitude. I don't want anything. I've *had* it with doing things for people.

And even as she reflects thus on the thanklessness of the universe, a brand-new puppy from Moti and Voti's latest litter wanders up on unsteady paws and piddles against her foot.

Dabbu stares down at it with huge, betrayed eyes, and sits down abruptly upon the platform around the champa tree.

'Dabbu mausi! Look. *Look!*'

Samar is lighting rockets in the driveway. The twins, seated on the stairs, are watching fascinated, their chubby hands clasped over their ears. Rocket after rocket sizzles, then ignites and shoots into the sky to explode with a satisfying bang. Samar grins.

'You should do that at night,' Dabbu calls out to him, her voice just a little shaky. 'It'll look much prettier then.'

'I don't want *pretty*.' Samar looks disdainful. 'Hey, Monu, c'mon, you light one.'

Monu shakes his head vigorously.

'Don't be such a phisaddi,' Samar says. 'I'll hold your hand. Come!'

Monu approaches, shrinking. Samar hands him the chid-chidding phooljhadi, then wraps his fingers around Monu's wrist. They lean down to the rocket standing inside the Campa Cola bottle together, hold the phooljhadi to the dangling fuse, and step back sharply.

Nothing.

A nervous giggle from Bonu.

The boys try again. The fuse splutters, flames lick at the base of the rocket, the gold of its wrapping slowly turns black, but there is no gorgeous hissing, no sudden shooting up from the mouth of the bottle into the white, waiting sky.

Somebody chuckles. The boys turn round.

'There's one in every pack,' Vickyji, lounging against a pillar, calls out to the disappointed trio. 'These Cock brand crackers come in packs of five – four light up nicely but one is always defective, you notice and see. It's how the firecracker company-wallahs make their profit. That one's the dud, boys, it won't light.'

Indignant protests from the children.

'But that's out and out *cheating*!'

'What *chors*!'

'We paid for *five*!'

Meanwhile, Dabbu, sitting under the champa, her chin in her hands, is hit by a supremely depressing epiphany.

I'm the dud, the one daughter in Ma-BJ's pack of five who fizzled out, achieving zilch. D for dud.

Tears rush to her eyes. She wraps her arms around herself tightly, leans back against the tree and lets them roll.

Dylan is having a hard time getting to Number 16. Traffic is clogged up all along Hailey Road. Freshly bathed people trying to get to work are now sweating and swearing with equal intensity.

'Madarchod, sadak pe tambu laga rakha hai!' fumes a man on a scooter. 'Who puts up a tent all the way across the road? No civic sense! Days of decency are truly over!'

He spits, rests his feet upon the road and manoeuvres his scooter around sharply, almost knocking over a shapely woman in a bright yellow nylon sari.

'Look where you're going!' she says shrilly. 'Blind or what?'

The man folds his hands in leering mock contrition and zooms away. Dylan, watching from his car, leans out.

'Are you all right?'

She nods. She has a broad face, big kohled eyes, a flashing nose stud and a thin maroon mouth.

'Thenks for aksing.'

'Don't mention it.' He switches his gaze back to the crazy pile-up of traffic ahead. 'Damn!'

'I can so you sortcurt.'

Huh?

It's the lady in the yellow nylon sari. She is leaning into his window, radiating an appealing smile and a strong scent of desi gulab. Dylan swallows.

'You want to go to Hailey Court?' she asks him.

'Huh? No. Number 16.'

'Same thing. I also want to go there only. If you reverse little bit and take a right after that paan sop and go down the back lane, you'll reach it quickly. I can so you.'

'Thank you so much,' he responds, pleasantly surprised. 'Please get in. Quickly. I need to get there fast.'

'So do I,' she says grimly.

Dabbu abandons herself to a good, no holds barred blubbering session. She hides her face against her knees and just lets everything flow, making good use of her loose sweatshirt to sop up the flowing liquids. Finally, she stops. Her eyes feel swollen, the rough ground is pinching the back of her thighs through her jeans, and she can sense a killer headache coming on.

'Damn it,' she mutters, straightening up and leaning against the trunk of the champa tree. 'This is *so* pathetic.'

Something falls into her lap.

Something light and soft and – she discovers as she opens her eyes – blue-checkered.

'Oh,' she says blankly as she looks up to meet Dylan Singh Shekhawat's part-sarcastic, part-ardent dark eyes. 'You.'

'Yes,' he says. 'Um... you have snot.'

'So what?' she says belligerently.

He grins. He is feeling suddenly, absurdly happy. 'So nothing. How are you?'

Dabbu picks up his handkerchief and blows strongly. 'I'm fine.'

Then why were you crying? he thinks but doesn't ask. Instead, he looks around – at the big tent, at the well-dressed children lighting crackers, the stack of boxed snacks and the obvious air of festivity in the house. To this, he adds her tears and a sudden fear snatches at his heart.

'So you're getting engaged?' he asks lightly. 'Should've invited us, na. We called you for our parents' anniversary, after all.'

Debjani frowns.

'I'm not getting –' she starts to say, but then she looks beyond him and gasps, 'Oh my god, what is *she* doing here?'

Dylan turns. 'Who?'

Dabbu clutches at her hair, shrinking behind him, then points with one shaky finger.

'Oh, her,' Dylan says. 'I brought her.'

'What!'

'Who *is* she?' he asks interestedly. 'She has a certain, quite *delicious* concupiscence.'

She punches his shoulder. 'Shut up! She's... oh god, Dylan, she's Chachaji's *rakhail*!'

'Raquel?' he replies, bemused. 'As in, Welch?'

'His *mistress*,' Debjani hisses.

Dylan's eyes light up with huge enjoyment.

'Chachaji has a mistress? And she's here at your big family function? Wow, you guys are pretty broad-minded.'

'Shut up,' Debjani says, appalled. 'This is an international incident. Poor Chachiji! I have to go and tell Ma right *now*.'

She starts to hurry away but strong fingers close around her upper arm. 'Oh, no, you don't,' he says, his voice like silk. 'You stay right here and talk to me.'

Oh my god, that was so *hot*, Dabbu, jerked backward, thinks chaotically, almost buckling at the knees. And he's here – he's here – he's here. I could die of sheer joy. Well, that's if he's here because he loves me, and not because he's really in love with Mitali and he's here, just to, you know, say thank you.

'I'm here to say thank you,' Dylan continues. 'Please stay and hear me out – your latest pity projects can wait till then.'

He loves Mitali, Dabbu thinks instantly, wretchedly. I was just a little rebound thing he had, a mad moment of insanity when he actually considered arranged marriage, and now he's back with her. He'll call me to the wedding and Anji didi will make me go, and I'll have to smile and maybe catch Mitali's bouquet (how humiliating!) and dance with horrible Donny Noronha all over again.

Dazedly, she watches the Hot Dulari sashay towards the main house. Eshwari runs up to talk to her.

'See?' says Dylan's voice from behind her. 'Eshu's got it. She'll head her off. Now will you please turn around and talk to me?'

Dabbu, glancing down as she turns to face him, realizes her right foot is drenched in puppy pee. Also, that he's still holding her. And that his sinewy muscular arm leads up to a strongly corded neck, to the jaw of a cowboy, to the mouth of an angel and to eyes that mean business.

She swallows.

'Yes, of course, let's talk,' she says in her mature newsreader voice.

Dylan sits her down upon the circular platform under the champa, and then sits down beside her.

'Thank you,' he says simply. 'For saving me. For saving the entire country.'

'Saving you equals saving the country?' Dabbu gives a scornful little laugh, looking down at her hands, twisting her ladybird ring. 'Wow, you have a high opinion of yourself.'

'That's not what I meant,' he says, and there is an edge to his voice now. 'I meant, you got them to withdraw the bill. You know that, right?'

She looks up. 'Yeah, I know,' she says, trying not to sound too pleased with herself. 'So, I'm not as dumb as you thought I was, huh?'

'I never thought you were dumb,' he replies, his voice warm. 'You're *smart*. You're one smart Molonchin.'

Dabbu, pleased but vaguely suspicious that he's being patronizing, looks down and away. A little silence follows, broken only by the heartfelt curses of the builder as he argues with the tent-wallah.

'So much money for a simple shamiana? Is it made out of diamond bricks and silver mortar? So sorry, I didn't realize, I thought it was cloth and bamboo only! You bloody thief and son of a thief!'

'It's stronger than these pigeonholes you built out of adulterated maal,' returns the tent-wallah, waving a contemptuous hand at the six-floor-high Hailey Court building. 'Two hundred litres of rain can fall on my shamiana and it won't collapse. Not even a leak. So cough up my money, makkhichoos.'

Debjani clears her throat.

'Uncle-aunty must be so happy you're safe. Did you get your accreditation back?'

'Yes, I did. *And* I got a promotion. And a bunch of job offers.'

'How nice,' she replies demurely. 'You're eligible again. Mangalorean maidens will queue up to marry you.'

'Dabbu, listen –'

'Don't call me Dabbu!'

'What are you so *angry* about?'

She turns away from him, her eyes starting to well up again.

One caveat, though. The sentiments expressed in the letter are slightly dated. Quite dated, actually. Remember that.

Debjani dashes her hand across her eyes. She knows why he's here. Because he's grateful. Maybe he even wants to marry her out of sheer gratitude or something. But gratitude isn't enough. Even gratitude with such a luscious butt.

She turns to face him.

'I'm not angry,' she says steadily. 'Those editorials you wrote were very courageous. You risked your life, Dylan, and your friends and colleagues rallied around you brilliantly. What I did wasn't really that important. You don't owe me anything.'

He frowns. 'Wait, I'm not the brave one, and I'm not here coz I owe you anything. I –'

But Dabbu has leapt to her feet.

'Fuck!'

Now what? Dylan looks around, thoroughly fed up, and spots a pug-faced lady – Debjani's weirdo aunt, if he remembers right – stumping down the driveway, brandishing a wicked-looking knife. She hurtles right past them, totally ignoring Dabbu's agonized wail of 'Chachiji, wait!' and turns a sharp left into the sumptuously decorated Hailey Court drive. The pink ribbon, stretched out from gatepost cherub to gatepost angel, snaps smartly into two as she walks right through it.

'Stop her, stop her!' gasps Samar, capering up and waving several spent rockets around agitatedly. 'The Pushkarni's upon her! She's going to go up to the sixth floor and push Chachaji right off!'

'What!' Dabbu whirls to look at him. 'How did you even think up something like that?'

'She *told* me!' he explains earnestly. 'She said the soul of Pushkar Thakur is inside Ashok chacha now so she has to kill him!'

A bright yellow blur streaks past Debjani. 'Hai-hai!' wails the Hot Dulari as she runs. 'Bachaaaaaaooo!'

Dabbu's jaw drops. She whips around, wondering what to do, and finds that Dylan has vanished from her side.

'Oh shit oh shit oh shit!' Eshwari runs up, panting, the rest of the family right behind her. 'I tried to stop the cow, but she pushed right past me and told Chachiji that *she's* the one who's moving into the flat with the Ant today. So then Chachiji reared, cursing, and said, May you rot in hell, may you be eaten by worms, may termites gnaw at your –'

'Anus,' Dabbu completes, her palms clammy. 'What do we do *now*, BJ?'

Before the Judge can reply, the twins set up a shrill rongta-raising wail.

'Dabbu mausi... *look*!'

And Dabbu, looking up to the terrace of the Hailey Court building, is hit with the cold thrill of foreknowledge.

A stout figure is standing upon the parapet wall, silhouetted against the noon sun. Flanked by the large black humps of two Sintex tanks on either side, it appears eerily resolute. Something drips from the knife it holds in its hand.

'Blurrrd!' screams Bonu in a high-pitched voice as a large clear red drop splashes on the ground between her feet. 'Bl-bl-*blurrrd*!' She turns around and clutches Binni, hiding her face in her kurta.

'The Pushkarni's taken over,' Samar says with stoic satisfaction. He puts a comforting arm around Eshwari's waist. 'She's going to jump.'

Don't jump, Chachiji, Dabbu thinks fiercely. He's not worth it. You're too good for this. Don't you *dare* jump...

⧫━◆━⧫

When Dylan, taking the Hailey Court stairs three at a time, burst onto the terrace on the sixth floor, he came upon an oddly calm tableau.

Peering from between the drainage pipes, he saw the back of a man he later identified as Ashok chacha, cowering behind Anjini, his handsome face slack with fear. He was swallowing drily and staring at Chachiji, who was standing in front of Anjini, clutching her bhindi knife. Anjini was looking beyond her aunt, at her husband. And Anant, with his back to Dylan, had just started to speak.

'Chachiji,' Anant said, and something in that quiet intense voice made her turn around. 'Don't you get it? He loves you.'

Chachiji looked at Anant, her face working.

'He just...' Anant paused. 'Just doesn't know how to show it. The thing is, you're so beautiful, and always surrounded by so many admirers... he's afraid you'll find him boring.'

Bit of a stretch, that, Dylan thought, looking at Dabbu's aunt's pug-like face. The Raquel Wench is definitely more alluring.

'All this stuff, it's just a silly misunderstanding. There has never been anybody for him but *you*, ever since the day he first set eyes on you.'

Chachiji looked just as sceptical as Dylan at this. But –

'Yes yes,' A.N. Thakur nodded with sweaty fervour from behind Anjini. 'The boy is telling the truth. Listen to him! He is reading my feelings for you like a *book*, Bhudevi.'

'He doesn't *care* that you can't have children,' Anant continued, and the throb of emotion in his voice was so real that Dylan pursed his lips, impressed. 'You're *enough* for him. You're all he wants. So please could you save all your loving just for me – I mean, for *him*, um... Chachiji.'

Chachiji's eyes narrowed. She whirled around to look at Anjini, whose eyes, boring into Anant's, were soft and shining like stars.

Chachiji gave one long, heartbroken, bloodcurdling wail, pushed Anant aside and hurled herself at her husband.

Dylan rushed in, trying to separate them.

But it was too late. Ashok Narayan Thakur had already slumped to the floor, blood spilling from his smart Charagh Din shirt. Breathing heavily, her hair like a wild grey storm around her head, Chachiji hauled herself up onto the parapet wall and waved merrily at the crowd gathered below.

'Hell-lo! Here I aaaam!' She put her arms out wide and flapped them gaily. 'Time for the Pushkarni to *flyyyy.*'

And then she walked right off the boundary wall.

Dylan, right behind her, had time for just one, crystal clear thought.

Two hundred litres of rain can fall on it and it won't collapse. Not even a leak. So cough up my money, makkhichoos.

'Here goes nothing,' he said under his breath as he threw out his arms and launched himself off the parapet wall, feeling the sickening suck of gravity hook him right through the mouth and the pit of his stomach.

Dabbu, standing transfixed below, saw Chachiji start to drop like a stone, bang on track to splatter like an egg on the cemented drive. But then another figure hurled itself at her in a flying tackle, propelling them both forward by a few vital feet, so that they fell down... down... down... and landed on the roof of the monstrous shamiana with a satisfying *whummmp.*

The shamiana shuddered, staggered, seemed miraculously to hold, and then collapsed. Chachiji, winded but mostly unhurt, was disentangled from various ropes and Dylan's muscular arms and taken into the house in the care of her sister-in-law. Anji, pink-faced and glowing, came racing down from the Hailey Court terrace, hand in hand with Anant, to report that Ashok chacha had cunningly been feigning death and had suffered only a glancing blow from Chachiji's bhindi knife.

❦

'But what about the Raquel?' Dylan enquires as he sits in the verandah with Dabbu, chugging down an extremely strong brandy and hot water, pressed upon him by the Judge. 'Where'd she go?'

Dabbu is valiantly trying to ignore the fact that Dylan's freefall has somehow caused his shirt to rip in seven different places, putting lots of muscular toffee-brown bits of him on display.

'She beat it,' she says matter-of-factly. 'Gulgul bhaisaab told her she could get involved in a police case, so she scuttled off.'

He grins at her, his eyes shining with a light that is at once cocky and caressing. 'So obviously she isn't honest and kind and brave. Like me.'

'You're *dumb*,' she replies warmly. She doesn't add that he's also swoon-inducingly, knee-bucklingly hot, a ripped alpha male in ripped white cotton. 'But I suppose people will say you were brave. Maybe,' her voice catches, 'Maybe Mitali will want to feature your amazing rescue on *Viewstrack*.'

He tilts his head, the long dimples flash and his eyes are so playfully challenging that Dabbu wonders if the brandy's already gone to his head. Or maybe he's just high on sheer adrenalin from that asinine plummet through space.

'What's with that bitchy little lip curl? Just now, when you said Mitali?'

She turns away. 'Nothing.'

'You're jealous.' He grins. 'Because I trumped your extempore speech on DD by jumping off a terrace eight floors high.'

'Six,' she tells him dampeningly. 'And this isn't kot-piece – there's no *trumping* going on.'

'Yeah,' he says, and the smile has gone right out of his voice. 'At least if this were kot-piece, we'd be partners.'

Silence.

'Dillu! How *brave* you were!' Anji rushes up and envelops Dylan in a soft, scented embrace. 'Well done!'

Binni hangs back a little, arms crossed across her chest.

'Yes, very brave,' she allows grudgingly. 'But what about your five-year-old girlfriend?'

Dylan reels slightly: is he being accused of paedophilia?

'She means your girlfriend of five years,' Anji explains. 'Juliet aunty told us about her. The one who works for *Viewstrack* – she studied with you also.'

Dylan's brow clears.

'Mitali's not my girlfriend,' he replies steadily. 'In fact, I think she may be in love with my friend Varun. She's a nice girl, though.'

Anjini waves a dismissive hand. She isn't interested in the 'nice' Mitali.

'See! I *told* you, Dabburam!' Then she remembers something. 'Did you meet Charles Sobhraj in jail, Dillu? Is he cute? Or is he creepy and old and chinkie looking?'

'I never made it into Tihar jail, actually,' Dylan admits a little sheepishly. 'Sorry.'

'Oh!' Anjini internalizes this. 'Oh, well, okay. Now listen, don't the two of you go planning a summer wedding just because you're in a hurry to, you know, *do it*. It'll be dreadfully hot, and Dabbu, your sari will go limp, and if it's white you'll look like one of those sad Benarasi widows. Now October is a good month – we'll get narcissuses and those lovely shaggy chrysanthemums...'

'Anji didi,' Debjani hisses, scarlet faced. 'Shut *up.*'

'Oh, but why, Dabburam? He just jumped off the tenth floor to save your chachi's life, sweetie, obviously he wants to marry you!'

'*Sixth*,' Debjani says again, rolling her eyes. 'And you can't just assume –'

'Yeah,' Dylan puts in. 'Don't go making any assumptions, Anjini. I could've done it out of love for Chachiji.'

Eshwari comes running up, hand in hand with Samar. 'What's happening, what's happening? Is the engagement back on?'

'Shut up!' Debjani hisses.

But Eshwari has made a discovery.

'He's *drunk!*' she chortles delightedly. 'Go for it, Dubz, take advantage of him while he's drunk! Grab him by the but –'

But before she can complete her instructions, she is pushed aside by an emotional Gulgul who appears out of nowhere, throws his arms around Dylan and kisses him fervently.

'You saved my mother!' he blubbers. 'I am in your debt for life!' And then, in a slightly altered tone, 'Arrey wah – solid muscle tone, ya. You're a jimmer! Where do you do your jimming?'

'Hello, namaste, I'm the dvelupper,' a man Dabbu has never seen before in her life pushes in and says hoarsely. He is flashily dressed and, being pale and hairy and knobby, somehow gives the impression of being made entirely out of ginger tubers. 'I dvelupped Hailey Court next door. After marriage, if your wife decides to sell her one-sixth share in this property and dvelupp it into an apartment building, please call me, okay?'

'This is ridiculous!' Debjani roars, her cheeks flaming. 'Stop it! Right now!'

Sheepishly, the Thakurs fall silent. It is an irreverent sort of silence, with a lot of eye-rolling and silent nudging and giggling, but it is silence, nevertheless. Dabbu frowns at all of them awfully, while behind her, Dylan looks on, his expression one of comic alarm.

The Judge and Mrs Mamta, shaken but relieved, walk out to the verandah and join the group of spectators. Dylan catches their eye from behind Debjani, raising his eyebrows in silent enquiry. They both nod – Mrs Mamta smilingly, the Judge resignedly.

'Debjani,' Dylan says, his voice very deep. 'Dabbu? Stop bullying everybody and look at me.'

But Debjani can't. Somehow, looking at her large, ill-assorted family is suddenly much easier than turning around to face Dylan's gaze.

'We can go away if you like,' Anji begins to offer but she's drowned out by a furious hiss of whispered objections.

'Nooo!'

'That's not fair!'

'I want to *see*!'

'This Anji always spoils all the fun!'

Slowly, Debjani turns around. 'If you ask me whatever it is you may be planning to ask me, in front of my entire snickering family, I will never, ever forgive you,' she tells him.

Dylan laughs, his eyes alight with possessive tenderness, wraps her fingers around his arm and then, ignoring the chorus of protests that rises from the Thakurs, walks her out of the verandah and into the garden.

He leads her into the annexe. Pausing halfway up the narrow

winding staircase, he pulls her to him. 'Now where were we?' he asks, his voice teasing.

She kisses his neck.

'Here, I think?'

His eyes darken. With a sudden movement, his hands come down to cup her face.

'Why did you do it?' he asks, his eyes stabbing hers. 'I was watching you from the lock-up in that wretched police station and I'll never forget how you looked at that moment. Seriously scary, like some nut-job suicide bomber about to blow.'

'Well, thanks a *lot*,' she begins to say indignantly but he interrupts her.

'Why'd you do it, Debjani?'

'Is that what you wanted to ask me?' she demands. 'Coz I was expecting another question *entirely*. And not th –'

He gives her a little shake.

'Why?'

She sighs.

'Well, I couldn't get your letter out of my head...'

'Ah! So Bonu finally coughed it up?'

'Yes.' She rolls her eyes. 'Which is a whole other story – but let's not get into that now. And then your creepy boss told me you were a snake and I almost believed him...'

'Hira? Where'd you meet him?'

'Never mind. But then that seedy little cat showed up. The one Moti was trying to eat that first day. So I *knew* you were telling the truth.'

His arms tighten around her.

'So when you made that newscast, all you had to go on was the *cat*?'

She nods.

'Weren't you scared?'

'Oh, no,' she says airily. Then she adds, looking up candidly, 'Well, I didn't know *then* that it was such a big crime to make up and read out your own news. If I'd known, I probably wouldn't have done it.'

'Such refreshing honesty,' Dylan says ruefully as he pulls her to him.

A few minutes later, Debjani emerges, rosy-faced and thoroughly kissed, and announces blissfully, 'You're better looking than all my brothers-in-law. I *think*. Because, to be fair, I've never seen the Estonian.'

He grimaces. 'Thank you. Am I also the better kisser?'

'You're goodish,' she allows, twirling a lock of his hair between her fingers.

His eyebrows fly up. '*Ish?*'

'Ish.' She grins.

'I'll show you *ish*,' Dylan says, his voice thick with outrage.

But Debjani pushes him away – not too far, just far enough to get a good look into his eyes.

'Anji didi's right, you know,' she says conversationally. 'October is a good month. Not too hot, not too cold.'

'Just like *you*,' Dylan murmurs, his cheek against her hair as his hands slide smoothly up her back, beneath her shirt.

'What are you doing?'

He smiles at her through spiky lashes, his gaze unfocused. She can feel his heart, it's thudding hard and fast, obviously he still hasn't got over that dive from the sixth floor.

'Checking for wings,' he murmurs as his lips graze her forehead.

'I *know* you have wings. Don't deny it – you hide them under your T-shirt and pretend to be a mere mortal like everybody else.'

Debjani wrinkles up her nose.

'But actually I'm a *chicken*?' she asks breathlessly even as she, very accommodatingly, lets him make an extremely thorough search.

Dylan has her pushed up against the wall, but at this he draws back, allowing her shirt to slide down again, much to her disappointment.

'You really don't know how to flirt.'

'I *know*,' she agrees fervently. 'Thank god we're beyond the flirting stage!'

Dylan stares down at her, a queer smile upon his lips, a what-the-hell, burn-the-boats light in his eyes.

'So will you be my Raquel?' he asks. 'And my wife? And my kot-piece partner for the rest of my life?'

There is a pause. A very long pause. So long, in fact, that he starts to feel rather uneasy.

Then she tilts her head.

'Is this proposal being made under the influence of alcohol?'

'No,' he replies steadily, kissing her fingers. 'It's being made under the influence of Dabbu.'

This draws an appreciative grin. But she quickly turns solemn again.

'Well, you're no Balkishen Bau...' she says, considering.

Then her arms go around him tight. She kisses his cheek, a kiss so full of hope and love and trust that it brings the sudden sting of tears to his eyes.

'So don't mind if, *just* for kot-piece, I pick another partner.'

⚊❁⚊

A very cowed Ashok chacha, with six stitches in his cheek and his stomach bandaged up, stands by and watches resignedly as Chachiji kicks over the cup full of genhu with her manicured foot and enters her Hailey Court flat, glowing like a new bride.

'Thank you, bhaisaab,' she tells Justice Laxmi Narayan as she puts a tika for him after the puja. 'You have kept my nose from being cut.'

'Yes yes,' the Judge says, looking rather cornered, and not wanting to talk about the cutting up of any body parts. 'Ahem! Mamtaji, if you are done, can we please go home?'

And so, after admiring the marble flooring, the modular kitchen and the stainless steel Diamond sink, the L.N. Thakurs return to Number 16. The Judge and Mrs Mamta retire to their room, where the Judge tries to take a nap, but is prevented from doing so because his wife is busy jangling open various Godrej cupboards, rootling through her caché of jewellery, watches, saris and perfume bottles.

'We'll need to do so much shopping!' she says. 'Thankfully I've already bought her wedding sari and we have enough pretty new salwar kameezes, but what will we buy all the honeymoon clothes with? They'll go to Goa, she'll need a new swimming costume, sandals, nightgown, nightie, underclothes – so many things! How will we manage?'

'Easy, Mamtaji,' he says. 'We'll economize by serving only mutton at the reception. Like we did at Anjini's wedding.'

Mrs Mamta sits on the bed with a thump. 'But these people are Christians. They'll want chicken and fish. Maybe even pork!'

'Then forget fancy underclothes,' the Judge says, reasonably enough. 'She's already caught the boy, he can't back out when he sees her plain cotton chaddis.'

At which aggravating remark Mrs Mamta bangs her Godrej almirahs shut and turns to glare at him, her hands on her hips. 'Maybe if you hadn't run up such a huge phone bill at Gambhir Stores, we would have enough money for her trousseau.'

'Ph-phone bill?' the Judge stammers weakly, looking undeniably guilty. 'What phone bill?'

'You *know* what phone bill,' Mrs Mamta says awfully. 'I asked young Mr Gambhir and he told me everything. I can't *believe* you could be such a lying, sneaking, cheating, two-faced hypocrite, LN!'

'I'm sorry,' the Judge says, red-faced and ashamed. 'I couldn't help myself. Especially after she had the baby. I had to get in touch again – I *had* to.'

Silence.

Then Mrs Mamta giggles. Just like her daughters.

'Does this mean we can invite them to the wedding, LN?'

'Of course,' he responds eagerly, relieved that she isn't angry, after all. 'Chandu, the Estonian and little Hendrik Lippik! That will solve our fancy underwear problem too! Chandu can choose it. And the Estonian can pay for it. Haha.'

Happier than she has been in years, Mrs Mamta kisses him on the forehead, leaves him to his books and goes off to sit with her daughters.

'Doesn't Chubs looks pretty?' Anjini asks with a proprietary air as she drapes Eshu's jade, green georgette sari over her tiny red choli.

'Yes,' Mrs Mamta sighs in satisfaction. 'She'll be Miss Modern too, wait and see – the third in the family.'

Jai Kakkar arrives to pick Eshu up half an hour later, very handsome in a formal shirt and tie. He is carrying a small posy of red carnations, which goes perfectly with her sari.

'You look *lovely*,' he declares, his eyes alight with admiration.

Ten minutes later, the doorbell rings again. Samar and Bonu answer it.

'Hi, kids.' It is Satish, reeking of aftershave. His shirt is crisply ironed, his upper lip and jaw have been scraped naked so scrupulously that angry little dots stand out on his chin. 'Is everything okay with Chachiji and all? That was quite an impressive thump. I saw it from my window.'

'She's fine,' Bonu tells him. 'Dabbu mausi's getting married.'

'Cool!' Satish grins. 'Congratulations. And... where's your Eshu mausi?'

'She's not my mausi,' Samar clarifies immediately. 'She's no blood relation.'

Bonu sniggers.

Satish doesn't notice. His eyes are searching the space behind them. 'So, where *is* she?'

'She left,' Samar informs him, not without some satisfaction. 'Jai Kakkar took her.'

Satish swallows. His eyes shut, just for a moment, and when he opens them again, he suddenly looks years older.

'Oh, of course!' He nods vigorously. 'I knew that! I thought I'd just check in case he was late. Because he's a little... undependable, you know?'

They nod.

There is a pause.

'You look nice,' Bonu tells him kindly.

'Thanks,' Satish smiles. 'Well! I'd better run or I'll miss all the fun!' He does a corny little disco move, pointing one finger into the air. 'Woo-hoo! G'nite, kiddos.'

And whistling softly, he turns around and bobs away.

ACKNOWLEDGMENTS

Many thanks to
Suneet Tandon and Rini Simon, for bearing with my many many
questions on what it was like being a newsreader in the eighties.
Mr Bhaskar Ghose, whose *Doordarshan Days* was a fascinating
and informative read.
Google, for all the dope on the Anti-Defamation Bill, 1988.
Satish Sridhar, for letting me cut-paste his name, surname
and persona.
Samar Singh Shekhawat, for loaning his names to two boys in
the book.
Mansi Jain, for the tedha naam Pushkar.
Nika, Nandu, Minni didi and Manu, for allowing me to swirl
them in a mixie and produce a smoothie called Debjani.
Tara, for being such a Bihari.
First readers Niret Alva, Niharika Alva and Shalini Beri, for all
their patient reading and critiquing. And Alok Lal, for providing
the closure on Chandu.
Anupama Ramaswamy, for the fab cover. Sudeep Bhattacharya,
for shooting the cover pic. Kavita Joshi, for putting me on to
Nakul Sawhney, who gave me access to both his cat and his flat.
My cover girl – she-who-shall-not-be-named.
My cover cat – Chuski.

Neelini Sarkar – perfectionist editor – who conducted many experiments to check if water mixed with Dettol really does look like susu.

Karthika V.K., who always provides fantastic direction and insight.

My three gorgeous and fabulous big sisters, to whom this book is dedicated.

My mum and her sisters, who were quite the original 'pricey Thakur girls'.

My nanaji, Thakur Dalchand Singh.

And, of course, the Lord Jesus Christ for teaching me both faith and patience in these last two years – and for keeping my family healed and happy.